THIS
BOOK
BELONGS TO

Havener

THE DISCOVERIES OF MRS. CHRISTOPHER COLUMBUS: His Wife's Version

a novel by

Paula DiPerna

THE PERMANENT PRESS
Sag Harbor, New York 11963

Library of Congress Cataloging-in-Publication Data

DiPerna, Paula.
   The discoveries of Mrs. Christopher Columbus : His wife's
   version / by Paula DiPerna.
        p.   cm.
   ISBN 1-877946-48-6 (cloth) : $24.00
   1.Perestrello, Felipa Moniz, ca. 1452-1484 or 5—Fiction.
   2. Explorers' wives—Spain—Fiction.   3. Columbus, Christopher—Fiction.   4. Explorers—Spain—Fiction.   I. Title.
PS3554.I64D57 1994   93-27525
813'.54—dc20   CIP

Manufactured in the United States of America

First Edition, October, 1994 -- 1,500 copies

THE PERMANENT PRESS
Noyac Road
Sag Harbor, NY 11963

To my mother, who gave me the gift of discovery

Acknowledgements

I am grateful for support to the Writer-in-Residence program at Thurber House in Columbus, Ohio, in particular to Michael Rosen, and to many others around the world, in particular Judith Cramer and Tom Wallace, my agent.

Many of these events happened;
the rest is not history.

Contents

Chapters

Chapter One

The Alien Sea

The cabin boy knocked, and I put my pen and paper away before letting him come in. I hadn't felt the time pass. He gently opened the narrow door, took the one creaking step down carefully, and steadied himself like a supple dancer against the slight lift and fall of the wide and unknown ocean that carried us swiftly away from home.

He reached for the hourglass on the Admiral's table, carefully loosening the leather brace as the last tiny white cascade of sand drizzled from the top chamber to the bottom. We counted on Juan to turn the clocks, so we could compare the hours and the passage of the sun. The thin glass tinkled against the scrolled hardwood dowels meant to protect it, a shapely fragile form housed in what looked like a small Greek temple rattling in the boy's hands, and he glanced at me with the taut, timid face of a young man possibly afraid he had been given too much responsibility. He didn't want to drop the glass, certainly not as I watched. His young lean body shook slightly with the effort of keeping balance against the roll, but he deftly rotated the fragile timepiece and the sand fell anew.

I followed him above deck and into the brilliant sunshine of our third full day at sea.

The Admiral, my husband, talked with Chachu, the boatswain, a wiry swarthy Basque who crouched in the hot afternoon sun replaiting fat gray ropes and neatly coiling them like a snake in a pile.

"He was a good choice, orderly and energetic," the Admiral observed to me, moving out of Chachu's hearing.

"Yes. Lucky for us Pinzon knew him," I answered, speaking of the Captain of our sister ship, *Pinta*. She was the nimbler, faster vessel, but I regretted mentioning the other captain as soon as I'd done it. Already the Admiral had had to order Pinzon to stay closer so that the three ships could travel shoulder to shoulder. My husband only nodded at the mention of *Pinta*, raising the collar of his maroon woven shirt as he did against the rising breeze. Though the Admiral was still a young man, his long thick hair had grown pure white, and it billowed in the wind like moving clouds. His glinting blue eyes drifted from mine.

He said nothing before leaving me on the foredeck with Chachu to fill the silence. The boatswain chatted on in his familiar, extravagant way.

"It is possible, I suppose, Madame, that we will sail on and on to nothing, or that great green monsters will rise from the waves and swallow us whole." Chachu gulped on his words, as if he had just seen the very creatures, rasping hot tongues on the horizon. Chachu had tapestry for imagination. But he was right to wonder. We had all heard of the great Sea of Darkness where none had ever sailed, of phantom virgin islands that tease and disappear before all who come too close, of the great wild whirlwinds of water that could suck us to the black bottom of the Ocean Sea. But the Admiral was convinced that valleys of gold lay ahead, a shining world of palaces inlaid with gems.

It was a tempting, magnificent prospect across untouched waters beyond all previously known.

Strangers bound on the same bold adventure, we comprised countless dreams, fears and feelings, and these made the vastness for me as much as the sea surrounding us that takes my eyes as far as they can go.

Here, the only real companion is a clear blue openness. The lodestone of our ship seems to cut azure glass, so luminescent does the water seem.

The Admiral writes down much that happens, as do I, though I haven't told him. My record is my own, to keep note of our impressions on a trip no one has made before, to float a frame on the moving sea of my mind to which random thoughts can cling before drowning, unheard or unshared.

And on a small ship, writing might be my only privacy.

Still, the *Santa Maria* can at times seem large, as one gradually gets to know its many nooks and corners. Underway, with full white sails against the sky, the emerald cross and herald of the Spanish Sovereigns unfurled and full, we look like a page boy in billowing blousy sleeves moving across a marble blue floor of court.

But at our departure, we had none of this elegance. There was only oppressive windless heat, and so our three ships left Spain pulled away by the ebb tide, our only hope in the dense, unmoving air.

We had all made confession, and attended mass to ask divine protection on our route. A small stone fountain shaped like a scallop shell caught a sparkling spring near the church, and the men filled the last remaining cask for our journey while the sunlight danced on the bubbling holy water. Then the quietude of St. George's gave way to the throngs of local people who stood on the river bank to see us off, cheering and shouting goodbye—goodbyes bequeathed in a touch, a wave, a word, hundreds of goodbyes from hundreds of faces—sailors, families, friends, wives. Could we really be off at last?

Then a man's hand reached above the tumult, and he tossed a single fresh red rose. The Admiral picked it up, somewhat surprised, and passed the flower to me. The people engulfed me in loud approving cheers, "God bless Dona Felipa," which filled my ears and trembled my bones, as if the crowd had climbed inside my body and we were, for one quick second, headed on the discovery as one.

"Long live the Admiral Colon," they shouted again as our tender was rowed out to our ship. Were we mad to leave the safety of this port, the godspeed of so many? Another rose landed in the water alongside us, floating easily, and whole, for awhile. Then the sea peeled the velvet petals loose one by one. Soon, as person after person tossed a flower, the blue sea surface rippled with magenta blossoms and petals, each a tiny fragrant ship, each a token of our leaving.

But the flowers cast to us soon drifted among other travelers, others also putting Spain behind, others setting out not on fantasies to a wide new world, but on shattered hopes to the limitless unknown of exile. Our great moment was not unmarred.

Months ago, the Sovereigns began expelling the Spanish Jews, and by ugly coincidence, the deadline for the departure of all the Jews remaining was the very day we left. Refugees poured into Palos from all over Spain. Around the harbor as we prepared our trip, I had heard that nearly 8,000 families had left in the months following the decree, and that thousands more had continued to be forcibly sent away before the terms of the order had been fully met.

[3

All during our days in Palos, great dirty barges carried away Jews, human beings who, from a distance, looked like piles of ragged cloth. The Crown stripped them of their Spanish citizenship, though many had lived in Spain for several generations. If they would not convert to Christianity, they had to leave.

Some local shipowners raised the price of passage to lurid levels to take advantage of the desperate circumstances. Meanwhile, few Spaniards offered the Jews the true value of their property and belongings and so, having no choice, the Jews were required to leave much behind, or accept a pittance for their wealth. The port of Palos wrung good money from the exodus, the demand for ships and crew much outstripping the supply.

Shortly after our arrival in Palos, I had asked the Admiral about the Jewish question. "Where are they going to go?" I wondered looking from our window as tender after tender rowed the new outcasts to their stinking vessels. "I have no way of knowing that," he replied, adding, "It is partly because of the demands of the Jewish arrangements, I suppose, that the Sovereigns did not pay prompter attention to me. All this has cost us much in time."

It was true that Ferdinand and Isabella had taken little interest in the Enterprise when the Admiral first proposed it. His bitterness laced his words as he said, "We cannot question the Sovereigns, and it is better the Jewish matter is behind us."

"But isn't Luis a Jew?" I asked. The Admiral had hired Luis Torres of Seville as voyage translator.

"Yes, but he has converted," the Admiral justified. "And he speaks Arabic." My husband had his reasons, I assumed, for thinking Arabic could be a useful language on this exploration.

I know the Admiral noticed the degrading state in which the Jews were travelling, for he lowered his eyes as one of their ships passed ours as we sailed away from Spain. We heard sad chants emanating, sung by those whose faces we could not quite make out, their deep voices rumbling like forsaken drums.

Not wishing to spoil the Admiral's greatest moment, I did not insist on the subject. As he says, the Jews, after all, are not our problem, and I had been writing of our leaving.

Our outfitting mission took place in Palos because two of the ships we would use were in port there. Palos had recently tried to shirk taxes by hiding the full value of its merchant income from the Crown. The Sovereigns found out, and fined the village the use of two caravels for one year, plus all food and sundries. These benefits were then assigned to us. Honest citizens had to bear the cost of the crime of their dishonest officials, but perhaps the whole town will gain in the long run from our journey, since a western route to the east would bring the Palos harbor many more years of shipping transactions.

Palos is an alchemist's child—a spicy cauldron of Spain and Africa and Arabia. Vessels of every size bob in the port, with hundreds of deckhands scurrying like insects and hunched under the burden of an infinite list of cargo. I had watched a very young boy balance on his head a wooden crate packed with urns of oil each at least his own height, negotiating the shaky plank walkway with bare feet.

The laden ships voyaged to Guinea, and the equator of Africa, exotic scented lands of a dark and distant continent about which I had been hearing, it seemed, for all my life.

The Admiral had hoped to provision in ten days, but the task in fact consumed ten weeks! True, disarray ruled the port in part because of the Jewish movements, but our greater obstacle was being strangers in the region and unknown to the many people with whom we had to work.

Which is how we came to know Sir Martin Alonso Pinzon, captain of the *Pinta*, and his younger brother, Vicente Yanez, who is in charge of *Nina*, the ships provided us in Palos. The Admiral also chartered *Santa Maria* to be our flagship.

The Pinzon brothers had been in Palos all their lives, and so were familiar to all on the streets and the port. Martin Alonso was a gentleman equal to any adventure, tall in bearing and charming in speech, able to turn a phrase to his advantage and quickly win a listener's goodwill. Pinzon had known my husband for several years and had discussed with him the idea of the Enterprise, although whether the Admiral had confided in Pinzon was not clear to me at the outset of the voyage.

Pinzon, on hearing that the Sovereigns had assented at last to the expedition and that we would leave from Palos, offered to join us and help the Admiral recruit men of good repute.

Pinzon is clearly keenly intelligent but at times enigmatic, even mysterious, though I could not say precisely why. He has very dark brown eyes that fix their subject in a stare, then loosen their hold with a sudden flicker of warmth.

His thick brown hair curls slightly at his collar, and he frequently winds his fingers through his full black beard. The Admiral and I spent hours with Pinzon at the harbor, and he introduced us as his lifelong friends with a major mission ahead. He approached each potential recruit as if the man were a partner already, as if Pinzon's words were the most important being uttered in Palos that day.

Pinzon dispensed compliments like sugar cubes, up and down the quay. "How well you handle that mast hoist, my comrade. . . .What are you fabricating there, good sailor. . . . Meet the Admiral Colon, surely you have heard of him. . . . A sailing? Yes. . . .Perhaps I could arrange it." In this way, Pinzon spread the word of the Enterprise, and we soon became as recognized on the Palos harbor as if we too had been born there. I wondered if the Admiral disliked the way Pinzon tended to draw attention to himself, for usually it was the Admiral who held center stage. But then, we had little choice if we wanted to be underway.

The Admiral assigned to me the business of securing foodstuffs. The staple was mainly of ship's biscuit, a ground bread of grain, oil and syrup—dull and dry to eat, but nutritious and long lasting. Plus sacks of beans and peas, wine, olive oil, vinegar, plenty of water of course, dried fish, salted meat and pork, live hens and pigs for fresh meat en route, salt, rice, cheese, figs, almonds—oh the list! It was my gathering of these pounds and gallons that led to what I would call the first Pinzon incident.

One morning when the sun was already hot yellow and high at only eight o'clock or so, I visited an oil merchant to sample his stock. The rotund man, not much smaller than the smooth heavy barrels lining his busy shop, amiably greeted me, perhaps knowing already who I was and the significant sale I represented. Tightly slipping sideways between his wares, he cheerfully let me taste from this or that urn. "This one, gracious Madame, will keep its texture even in the great heat of summer," he boasted, passing me a spoonful and holding his palm under my chin as I sipped. The oil indeed tasted lovely, like honey without sweetness.

As I was calculating as best I could how much to order, Chachu the Basque passed the shop, noticed me and came inside to be of help. He had been a member of *Santa Maria*'s original crew before the Admiral obtained her.

Chachu and the merchant worked out a delivery date, but Chachu set the conditions. "The lady will pay you after I have inspected the cargo once it reaches the ships. But don't worry," Chachu reassured the eager dealer, "all the charges are guaranteed payable by the order of the Sovereigns."

"Let me escort you home, my lady," Chachu then offered. A proper Andalusian would never have been so forward, but the more liberal Basque had no qualms. He was always gentlemanly, if somewhat lavish in his gestures, using his hands as much as words to convey his thoughts. "Do you see that wonderfully fertile hill?" he waved and traced the golden landscape across and up over the harbor. "Beyond all that, I was born."

Chachu spoke freely, as if he had always known me. "Frankly, Madame," he confessed, "I had my doubts about this voyage, and I had thought of leaving the *Santa Maria* to work on one of the Jewish ships." And, he further explained, a Basque to the core, "I didn't want to sail with so many Spaniards." Perhaps he already knew I was Portuguese.

"Well, Chachu," I answered, not taking offense, "how fortunate for us you changed your mind."

"Actually, Madame, it happened by mere coincidence. Just before I was to resign my ship, I spent an evening with some Palos sailors. They told me about Master Pinzon's idea, so I decided to stay, for it isn't every day such an expedition sets out."

I was startled at the words, "Master Pinzon's idea," but I did not interrupt. Chachu admitted that the thought of misty islands to the west en route to Japan appealed to him, as did the promise of an opulent court presided over by the Great Khan himself.

"Who would mind rubies for the picking?," Chachu speculated. "I might someday wish to marry, Madame, or maybe just please myself with the wealth."

He finished his saga by saying it was only the confidence the people of Palos seemed to have in Pinzon which induced him to join us. Then he added in doubtless afterthought of courtesy, "Though I had not heard of the Admiral before, I am sure his reputation must be as distinguished as Pinzon's, perhaps even more so."

He bowed deeply as he left me at my door. I decided to give Pinzon the benefit of the doubt, but what could Chachu have meant with "Pinzon's idea"? I thought perhaps Chachu had merely embellished or misheard, but a subsequent conversation set me wondering again.

One day not long after my talk with Chachu, Pinzon and I stood alone, watching cargo being loaded on to *Pinta*. Chachu talked gaily with his counterpart, giving sharp-eyed suggestions about the distribution of weight. Pinzon remarked good-naturedly that he envied our ship the services of the Basque.

[7

"Chachu was so eager for the voyage, he barely needed convincing," Pinzon told me offhandedly, adding "He was most impressed with the Admiral's thinking and skill."

This was the opposite of the boatswain's own account. Which version to believe, words changing like quicksilver as they pour from one person to the other on the waterfront, impressions melting into facts.

Pinzon spoke so convincingly to the sailors of the importance of a faithful crew for the Admiral that I was reluctant to think he would seek his own glory more than ours together. But was his pleasantry merely for my sake? This was a quandary I could not afford, unless I was willing to share it with my husband, which I was not. He would be annoyed and find me too protective of him. And what would be the basis of my worry? Pinzon so far had done nothing except help.

I could not also share with the Admiral what I can confess here, namely that I could not deny the power of Pinzon's ways. He appeared to live for his own diversion, taking a rash deliberate pleasure in his own words. I enjoyed his easy manner, though I was relieved he was on another ship, for his self-assurance gave me pause.

But I had not meant to speak so much of Pinzon here.

Much has happened in our short time at sea, including near disaster.

"The Admiral says the wind will wail tonight, and I agree," Chachu had observed, finishing his work with the ropes, preparing to move onto the next task. He seemed constantly busy, charged as he was with maintaining all ship's gear, keeping the belowdecks clean, the lines dry and the sails, our wings, intact.

With all this, I did not know when Chachu slept. But anyway surely not that night.

Without warning, shortly before dinner, the winds did come up suddenly, more fiercely than the Admiral expected. In minutes, it seemed, the sea rose in walls around us.

Seeing me, the Admiral ordered me off the upper deck and back to our quarters. "There will be enough for me to manage here, and you will not have the strength to cling to the fixtures," he cautioned and commanded.

He was right. The wind soon gathered full gashing strength, and great dark sheets of water swelled and hissed over the rails. It was as though we had become too confident of the calm, and the ocean swirled up angrily to demonstrate that all was never what it seemed. Before obeying the Admiral, I looked to the heaving *Nina* and *Pinta*, losing sight of them in the waves and heavy rain. *Santa Maria* was alone, the sky and sea a seamless mask of gray.

Chachu and the crew raced madly around the decks, yanking down the sails to keep them from being split in the wind, and doubly secured cargo crates, barrels and tables, for we could hardly afford either to lose them overboard, or let them tear loose to smash through a deck or wall.

Already chaos had taken over our cabin. I rushed to tie down the Admiral's compass and navigational tools, his books and my own. There were papers strewn like snowfall from the cupboards. The water had not yet washed in, but the wooden walls between me and the ocean felt only wafer thin, poised to rupture. I bent to collect things, and suddenly behind me, a wild explosion of glass, wood and sand, a piercing shattering noise—the hourglass had torn from its strapping and burst on the floorboards. I tried to sweep the gritty mess with a paper into my skirt.

But then, more thrashing. The ship swayed mightily, and a bench tumbled and pitched roughly across my foot. I scrambled to escape things falling and scraping by climbing up on our bed, there being no means of keeping balance, or forcing objects back in place. I rubbed my throbbing toes and cowered beneath the sloping seasoned timber, all that stood between me and the howling screaming seas.

Evening melted into night. All the time, outside the waters pressed, each wave angrily feeling for an opening, the most minor crack in *Santa Maria*'s body through which to seep, erode, then blow and force itself. But the ship did not lose her stride. Against the crashing pressure, she felt like a drifting mountain. And all the time, the Admiral did not come below.

I tried to stay awake, but riding the storm had exhausted me, and I finally lay down. My neck had begun to ache from bending— there was little room to sit upright on our bed tucked under the low cabin walls—and as soon as I let my body relax from the tension of resisting each buck and roll, I slipped into a superficial, tossed sleep.

I listened to my heartbeat through the straw matting of our bed like a besieged soldier straining to hear an approaching ally's horses, ear to the ground—the regular thump, thumping, thump, the roar and hurtle of the storm, the heartbeat again, then the rocking of the next long wave.

I wondered if the dying could feel the waning of their pulse. What would come first, the last beat or hearing it, and I rolled in and out of unquiet dreams until I thought I heard my own heart stop, a cold silence in the mattress. My eyes opened wildly.

The cabin door shuddered ajar, and I sensed light at last, not water, entering between the planks of the cabin walls. The sea seemed to have subsided. The Admiral was here, as was the beginning of the day.

He came to bed and I moved closer to him. He put my hand on his chest and held it there. His entire body felt warm and rushing, as if recouping from a race.

"It has begun to quiet," he said breathing more softly, "and we were able to approach the other ships. The *Pinta*'s rudder broke loose in the rough water."

Pinzon, he said, had relashed it, only to have it rip away again. The Admiral now had to choose between a return to Spain, where we could be sure to be properly repaired, or to carry on to the Canary Islands, which were much closer, but where the necessary boatyard was not at all assured.

"I've decided to risk the Canaries," the Admiral reported, "But the crew is exhausted and would surely prefer that I take this chance to make for home again." He worried that the men were already too dispirited to go on. "Perhaps it is all already lost," he said aloud, but as if to himself.

I moved nearer, wanting to share his ordeal. I was sure the men had admired him for meeting the storm by their sides. "They will not leave you," I murmured, and I longed for him to reach for me.

We had been discreet throughout the preparations and the voyage so far. The Admiral had not wanted to underline before his men that he did not lack the presence of a woman. He worried that his wife could become a wedge between himself and the crew. "Please understand," he had asked me.

I had, but not on this stormy half-night just turning into day. I wanted to be with him. I tasted the salt of the storm on his face as I kissed him, and touched my lips softly to his, to his cheeks, his eyes, until soon, loosening his clothes and mine, he returned my wishes, his full weight turning upon me.

I lost myself then, as I do now in the retelling, in his power, his desire, his mouth open and warm on mine, and in the memories of our earliest days and nights in Lisbon.

Brimming with life and passions, Sunday after Sunday he came to see me at my convent school, filling the afternoons with flowers and splendid tales of where he had been. Africa and Italy, and hundreds of places I had only heard of but yearned to see. Finally, after weeks of afternoons, there came an irresistible turning of time, the embrace that did not end, the first touch of fingers on the flesh, our beginning.

I remember that is how I learned how early birds begin to sing, that they sing when it is still dark, as early as three or four after midnight, well before dawn. For our first full night together, I never slept. He was so full of wanting me, and after, I just lay awake beside him through the entire night. I knew I could never deny what we had done against all convention, and despite what I had been told all my life since childhood would be a sin.

On the ship after the storm, it seemed again like the first shimmering night to me. Except this time, as afterward he slept and I did not, there were no songs of birds, for we were at sea, far from land, and far from any other life or sound, except our own breathing, and the now almost gentle movements of the alien sea we had survived.

Chapter Two

The Governor Must Be a Curious Man

As briskly as the seas had whipped into rage, they flattened, and the day after the storm we were an exhausted crew stalled on an exhausted sea. The wind, as if a child we no longer amused, ignored us altogether. Hot calm prevailed. The fury had blown itself silent and still.

A few men slept after the Admiral woke, their tired bodies wrapped in blankets tucked along the sides of the decks in a series of puffed coccoons. Chachu too, at last, found time to doze. Other men began the business of restoring order to the ship, removing soaked canvas shrouds, untying ropes and unwrapping cargo. The ship was coming back to life.

Above deck for a harrowing moment I thought the ship had now caught fire, but it was only the bitter black acrid smoke of burning tar, as Chachu's helper, Falguero the caulker, melted pitch to begin resealing spots between planks the sea had picked clean.

But instead of the gentle banter and talking common to sailors, in place of the occasional song and frequent shouting, the men were quiet. De Terreros, the steward, too had given up his music. On and off since our departure, he had played a small carved flute to pass the time and please the crew, but it now rested tightly in his sash, like a forgotten dagger.

"Their eagerness is gone after this false start," my husband said, noticing as well, as we drank our morning tea together. "I can feel it."

My husband could not look to Pinzon for support, for *Pinta* and Martin Alonso, had already sailed for Grand Canary, to seek repair while we made for Gomera, another island in the Canary group, where the Admiral would investigate the option of a new ship in case we had to replace the *Pinta* altogether.

He decided to share his plan with the entire crew and returned above deck to summon the men. The great ship swayed mildly, normally, reassuringly regular. All eyes searched my husband's for news.

He stood among the crew on the main deck, not on the forecastle above.

"My very dear voyagers," the Admiral greeted, in a rich comradely tone. "Thanks to your strength and courage, we have survived our first danger together. Be proud, each of you. Be content. Recover your energies. Today, no man has duty."

The men shifted and brightened. My husband knew how to begin.

"Our ship, *Santa Maria*, weathered things well. But *Pinta* as you may all know, now rides rudderless and leaking in the sea. It is impossible for her to continue in that condition, so I have decided to put in to the Canary Islands, not far away, to repair her or secure another ship."

A disappointed murmur spread among the crew. The Admiral, however, had expected that.

"I know, I know," he amply acknowledged, "I too would have preferred to see Spain again, to sleep in my own bed, to be at home. But think not of the past, the known. Think of the great mission before us. We together have a great destiny, all of us. We cannot go back before we have truly begun. The Canary Islands, particularly Gomera, are reknowned for hospitality. The Governor at Gomera will surely help us repair, reprovision and gather our strength again."

But then I heard the questioning voice of Cristobal Caro, the grizzled goldsmith. "And with respect, Admiral, what will happen," he asked, "if neither repair nor replacement are possible?"

Caro had been among the first crew to sign on, a native of Aviga, a hamlet near Palos. Since departure, I'd paid little notice to him, although he seemed willing to share the deck work with Chachu when the Basque asked him, without resentment.

In truth, the Admiral had not considered the twin-horned dilemma the goldsmith raised, so sure was he that the Canaries would solve our problem. And so, he seemed to hesitate in forming his reply. He could hardly promise the entire assembly that he would so soon return to Spain.

"A fair question, Caro," the Admiral began, too aware that much hung in its balance and his answer.

But then came the voice of Diego de Harana, the marshal of *Santa Maria*, a dashing gentleman from Cordoba whom the Admiral had met during the interminable waiting for the decision from the Spanish Queen. The de Harana family had helped my husband during his stay in Spain, according to him, showering their hospitality and friendship when he was most alone.

"Allow me, Admiral, to address our friend," the young de Harana interjected, turning to face the goldsmith.

"Why not, Caro, ask God what will happen if there is neither sun nor cloud tomorrow? Surely, if the situation arose, Our Father would develop the necessary alternative, but not before. The Admiral's plans are based on his years of experience in navigation in this ocean. He knows these islands. I would bet the Admiral Colon will be received as royally on the Canaries as in Spain itself, and that officials there would offer their own ships if we needed them. I believe all will be right."

Before Caro could reply, or even the Admiral, came other welcome words. Juan de la Cosa, *Santa Maria*'s actual owner and the Admiral's second in command, now also spoke, widening the path cut by de Harana.

"Yes, gentlemen, surely on the Sovereigns' territory we will be treated to all we require. After all, we sail for the King and Queen, and I would have chartered this ship to no one less than the Admiral here in charge. Let us not forget who we are."

The crew absorbed these words intently, for de la Cosa was a well-known merchant in the south of Spain who had given many sailors good employment. My husband, given respite to think while his allies spoke, now resumed persuasive control.

"Oh good and gracious comrades, your confidence is my guarantee. Believe and trust me, as these most worthy gentlemen have said. I shall not command you into foolishness. The Canaries will restore us. But today, little work. To each of you, I offer a cup of our finest wine. I thank you my dear friends, and I salute you all."

Caro gave a surprised smile when the Admiral broke from the crew to single him out, embracing him. On seeing this unusual gesture of solidarity, each man then eagerly sought to shake the Admiral's hand, each agreeing that indeed the Canaries was a good choice, each throwing in their lot with the new day. The Admiral had won.

Chachu now hurriedly hoisted a foresail at the Admiral's command, and the ship slid forward. The Admiral had swayed the crew, though he himself rippled with uncertainty.

"I am not sure if I fail in the Canaries that they will ever put out to sea again," he said with uncharacteristic self-doubt when we were once again alone. But he recovered soon enough. "God knows, though, I have done my best. We can only hope hospitality and good shipyards carry us over this next obstacle."

He sat down at his table in our cabin to calculate how far we'd come and the time we'd need to reach the island group.

Fastidiously, he drew a line, plotting his morning observations of the sun. His pen scratched busily, as if trying desperately to keep up with the mind and hand controlling it. The Admiral was so lost in his work, it was as though the ship and beams had fallen away from around him. His desk had become his only vessel, his ideas the only wind he needed now.

I stood behind, watching him concentrate.

His handsome compass consumed him. In a round pressed leather bowl, the magnetic poles shook the needle like the tremor of a finger. A miniature painting of a Genoese galley graced the center of the compass, many rowing hands symbolically and perpetually heading north. A Genoese friend of my husband's gave him the compass on his arrival in Lisbon and it had been his trusted tool ever since.

How many times I had stood, in a sense lovingly absent, outside the circle of the solitude he so often drew around himself. Even in our tiny room at sea, a gulf stood between us when my husband worked, and I watched, loving him without saying so, until, his thinking and planning done, he broke the bubble of silence with the shuffle of parchment maps and the rattling closing of his desk drawer.

Only when he turned from his table to again join the men did he notice me.

"Oh, I didn't realize you had stayed here," he remarked, a small smile on his face.

"A tribute to my dedication to letting you work," I replied, following him out to the main deck again.

We at last had enough wind to reach the skirt of Gomera, a brown muted island.

Santa Maria drew far too much water to approach the small village of San Sebastian. The Admiral hurriedly ordered a tender readied and lowered to take him to shore. But he was still worried about the mood of the crew.

"Listen well to the men while I am gone, Felipa," he instructed me, "for here we may win everything, or be forced to return to Spain."

I would have preferred to go with him to speak to the Governor, but he wanted to make the visit alone.

"What I need is to rely on you to be my eyes and ears on board," he said as he left. But he returned much sooner than expected, only half relieved.

"We must wait here," he announced to the men, again anxiously assembled on deck, "for the Governor has a ship we may engage, but the Governor is gone and due back in some days." Now the men heaved their chests with relief, delighted we would be in port that long.

To make good use of the time, the Admiral sent a team to replace the food, firewood and freshwater already spent. De Harana was in charge of water supplies en route, and before he went ashore, I spoke to him. "It was good of you to come so quickly to the support of the Admiral," I offered, grateful for his timely intervention.

"I could hardly do otherwise, my lady, and indeed I agree that your husband is right to have come here."

"Still had you waited even a moment more, the crew might have become too restless."

"We are all here to serve this great Enterprise, Madame," de Harana answered, bowing slightly.

He asked if I would like to accompany him to the water fountains and to oversee the provisioning.

"No, Diego, you surely can monitor this task well, and I have had enough of measuring and buying in Palos." We laughed together and he collected his men. I also preferred instead to watch another of the Admiral's projects, the redesigning of the *Nina*'s sails.

Since we left Spain, we had had trouble keeping our three ships together, as each had different designs, speeds and rhythms. *Santa Maria*, though stately and more spacious than the others, lumbers like a laden wagon, although as the storm proved, she held solid in the angriest of seas. In flat waters, though, *Pinta* cuts ahead neatly, while we, the flagship, trail behind. *Pinta*'s sailing, by far the fastest, both pleased and bothered the Admiral.

Nina, the least of us, is much loved by the Admiral. Her huge lateen sail makes her as maneuverable as a racehorse, according to my husband, but presents a great disadvantage if we cannot all keep together. So the Admiral decided to use our unexpected stop in Gomera to trim *Nina*'s sails to match *Pinta*'s design.

Nina's Captain, Pinzon's younger brother Vincente Yanez, about 30 years old, walked at the Admiral's side, listening intently as my husband outlined what he had in mind, posing only the occasional technical question.

Vincente often wore a pure white shirt, braided with black piping at the neck, blousing fully over black breeches, as well as a large silver medallion cross. He had a slender nose, fine skin, and very soft brown eyes. Beardless, he was still as striking as his brother, Martin Alonso, though much less outgoing. Yanez seemed to enjoy the chance to be both Captain and student learning from someone as experienced as the Admiral.

The sail work proved ambitious. Using an elaborate system of pulleys, a team of men pulled *Nina*'s main mast from the deck, and it resisted like a recalcitrant splinter. Once they had dislodged this massive centerbone, they hauled it forward and out and moved other beams around as if they were building the ship again. This all under a beating sun, and still with no news of the governor.

Nina's rebirth took two days with Chachu supervising the cutting of the new square-rigged sails, an adaptation the Admiral said he would have made in Palos if we had had the time.

It was amazing to me how the simple modification of a sail's shape could so much alter the ship's response to the wind. There was so much about sailing I still did not understand, despite my having grown up at the door of the sea. While I just looked on, the workers did not appear intimidated by my presence. I brought them cups of water as they sewed and cut, the new sails spread before them like bread batter.

These necessary tasks busied the crew and their thoughts had seemed to turn again to the future of the journey.

But the Governor still did not appear. I thought perhaps my husband had raised endangered hopes, for we had no assurance that the Governor's ship would suit us or be available to us for as long as we needed.

But when I questioned the Admiral about why he was so keen to wait, he seemed uneasy, so I did not press. He simply noted, sensibly I thought, ''We would be better off to have an entirely new ship. Then the men would not think we had among us a ship tainted by bad luck.''

At last, after another week of idling, consuming more food and water, Chachu spied the *Pinta*, swiftly gliding toward us, apparently fit and feisty.

"She will be here very soon, Admiral," Chachu called down from his perch on the mast.

Then, in pure coincidence, Chachu spied the Governor's convoy returning at the same moment from the other direction.

On seeing the *Pinta* fast approaching across the sunlit ocean, and the not-too-distant Governor's ships, the Admiral brightened considerably.

He greeted Pinzon warmly when the captain and his crew debarked and gave him a detailed tour of the remade *Nina* with obvious satisfaction and pride. "It was clever to alter the lateen, don't you think?" my husband remarked to Pinzon. But Pinzon took equal pleasure in his own accomplishment. "Yes, Admiral, quite brilliant, wonderful work," he said fingering Chachu's perfectly stitched sail seams. "But you must also visit the reborn lady, *Pinta*, more seaworthy and fleet than ever."

Pinzon's ship, repaired rudder firmly in place, did indeed look as solid and reliable as when we had left the mainland. Still, though, the Admiral wanted to pursue the matter of another ship. "I know you have confidence in your vessel, Pinzon," he explained after Pinzon had mildly protested that *Pinta* could be trusted now in any weather, "but we cannot know whether an entirely different ship would be preferred to one apparently well repaired. A ship once broken . . . "

The splashing of a vessel rowing toward us cut the Admiral's sentence, turning his attention. "The attaché would like to pass you an official note, Admiral" Chachu reported, having bent overboard to inquire the visitor's business.

The Admiral read the paper quickly. "The Governor wishes to see me right away," he elatedly announced.

"I must leave you, Pinzon," he said abruptly, and hastened back to *Santa Maria* to prepare for the meeting, as did I.

But once in our cabin, he again asked me to stay with our ships. "Please help me once more," he said. "You see how eager Pinzon is to promote the *Pinta*. Now that I am called to shore, I think it best for you to gather the details from Pinzon about the repair, its costs, its method, executors and so forth. Then I can later make a judgment about its quality and I will compare it with what the Governor has to offer."

The Admiral collected some papers and changed his cape as he talked.

"But wouldn't I be far more useful in a diplomatic meeting with a Governor?" I protested. "I hardly know what to ask Pinzon about shipbuilding, and surely the Governor might think it discourteous that I had not come as well. . . .''

No, the Admiral was adamant. "We must divide the tasks at hand, Felipa, if we wish to be fast on our way again. You are my only reliable source.'' He kissed the hand I had put on his shoulder and left for shore.

Meanwhile, Pinzon arrived on *Santa Maria*. "May I come in,'' he inquired, already walking toward my quarters.

His jovial, confident manner suggested he had amused himself well, despite the *Pinta*'s mishap.

"We had enough relaxed time to learn much of local lore and local life to tell you about, Madame,'' he explained, as if he had been gone on a visit of leisure.

Pinzon leaned against the Admiral's cupboard, while I sat on the bench at the Admiral's table.

"Grand Canary soil produces delicious swollen grapes, my lady,'' he began, his face somewhat bronzed by the sun he evidently enjoyed there. "So I have a present for you. Have any glasses survived the storm?'' He placed a black bottle of wine tightly sheathed in yellow burlap on the table in front of me.

"Oh, a few,'' I replied lightly, passing him two goblets from the small cabinet above the desk. "*Santa Maria* held her keel well, you know,'' I said, in a mild promotion of our ship.

"Indeed, indeed,'' he acknowledged lightly, already pouring from the flask.

He handed me my glass, then filled and sipped his own. "Still wonderful, this wine, unharmed by travel,'' Pinzon proclaimed, gratified.

"That delightful island truly brims with hospitality,'' he continued, "and all received us well. We dined richly on fresh delicious fish and crisp greens, and listened to the most lovely lyric ballads of the local sort played on a strange three-stringed guitar. And the people begged us to report on our travels. You would think we were heroes already, instead of sailors waylaid by the wind barely outside the sight of Spain. A pity you couldn't have been there.''

Clearly Pinzon had not worried much about us. I could picture him on Grand Canary, walking among the rolling vineyards and bustling markets, tasting this and that. He was right—the wine had a full fragrant body and bouquet.

Pinzon certainly relished voyaging, and he recounted details of the rudder repair as if the episode too were a part of the pleasures of travel.

"Of course," he recalled with amused satisfaction, "the workers at Grand Canary were amazed we had reached their boatyard at all, considering the extent of *Pinta*'s damage. And they were very impressed by our perseverance in such intemperate and wild seas."

Each time I tried to direct our conversation to what I wanted to know—"but what did it cost, Mr. Pinzon," for example—he steered the talk his way. "I have all the receipts, Madame, in my cabin on *Pinta*, but I made sure we were not taken advantage of, if that is your concern."

Eventually, Pinzon did answer all my questions, and our conversation, if not the most direct, had undeniably been very pleasant. Again, I found myself of two minds about this man.

Obviously, he was convinced that the *Pinta* repair would now withstand any imaginable wind and threat.

When Pinzon had finished his report, he turned his attention to me. "Madame, but I am rude," he said in mock self-scolding. "Do not let me be the only one to tell a tale. What of your sojourn here?" He listened attentively as I passed along our news, and the story of *Nina*'s "change of clothes."

His laugh interrupted me. "What a delightfully original description of the replacement of a sail," he remarked and though I enjoyed his appreciation, I grew uneasy when he fixed his active eyes on mine.

I gave him a full accounting of our present inventory, thinking it wise for him, a Captain, to know our overall state of supply, taking my turn to pilot the conversation.

In this way, we agreeably passed two hours, but soon we had both exhausted our tidings, and it was difficult to think of what to speak of next. I wondered about the Governor's meeting.

"He must be hungry for details," I said.

"Who, the Admiral?" Pinzon asked, somewhat confused.

I, of course, meant the Governor and pictured the Admiral, having finished his negotiation for the best ship available, not being able to tactfully take his leave.

"No," I answered, "The Governor. He must be a very curious man and full of questions."

Pinzon suddenly understood. "But Madame," he declared, "the Governor here is a woman like yourself!"

Now it was my turn to be confused—I had had no idea that the Governer here was female!

But before I could ask, Pinzon provided more information. "She is the Dona Beatriz de Peraza, a cousin of the Marquesa de Moya, of the family Bobadilla. The Queen Sovereign knew her well, having named her maid of honor. No doubt she met the Admiral when he spent so many months in Cordoba at the Spanish court."

This last thought spun around me. If that were so, would not the Admiral have told me?

Pinzon noticed my distraction, and begged his pardon to leave. "I am sure, my lady, they have had to talk of many issues related to the ships," he ventured, adding, "Surely the Admiral will be returning soon, and I ought to be back to *Pinta* and *Nina*. It is awhile since I have talked with my brother."

Pinzon left, saying, "Please finish the wine with the Admiral and give him my kindest wishes."

He summoned his tender and chatted amiably with the men who rowed him away.

I don't know how long I waited in the cabin, perhaps another half hour. It annoyed me that Juan had not yet replaced our broken clock, since we had many aboard, and time stretched immeasurably before me.

I was hardly relaxed when the Admiral did at last return. He had barely stepped inside our chambers when I asked about the meeting. "How did you manage," I said, not wishing to be the first to raise the matter of the Governor's sex.

"All is well," he reported simply. "We can have a ship, plus anything else necessary. And the Governor has told me of many visitors coming through this place, including a visiting Spaniard who happened just now to join us, who claimed they saw each year—imagine this—lands to the west of the Canaries!"

I ignored this last tidbit of important news, letting it wash over me like a weak wave. I had another aspect of the Governor's visit too firmly in mind.

"Is she rested enough from her journey to accept my respects?" I inquired. The Admiral at first looked startled, but then said, "Yes, if you wish, but surely it would not be necessary. I have already conveyed your greetings."

"No," I replied, "I think it proper, as we have a bit of time."

I suggested we go ashore that evening before our meal, and invite Pinzon and his brother. Then the Admiral could take the opportunity to hear firsthand about the repair at Grand Canary.

"As you wish, Felipa," my husband answered, replacing his portfolio on his table, then excusing himself to wait for me above deck.

San Sebastian thrived, a tiny harbor sitting at the mouth of a deep canyon opening on the sea. A large castle overshadowed the port.

The Admiral did not speak to me as we made our way, but instead talked to Pinzon barely without a stop. He deflected my every question about our sailing plans, returning always to his conversation about the rudder work. Could he have been angry with my forcing this extra trip ashore, I worried. I had begun myself to regret it, for now it was I who had added to the delay. Still, I remained off balance, curious to know this woman who might have known my husband, and I thought, having insisted, I had better see the visit through.

The Governor received us right away, and she was far more alluring and composed than I had expected, for somehow I had thought her distant post, perhaps a hardship, might have taken a toll. Her hair was wound in a perfect golden braid, held at the top of her head by a silver peacock comb. She wore a laced dress, the color of eggshell, a series of diaphanous layers of fine cloth. The Bobadilla initials were double embroidered into the waistband, resembling a wide-winged embossed butterfly in flight. The low neckline revealed her ivory skin, barely flecked, her chest there to be seen, the hints of the rising of her breasts. She was dressed for a gala Spanish evening event, not an island afternoon, and I had to admit she was very very beautiful.

The Admiral and the Pinzon brothers each kissed her hand, and I bowed.

"Please take some refreshments," she beckoned, "though we have assembled them hastily and I fear they may not be enough, for I did not expect so welcome a visit." She led us to a well-laid table of crisp linen and freshly washed fruit. Bright oranges like small suns lustered in a silver bowl, and clusters of perfect purple grapes tumbled over the sides.

"And do let us gather in the more intimate chamber," she added as she walked. But then Pinzon asked the Governor to briefly excuse the men, so that they could finalize the details of our departure.

The Admiral eyed Pinzon coldly, and disagreed immediately. "No," he protested, "it would be improper and impolite for us to absent ourselves."

22]

But Dona Beatriz delicately waved his hesitation away and purred, "Oh, Admiral, not at all. I know you must have important navigational matters to discuss, though I so regret your urgency to leave Gomera. Had you more time to spend here, you would learn my reputation for hospitality is indeed well warranted. Feel totally free to complete your business without us."

The men bowed deeply, and stayed in the outer administrative hall, while the Governor and I moved alone deeper into the castle. We walked along an enclosed breezeway and our footsteps echoed just enough to give the impression that our shoes were stepping across the floor first, and our feet catching up.

Once in the reception room, the Governor offered me a seat on a rich velvet sofa. She settled herself effortlessly, despite her abundant gown, in a heavy wooden chair which surrounded her like a half barrel, a Sovereign cross deeply carved in the base.

The Governor spoke first, asking of our voyage, our success, and my comfort in Gomera in a polite solicitous tone in keeping with the stature of our setting. And I answered without detail, distracted by her undeniable grace, but mainly by her youth. Surely she was younger than the Admiral, and by me as well, by about 10 years. How had a woman so young achieved this station, I wished to ask, but could not of course.

Instead I heard her begin, as Spaniards often did, with reference to my not being Spanish. "I understand you are from Portugal," she said politely. "I regret I haven't been there."

"Do not apologize, Madame," I replied. "After all I had not been to Gomera until just these last few days."

"True," the Governor answered, dipping her head, "You are kind to remind me." She passed me a tray of honey-glazed biscuits and began another line of conversation.

"How is it that you do not fear the sea?"

"My father was one of Portugal's great navigators. I grew up very near the ocean and . . . " I had not expected a woman of her breeding to interrupt.

"But that is quite another matter than actually travelling yourself."

"But Madame Governor," I urged, "you are quite alone on this remote island. Did you fear the trip?"

"No, surely not but . . . your father was?"

"Bartolomé de Perestrello."

"I regret I do not know your family."

She passed the biscuit tray a second time, but I declined.

"Nor I yours, Madame, but then great families of Europe often remain strangers to each other."

Her glare did not dislodge my own.

"Indeed," she responded coolly, "especially when we move about so much."

Then she looked away for a brief moment, back, turning now to a subject entirely new to me.

"Tell me, are you eager to accept my offer?"

"Offer?" I repeated, puzzled.

The Governor explained, "I simply wondered if you wished to accept my offer to the Admiral that you remain here on Gomera, rather than continue the journey, until we can facilitate your return to Spain." She touched her lips lightly with her napkin after making this proposition.

"How could I?" I replied, incredulous at the question. "I am needed, and I would never deny myself the experience ahead."

I did not wish to share with her all the years that had brought us to this point. But I wanted her to know that the Admiral wished me to stay. "It is important for the Admiral's wife to be aboard for morale," I offered, "and to share tasks, for this expedition is no easy matter."

"I do not underestimate the difficulties, Madame, rest assured, but you will be prey to strange peoples you might meet. I am concerned for you."

"Be assured, dear Governor, that your concern is deeply appreciated. But probably there are few dangers in Japan," I returned, hoping to dispel her sympathy and any impression that my situation was foolish. "And anyway, Madame, were there not until recently raw cave dwellers right here on the Canaries?"

The Governor laughed mildly, rearranging herself, both arms now resting less casually on the high sides of her chair, though the flounces of her sleeves and dress still fanned perfectly around her, giving her the appearance of a seated lily.

"Indeed, there were aborigines here before the Sovereigns conquered the group," she acknowledged, lifting a biscuit from the tray. "Did the Admiral tell you that?"

"Yes, he discusses many historical events with me, and I had heard it on my own."

"I see," Beatriz reflected, again taking a minute before speaking. I waited and prepared.

"But it does seem strange to me that in all the elaborate after-noons the Admiral spent at Court, and surely you have seen his many excellent models and exquisite gold threaded maps of the world, in all those days he spent at court—what I am saying is that I find it strange that I hadn't known the Admiral to be married." She settled back more comfortably in her chair again.

She spoke with such familiarity of the Admiral's navigational presentations that I could not mistake she must have been present frequently when he had made entreaties to the Queen in Cordoba while I had waited in Lisbon.

Beatriz completed her recitation. "Given how much the Admiral enjoys conversation, it seemed odd that he did not once mention that he had a wife." Now I was the one who could not find an untroubled way to sit.

I tried to respond. "Of course in those days the Admiral had much to accomplish, and so he might not have thought to discuss his family in the face of the greater business on his mind."

"Of course, my dear" the Governor agreed feebly. "And yet, well, as you say, it is not relevant now."

She put her slender pinky to the corner of her lips and added, "I do assure you that you would be welcome here if you are truly so uncomfortable on board."

"But I am not the least uncomfortable," I replied.

"Oh," she said doubtingly, now gazing away toward the ships. "I had another impression from the Admiral."

With that, I had had enough of this encounter. I disliked feeling this familiarity with my husband from another woman, and speaking with her of what he had or had not said.

I stood and bid us return to him. Beatriz said unhesitatingly, "Of course."

The Admiral's meeting too had quelled, and he and the Pinzon brothers were speaking of small matters when we arrived. The time had obviously come to take our leave of Gomera.

Beatriz protested roundly, urging us to have dinner with her at least. But, now I took the lead.

"I think not, dearest Governor," I said before anyone else could speak, "although that would be a most pleasant change. But we must return to our ships, after all. It is we who are in charge of so magnificent a journey. It would not be fair to leave those in our command alone on the last night in port." The Governor nodded her understanding, but I did not invite her to dine on board with us.

We made our farewells, and Beatriz spoke a few words quietly to the Admiral, then to Pinzon and Yanez. She clasped my hand and said, "I have so enjoyed meeting you, and learning another side of our great Admiral."

"And I you, Madame Governor," I said, only bowing my head this time instead of a final curtsy.

I wished to speak privately to my husband right away, to settle questions on my mind, but on the journey back to our tender, he excused himself to speak with Yanez, saying "I must make one more check of the new sails on *Nina*. And *Pinta* and the flagship as well."

Apparently, the vessel the Governor could put at our disposal would be even heavier than *Santa Maria*, and so the Admiral had decided to continue with the original fleet intact. He walked on ahead with Pinzon's brother, signalled a tender, and the two were rowed out to *Nina*.

Once again I found myself alone with Martin Alonso, who seemed delighted to be keeping the vessel with which he had started. "Good fortune for me, Madame, your husband finds this Gomera ship ill-suited for discovery. I am so very fond of *Pinta*, even more now than before the storm."

My mind catapulted back and forth. This meeting at Gomera disturbed me. Soon, I heard myself saying aloud, "How could one so young be posted so high?"

Pinzon immediately offered an answer. "If you speak of Dona Beatriz, that is not a polite story," he suggested in a tone which told me he only half wished to keep the tale to himself.

And I, I confess, more than half wished to hear it. I said nothing, guessing Pinzon would continue on his own, and indeed he interpreted my silence as permission to go on. Pinzon, I had seen, did not stand on ceremony.

He elaborated easily.

"The story goes that the King, our own Ferdinand, too much appreciated Beatriz, for she is exquisite, as we've seen, but what is not known is whether Beatriz too much encouraged him, so to speak. In any case, the Queen, not one to support intercessions, decided to relieve Beatriz of her role as court matron, assigning her instead to the estate of a gentleman who was Captain of Gomera at the time, de Peraza. Beatriz could not protest and probably did not wish to, for she must have known marriage to the Captain could likely ensue. For his part, de Peraza was charmed, romance took its course, and Beatriz became his bride. When he died, Beatriz inherited his title.''

Pinzon tossed a stone in the harbor, as if to punctuate his recitation. Clearly, stating the facts entertained him and he did not bother to excuse himself for intimating that an illicit flirtation had passed between a Sovereign King and Beatriz. I had to admit I could easily picture the vexed Isabella banishing the lovely woman; Beatriz obviously knew her appeal to men.

Just as we reached the tenders, Pinzon apparently felt compelled to add, as if reading my thoughts, ''I tend to believe the rumor myself, for after all Beatriz is one of the most magnificent women in Spain. I can well imagine Ferdinand's eyes travelling her shoulders and he would not have been the only one to wish to. . . .''

He stopped abruptly, this time perhaps aware he had gone too far. I felt my eyes fill, for now to hear Pinzon too speak so admiringly of her, and to me as if I were his crony, not the wife of the Admiral, not also a woman—I suddenly felt unpleasing and invisible. Awkwardly, Pinzon, detecting my near tears, excused himself.

''Oh Madame, I have offended you somehow. Do not feel distress about such a harmless story.''

He tried again. ''My dear Madame,'' he began, reaching for my hand then thinking better of it, ''you who are so courageous as to join us, I did not mean to say all that I have.'' For the first time since we'd met, Pinzon was stumbling on words.

''Perhaps, I'd better rejoin my ship directly,'' he decided, ordering his oarsman to take me back alone.

Santa Maria swayed lightly, silent in the night, her decks empty. The Admiral had not returned yet.

It had been a bitter troubling evening. Had I been too hasty to go ashore, then too hasty to leave? Had I said something untoward that caused the Admiral to reject the Governor's offer of a ship?

But why had he told her I wished to leave the voyage, if he had at all. Had something passed between them once he wished me not to know? Did Pinzon know instead? I saw his confident bemused face recalling the scenes of Cordoba.

I had no choice but to wait for the Admiral, needing his embrace and conversation and the calm to talk things through. But my husband would be a while in coming.

''The Admiral sent a message that he has been detained, Madame, and he begs your leave,'' the page announced from the doorway of our cabin. "And he suggests you not wait to dine with him."

I responded by telling the page to summon me a rower so I could join the Admiral.

"All the tenders are in use, Madame, I am sorry," he replied. I was shipbound, with no means to send the Admiral a single word.

I ate alone in our cabin, letting my eyes rest on his desk. I fingered his velvet capes, his leather doublets, the blue woolen captain's cap he rarely wore, the corners of his many papers. I watched his Genoese compass galley bob in its holder. I walked around the cabin, then above deck a moment, then below again.

It was a restless awful night, numb with wondering. Could the Admiral, like Ferdinand, have once been tempted? And what if yes, temptation means nothing. The dread conflicting thoughts continued. But what of the time the Admiral spent in Spain? Had he really never spoken of me?

And Pinzon? Why was the Admiral so eager to have me check on Pinzon's actions? Was a friction brewing around this man? Still I had to admit I had hated feeling so much less than Beatriz in Pinzon's eyes as he described her charms.

I wanted everything back the way it had begun. My husband here with me, Pinzon safely commanding his ship where I did not have to hear his gay chatter and his gossipy intimations. And all of us well underway.

The Admiral loved me. "Things will come right again," my inner voices consoled. This Gomera stop had been legitimate, after all. Hadn't the Admiral heard necessary testimony of lands, not east, but west? Of course, the gathering of these corroborations made our visit here invaluable. For this alone, he would have had need to speak with the Governor at length. Ought I not have thought of this aspect of it before?

I pictured our sails sometimes twisted in the wind, then coming around in time to their true position. So it would be, I thought, with us.

I had magnified this Gomera, this delay, this business of the ships, and in one quick sunrise, it would fall well and long away.

I gradually let my worries go, and welcomed the drowsiness. I wanted to be tired enough to pass the night without once stirring, not even for the Admiral, thinking now that time and rest, not talk, were the cures for my distress. And love? That night at Gomera I did not even wish to know if the Admiral would want me. It was my turn to think it better to be discreet.

And so I won the peace of mind I sought. And it was already daybreak before I knew we had slipped from anchor and had put the Canaries behind us, so sound had been my sleep. I had not felt the Admiral return, and when I woke he was already above deck, for I heard his voice. There would be no chance to speak soon about the preceding day's events, but perhaps just as well, for what had burned through me then seemed weakened now, gratefully less urgent and important.

I took refuge in our rekindled journey. In the morning the sea was rippling blue, majestic, ours. And I decided that what had happened here was just an insignificant distraction compared to all the magic that surely lay ahead.

Chapter Three

The World Expands

In a story such as this, perhaps it would be useful to explain how I met the Admiral and came to be travelling with him.

I am Felipa Moniz de Perestrello and I married the Admiral Cristobal Colon in 1479.

My family records are incomplete, but I was born in Lisbon in 1453 to the comfortable and well-regarded home of my father, Don Bartolomé Perestrello, and mother, Dona Isabel Moniz, both of Portugal. My father's family, of wide repute in Italy, emigrated to Portugal in the 1300's, and he became a leading figure in Portuguese navigational affairs, an explorer of the Atlantic coasts. The Moniz family of my mother was noble, long and deeply rooted in Portugal, with many relatives and acquaintances at the court of the Portuguese King.

The Admiral's personal archives too are unreliable and he speaks little of his past. As best as is known, he was born in Genoa, Italy, in 1451, the son of a wool weaver and teacher of textile skills.

The Genoa of the Admiral's youth was by all accounts both a grimy and a gracious port, known as Genoa the Superb, a seafaring city-state rival to the most serene majesty, Venice. Trade on the oceans brought income to the city, and the Genoese grew affluent, decorating their palaces and public buildings with frescoes depicting such mythical exploits as the muscular labors of Hercules. Helmeted heroes looked down from the facades of the homes of well-to-do shipowners, patrons of the arts by having become patrons of the sea. Through this painted keyhole of Genoa Superba, my husband peered out to the Mediterranean and his destiny.

By then Northern Africa, the Aegean and Asia Minor were well known to the Italians, and galley ships rowed by scores of strongbacked men and boys traded back and forth among the continents.

and a powerful force in the country's economic life. The Admiral might well have heard of my father during this time, though he said he did not know who I was when we first met.

But despite the occupation of Lisbon, the Admiral remained somehow unfulfilled. His business did not earn all he had hoped, and he was haunted, I suspect, by the memory of his father's debt-ridden life in Genoa.

He began attending weekly Mass in Lisbon at the public chapel of the Convent of the Saints where, as it happened, my family had sent me to finish my studies.

The Convent was a beautiful, if unlaughing place, rambling along a high hill of Lisbon, its several cream-white stone abbeys set in a flourishing garden meandering gently in two levels along the banks of the Tagus River. Large swaying palm trees overlooked the great sailing ships at anchor off the piers. Lemon trees bloomed and every perfect narrow white stone path was lined with oleander, or bright dragonfly plants, flaming red against the deep overriding green.

Our sleeping quarters framed the garden, and thick ivy fluttered in the breezes, covering the walls, surrounding, yet not obscuring, each tiny window like eyes squinting to view a world perpetually closed out.

A spiritual refuge, All Saints also gave relief from the pressing heat of the city, for it was always cool under the flowering trees that bent over the path leading up from the street and into the cloister.

The religious Order of St. James founded the Convent over a hundred years before my stay as a secure place for the wives and daughters of Knights who had left Portugal to battle in the Crusades. Once safe inside, the women swore to obey the sisters, to live simply, follow chastity and await the return of their men. Gradually, the convent evolved into a school for younger women whose prominent families wished to see them live a quiet reflective life until they married, if they ever did. In the meantime, they would meet only women of a similar social standing so that their ideas and behavior would not be too much shaken.

From the outset, though, All Saints was not an ideal setting for me. I was hard-pressed to settle for life inside these unvaried surroundings, where practically no news entered and where absolutely no gaiety set foot.

I craved the nourishment of my youth, memories of the constant visitors to our home with tales from afar, their talk of exotic coasts

[33

and men as dark as jade with gold earrings in one ear, of silver flying fish skimming the surface of the sea, of exciting things beyond my reach but not my dreaming.

There was none of this at the convent. All Saints let in no air, no imagination, and I had never agreed with the choice of my school. "Please, I would rather not study at all than go to All Saints," I remember begging my mother.

"Darling, I cannot allow that," my mother had replied, winding a fine white ribbon into my hair as she had done when I was very young. "If your father were alive, perhaps we would have another choice, but . . . "

When I was only eight years old or so, my father died, we had to leave Porto Santo, and my mother could no longer be certain of income. By then, my younger brother had been born, to whose future she would have to attend. She provided for us many years alone, but it had begun to wear on her. Her once lovely face was more easily fatigued, her forehead creased, her long brown hair grew nearly all gray well earlier than it should. She told me simply "It would soothe my mind to see you at the convent."

I had little choice so I entered at the age of 18, expecting fully to regret each day. And I did, with every basin of cold water brought to us in the mornings by the good sisters so that we would learn to appreciate the hot. We were encouraged to be quiet, always. The doors to our rooms were low, so we had to bow our heads to enter. Even the steps up the convent slopes were diminuitive, placed very close together, seemingly to promote walking on tiptoes.

But the greatest struggle of my stay at the convent was the battle for writing, a skill that was flatly denied us.

Reading was all right, even encouraged for most women of our social position, so long as we emphasized religious works and did not solicit other books from visitors. Exceptionally, I was allowed to bring one of my father's books on geography, and one of his cartographic binders with me when I entered the convent, but I was forbidden to exchange these materials for others when my mother visited me. And so I read and reread them, and for diversion I would have liked to add to the binder and make notes, but I could not, having never been taught to write.

I asked, then begged, for parchment and ink, season after season. "No value will come of it," the nuns always refused, or "That is a gift you must earn in the afterlife," they intoned. To deflect me, they often recommended that I occupy my hands instead with the silk-stitching linen embroidery for which "All Saints women enjoy a fine reputation." I protested that I had heard women in other countries of Europe were learning to write.

"Not at All Saints," came the constant crisp reply.

But one night, a sister closer to my age listened at my chamber while I recited prayers, as was the custom. Once I had finished, when I thought she might still be within hearing, I added a line of my own words that I had memorized. The sister must have found them pleasing and sufficiently chaste, for though she said nothing at the time, she did at last acquiesce to my wish to write when I next raised the subject, saying "I see that you will write in your mind regardless of what we forbid."

I can hear her now, whispering her breaching of the rules, "Do not boast about this among the other students, Felipa. You must keep this learning to yourself."

She also imposed the condition that I make an extra vespers each week, to which I immediately agreed. Then one morning, as the rattling wagon that delivered our foodstuffs weekly from a farm just outside Lisbon prepared to leave the cloister, a slat fell loose from the bottom to the ground. No one noticed except me. I seized the rough knotty board, hid it under a bush, and when I was sure it had not been missed, I smuggled it to my room and built a makeshift desk across my rough stone window sill.

And even about this ill-gotten, non-standard furniture, my confidante did not protest. I don't know why she helped me, this sister Maria Hidalgo, her habit and robes so tight and stiff around her face that her cheeks puffed against them as if filled with air.

She never would say, and soon I stopped pressing her to explain her sudden change of heart. I had the impression she would feel free to continue teaching me to write only if she did not too directly acknowledge it was going on. I saw that reason could be separate from faith. I did not have to know her rationale; I was getting what I wanted.

Slowly as she read a prayer aloud, I learned to distinguish each sound. Then she taught me how to represent sounds as letters and letters as words until slowly an embroidery of thoughts found life on paper.

And this was how I came to the Admiral's attention. He had come first to mine, however, as I had seen him well before I believed he had noticed me. He was very handsome, his bearing sturdy and determined. I spotted him week after week at Mass, though I could never tell if he wished to speak to me, for he gave no sign of that.

One Sunday, after services, I returned to my room to retrieve my notebook before I took a walk and on the way back to the convent garden, I saw the Admiral, listlessly strolling alone. He wore the most beautiful deep forest green tunic, and nut brown fine leather breeches. He glanced at me across the path but did not approach. I sat on a cool contoured gray stone bench, but it was only when I began writing that the Admiral came nearer, removing his cloth cap and squashing it firmly under his arm. His hair was at the time fiery red though nevertheless I could see strands of gray arriving. His eyes sparkled with intensity, a crystal merry blue.

"Why do you write?" he asked, the first words he ever spoke to me.

I was startled by his forthright probing manner.

"It is rare to see a woman with pen in hand," he solicited again.

"I hardly know how to explain it," I began, having never been asked by anyone. "I write my thoughts, I suppose. It has become my passage to life outside All Saints." Indeed writing had become the same to me as breathing.

The Admiral smiled warmly. "I see. As for me, I've relied on sailing, and there's been much of that," he replied. There was a charming accent I had never heard before to his quite correct Portuguese.

"It's Italian," he told me, relating his Genoese origins. He told me of his chartmaking business and its demands, and said that his acquaintances in Lisbon had suggested he take his much needed weekly respite at All Saints. But mostly he spoke of his travels; oh his travels, including, he said, to a land north and west called Iceland.

"Few would believe I've actually been that far," he noted, "but I have."

His manner was so assured, and his experiences so unusual that in moments I was mesmerized by his stories.

Soon our words cascaded one across the other, until it was impossible to know whose sentence had begun first. We spent the afternoon talking of our different worlds and only when he was about to leave did the Admiral confess to having noticed me once several weeks before.

"Why did you not speak then?" I asked him.

"There was never the occasion, nor perhaps the courage, Madame," he gallantly replied.

"Perhaps if we meet again I will have learned some Italian," I joked.

"Does my Portuguese displease you?" he quickly sought approval.

"Oh no, you speak beautifully. I am studying Spanish, but perhaps Italian would be more worthwhile."

"Continue your Spanish, my lady. It can never hurt to know the language of your nearest neighbor and border state."

"If one had to know the languages of all the lands you have seen," I admired, "one would never be finished studying."

The coincidence that this foreign man so in love with the sea would drift into the life of the cloistered daughter of a navigator stayed with me all evening.

There was no time to waste after that, for soon, we were meeting in the garden each week. Soon too, I was falling in love with him, and when the sisters noticed, they withdrew their permission for my afternoons free of chaperones, accusing me of flirtation and warning of ill to come.

Finally, as I've said, the Admiral and I could tolerate no more restriction. He came to my room, and I did not refuse him. He wished to marry me.

My mother consented to my departure from All Saints to prepare for the wedding, ignorant of how we had already flouted the rules. Nevertheless, she liked the Admiral by instinct, despite her not knowing his family, or very much about him for that matter, for he spoke to her kindly and patiently. Too, perhaps she respected and understood my choice, having been herself the wife of a navigator.

But above all, I think she was joyously surprised, for probably she had doubted I would find a suitable husband and thought that at least the convent would provide for me if she could not one day. So, the Admiral won her heart completely.

We were married at the Church of Do Carmo, Lisbon's imposing great white Gothic cathedral, already nearly a hundred years old. The center spire, it was said, alligned with the full moon, and a dozen towering arches shaped like horseshoes, each carved braided stone painted with gold, marched down the center nave.

But despite the grand setting, our ceremony was frugal. Most of my relatives were out of Lisbon at the time, it being summer, and they sent only their good wishes and regrets. The Admiral invited a few Genoese clients and after the blessing, we happily chatted in the square in front of the Church, as pigeons splashed madly in the fountain and townspeople watched.

I hoped that perhaps later we would have a larger, more festive wedding dinner, but for the moment we had other plans.

We intended to sail first to Madeira with my mother where her family had property and where my father had been well known, having been among the original explorers to claim Madeira for Portugal. Then we would move on.

My brother had inherited my father's captaincy at Porto Santo and my mother wished to see to the status of his claim. Also she suffered chronic chest discomfort in Lisbon, and wished to leave her house in the city for awhile.

The Admiral, for his part, had no permanent home in Portugal. His rented rooms in Lisbon were cramped and stuffy; he said he needed a rest from his business, and the fresh smell of the sea free of the city's stench. As for me, I was delighted to return to the scene of a childhood so amply filled with fun and mystery.

So, married and untethered, we poured our youth together and left for Porto Santo.

Chapter Four

The Sea At Porto Santo

"Are you sure you want to go to that small forsaken island again?," my grandmother had skeptically asked when we stopped over en route on nearby Madeira. She lived in the coastal town of Machico, which had been the first landfall when the Portuguese King's explorers, including my father, had discovered the island. Machico grew quickly, attracting foreigners and Portuguese to the new Madeiran colony named for the lush woods that swept over the gentle slopes.

But now, Funchal, newer and better situated, had briskly eclipsed the original settlement. To my grandmother Moniz, though, Machico remained the authentic center of things, and she would have preferred that my wedding, however small and limited to family, be held here. Her villa overlooked the splendid green Machico River valley, commanding the eastern coast, and to my grandmother no other place on earth was as important or appealing.

"Yes, mother," my own mother replied with certainty, even though she had not lived on Porto Santo for many many years. She rested her fine white porcelain cup on the table as she rose to excuse herself briefly from where we—the Admiral, my mother, and I— sat having tea with my grandmother on her great wide terrace. And she added neatly, "I've always been happier at Porto Santo; we have responsibilities on the island, and money goes further there."

I knew that my father's death had put my mother in reduced circumstances, and though I also knew she had money of her own, from the Moniz side, she preferred to live as if that fortune did not exist. "We'll always have what my parents have and after me, it will be yours," my mother had assured me once, "but let us try to live on what your father provided." She had loved my father deeply, and always wanted to believe he had left enough.

The Admiral of course did not know the exact details of our finances, for my mother and I rarely spoke of money, even among ourselves. But he could judge wealth, and admired my grandmother's house.

"I adore the fragrances here, my lady," he complimented my grandmother, fingering the young orange orchids which reached over the balcony from the trees around us. The villa nestled among resplendent forests, and it felt as if these bushy branches could swallow the house whole at any time.

"And," the Admiral added politely, "we are grateful for your hospitality. I am so sorry you could not join our marriage celebration in Lisbon."

My grandmother, a fiercely proud and remote woman, gave much importance to Portuguese tradition. She had been among those of my relatives who had not travelled to Lisbon for the ceremony, pleading distance and lack of forewarning, and I could tell she did not feel at ease with my husband, whose family and origins she did not know.

"Thank you for your visit," she dryly replied to my husband, "and be assured that I too wish my granddaughter's wedding could have been attended by the proper people. I am glad you enjoy the grace of this island, for it is rare that someone who has not been born here can truly appreciate its advantages." She turned and left us.

"She is a difficult woman," I consoled him. "Don't be hurt by her indifference. She never fully warmed to my father either." I caressed his shoulder.

"I've seen more of the world than she ever will," he remarked bitterly. "I was simply being polite to her. The truth is that her lovely little Madeira is hardly the eye of civilization." The Admiral could be crisp, even when it involved my family.

He glanced back over the balcony, and flicked a tiny orchid blossom into the canyon below.

"Don't worry," I offered, slipping my arm through his. "We will have no one to answer to at Porto Santo."

We left Madeira the next afternoon, and our bark made its untroubled way across the ocean. In a few hours, we could see our island. From a distance, it resembled an empty windblown mound, a tan shadow on an iridescent blue-green sea.

Soon though, the features sharpened, and we rounded a black rock point. We began to sail along the southern coast of Porto

Santo, up along the golden crescent of sand that was the island's lovely lip—there was no other beach like it in all of Portugal as far as we knew. The Admiral smiled broadly at the sight of it.

"Ah-hah," he said with gusto, "*that* they certainly don't have in Machico." I was glad he found such pleasure in it, as we sailed on, never taking our eyes from the beach.

My father had discovered Porto Santo and Madeira on the same trip in 1418. As a child, I heard him tell the tale of how a fierce gale had blown the explorers off course, and they lay down on deck resigned to death, only to raise their eyes on the welcoming coast of Porto Santo.

"The recipe for discovery," my father often observed, "includes an ample ladle of chance."

Later, the King dispatched my father to settle the uninhabited place, which though forbidding, would support villages on olives and figs until food crops could take hold.

My father relished the assignment, and arrived in Porto Santo laden with grain and seedlings, eager to plant and start a settlement. He carried plenty of livestock also to tide the colony over in its early days, but he didn't know a pregnant rabbit was among his animals. She gave birth on arrival, and the creatures so exploded in number that soon every inch of green ground cover had been eaten and Porto Santo became just a mass of loose-blowing sand.

As a result, the Portuguese had to postpone their settlement until some greenery had grown back, and in the meantime shifted their main colonial efforts to Madeira.

My father felt like a fool. He requested reassignment and left Porto Santo, but was ordered back by the regional Governor to try again. But the colony never regained its initial prominence. My father died on the island when I was just a child, disillusioned with his plans for this rugged land.

The wide beach broke the rocky coast and was the only site on the island for disembarking a boat. The captain dropped our sail, and we glided in, riding the small waves.

The Admiral jumped out first and lent me his hand. My bare feet sunk down to the ankles in the wonderfully warm sand. The sparkling clean sea swirled around my legs—I was so glad to be here, so glad to be somewhere that felt like home.

It took only a little time to unload the boat, for we had packed few belongings. My mother would join us later, bringing what might be missing once we had made an inventory. She had stayed on at Machico to visit longer with my grandmother and, I suspected, to allow the Admiral and me time alone.

There were already several hundred people living in Vila Baleira, the administrative center of the island. It crowned the northern end of the beach, the island's tiny gateway. Its only two paths crossed at the Plaza Perestrello, the square named for my father, which was the island's central meeting point. Just there too was the only church, the sun-bleached Santa Piedade, where my father had been buried. A few houses and shops formed the village's hub, a huddle of cut stone buildings at the top of a dusty hill.

The path to our house crumbled underfoot. In fact, soon after disembarking, I began to feel the baking, still sensation of the desert all around us. We walked in single file up from the beach, and several men, barefoot, managed our sacks and baskets. We had brought many bananas from Madeira and Seixas, an old fisherman who used to work for my father, carried them in a large woven wicker urn, usually reserved for fish, on his head. There was no wicker growing yet on Porto Santo. "It's from Madeira," Seixas explained when I complimented his fine basket, "like everything."

In a few hot minutes, we reached the track that led in a dusty elbow off the Square to the quarters of my parents. A white stone wall ran unbroken until it reached a set of double wooden doors, cracked in the heat like aging skin. But the bougainvillea my mother had once planted now poured over the wall into the road like a waterfull of beautiful magenta rain.

Seixas turned the rusty key, and we pushed the door back against the dried weeds that had grown up around the empty building. With a long machete, Seixas chopped a vine that held half the door fast, and with one straight blow seemed to slash away years of slumber. "Wake up, house," Seixas yelled gaily.

"Not likely," the Admiral murmured, gazing in dismay around the garden. I had to admit the building seemed hopelessly lost to time, but there still were the four wonderful tall palm trees I remembered, rustling like whispering children in the breezes that blew off the sea.

Several cactus had taken root too, their wild spiky leaves dancing like spiders at the feet of the palms. It was a disordered, abandoned beauty, and easily reclaimed. The property was grownover, and the house humble, but I thought it could be very welcoming with a little time and care.

We climbed the several stone steps to the second floor of the cottage. The Admiral glanced around. "Where is the cooking done?'' he wondered, not one to usually pay attention to household features.

"Downstairs," I answered.

"And where do we sleep?"

"Here," I replied, as we stood on the somewhat more spacious second floor, where one oakwood bed and bare dressing table remained. "But we will of course add some furniture and ornaments," I assured him. My parents had lived in this cottage when they had first reached Porto Santo, and I could imagine it with brightly colored cushions on the bed and richly woven draperies. The walls were made of many gray flat stones that fit together like a rough puzzle.

"But is this all there is?" the Admiral questioned.

"Well, yes," I answered, somewhat embarrassed suddenly to have believed the house would suffice.

"And your mother?" the Admiral continued.

"Her house is on the other side of the property," I explained, pointing out a much larger stone building, the official Captaincy residence, fitting into ours like a tree trunk to a branch with a common garden.

The Admiral eyed the adjacent property, and quickly said, "Why don't we stay there for the time being, until your mother arrives?"

I saw no harm in that, though it hadn't been my plan. "Well, why not," I replied, "since it will certainly take some time for us to arrange the household here."

So I instructed Seixas to put our personal belongings in my parents' bedroom, and all the foodstuffs in the old Captaincy granary behind the residence.

"Yes, right away," Seixas obeyed happily. "I am so glad to see these buildings lived in again."

I stood a while at the top of the steps. The hills were low and brown, the only trees tough sparse juniper. The only green pockets were wispy reeds drinking from alongside the hidden freshwater springs that made life on the island possible.

The eye excuses a lot of brutality in a landscape when it is an island, I thought. Though I was deeply fond of Porto Santo, the land was exceedingly dry and barren, if one had to be objective about it.

But I did not. I could embrace this island unabashedly, for though I had been barely ten years old when we had left Porto Santo, I felt the bold spirit of the place, eternally familiar. My life was beginning again here.

The Admiral was busy downstairs, negotiating with Seixas for the hiring of staff. "I thought you would need some help to make the quarters liveable," he said to me as I joined them in the garden.

"Perhaps we ought to wait until my mother arrives," I replied, hesitating, wanting to consult her.

But the Admiral eyed me firmly. "Felipa, either we are in charge here, or we are not," he said somewhat impatiently. Sexias looked away, as if to give us privacy.

What the Admiral said was true; we would have to make some decisions on our own, and so I agreed to the hiring of two persons, plus Seixas and his wife to cook and keep the household.

"But not until we have been here a few days," I stipulated, wanting a bit of time alone with my husband. "Just a breathing space?" I said gently to him.

"If you like," he answered, "though I would prefer to have these people working right away."

He walked out onto the street and entered my mother's house from the front. There was no comparing the two dwellings—naturally the Perestrello Captaincy House had the amenities it should. There was the official receiving room with the yellow and blue satin flag of Madeira still folded on a side table, the several bedrooms each with a long window to the garden, the stone oven cut like a great vault in the lower kitchen wall, the still-polished oval dining table that could seat at least a dozen guests, and of course my father's study.

The darkened rooms were cool refuge from the sun outside, and though the house had been empty so long, I felt it to be breathing with us. The Admiral soon deposited his papers on my father's table. He had brought along his most important maps, many books, and a cork and leather box he used to store his rulers and measuring tools.

He began to arrange himself as if at home, opening the drawers of my father's cupboard, removing the remaining odd articles—an apparently unused burlap sack, an empty smoky blue glass decanter, and a single blue and white porcelain tile, perhaps a sample of a pattern my mother had hoped to use in her planned redecoration of the church. My husband examined each of these abandoned objects, then consolidated them in one drawer, filling the rest of the cupboard with his own items he had brought from Lisbon.

He became aware of my gaze, and turned to me. "May I get you something?"

I was uneasy, I confess, with our simply moving into my parents' home and making it our own, even though my mother had not forbidden it.

"Must we move aside everything that isn't ours?"

He approached me slowly, and took my hand. "Felipa, it is perfectly appropriate that we stay here. Your father was captain of this island; your brother will eventually be captain. You are the family representative for now, and I am your husband. Your mother would approve, I have no doubt."

Then, he added with a slight hint of sarcasm he guessed I would take well, "and we know were your grandmother here, she would most certainly have it no other way!"

I had to laugh with him, for surely my grandmother would never have cut through the bramble to take up residence in a two-room rough stone cottage. My husband was right. There was no good reason not to live in the Residence for now. The Admiral returned to his unpacking, and I to mine.

In a few minutes Seixas had cut away almost all the brush between the two houses. I pushed the garden door open from the inside, and it scraped grudgingly along the stone. It would need replacing. Yes, there would be many little tasks to do here. I felt busily content.

Seixas defied age, though he had been on the island already nearly 30 years when we arrived. He had a toughened face like the rocky soil he had left in the Algarve to join my father's first group of settlers on Porto Santo. His thick brown hair curled tightly like woven wool on his head, and he had deep brown eyes to match, though one eyeball was acquiring a yellow tinge, from "maybe too much white wine," he said offhandedly.

He always wore a shirt of roughly woven blue cloth, which hung loosely on his frame, and brown breeches, tightly fitting up to the knee, but very baggy everywhere else. He had tied two rope loops to a brown burlap sack, and he slipped his arms through them so he could throw all his fishing gear in it on his back, including fresh torches to be lit at sea during the night fishing for which the islanders were known.

The unusual back sack left his hands free for carrying his catch, sometimes six or seven huge slithery espadon at a time, long black fish like thick snakes, speared through the gills by a sharpened stick. Seixas knew how to improvise.

He had been especially valued as an early settler for his skill at wheat growing, which he had learned in the Algarve. One of the

Crown's motives for colonizing new lands was to augment Portugal's supply of food. But wheat proved nearly impossible here and, as always, the rabbits were easy to blame.

One afternoon shortly after we had arrived, we began to refit the withering grape vines in our garden. Seixas and I worked together in the sun, Seixas in his usual costume, and me in my new lightweight garments which would have been frowned upon in Lisbon but which made good sense on the island. I had made a loose-fitting suit of white trousers for myself. In fact, I had simply sewn a skirt up the middle, but so loosely that anyone would take the ensemble for a dress. It was wonderfully comfortable in this climate.

"You know," observed Seixas, his every step raising dust, "it is unlikely that wheat could ever have been successful here. The soil is too dry. It is not correct to say Don Bartolomé's rabbits ate everything, since there wasn't much growing here when he arrived, and the springs would never be sufficient to water a wheat crop."

I appreciated Seixas' words, and knew he was being kind. He continued, tying each vine carefully with a piece of golden yarn as I held it back for him to reach around. "Your father kept soliciting funds for desert plants, the only fruits and crops that would grow in this soil, but the Crown would hear only of wheat. They had boasted of their plans, and it was surely not your father's fault that the cultivation did not take. Porto Santo could export to the world if it respected its climate, and of course looked to its real treasury, the sea."

Wheat failing, Seixas had lost no time learning new skills and now believed he saw the future.

"How many times did I tell your father, 'Don Bartolomé, Portugal could be the mistress of the age if it took to merchanting the sea.' If he only knew how many fish I'd seen swirling around out there, cyclones of sardines, espada, all kinds of fish."

Seixas, it seemed, had become a fisherman with a flair for Empire. But surely he had seen much in his long life. I knew that Portugal hadn't yet surmounted the wheat problem. In Lisbon most grain was imported from Spain, Italy and northern Africa.

"Your father knew these problems perhaps too well," Seixas observed. "He understood that the grain shortage came from King Alfonso's giving away so much royal land to aristocrats who did not properly cultivate it."

Indeed, it was hard to understand why the Crown bought wheat abroad when so many of its own fields lay empty and untended.

"And the grain we receive here on Porto Santo?" Seixas questioned. "I call that 'ocean wheat' because it seems to grow on no land at all."

"What do you mean?" I asked, having noticed intermittent grain supplies arriving and always assuming they came from Madeira.

Seixas easily tossed out his theory, suggesting casually, "I think it is contraband. If the Crown had legal wheat to spare they'd never be selling it to Porto Santo—they'd be trading it for African gold."

I still did not understand. "Why would the King do that, if as you've said, wheat is so rare?"

A flutter came to Seixas' dark eyes, his sudden recognition of how little I really knew about these matters.

"My dear Captain's daughter," he began with the pride of one about to present a noble lesson, "did you not hear in Lisbon how much our King loved that glittering metal? Did you not know that he even minted a new cruzado of nearly pure gold? I think that was the very same year the officials in Madeira told your father the Crown could not afford to send us an irrigation engineer." Seixas frowned in sarcasm.

I watched him work. He handled each vine with his fingertips, draping each plant just so, as if he wished to be sure the vine would be comfortable in its new position. In his gentle unquestionable expertise, he seemed born to this land, respecting its gifts as well as its rude surprises of drought and despair. Seixas' schooling came to him through living, as did his opinions of the King and the possibility of stolen wheat.

Alfara, Seixas' dour wife, was also ever-present. At times I wondered if she had been schooled by the sisters of All Saints. She always wore a thin black shawl and did her work in virtual silence, barely saying good day or good night, never humming, nor laughing, only hinting at a smile. Yet the hint seemed genuine, as if a much fuller smile lurking within might any second brighten her face. She became outrightly joyful, for Alfara, at the sight of her husband, following his every move with expectant eyes like a cat's stalking a sparrow on the ground.

Perhaps she thought Seixas spoke enough for both of them. In any case, Alfara moved through our lives as lightly as a shadow, as indispensable as Seixas.

Little by little, we coaxed our garden back to life, and it gave me much pleasure to watch a healthy vibrant green return, and the shimmering yellow of the lemon trees, the hushed pink oleander, and the ever-prospering flowing crimson of the bougainvillea.

The cottage too was coming along. There had only been a rough black wooden table in the kitchen, with four unsturdy chairs plus a small stool with only two legs. Seixas, as a surprise gift to me, took it home one day and carved and added the missing leg. He said it had been my favorite seat as a little girl, though I didn't remember it.

With the cottage chimney opened, we could enjoy the pungent fresh scent of juniper wood fires, although Seixas worried once that "too much cutting of wood will be worse than rabbits."

Upstairs in the room which would be the Admiral's and mine, I had added a lovely sofa constructed on the island with a rich dark wood frame, and large heavy straw pillows which Alfara covered with exactly the sort of milk-colored embroidery the sisters at All Saints had called "gentle proof of gentle hands."

I had brought along the only embroidery I had managed to produce, two armchair sleeves, decorated with the crest of the convent. The sisters could never have pictured I'd put them to use on Porto Santo, as far from All Saints as it was possible to be and still remain in Portugal.

It was easier to have household errands done in Porto Santo than Lisbon, for Plaza Perestrello provided all that one needed for the time being—a grain warehouse, a public kiln, and fish and vegetable market stalls. There was Arabel, the Galician furniture maker, and Diego, a Portuguese potter from Cascais, who worked clay and stucco with the subtle dedication of someone carefully polishing a peach. He had an amazing knack for bringing texture out of stone, and the long-lasting quality of his bowls and goblets earned him a steady loyal business.

But apparently artistic yearning smoldered unfulfilled inside Diego and he had taken to decorating the chimneys he made for new cottages with ceramic birds.

At first, few people noticed. Then, gradually, Diego's birds became a bubbling topic of island conversation.

One morning, I visited his shop and Diego lamented that one of the elder citizens objected to the birds, claiming they were becoming too commonplace.

"Imagine, madame," Diego began good-naturedly, "since the Portuguese first set foot on this island, straight plain chimneys ruled, and he did not find it dull. Now a few birds appear, and he complains. It is not as if each bird were the same." He wiped his brow with his sleeve, since both hands were full of the oozing grayish stucco he was readying for spinning on his wheel. He looked like a tree of wet cement.

"What did you reply, Diego?" I wondered.

He shrugged and nonchalantly said, "I simply told him that when you have your fingers full of lovely soft clay, and you live under such a blue sky, it is impossible *not* to make birds!"

Diego's shop filled with his deep self-satisfied laugh.

Not far away, there was the large public fountain. The island water system fascinated the Admiral. He paid little attention to the garden, less to the renovation of the house, and almost none to our neighbors. But the waters of Porto Santo—these he studied as closely as his navigational charts.

Pumping water vexed everyone, and my father had had the idea of using windmills powered by tiny triangle sails like ships to turn a pump wheel, but years passed and the scheme had not caught on. Slowly now, islanders saw the merit of the system, and the Admiral occasionally supervised as the first mills began to be installed.

Somehow, in this land that might as well be Arabia, springs surfaced in unexpected places. One afternoon, the Admiral returned from a walk completely elated, having seen the remarkable spring of Fonte da Areia which had been wastefully flowing freely to the sea from between two cracks in the earth before it had been tapped.

"There in the middle of a blowing desert, clean water," the Admiral described enthusiastically, "shining like glass, slightly salty but still good to drink. There is more water on this island than I thought."

"Yes, but still not enough for wheat, according to Seixas," I replied.

"Ah yes, Seixas, your encyclopedia," the Admiral acknowledged. "He was very fond of your father."

He poured some spring water from his flask for me to taste, and went on.

"Your father tried installing settlements in the north, if I am correct?"

"Yes, but it was very harsh."

"So it is," the Admiral agreed. "Did your father leave any charts of the area?" he wondered.

"Not that I know of," I replied, trying to picture the far hillside of Fonte Areia where I had never been.

The Admiral promised to take me one day, and headed for his study.

But I too had something to share that afternoon. "Stay there a moment," I ordered lightly, "and close your eyes."

I stepped quickly to the garden and returned with a large bunch of the first grapes of the season.

The sun had worked its wonders, and the yellow-green beads swelled.

The Admiral fidgeted. Generally my husband disliked games, but he went along.

"Guess," I said, feeding him one plump delicious grape.

"Ah yes," he identified quickly, as he bit through the skin. "From your garden perhaps?"

"From our garden, darling," I replied, running my forefinger along his moistened lips.

He opened his eyes. "I didn't have much to do with it," the Admiral observed, now standing, happily plucking another grape from the stem.

"Maybe not, but this is our house and so, our garden," I responded. The Admiral smiled and said only, "Thank you, Felipa, I know."

He returned to the work table where he often withdrew for hours, drawing maps and making calculations, and even then, I did not pose questions in favor of his solitude and privacy.

We had gone on living in the Residence, though our own adjacent cottage was by now ready and comfortable.

But the Admiral had been right—my mother's house was so much bigger, we were two, and she was not yet here. We continued to sleep in my parent's bedroom and I used my mother's sewing room, not to sew, but to store dried plants in clay jars that Seixas kept bringing me as proof that Porto Santo's vegetation was recovering on its own.

"Native plants," he would say as he handed me one gnarled cutting after another, "that's what will make the island green again." Often Seixas did not know their names but when he did, I jotted it on a small piece of paper and put the slip in with the plant.

One day, Seixas arrived holding a handful of purplish burrs. He popped one open, revealing a sac of tiny reddish seeds, then smeared a few between his fingers, coating them with a vivid red resin. "We call these dragon's blood," he explained, playfully streaking his nose and cheeks with the waxy paint. "There are plenty of dragon trees on the north side of the island," he informed me. "A lot of money could be made in farming them for the dye."

I added a few of the seeds to my collection.

Since our house stood at the top of the path leading to the sea, each morning fishermen returned, dragging their slinking espadon, their skin black as the night in which they were caught, their eyes and mouth locked open in the shock of death.

"Espada, espada, espada today," the fishermen would call. Not that we didn't buy most of our fish from Seixas, but the Admiral believed we should buy from as many fishermen as we could since we were, as he liked to say, "the island's leading citizens," to set an example. I somewhat agreed, but let him haggle over prices, since he enjoyed it and I did not.

During this time, Porto Santo life was simple, and our days passed in pleasant predictability. If the fishermen didn't wake me, I woke to the long gentle rings of the church bell sounding the start of the day at six. I heated water in a large copper pot, burning the logs Seixas kept stocked. With this we washed, then had some broth until Alfara, Seixas' wife, arrived to prepare the Admiral's breakfast. I never felt hungry until noon, but he enjoyed a morning bread and tea.

It was always lovely enough weather to work in the garden, and I did so religiously, alone or with Seixas and Alfara, who taught me everything they could. And how blissful to have our magnificent view at the same time. If I stopped to stretch or take a cooling drink, my eyes were the first part of me to feel refreshed. Through our now flourishing greenery, the pure blue sea beyond lay endless, interrupted only by the triangular Cima rock offshore, resting as naturally on the sea as a peaked cap on a clergyman's head.

Alfara made our lunch, almost always fresh fish accompanied by a soft brown farina. Occasionally she would blacken this mealy grain in hot oil, and serve it with honey, a delicious crispy dessert. And we always had our lovely grapes, themselves sometimes as golden as the honey.

Then we slept while Alfara restored order to the kitchen. In the afternoon, I usually walked to the square, surveying what new items had arrived from Madeira. Sometimes the Admiral joined me later, and from the stone bench in the square where we often sat, we could see the flat blue-black horizon.

The Admiral mused over the unchanging weather, so much more stable than on the Portuguese mainland or Italy, but occasionally the water would ruffle into a patch of black.

"It is as if ink were flowing into the waters," the Admiral said one afternoon, commenting on the changing sea surface. Then the wind would shift suddenly and the sea would be a settled blue once again. "The currents here must have something to do with why the weather is so constant," the Admiral thought out loud.

In these languid days, water and weather ruled our existence, not distant official decree.

The settlement of Porto Santo was still formally in the hands of my brother, but he had shown little enthusiasm for it and had been called on a mission to Africa before ever returning here. The island's actual Administration rested in unclear hands, no governor having been assigned. Still, somehow, in the absence of any true government, the supply boats came and went—loaded with the goods of daily life.

And there were always sacks of new seeds and new cuttings arriving—the settlers continued despite bad results to try to cover the island with imported plants.

It was strange how I so rarely thought of my father in Lisbon, but here his memory was vivid. Now and then I would walk to his tomb. There I listened to the silence, undisturbed except for the light shrill sound of a nearby cricket, chirping somewhere in the church against the mottled stone.

Santa Piedade was beautiful, with an elaborate dark wood choir stall carved with flowers and the Madeira cross. It was, besides our own garden, the coolest place on the island.

On Sunday morning early, no one stirred. The square was tranquil, the only noise the trickling sound of the fountain, the swish of the palms in the breeze, and the legato hollow call of a morning dove.

Until time for Mass. Then when the bell of Piedade called, silence became sound. Doors opened and people began clamoring up the paths to the Church.

From Camacha and Sera Fora, the furthest settlements, donkeys carried men and women into town, their bells tinkling like early light through the plaza.

The Admiral and I attended mass regularly, and Father Palmeira always waited until we had been seated before beginning. In the chapel, motley voices sounded as one, as all villagers sang, trained by the priest in ancient Christian hymns. Save one woman whom I could hear but not see in the crowd, whose voice always rose like a crown above the rest.

At these times, I often thought of what my father must have hoped to accomplish in this tiny place, an exciting new beginning for those who wished to live at the ocean boundary of a world we were just coming to understand.

And I thought of his frustrations, pushing settlements further onto the dry hills, under orders, against his own judgment, then loyally taking the blame when no settlement could truly prosper and his dreams collapsed.

I scanned the faces of the islanders, beautiful faces with clear eyes the color of ground coffee, skin darkened by the sun and streaked a little by the salt, faces of people who worked hard and lived hard—Alfara, Seixas, Arabel and the others. What were their chances of making good here, even now?

Our neighbors on the island lived on faith that progress would reward them sooner or later, but the Crown provided few services to its colonies once it laid claim to the lands. Poor father had tried, and I wondered if even my husband could overcome the difficulties were he to be the governor.

In the market, foodstuffs were suddenly available, then suddenly scarce, dependent on uncertain shipments from Madeira. One day, the fruit vendor dozed on his green melons, he had so many to sell, and next day they were all gone, and none would arrive again for weeks or months. And despite the success of the fountains, there simply never was enough water when and where the villagers needed it.

We, of course, had help in coping with the vagaries of life here. Alfara insisted on doing most of our shopping and Seixas kept us in fish, and news of the village. The Admiral had also hired two boys, Henrique to manage the household water supply and Pietro to make sure the oil lamps were always full, since often the Admiral worked on his maps late into the night.

The staff was large, I thought, and I had begun to worry that my mother would think us wasteful.

"I doubt she will," the Admiral assured me once when I raised the question to him. "These are minimum services and we do not have the time to do the tasks ourselves." Our expenses were trivial, in truth; the money my mother had provided us was certainly sufficient. And we were, after all, in the absence of a true captain of the island, the exemplary household.

In fact, occasionally a passing ship's Captain would send a message asking if he could be received by the Perestrello family. The Admiral at first disliked accepting, but felt it his obligation. However, as the visits increased, he seemed to enjoy them immensely, and despite our distance from more populous places, he did not lack for contact with the world of navigation.

It was like my childhood, when passing ships put in on the island and I had listened to their tales of the sea beyond the horizon, for it was, after all, the age of the oceans—local, distant and unknown.

One captain spoke to my husband about the hazards to shipping just offshore posed by Cima rock. "Perhaps," the captain suggested, "you can have a beacon torch there at all times, certainly on moonless nights."

The Admiral immediately understood. "Yes, my captain, splendid idea—good idea," he said, "and we'll go one better. We'll arrange for a small chapel to be built on the islet to bless the ships, beacon or not."

"Wonderful," said the ship's captain, and they drank to the plan. I found myself smiling at my husband's audacity, knowing he had no authority at all for promising a bonfire, let alone a church.

Often, large vessels put in just for water, as did one day the captain of the vessel, *Guinea Costa*. He had heard of the Porto Santo springs and thought it best not to sail onto Lisbon without replenishing. As it was nearly dark when his crew had finished filling their jugs at the Square, I sent word to Seixas to invite the Captain to join us for dinner.

"My dear Madame Perestrello," the captain greeted me when he arrived at the Residence, "how honored I am."

"You are welcome, of course, Captain, but I am the late Governor Bartolomé's daughter, not his wife. I am the wife of the navigator Colombo," I explained to clarify the family links before the Admiral joined us.

"Oh, excuse me. I hope to greet your husband, of course," the Captain replied courteously, as Alfara offered him a basin of water with which to wash his hands and face. The Admiral came down from the study and the men shook hands enthusiastically.

We enjoyed our dinner and the Captain proved an animated storyteller. As the Captain chatted on, my husband's interest climbed.

"There appears to be no limit on what the Crown will pay to find new lands," the Captain noted, "especially if such lands could be shown to lie in the east. The King Alfonso aches to round the Cape of Africa, to the point that he rented the African trade monopoly to a merchant named Fernao Gomez. If Gomez discovered one hundred leagues of African coast a year, he would be granted exclusive rights to all commerce, except ivory, reserved to the Crown. But I know he took on ivory from time to time anyway.''

The Captain took a sip of wine, and the Admiral posed his questions sharply: How much longer before the Cape voyage could be made; what was the cost of a journey to Guinea in manpower; what were the latest estimates of the distance the Cape lies south of Guinea, and on and on, registering it in his mind so he could later transfer all the details to his maps upstairs. But the Captain had only his best guesses to offer.

''It is difficult to speak of sea travel with precision,'' he replied. ''The King has put his son, the prince Joao, in charge of all these navigational matters, and he too searches constantly for information. The sailors send him frequent reports, and all expect to see the land of Antillia, and the San Borondon, said to lie off the Canaries. The islands seem to be there, then vanish as the ships approach. But surely Don Bartolomé Perestrello had many useful notes on these matters?''

The Admiral glanced inquisitively at me, but I did not reply. He leaned in close to the table, as the captain used the rim of his plate to demark the coast of Africa. The Captain pointed with his carving knife how far south he had traveled: ''Here, I would say. That is where I could have left our last stone pillar. The Crown requires that, you know, that we mark our journeys.''

But, a few glasses of wine ahead of us, he confessed loosely that he had sailed further than he would report to the Crown for now, since, ''then my next voyage will receive additional funding to cover miles I have made already. The Crown is not really interested in where we have been, only where we have not.''

The Admiral feigned disinterest in the levels of financing available, but the Captain added without prodding, ''It's worth hundreds of sovereigns a day to the King to collect the spices of the African coast, and specimens of everything that grows. But many men are dying of sicknesses and misery there, though no one speaks of it.''

''And have you seen much of the local people?'' the Admiral prodded.

''Oh yes,'' the sailor answered, his eyes now full of drink, his voice relaxed and his mind burgeoning with fantastic truths only he had witnessed.

Slowly he began the tale of Caramansa, a chieftain of the African Gold Coast where the Portuguese King wished to build the first permanent Portuguese settlement.

[55

"Diego de Azambuja, a great sailor, was named Ambassador, and I sailed in his fleet of twelve ships," the Captain began proudly.

"Caramansa had seen a Portuguese ship or two," the Captain recounted, "but never a fleet so large it filled the bay."

The African, by the Captain's account, was stately. His tribal lieutenants preceded him as they walked to meet the Portuguese, tall black men as straight as palms, wearing little clothing, their nudity made up for by many streams of necklaces of ivory and gold and white polished jaguar's teeth. The tribesmen blew long ceremonial notes on swirling sea shells, announcing the arrival of their King; Portuguese trumpets answered. Then, Caramansa stood alone, his aides holding an enormous flaring palm branch to shade him as he walked. The two leaders advanced.

"It was an extraordinary moment," the Captain recalled, "not calm, but not tense either, for no one really knew what to expect next. Then, Caramansa did a shocking thing. In front of all of us, simply snapped his fingers and shouted 'Bere, Bere' meaning 'peace, peace.' But we didn't know it at the time. Scores of naked black men stepped up to us. They wet their fingers in their mouths, wiped them dry on their bare buttocks, and only then offered their hands in greeting."

"But why?" I blurted out.

Apparently, before distinguished visitors, the Negroes licked their fingers to prove that their hands had not been previously dipped in poison. No warrior would suck a deadly potion, it was assumed.

"It's a gesture an inferior grants when receiving a superior in Guinea," the Captain explained authoritatively.

But, Caramansa at first refused the Portuguese proposal for a fort. "He made the argument that though he liked the Portuguese and our splendid ships, friends should not spend too much time in each other's midst."

"A clever man," the Admiral observed, "but what then? How did the Portuguese succeed?"

"As usual," the Captain replied, "with trappings—brocade cloth woven in Flanders, damask from England, sealing wax sets from Italy, bracelets of glass beads and basins of polished brass. The Africans will barter a bushel of malagueta pepper for a single brass bowl."

56]

Since the fortress adjoined the tribal village, eventually the Portuguese colony pressed at the boundaries. Some tribal huts had to be razed.

"We smashed them as the villagers watched," the Captain reported, "but we gave them as much new cloth and jewelry as they could carry on their bodies, and they marched deeper into the forest and built their huts again."

Such was the tale of the establishment of the great St. George's Castle at Portuguese Mina.

"We see that Africa consumes much material and navigational attention," the Admiral edged the conversation, baiting the Captain again.

"Indeed so. And for Africa, the Portuguese engineers have much improved ships. They have so nearly perfected the caravel that I've heard the design plans are now a state secret. The King banished a builder just for speaking to a comrade about the round shape of the bow."

The Admiral remained transfixed; the sailor talked on.

"The Crown recently doubled the bonus it pays to builders of larger ships—two gold crowns for every ton we can load below deck. And all the pine woods of Portugal have been put at open disposal of the shipyards. Anyone who refuses to sell trees to shipbuilders, or charges too high a price, risks a fine or jail. Even hunting privileges are no grounds for exemption. No carpenter can stop work on a ship until it is finished, no caulker may look elsewhere for a job and . . . " The Admiral interrupted.

"And have you news of the furthest trip of these new vessels?"

"None of us is permitted to say where we have taken our caravels. If we do, we risk prison or worse."

Then a crack creeped into the voice of our Captain friend as he travelled back to Africa, back to a single flaming night. His eyes began to glisten as he recounted.

"Once a Portuguese commander even received orders to burn his own boats because they were of the old urca design. Our great King wanted to scare his opponents, mainly the throne of Spain, into thinking that only our newer vessels, the Portuguese caravels, could attempt to round the Cape of Africa. He didn't want it known how far the old urca ships could actually reach. So he ordered that ships of his own fleet be burned."

The Captain stopped suddenly, now aware that perhaps with this last tale he might have revealed far too much about the strategy of the Crown.

"You will keep my confidence, of course," the Captain asked us pleadingly."

"Of course, my fellow, I would not betray a fellow seaman," the Admiral answered, pouring the sailor a final half glass of wine. "As you see I am not keeping notes," he added.

Then Seixas lit one of his fishing torches and escorted the Captain through the darkness to the beach where his men waited to return him to his vessel anchored between Cima and Vila Baleira.

A full moon hung low and brilliantly white. While the Admiral worked in his study on his charts immediately incorporating the Captain's information about routes and coastlines, I sat on our terrace thinking of polished brass bangles, wild black pepper and smooth white ivory.

I gazed out for a long time under the sky shattered by thousands of stars like chieftains in the night where Africa and the East converged. In this farflung tiny Atlantic seaport, we lived between memories and imagination, neither truly settled nor truly cast away.

Chapter Five

A Shift of Wind

These Porto Santo days felt magical to me then, as our world was entirely of our own making.

Yet, after the visitors had left, and the exotic sailors' talk had waned, one could say that Porto Santo was about very few things— palm trees, and dusty twisted paths—and, of course, its stunning long, ranging beach that pressed along the coast until the tip of the island, nine golden miles.

When my father busily governed here, and I was a child, my mother took my brother and me onto this beach day after day, winter and summer, for the temperature almost never varied. We splashed in the sea, then covered ourselves in the wondrous sun-heated sand, my brother burying me, then me him, each pretending to abandon the other under a blanket of beach, wailing until we couldn't stop laughing. We hid in the tall beachgrass, where dried sea salt clung to the soft black-green shrubs like age in a graying man's beard. I remembered the joys of the Porto Santo beach as a constant in our lives.

And it was still my primary pleasure on the island. Rolling in a perfect crescent, the beach gathered the sea to it like an island woman gathering grapes in a wide-cut skirt.

The occasional rough night sea pressed out a flat patch of sand and trapped shallow pools of seawater, by morning home to count-less tiny shrimp and slimy weeds with small air sacs to keep them afloat.

On this beach there was always something to see, particularly pieces of smooth gray wood worked into shapes by the sea, the driftwood of Porto Santo drifting in from nowhere.

I had loved collecting this soft beach wood as a child, and had begun again, setting a piece on virtually each shelf of my father's study and in the cottage bedroom—a wave-worn fish, a twigged cross, a smooth fat heart—all sculpted by the ocean.

How ceaselessly I walked the beach, sometimes alone, sometimes convincing the Admiral to come along. In a way, it was where he came alive.

Rugged mountain walks and mysterious springs, yes, he was interested, but horizons, openness, the next place—these seemed to be the sensations that truly stirred him.

Here the Admiral released his soul, as if throwing open the shutters on a long siege of winter. Often it was like talks of our earliest meetings, and he repeated and embellished his many tales of Iceland, Chios and beyond.

He enchanted me with stories—he'd even been to Lombardy, where the Perestrellos, my father's family, had come from.

"Yes, Lombardy is always fighting with Tuscany over whose Italian is more pure," he observed cynically, "and they have little use for Genoa, despite all the money there."

Even when it rained, which was rarely, we did not hurry to leave the beach. Instead we watched the raindrops land and scatter in the sand like rye seeds in bread.

On the Porto Santo beach, the Admiral grew boyish, and we made a game of the circus of debris that fell constantly at our feet. Once in a single spot, we found a group of particularly smooth driftwood pieces, all similarly buffed, plus a cluster of well polished stones, all whitish-gray, embellished with a single white stripe.

The Admiral saw a family pattern immediately. "Ah, our dear relatives," he said impishly.

"Here is your grandmother," he announced grandly, plunking a stout bit of wood down in the sand. He had assigned her a flat gray piece, shapeless but ample. I could not be angry at him. How could he like her when it was so obvious she would never accept him?

"And here is all her money!" He shook a long black seed which made a rattling, hissing noise.

I had been collecting these strange flat casings for months, having never seen them before. Neither had the Admiral, but he had not paid any attention to them. Even Seixas did not recognize them. They were a dark velvety color, like Moors.

The Admiral cut one of the pods open and counted out the seeds as if they were coins. "We must be nice to grandmother, for here is all her fortune," he teased.

60]

We laid out grandmother's counting house next to her plump wooden person. I felt mischievous and wonderful.

"And here is your sweet mother," the Admiral continued. He put down a smoothly worn and delicate curved stick branch to which a single seaberry clung, as well as a lovely translucent white stone. I approved.

"Could this be your beloved cousin, Tristao?" the Admiral mocked, and lay down a single thin piece of wood, Tristao indeed being very slender, both in mind and body. I laughed for it so resembled the silly Tristao, and the Admiral had cast him perfectly, even though he had never met my cousin but had only heard of him from conversations with my mother.

"And here is the ever-necessary Seixas."

For him, a solid stick, worn into an obvious swirling curve, in fact worn like a fish hook.

The Seixas wood gave me a second of pause. "You know," I said, "it might really be a fish hook," for it did seem deliberately carved. I took another look.

"Where could all this material be coming from?" I asked the Admiral, who had been studying the currents around the island.

He scrutinized the object.

"I suppose it could have been dropped by a fisherman nearby and washed up here. Still, I've never seen one like this." He put the wooden hook in his doublet pocket and we went on with our game.

"And here is the great Governor, Signor Bartolomé!" The Admiral lay down a regal piece of wood, one side scoured into tiny peaks, like waves at sea.

Soon we had most of the extensive Perestrello e Moniz family tree assembled on the beach.

"But what about your family?" I asked. "Surely it is only fair that I have some relatives to make fun of. I know nothing about them, in fact."

The Admiral seemed to recoil.

"You know my father's name, and my mother's. That is all I know. No one keeps lineage records on weavers of Genoa," he answered bitterly.

There was no getting him to speak of his family, and so I did not force him. On the beach we had a refuge from the somber, fitful attitude that often plagued this complicated man I had married.

Here, we were together as nowhere else. He sat close, one leg bent and one leg straight ahead, one arm resting on the crown of his knee. With his other hand, he sprinkled sand on my bare feet, tickling me. "How I dream of you," I whispered, enjoying so the caress of sand falling across my skin.

The Admiral said nothing, but continued trickling sand.

I pressed the conversation. "And you, what do you dream of?" I asked. It was the sort of question I knew in advance he might not know how to answer.

"Me? I hardly dream, except of other places, though I am pleased to be in this place, right at this moment."

It was as close as the Admiral got to introspection. I leaned my forehead to his, and he embraced me. I felt his heart, his pulse, and I was never so happy with him, or with myself, as on such moments on the beach at Porto Santo. Yet, he didn't have to tell me of his restlessness—I knew he was both beguiled and bored here.

I thought he might wish for other company, but whenever I told him of the many invitations we received to dine with various island citizens, he sloughed them off, saying he did not wish to waste his time with "provincial transplanted people."

I had hoped he would show some interest in the Captaincy, for I was sure my mother could arrange for him to have the title if he wished, my brother being indifferent to the post, and an administrative decision having to be made soon. I longed for him to agree, for we could make of Porto Santo anything we wished.

I had my chance to raise the subject one day as he traced a piece of the driftwood he had noticed in my collection.

"Is the wood always on the same part of the beach?" he asked me as I entered his study.

"No, it lands at random but Seixas says they have been seeing it for years," I answered.

"Seixas again," he replied, somewhat disparagingly.

"Does he displease you?" I asked.

He did not answer. I approached him, but he looked up only for an instant.

"It is strange there aren't better maps and records of this settlement," he said.

I decided to broach the question of the Captaincy.

"Well," I said, "if you were in charge there could be."

"Perhaps, and then I could even be paid a pittance for governing," he answered sarcastically. "Felipa, really, you amaze me with your idea. This is a very small island."

"Yes, true," I acknowledged, "But we could be fully in charge. And we've spoken often of the business of finishing the settlement, the import of African plants, and . . . "

My husband cut me off.

"Joao Esmeraldo has written me, offering me a share in his sugar trade."

"But I thought you detested merchanting," I replied, surprised.

"African plants, no. Wicker roots, no. But sugar—maybe. It is lucrative. At least, Esmeraldo has made a fortune at it."

Esmeraldo was an Italian merchant who had been among the Admiral's Genoese friends in Lisbon, and his proposition was news to me.

"Well, I, please . . . let me think about it," I said and walked out into the garden.

The Admiral followed me there, carrying a small dossier.

Seixas was grading the dirt around the base of the palm trees, but he slipped discreetly away. The Admiral called him back saying, "Seixas, no need to go. This letter also concerns you."

A boat had arrived that morning from Madeira with supplies, including mammoth fruits, lemons the size of melons and melons the size of sacks of grain. Seixas had brought some for us, and apparently Esmeraldo's letter for the Admiral.

The Admiral began reading aloud:

> "Dear Colombo:
> I have heard through our Genoese acquaintances that you are still living in Portugal, in fact close to my own new home in Madeira, and that your attachment to this nation remains firm, formalized as it was by your marriage to the Dona Felipa Moniz e Perestrello. Perhaps you will recall our last conversation about my aspirations for the sugar trade, and your interest, which came again recently to my mind. Indeed my greatest hopes have been met and . . . "

The letter continued, full of dense references to measures, numbers and tonnage, and other details of the successful sugar business. Seixas found it difficult to follow, as did I. The Admiral noticed our empty eyes and stopped reading, excusing Seixas who on leaving murmured only, "Sugar will never grow in Porto Santo if that is what he wants to know."

The Admiral smirked slightly, but excused Seixas' impatience.

[63

"It is not about planting sugar here," he stated.

I had met Esmeraldo briefly at our wedding. He was now apparently doing well and installed in Madeira.

"He is inviting us to visit him in Funchal—that is the sum of it," the Admiral announced as he rose and walked over to the vines. He picked a handful of grapes, placed one in his mouth, and then one in mine.

"Oh dear," he mused, his fingers light upon my lips, "excuse me, ought I to have first licked my hand free of any unsavory substance, like the African princes?"

"That was only for inferiors to superiors," I joked back, kissing my husband's fingertips in reply.

Funchal seemed eons away, for we had, at least I had, become so settled here.

"Esmeraldo surely will provide wonderful entertainment and conversations," the Admiral continued. "And I am rather interested in this sugar business, you know."

Then he put a finger to my cheek.

"And wouldn't you enjoy a break as well?" he asked. "It's rather a long time since we've had news of your mother. We could bring her back with us, and I think the preparations of the house are a little tiring for you . . . "

His eyes caught mine and held them.

Then he spoke the simple truth. "Felipa, Porto Santo is a very limited place. I would just so enjoy a visit to Esmeraldo."

At such moments, I felt near despair, for of course he was correct. Porto Santo was a lost pebble in the sea compared to Madeira. This small island was the stuff of my family, my history. It was my childhood's cradle, not his, and perhaps I was too blinded by childhood memories to understand my husband's longings.

He said he had already learned the next sailing to Madeira, and had only to reserve the places.

I nodded my agreement, realizing that if I ever hoped to truly share this place with him, I would have to grant him this change.

I knew too that I could enjoy seeing Madeira again, and that my mother would be pleasantly surprised, and so when Seixas returned to the garden, I suggested the Admiral send him to book our trip.

"I only agreed because you plied me with these," I teased, kissing his fingertips again after he had pushed the last grape across my lips.

"Don't give all your secrets away, my dear wife. Remember the lapse of the Africans," he said nuzzling the back of my neck briefly, leaving me among the refreshing breezes that had, as was their way, gently and slightly changed direction.

Perhaps I did need a breath of city life. Perhaps if for now I could love this island less, when we returned, the Admiral could love it more.

Chapter Six

Esmeraldo's Dinner Party

The waters of the port at Funchal barely rolled, and a small jetty had been constructed at the foot of "Rua Esmeraldo." The street had been given the merchant's name, so prosperous and notable had he become for having seized the initiative in the new business of sugar, brought to Madeira from Sicily.

Funchal had by then about a thousand people, who earned their livelihood from planting wheat, sugar, cereals and, extravagantly, flowers. All around, there were scents and colors—sun yellow and flame orange, heartblood red, mimosa, hydrangea, hibiscus.

I had forgotten the lush valleys, sometimes steaming after a rain, vapor rising from the moist fertile earth. I had also forgotten how stunning a contrast with Porto Santo Madeira made, the larger island seeming the elder, more voluptuous sister.

Several barechested boys dove into the clear sea, splashing in a melee to recover coins tossed by disembarking passengers. "Throw to me, to me," they clamored.

"Here's a fortune to carry our luggage to the Casa Esmeraldo," the Admiral proclaimed, hurling a coin as several boys dove boldly.

"No, no signor, don't pay them!" another young man cried from the quay, "Signor Esmeraldo sent us to help you." He stood with a dusky partner, also naked to the waist and barefoot. Soon the two had swept up our sacks and strung them along a heavy pole.

The one wet boy who had retrieved the Admiral's coin watched with fearful eyes, not knowing whether he should now forfeit the money.

"Keep it," I said. "We'll pay the other boys too." The boyfish smiled and jumped back in the sea.

"Casa Esmeraldo is this way, not far," our young guides gestured.

Esmeraldo's house, naturally, was commanding. An unusual double window of two slender arches dominated the face of the building, and small lion heads roared from the top. The facade was unique in Funchal, and talk was that Esmeraldo had had the stones carved in Italy and transported one by one to Madeira.

Esmeraldo met us at the door, dressed in black breeches and a red and green velvet tunic with the bright yellow cross of Madeira embroidered on a sleeve. His looks were plain, though his rather lumpy nose was offset by fiery solicitous eyes. He was partially bald, and his dark brown hair spread over the top of his head as thin and separated as a comb itself.

Nevertheless Esmeraldo did not shrink from attention.

"Ah, my dear Colombo," he announced joyfully, "welcome to my home, humble though it may be." Esmeraldo spoke rapidly in Italian and embraced my husband warmly.

"Hardly humble, I would say," the Admiral replied in Portuguese, I assumed to signal Esmeraldo that I did not understand their native tongue. We entered the cool structure, a palace really, built of solid stone that let in no heat, the only place Esmeraldo's velvet clothing could be tolerable in the humid climate.

"Soon I'll build you such a home if you want," Esmeraldo pronounced, placing an assuring hand on my husband's shoulder. Esmeraldo had been building houses up and down the street, selling them at a profit to his merchant friends. He offered us lunch, and asked me to see if the suite he had chosen would do.

Each room had a balcony onto the street, including our guest quarters, and above, a third floor terrace extended across the entire width of the house. The view of the harbor was unimpeded—still blue sheets of water, and hills pouring into the sea in graceful green waves.

From there I could see the Chapel of Santa Clara, once the outer limits of Funchal. Now, though, the town marched steadily toward the small white building, practically reaching the base of the hill where the Church itself stood. The growth shocked me—flailing in all directions, Funchal was no longer a town I knew.

We reassembled in Esmeraldo's sitting room, and our host poured us sweet red Madeira wine from a heavy cut crystal decanter encrusted with rose patterns. Wine grapes had been introduced shortly after the colony began, and soon Madeira began producing one of the most prestigious wines in Portugal. I stayed briefly with the two men.

Esmeraldo courteously asked about my mother's health, and my grandmother and our journey, and then said, "And how do you find Funchal after your sejour away?" He had begun now speaking to us both in Portuguese.

I told him the size of the city startled me.

"Yes," he interrupted before I had finished my sentence. "It's remarkable, really. There is talk of building a cathedral, and walkways to be inlaid with the black and white tile swirling patterns so popular in Lisbon. Too bad your father could not have brought Porto Santo up like this from behind."

I did not like comparing the islands, nor Esmeraldo's patronizing tone. In truth, I had not liked Esmeraldo much on our first encounter in Lisbon, for he had made several awkward jokes at our wedding about women abandoning the cloistered life for "the bridle" of marriage that only he found funny.

"Porto Santo could thrive too if it rained as much there as in Madeira," I replied, "My father got the least of the colonies to work with."

"Oh, I certainly did not mean to impugn your father," Esmeraldo hastily answered, trying to smooth over his remark. "He was after all an Italian like ourselves, a great man from whom your husband might have learned much. I certainly had no intention to belittle his settlement."

"Of course not. Our host is too polite," I quipped. Suddenly hot and tired from the journey and the sweet wine, I excused myself.

In our room I opened the door to the balcony, and rua Esmeraldo was filled with mid-afternoon quiet. I fanned my face, loosened my dress, and drowsily lay down on the ample bed.

I did not wake until I heard the regular rhythm and shushing sound of a wicker scoop being put in, then out, in, then out, of a sack of grain somewhere below.

I wanted to be outdoors. I returned to the salon and found our host and my husband just where I'd left them. They had apparently not taken siesta and not moved except for Esmeraldo to collect his long narrow account books to show the Admiral. The two chatted in Italian and though Esmeraldo moved to bring up a chair closer to them for me, I declined and left to take a walk.

Esmeraldo's house was situated at the true center of Funchal, and the quarter radiated business, everyone doing, making, selling or buying something. There was constant bargaining, arguing over this or that price.

Goldsmiths and tinsmiths tapped on jewelry and buttons and other useful and useless objects, their work a series of flat tinklings and thumps. I listened to the sounds of the city I had not heard in so long.

I walked up the hill of Rua Ferreiros. All along the street, wooden scaffolds braced new houses under construction—many of two stories, many with elaborately swizzled wrought iron balconies, and great arching doorways two carriages wide. Some windows were framed with carved wood ornaments, intricate vines fashioned like lace out of wood. Money was speaking in Funchal.

It was still very hot, and I doused my face in a fountain. An elderly woman flower vendor sat there, happily sucking on a large vermilion fruit with a very smooth skin. It looked so refreshing, and soon she noticed me.

"Ameixieira," she explained, naming a fruit I had never tasted, and she pointed to a shop doorway further along the street where I bought some wrapped in a package of leaves.

They were luscious with tart delicious juice.

I strolled back to Esmeraldo's, delighted with my outing, and found the two men still talking accounting, as if they had been forbidden to leave the room or the subject.

"Esmeraldo has been explaining his difficult tax situation," the Admiral began as I joined them.

"Yes, and it has grown worse lately, my lady," Esmeraldo echoed. "The Crown has removed Madeira's favorable tariff status and costs have soared for what we sell and what we must buy."

I asked if perhaps that was the cause of the extensive bickering over prices I'd heard in the street.

"Oh yes, surely," Esmeraldo remarked, adding, "The situation grows more tense each day. It would be so helpful if the King could be induced to change his mind."

"Perhaps, but the King's mind seems fixed on navigation," I replied, loosening the palm wrapping of the fruits.

"Indeed he is," Esmeraldo noted, "which is good for your husband's business but not for mine."

"But I thought you were doing so well, Signor Esmeraldo," I observed.

"I am, I am, dear lady, do not fear for that. But still one must think of the future."

I offered the men the succulent ameixieira.

"Oh yes, these are common now," Esmeraldo commented matter-of-factly as he helped himself, "Eastern plums from an imported seed. We have been growing them here for some time. In fact, I'm serving them tonight at the dinner in honor of you and your husband, as well as something very new, damasquero apricots imported from China. Our compatriot Marco Polo has provided the dessert table tonight!"

He smiled the contented smile of the host who had thought of everything.

"Oh how marvelous," I replied, not being able to think of anything else suitable to say.

"See," Esmeraldo then nodded knowingly to my husband, as if I had just provided irrefutable proof of some point already made, "a woman can be made happy with so little effort."

I bristled, and my husband made no acknowledgement. I decided to say nothing. The Admiral spoke first.

"Our host was concerned about your wandering in the town alone," he explained as he stood, as if to forestall Esmeraldo's saying more.

"Yes," the Genoese interjected nevertheless. "A woman of your status ought not wander unescorted. Funchal is not Vila Baleira, Madame."

In truth I had become so accustomed to walking at will in Porto Santo that an afternoon alone in Funchal had seemed second nature to me.

"Our host needn't have worried," I replied, taking the seat Esmeraldo pushed toward me. "I was well protected by the swirl of business all around me. Your house could not be more at the heart of things, Signor Esmeraldo."

"I require centrality, Madame, but truly I would not want my neighbors to think my guest so displeased with my hospitality as to venture out alone."

He ought to have stopped there, but felt compelled to add, "I've learned that Portuguese women can be very independent, despite the dependent facade they perfect. Not every woman would insert herself as you have at Porto Santo . . . "

With this, the Admiral rose to intervene and defend Esmeraldo, sensing me tensing. "Felipa, please," he hastily began, "surely Joao meant to give you no offense."

Esmeraldo too came to his feet. "Of course dear Madame, I simply meant that women were more than they seemed and . . . "

I thought it pointless to go on, so I coolly pardoned Esmeraldo with the words, "We are all more than we seem, Signor Esmeraldo. Until dinner."

I left them, and when the Admiral came up to dress for the evening, he begged me not to hold a grudge. "Esmeraldo's not skilled at conversation perhaps," my husband defended.

And to lighten the moment with a now familiar tease, he added, "Esmeraldo is really no more thoughtless than your grandmother." I had to smile.

As the Admiral pulled on the black silk Venetian slippers he had decided to wear that evening, he continued, "Esmeraldo can be boastful, true, but he is very successful, a good businessman and has made a lot of money by cajoling and joking. It's not always in the best of taste, but he means no harm."

"But I am not a customer," I persisted.

"I repeat," my husband answered, "he meant no harm and perhaps he does not know how to speak to a woman, still being a bachelor. And he is very tense about the taxation situation. In fact, he had thought that perhaps your family might have some influence over the matter."

"How could he imagine my family would intervene for him?"

"Not for him, for Madeira."

"Esmeraldo's future and Madeira's are not necessarily the same, you know," I answered. "Defend him if you want, but I . . . "

The Admiral interrupted me, now somewhat sternly.

"Felipa, you don't have to like him for me to do business with him. Let us drop the subject at least for tonight. If you don't want to help him, fine, but Esmeraldo has information I need."

The Admiral finished dressing, and left to join the guests. I took my time. When I arrived, Esmeraldo rushed to meet me at the entrance of the garden, and offered his arm.

"Oh, Felipa, good. Now we can begin," he said jovially, and we walked into the dining hall where the King himself could have felt properly and opulently received. Esmeraldo, true to form, had totally avoided moderation.

The table seated at least 30, though we were fewer, and at each place, there was an embossed name card held in the crowing mouth of an individual tiny silver rooster, the Madeira symbol Esmeraldo seemed to love. Small crystal trays were heaped with condiments. Mandolin players installed themselves in a corner, discreetly playing lilting Madeiran and Genoese songs. Servants began by offering cubed fish of great variety, followed by a parade of roast partridges stuffed with island raisins and herbs, cakes of finely ground wheat, and spiced jellies.

Wine flowed abundantly, including sparkling imported Italian selections with which Esmeraldo toasted the Admiral, calling him a "new star in the sky of navigation." Esmeraldo introduced me as a "finely fit partner, the daughter of one of Portugal's leading explorers."

A kindly Signor Ettore sat at my left, another Genoese merchant residing in Madeira, who made pleasant distracting conversation comparing Madeiran and Italian vineyards. Esmeraldo occasionally leaned across me to listen and add his opinion, referring now and again to the new trade laws, and if only they could be changed.

The Admiral, for his part, chatted amicably with the merchants about his early travels and the prospects for the sugar business. Save for one other wife, I was the only woman. After dinner, when we moved to the garden for our dessert of Marco Polo's fruits, this lady, a Signora Grucci, sought me out to congratulate me on my "obviously gifted husband."

I thanked her and she added, gratuitously, "I think our host, well intended as he is, has always been a little jealous that the Signor Colombo married so well, and so easily." I was beginning to wonder if tactlessness was a special Genoese quality.

Signora Grucci caught herself. She recovered, saying "Oh Madame, I simply meant that Esmeraldo believes himself so talented as well, and . . . "

"Do not worry, Madame, you meant no offense. Signor Esmeraldo will surely find a wife to measure himself by soon enough."

I joined the Admiral at the other side of the garden, taking his arm, and he put one hand over mine as he spoke. All stood in rapt attention, as he described his thoughts about measuring the world and all the places he had been.

The guests peppered him with questions, as if privileged to be shoulder to shoulder with a keeper of wonderful secrets.

"Is it true that there are spurts of boiling water in Iceland, blowing up from the earth?" A guest wished to know.

"Ah yes," he answered, crouching to the floor, then widening his brilliant blue eyes and bursting to his feet to imitate the unleashed gush of water. All the guests applauded his living geyser with affection and delight.

He spoke easily of the far Mediterranean, of Chios, of Guinea, tales I'd heard before but enjoyed hearing again. He invoked African breezes, and the tallest prince, Caramansa, repeating the Portuguese captain's stories of Mina as if he had been there himself. He held the audience spellbound with his travels, until one admirer wondered when we would know when we had found all the land in the world.

The Admiral paused briefly as his audience waited in silent expectation, then replied, "When we have the courage to send the greatest among us to make the greatest voyages."

The crowd murmured its agreement.

"Is it true you clung to an oar and rowed six miles to Lisbon?" another admirer asked with obvious esteem.

"Yes, hard as it may be to believe. I did . . . "

Esmeraldo interrupted.

"I attest, I attest," our host earnestly corroborated in high-pitched tones, raising his right hand as he spoke. "This is how we met, for kindly Genoese I knew living on the coast nursed his wounds and rested his swimmer's bones."

Respect for the Admiral beamed on the faces of the dinner guests.

"I attest you can believe even the most fantastic tales this gentleman tells," Esmeraldo gushed, taking an empresario's credit for having brought the navigator Christoforo Colombo to Funchal.

And on the evening went, until I excused myself to sleep, leaving the Admiral surrounded by Genoese, now speaking only in Italian, the wine laying waste to even their most practiced Portuguese.

In the morning, Esmeraldo's chambermaid woke us with warm milk sprinkled with, of course, sugar, and the Admiral told me of the latest plan Esmeraldo had proposed.

"He will give you a boat to Machico any time you want. You can visit with your grandmother, collect your mother, and then sail directly to Porto Santo. I'll stay on here awhile, join Esmeraldo on a merchanting trip to the Grand Canary, and meet you at Porto Santo later on."

The thought of this expedition seemed to greatly please him, though I was ambivalent.

"Apparently, you have already discussed this in detail and consider it a wonderful idea," I said. The Admiral smiled, and I deferred my answer until Esmeraldo himself brought the subject up later in the morning.

"It is sensible, Madame," he began in his practical coaxing way. "Machico is on your way home from Funchal, and Porto Santo is on my way home from the Canary group. I've always wanted to see Porto Santo, and I'll be happy to put in there to leave your husband off. For now, he can stay behind to savor more of city life—the people here cannot get enough of him. And I guarantee he will be back at home before you yourself!"

The thought that, if I were not at Porto Santo when they arrived, I would not have to host Esmeraldo, tipped the balance for me. In truth, I agreed because I knew it was what the Admiral wanted.

"I will not be missed at Machico," he said. "I feel I am not welcome there and I would love to sail with Esmeraldo for awhile. I really would, darling."

He kissed my forehead. He wasn't wrong about my family. Except for my mother, I had had little support in my marriage. Not only had few relatives attended the ceremony, few had since invited us to visit or sent a gift or offered any of the niceties usually substituted when relatives cannot attend a wedding.

To my grandmother, the Admiral was no more than a non-Portuguese itinerant, a handsome foreigner with no past who had rescued her granddaughter from the convent. I could not deny her resistance to him.

And so in a way, I was secretly relieved he would not be coming with me. I had tired of trying to please my grandmother. I could visit her, pay my respects, and love her, for I did, but I was weary of trying to redeem my husband in her eyes. Alone, I would simply be her granddaughter, still a Moniz, untainted, the Moniz she had always preferred.

I took my leave of Funchal soon thereafter, and the Admiral and Esmeraldo saw me off at the pier.

"Thank you for your visit," Esmeraldo said gratefully, gesturing graciously. In the last days of my visit, he had somewhat curtailed his flamboyant speech and governing attitude, and I found myself tolerating him better. I had to admit he had been a flawless host, and the vessel he provided me was handsome and sturdy. "Thank *you* Joao Esmeraldo, for all your kindnesses," I answered.

The Admiral embraced me, and I kissed his cheek. I very much disliked saying goodbye to him. "I promise I will be there before you," he said to reassure me. But my eyes filled with the hot tears of parting. Why did I always feel there was so little between me and losing him?

Chapter Seven

The Great Idea

My mother and I returned from Funchal in a month's time. Seixas and Alfara waited on the beach, along with a group of fishermen to carry belongings. And to my delight, as he'd promised, the Admiral with no sign of Esmeraldo.

Seixas carried my mother ashore with the grace of a ballroom dancer. She embraced him and Alfara tenderly, nearly crying for she hadn't been here, where she had come as a bride, for almost 15 years.

"It is all nearly unchanged, Mother," I chattered as we walked the familiar path. But my mother only half listened. Her eyes scanned the harbor, the rocky hills, the crescent beach, the sandy flats and the blue sky broken only by the sharp intrusions of tall wavering palms, drinking in her memories.

I led her through the cottage to the garden door, wanting her to see all we'd planted first. She was amazed by the verdant spectacle, saying "My dear, it is as if I had never left."

She immediately fingered a fresh pink oleander, and some grapes, delighted at the life that had flowed into the places she had had to leave behind. Then, as if by instinct, she pushed open the door to the Residence.

I was at first bewildered, and then I realized—the Admiral had not moved us back into the cottage! Our belongings, our lives, lay bare before my mother, in her house, as she went silently from room to room. My clothes in her cupboards, the Admiral's papers strewn on my father's tables. My husband had vacated nothing, though we had agreed to it long ago.

The driftwood and seed casings and plant samples covered every available shelf. It was inescapably clear that we had usurped her home.

"I'm sorry, Mother," I rushed to apologize, "all this should have been taken out."

The Admiral said nothing except, "Yes, we ought to have resettled ourselves." I glared at him, truly angry with him for the first time I could remember. Why hadn't he done the moving we had planned?

But my mother made not a single comment. She left the Residence and walked across the garden to the cottage, surveyed our smaller kitchen, climbed the steps to what should have been our bedroom, and looked across the sea to Cima. "The view is better from here," she proclaimed, adding "I will take the cottage and you both may stay where you are."

I would not hear of it and begged the Admiral to ask her to reconsider. He however said only "Your mother knows her own mind, and the cottage is indeed better suited for one than two." I was exasperated.

My mother, though, soothed me. She came down the steps and held my hand briefly. Out of his hearing, she said, "He is your husband, Felipa, and he needs a work space, a place to be with us and away from us. Let him have the house. I have already lived there; the cottage suits me better now."

I embraced her. I knew that neither I, nor the Admiral certainly, would have so easily surrendered the house in which we had gathered the richest memories of life, had either of us been in her place.

My mother had brought many family belongings from Machico, including a set of unused pure linen hand towels I had never seen before, embroidered with the Moniz crest of five stars set in a circle below a full-maned lion. She had also bought several locked oak trunks covered with brown burlap that I did not recognize. She explained simply "They are family papers I have been storing at Machico. They belong in the Residence."

The Admiral waited in the garden, sensing my displeasure.

"I meant to discuss this with you in Funchal," he began, "as I have been thinking for quite awhile of asking you to consider our remaining in the Residence."

"How could I have known that was your intention?" was all I could reply.

"It just seemed more appropriate since, after all, it is now to us that the visiting ships pay their respects. Esmeraldo says that he has often heard talk in Madeira of our hospitality to seafarers. I thought we might wish to maintain our role and reputation."

His reasoning, of course, pleased me, for it seemed he might be now giving serious thought to assuming the Captaincy. But I did not mention that, and I left him to join my mother and Alfara, who was already busy with preparations in the kitchen.

At dinner, the Admiral told of his trip to the Canaries.

The Spanish colonies were prospering richly, sugar was blossoming in harvest, although the islands were by nature dry and barren and suffered as we did for lack of water. The Admiral said the Canarians had not yet thought of attempting windmills, and I joked that, in that at least Porto Santo could be said to be ahead.

The Admiral too noted the animosity between the Spanish settlers and the Portuguese, each Crown then vying for control of the islands, although he explained, "As Italians, Esmeraldo and I moved freely and inconspicuously between the two."

Esmeraldo, it seemed, had skillfully nurtured his business relations, managing to alienate neither Spain nor Portugal despite their being always at potential odds. His ships were lavishly received in ports of both countries. In Grand Canary, according to the Admiral, there had been many dinner parties and gatherings, "Many more widely attended than even those of Funchal," he noted with deep satisfaction.

At night, the Admiral embraced me, declared his deep need for my love, and we slept warmly together. And in the morning, rather than beginning his day in his study, I found him in the kitchen, chatting amiably with Alfara about the price of farina, of all things, and Alfara, remarkably, chatted back. The journey seemed to have heartily agreed with him.

Again we settled into the quiet Porto Santo pace, my mother taking great pleasure in her return to the island. We walked on the beach, and she easily assumed her role of respected elder lady, relishing the greetings of everyone in the village as she passed. She did not seem to mind the heat, preferring it, she said, to the steaminess of Madeira. And it was true that even in baking Porto Santo, the evenings cooled to perfection.

In fact, in our garden at night the air seemed so fresh with jasmine and frangipani and the sea, I could hardly believe that all around us still was the desert created by the rabbits of my father's unintentional error.

We sat at the table one evening talking of this, and I remarked, "I still cannot decide whether it was the island, or my father, who was more the victim."

"Surely, your father cannot be held accountable for what he did not intend," the Admiral replied, taking my father's part immediately.

"No, my father could not foresee. . . . I just think it could have been so much worse."

Indeed it had been lucky that few citizens had been settled on Porto Santo before the first colony had been abandoned.

"Are you quite sure your father was on the original journey to Madeira and then to here?" the Admiral suddenly asked.

My mother said nothing, but I answered, "Of course. Why do you ask that?"

"Curiosity, merely," he answered, "and Esmeraldo implied there was some confusion about it." He sliced one of the last large ameixeira plums we had brought from Madeira and passed it among us.

I wanted to know by what right Esmeraldo questioned my father's reputation. My mother then intervened, calmly, saying that my father had been plagued throughout his career by rumors that he had not actually been among the explorers to discover Porto Santo, but that he had been merely sent later to supervise its settlement. I had never known of that dispute.

"But surely," I protested, "there are records."

The Admiral then noted that, according to Esmeraldo, the Perestrello archives in Madeira were incomplete.

With this, my mother excused herself, and we retired. The Admiral worked into the night on a route map of his journey to the Canaries, and I did not wish to speak further of my father.

I did, however, rekindle the subject with Seixas one afternoon when the Admiral and I joined him on a rare daytime fishing trip. Seixas had simply replied, "Don Bartolomé, as far as all of us ever knew, did land here on the Crown's first voyage. No one had reason to think otherwise." For me, that laid the matter to rest.

One day shortly after this, Seixas sent word that the ship, *Guinea Costa*, was again offshore, with two smaller vessels, wanting to resupply with water. Soon enough, the same captain and his colleagues arrived at the Residence to bid us greetings.

The Admiral was delighted to see them, and as before, the conversation turned to Africa and the longing for the Orient. Ships were constantly being outfitted in Lisbon; fortunes were mounting. The East was magic powder to the Crown, and all of Portugal was heady on its scent.

The Admiral's eyes brimmed with interest and many questions. He invited the men to his study, and they pored over his maps, each ship's captain outlining his last voyage, and the Admiral writing intently, now having the confidence of the men, who gave their true routes and actual distances to him, not the false mileage they reported to the Crown. The Admiral probed them for an estimate of when the King would have the means to fully round Africa.

"It would take a man of your navigational experience and knowledge even to try," the *Guinea Costa* captain replied. "The grip of King Alfonso is faltering. His son, Joao the Prince, grows more potent everyday, but he is distracted by wars and problems with the nobles."

The Admiral savored such conversations, which kept us at least generally informed of distant news and events. And too, he still profited from our surroundings, paying great attention to what we observed at Porto Santo, the changes of wind, the darkening of water to signal a new sweep of current, and the flight patterns of the marine birds.

Soon, a full year had passed since our return from Funchal, nearly two years on Porto Santo. To mark the occasion, and to my deepest surprise and delight, the Admiral presented my mother with what he called "The first complete map of the island of Porto Santo," showing the slope of the hills, each bay and indentation, the wind and ocean current patterns. It was magnificently precise, beautifully drawn, impeccably lettered. Every detail of the island was here, including vegetation and the route of the known springs. No one had ever compiled such information before. My mother was speechless with gratitude; I was enthralled.

The Admiral enjoyed the satisfaction of having given us this pleasure, and then withdrew to his study. I followed, wanting to be near him, and as he drew, I stood behind him, massaging his neck and shoulder. He removed my hand indifferently, and put it out of his way next to the sheaf of paper on which he had been writing.

The oak table should have been rock steady underneath, but through my hand, my entire body quaked.

I tried to thank him for the gift he had given my mother, to say how much it meant to her, and to me. But he merely waved my words away. I began again, but he interrupted in a cold impatient tone, saying, "I did not make the map for gratitude. I made it to amuse myself, to pass the time, to produce something to account for all these damnable endless days and hours . . . ."

He stopped himself.

I left.

My mother sensed something had gone wrong. I tried to explain what had happened, but I didn't want to involve her. She could not, after all, help me to understand my husband. I did not wish her to be hurt by his brooding, his apparent lack of satisfaction, his volatility.

I tried to go on with life as before, but the Admiral's bleak spirits continued. He could not express himself to me, nor I to him, but I worried that my joy in Porto Santo had blinded me to his slipping away.

One day, however, my mother found a way to intervene, her own way to try to please him and lift his spirits.

She called me to the cottage and explained that she planned to offer him all my father's papers.

"The Perestrello archives in Madeira are incomplete indeed, as Esmeraldo says, for good reason," she confided. My father, she said, had not trusted all his papers to Crown officials out of his own bitterness and what he considered their ineptitude with respect to his suggestions about irrigation and cultivation at the first Porto Santo colony. My mother believed that since my father had never supported the Portuguese incursions to Morocco, the Crown in turn undermined him in Porto Santo.

In any case, rather than entrust his most important documents to the State—his personal maps and diaries as well as two trunks of maps and notes passed on to him by most navigators of the age— he gave them to my mother for safekeeping, on the promise she would keep them for exclusive family use. The documents represented a lifetime of experience with the sea and navigation; I doubted whether another such comprehensive collection existed in the world.

"The time has come," my mother decided, "for these papers to be put to service. Your husband can properly understand them, and use them well. They will occupy him and perhaps lay the doubts about Bartolomé Perestrello to rest."

I knew that my mother's gesture was one of great love for me, for the rightful owner of these papers ought to have been my brother.

I thought she should convey the news to the Admiral herself. That afternoon after lunch, I let the two of them walk alone in the square.

Then, as soon as they returned to the Residence, she summoned Seixas to bring the locked trunks she had brought from Madeira to the Admiral's study. "They are yours," she announced. There, saying nothing else, she opened them with tiny keys she held pressed in her palm and began presenting the Admiral leather portfolio after portfolio, each embossed with my father's seal, each tied with gold satin ribbon, each stuffed with papers and drawings. My father had gathered much material, much of which had been known only to him.

The Admiral was silent too, taking each bulk of documents and carefully placing them in piles on the long sidetable near his desk.

"I have no words, Madame," he said at last, and my mother embraced him; then she and I left him alone.

I waited awhile for him to join us in the garden, but he did not. I hesitated to disturb him, but I was so impatient to know his reaction to the gift. I knocked gently at his door.

"Come in," he shouted. He was already engrossed in the material, which was strewn here and there.

"Are you happy, darling," I whispered, softly fingering his hair. A chilling uneasiness overcame me when he said, admittedly in a lightly joking way, "Of course, I am happy. Here is your dowry at last."

He knew immediately he could not unsay it.

I buried my face in his chest, and he took me in his arms, trying everything he could to explain. Of course, he hadn't meant "at last"; of course, he hadn't been waiting for this; of course, the papers were not the most important thing to him.

"Please forgive me," he begged. But still I cried and cried. At last he proposed we walk on the beach, knowing I loved it so.

I agreed because our beach walks had remained, despite his increasing remoteness, our most meaningful moments on Porto Santo, important times because only then did the Admiral speak of what he thought.

We had continued to examine every bit of stone, and ground glass, and beach wood, as if they were messages from our future, and in a sense they were.

Through the visiting sailors we had heard of a pilot in Lisbon who had found a piece of wood on a beach, seemingly carved but not by the sea, similar to the driftwood we had been picking up. And to add to the hook we had collected long ago, we had also since found another piece of whittled wood, gray from exposure to salt and formed to a point as if by a man in need of an arrow. We never used such weapons in Europe.

Also, there were bits of yellowish wood in natural jointed sections, unknown in Africa, but perhaps the bamboo of China and the East washing up on our Porto Santo shores?

So much floated, seemingly able to survive in the sea forever, washed offshore by a wave and carried thousands of miles by a wind. Porto Santo was a trap in the middle of the world; the beach had remained a library of evidence of lands we did not see.

Where was all this seagoing debris coming from, and what pushed it to drop at our feet? Yet instead of taking pleasure in these speculations, the Admiral had continued to seem so unfulfilled, so frustrated, and distracted.

That afternoon I could no longer contain my feelings. He had hurt me deeply, and I begged him to explain.

"What is it, my most dear love?" I implored. "For all these weeks and months, why do you brood and sulk? I beg you to explain. Please tell me why you are so unhappy, when all is so perfect in our lives. We have this lovely place, now you have my father's work, we could have a child . . . "

He simply looked at me and announced what had been his obstacle. "I want to find the way to the East. I want to make a great voyage to the East, to go to those lands. I cannot listen any longer to the tales of others. I feel I was born to do it and I don't want it to happen without me."

He measured and remeasured the world, he confessed, hoping to find the distance lesser, Asia closer to us, reaching out into the eastern sea close enough to throw a stone. He seemed to be groping for the formula, as if it was the port of entry to his soul. He wanted a destiny.

We walked further along the crescent of sand the color of the gold of the East for which he seemed to yearn, and it slid across my bare feet like Eastern silk.

I held a bit of beach wood I had collected along the way, a survivor of some wild and wayward journey ground to the smoothness of stone, no longer mysterious, suddenly a clue between my fingers.

I formed the words that then seemed so simple, rising up through memory.

"Why not," I said clearly, the driftwood now a wind-lashed omen in my palm, "try to sail west first? I've heard an Italian mathematician has once proposed it."

Chapter Eight

The Birth of the Enterprise

A western route—I had said it. And once said, where no one else could hear, the idea became the fusion of our minds at that moment. It felt logical and unquestionably easy to stand ankle deep in the Porto Santo sand and tell the Admiral all I knew, so much did I feel a part of him, so much did I love him.

I had not meant to be so matter-of-fact, but I was merely referring to a proposal contained in a letter I had heard of long ago while studying in Lisbon. It suddenly seemed immensely relevant.

My cousin, the Canon of Lisbon, had been to Rome on royal Papal business, and there met a great Italian physician and geographer, Paolo Toscanelli. An astrologer as well, Toscanelli, counseled the Medici family, determining politically auspicious moments by reading the stars.

On his return to Lisbon, much impressed by the Italian's omniscient skills, the Canon reported to Alfonso V, the Portuguese King at the time, who then told the Canon to solicit the Italian's advice about the shortest route to India.

Toscanelli had great faith in his fellow Italian, Marco Polo, swallowing whole the latter's tale of the palace of Cipangu and the Eastern court of the Great Khan. Toscanelli replied to the King, sending a letter and a map, suggesting that the shortest route to the East was to the west, and not around Africa, as the Portuguese were so busily trying to accomplish.

But the King, unconvinced by the Italian, and already heavily invested both politically and monetarily in his chosen route, ignored the letter and the map, flatly dismissing Toscanelli's advice.

"Most likely," I continued to the Admiral, "Toscanelli's documents lay somewhere forgotten in the royal archives still."

[83

My husband, knowing no one at court, would have had no means to hear the Toscanelli story, but I had been aware of it for years through old family friends. The importance never occurred to me until that moment on the beach. The discarding of Toscanelli was simply another bit of gossip in our family repertoire of tales about Alfonso's lack of vision.

But my news stunned the Admiral.

"My god," he uttered. "My god, if I had only learned of this before."

He embraced me joyously, and from that moment, he talked of nothing else but sailing west. Within minutes, he formed a plan, and I was swept up in it, agreeing and promising. Yes, yes, my darling, friends can help us find the Italian's letters in Lisbon in the archives. Yes, we'll return immediately there. Yes, my dearest darling husband, we will tell all who will listen of this plan, and yes, of course, we shall somehow find the money.

Suddenly on the beach so much had become clear and wonderful. The west.

Of course, I thought, the currents that pounded Porto Santo came from the west; the rough bamboo cuttings landed from the west; the driftwood settled randomly, but randomly from the west.

"We must not refer to it publicly for now," the Admiral cautioned.

"We can refer to it as 'The Enterprise' between ourselves," I suggested, as a code word for what we meant.

The Admiral scratched his voyage in the sand.

"Spain is here," he poked with a stick. "Japan will be here." On our beach map of the world, the continents were as far apart as a forefinger and a thumb.

"And I promise her a pearl-encrusted palace when the Enterprise is through," the Admiral shouted with an empty beach as witness, then covered me with kisses that swallowed half his words.

At last I had found the key to his troubled spirit, and it had unlocked his fervor once again.

"Why not go west?" I ought to have said it before.

I felt at last his full partner, and that the anxieties of our recent days had melted into the single path of fate.

The Lisbon to which we returned, full of the prospects of our plan, remained as humid and breezeless as before our marriage, but trade with Africa, now a monopoly business of the Crown, boomed more than ever.

On the Tagus, ships were loaded below the waterline with sacks of fruits from Guinea or Morocco, and rippling with the activities of the Negroes, newly imported from Africa to be profitably sold as workers since the settlement at Mina had spawned a steady slave trade. The Lisbon population took this in stride, finding the dark races inferior to our own, and reaping the significant financial benefits of the commerce of the Empire, in ivory and pepper, wax, Arabian horses, dates, myriad new products, just as we had heard from the sailors who put in at Porto Santo.

The Negroes, black and beaten, nevertheless held themselves in stately posture. One of them might have been a prince, a Caramansa, a leader of his land who had welcomed the Portuguese and bartered food for bangles, soon to barter flesh and blood. "Six or seven Negroes for a horse," our *Guinea Costa* captain had reported. Still, however, it was like the Jews when we sailed—there was so much else to think about at the time.

The very air of the capital buzzed with trade and the adventure of reaching the newest furthest point. But always, the eyes of Portugal looked east via the south. Alfonso II had died; his son, Joao II, now reigned in his own right. The national pulse throbbed with the prospect of rounding the Cape of Good Hope, the elbow of the known world, and gliding then up to China and Japan.

But now here was another idea.

"There would be no official reason not to read Master Toscanelli's letter again, Felipa," my cousin, the Canon, analyzed, as we sat in the throne-like velvet chairs of his study at Court.

He was fastidious, impeccable in his choice of furnishings. No shimmering glass vase, no pure silver candlestick, no scarlet feather writing plume, was ill chosen or inelegant.

My cousin put an index finger to his face, tracing his throat, as if ever so vaguely reassuring himself he had no unwelcome blemishes. He was vain, but I liked him. The Canon completed his thought, saying, "Although I am not exactly sure what my legal position would be, or even if I could find Master Toscanelli's correspondence now."

I had spent several months trying to arrange this audience with Fernam Martins, one of the busiest men at Court, the Canon of Lisbon, ecclesiastical advisor to the Crown. He had been away traveling in the rural areas, then his secretary misplaced my appointment approval note. Finally, my cousin waved away formalities and found the time to see me.

We had not been confidantes as children, he being quite a bit older than me. But he had been a frequent guest at my parent's home, his father and mine being distantly related. He had once intimated to my mother, without my asking, that I would be unhappy at the convent school. That unsolicited intervention on my behalf, however futile, had formed a certain bond between us, and I groped now for a way to convince him to help.

Martins was a learned man, with active dark brown eyes. He had grown portly with age and rich food, but nevertheless retained a spry informed manner. He was greatly trusted by the Crown and the Pope, responsibilities he took very seriously.

"How is your mother," Martins wondered good-naturedly. I replied that Dona Isabel bore her age well, but that her breathing troubles had returned now that we were back to the dampness of the city. We had indeed left our lovely island hastily, leaving Seixas to keep the houses intact until we better knew our plans in Lisbon. Martins sat straight in his chair before many shelves of books bound in caramel colored leather and lettered with hand-stamped gold leaf. I saw a way to bring up Africa.

"The bindings on your volumes might have just arrived from the mines of Mina," I commented, scanning the luxurious library, adding, "My mother gave my husband all my father's papers, you know, for she loves and trusts him very much."

The Canon had once looked over some of my father's collection and was vaguely familiar with its contents. He clasped both hands together and they disappeared under the great wide sleeves of his rust-colored garment. He had also always held my mother in high esteem, I thought, for although her family had been pretenders to the throne, she remained loyal to the Crown. The Canon, as if hearing my thoughts, said, "Your mother has always been so kind to me despite the differences of her family with the Court I serve. It impresses me how she avoids the blurring of blood ties and politics."

He paused, then added, "It appears you have been much help to your husband. Have you any children?"

"I love him deeply," came my immediate reply, not answering the question directly. Children had become a sore subject between the Admiral and me. He wished to postpone our family until the Enterprise was en route. I had not settled the issue in my mind.

"He is somewhat Italian, isn't he?" Martins asked, an eyebrow arched slightly and a slight aspersion creeping into his voice. "By somewhat, of course I mean that he is not a Florentine, like Toscanelli.''

"Yes, he is Genoese, but as much a dreamer and an artist as all Italians, and also very hard-working," I replied, now wishing that the Admiral had come along for I knew how much Martins admired Italy. We had decided it best for me to visit alone first, so my cousin would feel he could speak freely.

The Canon said no more for several moments. Then, he thought aloud, "In principle, the letter belongs to the State, though addressed to me. But the State is not interested in it. Toscanelli's theory too overtly contradicted Alfonso's view, and his son, the present King, did not take Toscanelli seriously at all. They did not even wish to have the correspondence formally indexed, and without that, in such a cold dark cavern, it would be very difficult.'' My meticulous cousin's voice carried dread of the dirty archives.

Martins continued deliberately, as if dissecting his thoughts into individual words to examine their validity one by one. "But, on the other hand, I believe there is no official interdiction on viewing it. I could show it to you as a family member, that is if we can find it at this late date in the vault of papers. But it could not leave the shelf. Agreed?''

I was halfway there. It would not be enough for me to read the letter; only the Admiral would be able to decipher what I assumed would be complicated mathematical talk of longitude and latitude and circumference of the world.

"My husband cannot come?'' I gently pushed the Canon.

He smiled and lowered his eyes. "I suppose it makes no difference, as you are married to him. But three will be a crowd in the darkness of the archives, I assure you!'' It seemed to please him to give in.

I had gambled that I would be able to move Martins to our side and was bursting with the news when I returned home, delighted to tell the Admiral of my victory.

"Martins will take us through tomorrow morning before his first day's meeting,'' I reported excitedly to my husband.

"Wonderful.'' he answered, "Then we must sleep well and early tonight.'' After dinner, I rested my head on my husband's shoulder and hoped he would compliment my success.

He brushed a finger through my hair, and kissed my forehead but said nothing. Two candles flickered on the wall.

But thoughtlessly, and to prevent so soon an end to the evening, I raised the subject of a child, my cousin having made me think of it.

I had not yet become pregnant, despite our many times together, and the way the Admiral now made love—withdrawing just before, which I had never felt comfortable mentioning—I knew I had little chance to conceive.

I was already 27 and perhaps it was by then too late. But such private womanly questions—I felt as though I had swallowed a cold lump whenever I tried to speak of them with my husband. He, however, consoled me.

"Felipa my dearest wife, we have so much yet to accomplish on the Enterprise, and you are so involved, we cannot also add a child. Please let us not create a source of argument about it."

He still kept his arm around me. I began to speak, but he stopped me with a kiss, and words I hadn't heard in a long time.

"I love you, this you know, so please let us not be distracted now, before the plans are settled. Please believe me, as you believe in me."

His blue perfect eyes penetrated all my fears and discontent. It was enough to hear he loved me, for I needed these reassurances more than I liked to admit.

Of course, he was right. There was still the Toscanelli letter to find, much maneuvering with more cousins and friends at Court, and eventually an audience with the King himself. I had to be a public person, free to go out, be seen, and though I burned for a child of ours, it would happen, I was sure, once the other matters were underway.

We darkened the room and went to bed. I did not face the Admiral, but instead slipped into the crook of the arm he placed over me like a great safe coverlet. He rested on his cheek, his face brushing my back, and our bodies fit roundly and perfectly together like two spoons. But we did not move to embrace.

I filled up with wanting him, edging closer to him, then pushing the thought away as my husband's sleep grew deep and settled, and soon, slowly, so did mine.

In the morning, we stood in the Canon's antechamber.

The Admiral dressed regally, having worn a maroon tunic over a pure white shirt whose collar neatly rolled up and ruffled over the neckline, a cross embossed just under a shoulder, and his usual fine bronze-colored Italian leather breeches.

He presented his hand forthrightly to the Canon, kissing his Papal ring as was proper even among relatives, then noticing my cousin's other jewelry.

"I see you have a magnificent coral finger rose," the Admiral complimented. Indeed, the Canon wore an exquisitely carved tiny flower.

"You are astute and kind to notice, for these rings are quite rare," the Canon replied.

"And difficult to craft," the Admiral continued knowingly. "I have seen the fishermen dive just under the sea surface, off the Italian coast, to cut coral branches and then sell them to artists to work."

"Yes, mine comes indeed from Ostia," Martins agreed, twirling the ring on his finger.

The Admiral knew Ostia it seemed, taking his cue.

"A lovely restful place. Even the Romans enjoyed it for respite from the insalubrious inland."

"Bravo," Martins commented, obviously pleased, "you know your country well, Signor Colombo."

Then the Admiral lost no time thanking Martins for his confidence in us, and his help.

"We will be eternally in your gratitude," the Admiral said sincerely, "and so might be the world," he could not resist adding, catching Martins' full attention with his remark.

"What a very grand Italian notion," the Canon warmly returned. "Perhaps you are right," he reflected. "That would please me, as I have long admired the thinking of Doctor Toscanelli."

He breathed in slightly. "He is such a handsome and delightful genius. I was sorry when nothing came of his letter and he did not come to Lisbon. Did you know he had designed the sundial of the Florence Cathedral?" The Canon and my husband chatted on about Toscanelli's brilliance, and Italy, as we pressed ahead toward the inner chamber.

I had never seen such imposing rooms as these. Enormous wooden racks stood like rock promontories all around us. I had expected to be among magnificent and rare manuscripts, as carefully preserved and tended as vintage wines. But not so.

"You would think these documents were prisoners," I murmured to my cousin, who did not need to have his attention called to the dinginess of the place.

"Have you so soon forgotten, dear cousin, that it was you, not I, who was so eager to penetrate this literary labyrinth," Martins replied, a friendly lilt to his voice. I believed that, but for the grime, my cousin savored the search.

He cut an amusing figure, today clothed inexplicably in the whitest of clerical garments, ambling among lost papers, some piled higher than his slightly balding head, holding his robes just above the floor, as if fording a stream of putrifying water instead of a carpet of innocuous dust.

But still it wasn't pleasant. The rooms were unventilated and dark and mildewed.

Several hours passed and we had examined many large piles of forgettable invoices, lists, inventories, receipts and letters, all to no avail.

"But the letter was only six years ago," the Admiral bemoaned, frustrated at the mass of material we had already perused.

"Yes," the Canon acknowledged, "but you have no idea of the volume of royal and theological correspondence that can accummulate in even that seemingly short period. I doubted we would find it."

"We must continue looking," I urged Martins. "Please stay with it a little while more." The Canon acquiesced. I smiled my thanks and wiped a black smudge from his cheek. He whispered to me kindly, somewhat mischievously, "He is more charming than I expected, dear cousin, and I do see that you love him. Let us go on, if we have come this far."

We reached a cul-de-sac, with a large oak table along one side, itself the length of one entire wall. Martins rested the candlestick on it, using the weakening candles to again light fresh ones he carried in a red felt pouch. After this, we had only two new candles left.

There was another tall rack with stacks of materials, and many small wooden lacquer boxes, sealed and closed, too small, we thought, to contain what we were looking for. The table itself had several drawers, and underneath it, there was a large wooden chest trimmed with tarnished brass and tinged with mold, unlocked and entirely empty.

We checked each of the table drawers, each also empty. Martins mumbled that he had known at the time he ought to have catalogued and stored the Toscanelli documents himself. "Without a proper index it is absolutely impossible," he said, stating what we were finding out ourselves.

There remained the rack against the wall, packed with dossiers tied with ribbons and braided cords, piled like dinner plates nearly to the ceiling. Even I dreaded the task.

But then all three of us noticed that in the middle of this last tall stack, a single sheet of parchment protruded. "For fun, and nothing to lose," said Martins dryly, pointing overhead with his chin, "let's begin with that little beckoning flag up there."

He and the Admiral stood on the chest and gently lifted the top half of the stack so I could carefully slip the oddsize manuscript out. The file was not too thick, but there seemed to be several double folded sheets inside. My cousin and my husband scrambled down to have a closer look. There was no label on the outer cover.

Only when we undid the packet tied with vermilion ribbons did we find the tiny paper of identification loose among the documents: "On the Matter of Paolo Toscanelli, June 25, 1474, correspondence between said physician and the Canon of Lisbon, Fernam Martins, at the direction of Alfonso V, Sovereign King of Portugal."

We whooped with pleasure. Martins too. "How clever of me," he delightedly congratulated himself. "That is my writing. I must have included this irrefutable note as an afterthought."

Incredibly, the paper that we had spotted first was Toscanelli's map itself, appended to his letter.

Immediately the Admiral took the chart in his hands and spread it across the long table.

"Extraordinary," he murmured.

And it was.

For one thing, the coastlines and land masses were painstakingly drawn, and the map itself trimmed around the perimeters with gold.

All the sea was colored a heavenly blue, and unlike most maps I had seen before, Europe was not at the center. Instead, Europe travelled off to the right, a mere border on the page. Our continent had its familiar form edging the Mediterranean—the Italian boot, the Iberian chin. But, Europe on this map was of secondary import.

Instead, most of Toscanelli's map was water, marked MARE OCEANUM, save the islands we knew—the Azores, the Canaries, Madeira, even the speck of our own Porto Santo.

The left side of the sheet was critical. There, commanding our eyes, were many outlined fluid white forms, blank, unknowns, islands exploding off a large mainland called "Cathay," one larger than the rest, a vertical long land called Cipangu—Japan.

And between Europe and these eastern lands, what looked like a reasonable distance of absolutely nothing but Toscanelli's majestic, uncharted blue.

"Listen to this," Martins commanded, now as excited about finding the documents as we were. He began to read aloud.

"'Paolo, the physician, to Fernan Martins, Canon of Lisbon, Greetings: It pleases me greatly to learn of your familiarity with your Most Serene and Most Magificent King . . . '

"You remember," Martins pointed out "it was I who recommended the King seek out this great gentleman's advice."

He continued reading: "'And although many other times I have discoursed of the very short route from here to the Indies, where spices grow, by way of the sea, which I hold to be shorter than that which you follow to Guinea, you tell me that his Highness would now like from me some explanation or demonstration in order that he may understand and that he may be able to take the said route . . . '"

"What does he say about Cipangu?" the Admiral interjected, obviously trying very hard to restrain himself from taking the letter from my cousin's hands to read.

Martins scanned the pages. "Let's see, yes, here he says: 'Know that in all those islands only merchants live and traffic, informing you that there is as large a quantity of ships there and of mariners with merchandise as in all other parts of the world . . . '"

"No, that is not it," the Admiral interrupted again. "There must be some references to the route and some mention of gold. Read on please."

Martins did.

" ' . . . and this country is most populous and there are many provinces and many kingdoms and cities without number under the dominion of a Prince called the Great Khan, whose name means King of Kings' . . . "

Martins broke off, saying "No. I see myself that is not it. I will read on." His eyes moved wildly around the page.

"Ah yes, here we have some pure Toscanelli. He always loved elaborate buildings as much as he loved to dote on the stars over Tuscany. In this paragraph, perhaps . . . "

He read grandly: " ' . . . Upon one river alone, 200 cities are situated with marble bridges very wide and long and adorned with many columns. This country is as rich as any other that can be found . . . ' "

Martins stopped again, pulling the Admiral's sleeve, urging "Here, Colombo, listen well, here is what you want: 'But also gold and silver and precious stones . . . a great city of Quinsay . . . ten marble bridges.'"

"But that is not yet Cipangu!" the Admiral bellowed with frustration.

"Nor the way to get there," I added, now wanting desperately too to search the papers with my own eyes.

"Yes, yes, I am sure we will come to that," Martins nodded, his rose-ringed index finger passing madly from word to word.

"Yes, just a second, here are some very precise calculations . . . here it is. Yes."

The Canon cleared his throat and read the words we had been waiting for:

" ' . . . as far as the most noble Island of Cipangu, there are ten spaces, which make 2500 miles, that is to say 225 leagues, which island is most fertile in gold, in pearls and precious stones. . . . Thus because the way is not known, all these things are hidden and covered. And one can certainly go to these places. . . . I therefore send His Majesty a chart drawn by my own hand . . . upon which is laid out the islands which lie on that route, in front of which, directly to the west, is shown the beginning of the Indies. . . . And do not marvel at my calling 'west' the regions where the spices grow, although they are commonly called 'east'; because while one who goes overland to the east will always find the same lands in the east, whoever sails westward will always find those lands in the west.' "

"That is all he says?" my husband cried out, incredulous.

Martins now bridled. "My gentleman, this is already quite a gift of God. Toscanelli ends with a most courteous greeting: . . . 'And this to satisfy your requests as much as the brevity of the time and my occupations have permitted.'"

The Canon somewhat curtly said, "I would be most satisfied with this, if I were you, my cousin's husband, and . . . "

"We are, Canon, excuse me, of course we are so wonderfully satisfied and most grateful," the Admiral recovered. But he added quickly, "I must copy it."

"Here?" Martins replied, shocked.

"Yes, and now," the Admiral replied, "for I must study it more carefully at home."

Martins reluctantly consented, gingerly handing over the documents. The Admiral had brought with him a navigational text he had intended to show Martins, and in its margins, he now hastily hand copied the complete Toscanelli letter, and redrew the map on a sheet of blank paper he had also brought along.

While he worked, Martins and I moved out of the airless corner and my cousin inquired about what we planned to do next. I told him we hoped to mount an expedition to Cipangu, but he reeled and cautioned me at the expense.

"Frankly, Felipa," he said, "this plan was once rejected by a King as too costly and silly. Are you not daunted?"

I did not have a ready answer yet, admittedly.

Martins continued with concern. "Is it wise to become so, shall we say, involved?"

"I am committed to my husband," I answered.

The Canon simply bowed his head, saying in a low voice, "As you wish, my cousin, if you wish."

The Admiral finished his copying, and he and Martins replaced the Toscanelli file just as we had found it. We returned to Martins' study quickly, to stay ahead of our last candlelight.

We had passed no one in the corridors, and we swore to the Canon we would tell no one of our visit. Once back in his chambers, my cousin efficiently resumed his formal clerical posture and attitude, brushing and straightening his clothing.

"Bless you both," he said as we left him, laying his hands upon our shoulders. He retired swiftly toward his inner office, where he had an appointment waiting, the last tail of his long white robe soon fluttering out of sight down the hall.

We hastened home along the Tagus, the Admiral taking long steps, eager to study the new material. It remained now only to open the door to the King of Portugal.

Chapter Nine

The Secrets of the King

A light breeze of dawn pushed the gauzy lace curtain away from the window. I shut my eyes again, and saw her still, a woman trying to hold on to sleep, as if to stay astride her horse, leaning into the clean leather sighs of the saddle, to ride all night, ride and dream . . . close your eyes or morning will come. The hoofs stepped out their message.

She hunched over the horse's chestnut neck and slipped her hand under the black glistening mane . . . my pillow, where were my hands, here, but where was the sweetness of rest, the remains of sleep?

I turned on my back and gave in to day. Streamers of light circled me, dancing on the walls and ceilings like votive candles in a cave chapel. My husband rustled a little, stirred, and inched slightly toward me. I did hear horses outside clopping, and the voices and laughter of people, but it was too early for a gathering.

I opened my eyes, finally, and left the bed to look.

An elaborate royal procession wound through the streets. Of course. I had forgotten it was Sunday, though the King had not used the route below our house before. Joao II had taken to riding publicly through the city each week, partly it was said because he wished to keep direct contact with his subjects but also to put to rest rumors that he no longer felt safe in Lisbon. For since the beheading of the Duke of Braganca for treason a few months before, the capital rippled with reports of treachery against the Crown, real and imagined. Though the Duke had been the ringleader of the attacks on the new young King, some of Joao's advisers believed danger still lurked among Braganca's accomplicies awaiting their next opportunity.

But clearly Joao remained in control, and he was very popular. Up and down the street, royal satin bunting draped from household windows, loyal citizens baring the crimson and sapphire blue colors of the King. Those who had no official banner draped their finest small carpets, or any gaily colored cloth.

And then there were the minstrels. If their chinking tambourines did not wake the Admiral, their heraldic kingly trumpets did.

My husband rose from the bed to survey the commotion, rubbing his eyes.

"Good god, Felipa, what's all the . . . oh. I see." He peered down.

"If we wait, we'll see the King," I said with excitement, "for the entertainers usually signal he is not far behind."

Sure enough, pure white horses pranced high below, as if stepping on hot stones, pulling a gleaming carriage. But the King did not ride inside. He rode ahead, on a single magnificent horse. I had never seen him this close before.

He wore no armor, though he rested one hand on the sword jutting stiffly from his side. Footsoldiers surrounded him with a forest of spears, walking alongside.

The crowd cheered and roared, and he returned their warmth with a full wide smile. His bright alert face shone in genuine pleasure as he turned his head first to one side, then the other, greeting and waving. His black beard came to a rather sharp point, yet on him, the effect was not stern, but instead seemed to enhance his authority and confidence. He wore simple clothing for his rank— a brilliant blue tunic, its long ample sleeves cut with slits through which his hands could slip, to give the impression he wore a cape, and flaming sunset red breeches fitting tightly into polished black boots that came nearly to the knee.

A royal medallion bounced against his chest, but he carried no sceptre of office. He wore no Crown, only a brown beret somewhat rakishly tipped toward one eye, trimmed with thin gold braiding.

The Admiral was mesmerized.

"Don't we have anything suitable to drape from our window?" he worried, swept up in the aura of the pageant.

"Perhaps the Moroccan weavings my grandmother gave us," I suggested. They were magnificent tapestries, depicting the triumphal entry of the Portuguese to Tangiers. In fact, the weavings would be perfect, I realized suddenly, for they depicted the young Prince before us now a King, then only sixteen years old and already a key figure in his father's conquering army.

My husband opened one of our cupboards and unrolled the emblazoned cloths out the window in full view of the King, who waved his acknowledgement, though he would not have known who we were even if he could have made out our faces from the street. Soon, he had ridden beyond us, and the full parade moved on.

"Well done," I smiled to the Admiral, "a good first impression." He nodded and followed the procession with his eyes until even the loudest trumpet fanfare had faded away.

"A splendid sight," he remarked, very pleased and impressed, as he rolled our tapestries back up from the window sill. "I see why they called him 'The Perfect Prince.' "

"Yes," I agreed, "and by all accounts he has become a good and worthwhile King."

My father had served Joao II's father, Alfonso V, the King who had rejected Toscanelli's advice. Alfonso had always doted on his son, Joao, who by the time he was sixteen had been knighted in battle. Groomed early for the throne, Joao had participated in important negotiations, including the ever tense relations with the court of Castile in Spain. The prince became a true extension of his father, the King's only real confidante.

During a journey to France, the aging Alfonso slipped away from his palace guard and disappeared for days to meditate in a monastery. Only Joao's pleading induced him to return home. But though the palace kept up appearances, Alfonso had virtually abdicated in favor of his son. He lived the last days of his reign as a monk in a monastery close to Lisbon, paying almost no attention to affairs of state. Joao ruled quietly by default until his father's death.

His accession in his own right infused the country with terrific energy. The interminable war in Morocco and Alfonso's eccentricities had worn down the Portuguese, and Joao symbolized youth and promise—a vigorous handsome man, crowned at 26, four years younger than the Admiral, two years younger than me.

To begin with, Joao undid most of his father's land policy, returning much untilled land to the title of the Crown, so it would again be planted to relieve food shortages. He also reduced the pensions paid by his Treasury to relatives and vassals, monies that had been granted by Alfonso in return for their acquiescence in his unorthodox reclusive reign.

Of course, Joao's reduction of various aristocratic privileges was a root of the Braganca conspiracy, for not all the lords agreed with the new King's approach. But Joao's plans were working—talk was that food production had increased, and the people could more easily buy grain. One by one, the King was ferreting out his enemies, and developing new friends.

Joao relished his role, and this too endeared him to the country. One heard of happy parties, troubadour competitions—events not lavish, but truly royal. In addition to his weekly processions in Lisbon, he often travelled in Portugal—to Evora, to Sintra—to show himself to the people.

But above all, he had gained respect for the supreme gesture he had made to quell tensions with Spain. He had placed his only heir, his most beloved son, as collateral for the treaty he had recently signed with his cousin, Isabella, Queen of Spain, herself a force to reckon with, as we of the Enterprise certainly know.

Tensions with Spain had erupted into battle shortly after my marriage. The two shrewd leaders knew a peace treaty between such chronic rivals would need to be sealed in some inviolable way. So, while my husband and I had been on Porto Santo, Joao not only betrothed his adored five-year-old to Isabella's eldest daughter, then age 10, he had also agreed that the two children would be raised in the impartial custody of their mutual grandmother in a Castle at Moura, totally incommunicado except for the right to parental letters, until their marriage. Then Spain and Portugal would be, in theory, forever allies. In the meantime, the precarious peace rested on the fact that the lives of two star-crossed children would be at risk should either sovereign attack the other.

"What a remarkable plan," my husband commented, as I told the Moura story over breakfast.

In fact only this month, as we began to form the Enterprise, the Spanish Queen and Joao had abrogated the custody terms of the treaty. They decreed that the peace would depend on royal word, rather than this strange exile of their children which none of the parents could bear.

Joao had the right to look enraptured as he marched through Lisbon—his only son had just returned to his family safe and sound.

"So the Portuguese King's story has had a happy ending," the Admiral observed, pouring himself a second bowl of tea. So it seemed, and all the better for us.

The days and weeks began to run together and the Admiral lost himself in essential reading and writing. He examined the works of all the great geographers again—Ptolemy, Marco Polo, Marinus, even the Bible—industriously making notes in the margins of his books, all to prepare the argument for the King.

Too, he often spent afternoons in the Genoese quarter, in order, he said, to remain informed about navigational news that his compatriot merchant friends were in a unique position to collect.

And I was equally plunged into the tasks at hand. I busied myself with trying to visit friends and relatives, soliciting their advice on how to bring the Enterprise to royal attention. But people had moved away since my marriage, and the task of reconstructing my life before Porto Santo moved much slower than I had hoped.

One afternoon, I took lunch with my mother in her room, and sat at the foot of her bed. The shimmering satin canopy draped like a white waterfall from the bedposts, and she spoke gently.

"This matter takes all your energy, my dearest daughter. Perhaps this is why there are yet no . . . "

"Mother, I do not think so," I answered, knowing exactly the subject she wished to discuss. "I am not fatigued, nor is the Admiral. Partly we are not wishing for it, or trying, or perhaps I simply cannot conceive."

I could not of course share all my intimate feelings with my mother, for though I loved her, we had never been openly confiding, and it was uncommon to share with one's mother such preoccupations as I had about my own motherhood.

"We will eventually meet with the King, I am sure of it. It is simply a matter of time," I told her as my mind spun to the future. I had promised myself to speak with my mother about subjects other than the all-consuming Enterprise, but she insisted on this track.

"Dear Felipa, if the King refuses to see you, and he might, for the plan is quite unorthodox, and the Admiral's hopes quite lofty, and . . . " she said, then stopped, her voice cracking a little. Her servant poured her a glass of water, and I wished I had thought to do it myself. I asked the servant to leave.

"It is a good plan, mother," I defended, "I believe in it. The Admiral has learned much from the Perestrello papers—there are even references to western lands. It is quite remarkable how much no one but father seemed to know."

This pleased her and we talked a bit more, about my brother administering in the Azores, from whom there had been little news. She asked too if there had been any messages from Seixas or anyone at Porto Santo, or from my grandmother, but I had nothing to report. Then my mother returned to the discussion she had begun.

"If the King rejects . . . "

"Mother, if he does, I have already promised my husband I would pay some of the costs myself, not all, of course, for we cannot, but enough to begin." Since my mother's illness, she had allowed me to take over the family finances.

"It has already been decided," I continued. "But please don't worry. I won't be wasteful, and we will always take care of you well."

She was too tired to protest. She closed her eyes.

My mother, how little I knew her really, or she me, and yet we were so similar. My mother, who curled my hair when I was a girl with strips of cloth that left long soft tendrils when she removed them, who told me tales of wounded slate gray seabirds we could nurse back to life if they landed on our Porto Santo windowsills. My mother who followed her husband to an island pinhead in the sea, and loved it more than the opulent society into which she had been born. My mother, who now doubted what I was doing was best.

She was asleep. I bent and kissed each of her eyes. Downstairs, the Admiral asked me, "Is your mother well?"

"She is worried for us if the King denies . . . "

"If the King refuses, he ought not be King," was all the Admiral had to say.

We had made plans to spend a Sunday afternoon at the home of my dearest and oldest friend, Nicola de Resende e de Vicosa, with whom I had at last been able to rekindle contact. She had only recently returned to live near Lisbon from Burgundy, where her husband had been Ambassador. It was a great advance for our plans that Nicola now lived within a day's visit.

Nicola had been my best companion as a child, and we swore to be lifelong friends. I had not seen her for many years, for she did not attend All Saints as I did, having earlier married the Duke of Vicosa, leaving Lisbon immediately to travel with him.

At first, the Admiral protested because he had wanted to conduct some business with an acquaintance of Esmeraldo's in the city, but he soon understood the potential for the Enterprise that Nicola represented.

Her husband sat on the King's most trusted Council, and Nicola consequently enjoyed much privileged information. She also was in charge of soliciting all private subsidies for the construction of a new public hospital in Lisbon, Queen Leonor's main occupation these days now that she could devote time to it free of worry for her son. The Crown had long planned the hospital to cope with new plague cases but, heavily committed financially to exploration of the seas, counted on the nobility of Portugal to help support the charities.

The hospital project had resumed full throttle lately, and Nicola knew almost all of Lisbon's involved and leading families.

"And in addition to that," I explained, as my husband and I waited for Nicola's carriage to collect us, "Nicola is a cousin of Garcia de Resende, the King's personal secretary and poet to the court." In one fell swoop, if she were so inclined, Nicola could be of tremendous help.

It was a warm but sunless day so far. My mother had first intended to come along, but had changed her mind fearing a rain that would leave her chilled on the journey.

"It's always cooler in Sintra," she observed, seeing us off, "so I'll be better here at home. My own friend, Dona Maria, may well visit. Feel free, my dears, to spend the night in Sintra if you wish, for I'll be in good company."

She kissed us both goodbye when the Vicosa coach arrived. We rattled through the narrow streets and down the slopes of Lisbon until we reached the Tagus.

Our greatest poet said that Lisbon is "the princess of the world . . . before whom even the ocean bows," and it was true. The Tagus River was filled with possibility, nourishing the sea with convoys of ships bound on discovery, as soon I hoped, would we.

Talk took some effort in the carriage. The heavy-footed horses drowned our words in clopping on the stone, and even the plush cushions of the carriage did not absorb the shock and thrashing of the rutted roads. We conversed little, each gripping tightly the gold braid loops hung inside the coach.

"This will be worth it," I said into the Admiral's ear, as we tumbled into each other and laughed heartily at being tossed about like juggler's fruits.

Soon, though, the jostling city streets lay well behind us. We had left Lisbon by the west gate, and travelled through fertile valleys that were the bread basket of the country. The fields were lavishly untidy with bundles of harvested wheat tossed this way and that, like the golden unbrushed back of a palomino horse. For awhile, the warmth and well-being lulled me to sleep, my head slipped to the Admiral's shoulder, and it was only when we began to climb slightly toward the peak of Sintra that I woke again.

"Is that a Moorish tower?" my husband asked, never having been to Sintra before. He had seen the first sign of the village, a vestige of the Arab occupation.

"Yes," I answered, "and just ahead the spires of the King's palace." For centuries, Portugal's Kings had spent summers at Sintra, and the black slate cone chimneys were so sharply pointed, it was as though the workmen had rounded them off with the finest barber's razor.

Joao II had chosen the hillside setting for his coronation, holding a fabulous ceremony of midnight fireworks which, I had heard, bathed the castle in fiery bursts of red and gold light.

A carved stone greyhound guarded each side of the entrance road, but there was no gatehouse. At least a dozen carriages stood in line in the oval roadway before the house, their drivers milling around together in the apple orchard out of the sun. At Sintra, surprisingly, there was no hint of the filmy clouds we had left in Lisbon.

I hadn't thought there would be so many people—Nicola had simply said "an outdoor luncheon."

"So much the better," the Admiral observed. "More guests, more opportunity." He breathed the warm fragrances deeply, apparently quite happy to be there now that the journey was over.

We waited the merest moment at the open door of the Vicosa palace, looking straight through the house into the garden. The other guests, attired in the pastel colors of summer, walked this way and that across the perfect grass.

"Felipa, Felipa, how wonderful you've arrived," Nicola announced, rushing toward us seemingly out of nowhere, throwing her arms around me, as if to embrace away all the time we had been apart. My girlhood flashed across my mind—an instant of memory against the passage of many years.

"How lovely that you haven't changed," she said, stepping back a little, "The island life agrees with you so."

Nicola herself looked radiant. She wore two braids over the top of her head, and the rest of her soft brown hair fit neatly into an exquisite lace net headdress tucked gracefully behind her ears. Her vibrant rose dress had tight-fitting sleeves puffed at the shoulders and came only to her ankles, an innovation for the time, and she carried a white silk purse just the size of her dainty hand.

"This is my husband, Nicola, whom I am so very very pleased to present, the navigator Christoforo Colombo," I began, using the Italian pronunciation of the Admiral's name. He bowed gallantly, and kissed Nicola's hand.

"I so love Italy," Nicola responded, her still youthful face full of genuine pleasure at our presence. "I have been there several times and each time I never wish to leave. You are so very welcome at our home."

Right away then, the trim figure of the Duke appeared, lovingly introduced by Nicola, and we four chattered on, as if we had all been raised together, about the journey from Lisbon to Sintra, the wonderful garden, the party ahead.

Nicola and her husband escorted us to the central lawn, where a long banquet table lay bountifully set with several huge roasted waterfowl, deep ceramic bowls of grapes and other fruit, many sparkling crystal decanters of wine, pewter pitchers of clear mountain water, whole baked fish, sliced wheels of lemons the size of oranges, and amiable conversations all around.

Nicola then began introducing us to many people, some of whom I had been trying myself for weeks to find, people I knew and didn't know, cousins, friends of my family, Portuguese from Lisbon, Evora, Albufeira, some with whom I could even claim passing acquaintance from my childhood days.

The array of guests was dizzying and the Admiral and I circulated under Nicola's guidance, somewhat like snakecharmers from afar, as Nicola made much of our "adventurous living" at Porto Santo as she moved from one inquisitive invitee to the next. Her doting did not escape the notice of the others, enhancing our stature in their eyes, for after all, we were quite new to Lisbon.

The Duke then discreetly whispered that Portugal's Ambassador to Liguria in Italy wanted to meet the Admiral, and deftly separated my husband from my side. My husband, for his part relishing the opportunity to meet the diplomat, eagerly followed the Duke.

Nicola then steered me away to a corner, like a shepherdess leaving the flock while she tended the newest lamb.

I was glad for the chance to be alone with her, for it had been so very long since we had seen each other. We sat on a white bench in a small orchard off the main garden.

For awhile, we simply caught up on our lives since our marriages. There was so much to tell! My days at All Saints, her marriage, her life as a duchess, mine as a navigator's wife—so many details since we had taken separate roads, including our indiscretions. Nicola confessed that she had had to elope with the Duke, so dead set against her marriage had her parents been because the Duke was more than 10 years older than their daughter.

"For awhile it looked as though I would have to climb down a ladder under the cover of night to the garden to escape their monitoring," Nicola laughingly remembered, "but fortunately even parents have to sleep. I bided my time until at last one day I found the courage to walk out the front door while my parents dozed after lunch. But my parents love my husband now, and all is forgiven."

Then I confided that I had sneaked the Admiral into my All Saints bedroom long before we were married, and we giggled about all the embroidery I never did. We were delighted with ourselves, for we didn't know whose behavior had been more scandalous. Oh, it was so good to have a confidante again.

But Nicola knew there was a real matter at hand, and began the necessary conversation. I had written her about the Enterprise, asking her to keep the plan to herself until we could discuss it personally.

"Felipa, I admit your husband does seem brilliant, but this western route to the east, isn't it mad? When did he think of it?"

She was the first to have asked me this question.

"Well, I suggested . . . ah, Porto Santo was the source of much of this," I replied, avoiding the issue of who was author.

"I see," Nicola nodded, pursuing it no further.

"It's not mad at all," I continued, thinking it best to speak of the evidence we had. "In fact, we've seen it referred to in the earliest papers my father left. The western route would be much shorter. My husband has proven it with mathematics. His calculations are unique; he is a scientific Marco Polo, and he has sorted out many false land sightings from true ones. Between the new maps he has drawn and those from my father's archives, we may know more about the oceans than the Crown, Nicola." The thought was amazing even to me, now that I had said it to someone else.

"What makes you think the King will support this venture?" she persisted. "After all, you know how the Crown worries about money, and Joao already turned down this idea once, didn't he, when he was prince and his father asked his opinion on the Toscanelli letter?"

Good for the well-informed Nicola.

"But think of it," I replied, feeling myself fill with the excitement of the times. "Now that the prince is King, it is a new day for Portugal. Gold is pouring in from Africa. It is Joao's chance to retrieve the idea and launch a great surprise advantage on all the thrones of Europe. Now that we have the evidence from my father's files, the time has come to seize the concept of a western route, a commanding gesture for a new King to make."

Nicola listened with interest.

"And how did your husband hear about Toscanelli?" she wished to know. "Did he know of him through his Italian connections?"

"No," was all I said.

"I see," Nicola replied, at once putting the pieces together. "And then you asked Martins, no doubt, to help?"

I said nothing.

"I understand, Felipa. I would do the same for my husband."

Then Nicola took me by both shoulders and looked me straight in the eyes.

"You know I love you as a sister. If you want to meet the King, I will try to help. But I feel I must be honest." She held me fast and went on.

"Some of us are worried for you," she said frankly. "Your husband must be more discreet."

I was stunned. What did she mean?

Nicola collected her thoughts and spoke again.

"Of course, as I promised you, I haven't spoken to my husband of this western voyage proposition, and I will not for now. But you should know the Duke has asked me why your husband is so eager to discuss the personal matters of the King."

"My goodness, Nicola, what sort of matters?"

It seemed that not all the news of Lisbon had reached our Atlantic island. I had never heard, for example, of the King's illegimate son, of whom Nicola now reported, nor of Joao's apparent serious and tormented love affair with the boy's mother, the Spanish princess Ana de Mendoca. And though these circumstances mattered little to the Enterprise, according to Nicola, the Admiral had been talking around Lisbon about them.

"Your husband is frequently among the Genoese, of course, and they like banter. Felipa, all of Lisbon knows of the King's other life. That is not the point. Despite the Queen, the King meets his mistress often, and he loves her deeply. But it is an unspoken subject, as you must understand. Also the Genoese community here grows larger every day. They control much of our commercial life now and their success is resented. It would be better if your husband were not so involved in their gossip. Am I being clear?"

She was. But how did she know so much about my husband's movements?

"There is more," she continued, obviously wishing to set the full record before me.

"According to the Duke, your husband has also been peculiarly interested in the Crown's private monetary transactions."

I was astounded.

Nicola wanted to be generous. "Perhaps it is simply your husband's curiosity," she granted. "But as a young prince in charge of Morocco—I swear you to secrecy Felipa—the present King may have sold arms and swords to the Moors and Berbers to encourage their battling among themselves, even though the Pope had forbidden such sales to infidels for any purpose. For some reason, your husband has been gathering information about this, names of potential traders, apparently for Genoese friends who may wish also to establish themselves in this weapons business."

Suddenly it was chillingly clear. Esmeraldo.

"Someone, no doubt, has put my husband up to it for personal gain," I confided, "for I assure you this sort of trade is of no interest to the Enterprise, or us."

"I believe you, Felipa, but suspicion of him will undo all your best efforts on his behalf."

I wanted to know how she had come by so much information.

"Felipa, you must remember you have been gone for a very long time. Your family is loosely tied to the Bragancas, though your mother has always been above suspicion, and now you are returned to Lisbon with a dashing foreign husband who has easily travelled the world, easily crossing many borders, and who now asks unbecoming questions. There are eyes in many walls in Lisbon."

"So, are you saying he is being followed?"

"I have had it stopped for now," Nicola divulged.

She seemed to dislike the spying as much as I did.

"Felipa, try to understand," she appealed, "these are gay but dangerous times. First Braganca's execution, and then just recently. . . . Felipa, good god, the King had to stab to death his own cousin, Viseu, who stood at his bedside ready to assassinate him as he slept."

106]

I had had no idea the plotting had reached such dimensions, or that the King's life had ever been at such extraordinary risk.

"Felipa, my dearest friend, the Crown is precarious," Nicola implored. "Please see the matter from my point of view. I am simply warning you so you can warn him, and win."

I embraced her fervently, for she had put her obvious love of country on a par with her love for me. I asked a final favor.

"Will you speak to my husband about the Genoese, for he will believe it and accept it more readily from you, I think."

Nicola agreed, if I in turn agreed to keep our conversation entirely between ourselves. She also promised to try to arrange an invitation for us to a palace function where the King would be present, and where the idea of a meeting about the Enterprise could be initially broached.

It would be arduous, and we would have still to meet many people between this Sintra afternoon and the King, to gain the confidence of the royal circle, deepen the Admiral's reputation, and endow the Enterprise with stature without giving the matter away too soon. But she would help.

"Good luck, Felipa," Nicola wished me, just before we returned to the party. "I am not sure that even I would play your role."

"You would indeed, Nicola, for aren't you already?"

"We understand each other too well," she answered, and we walked back to the group arm in arm, just as the Duke was gathering everyone to the table and beginning to look for his wife.

But before the meal, Nicola had a final errand. She left me, walked up to the Admiral, cupped her hand under his elbow and edged him out of the hearing of anyone, and spoke intently. When she had finished, the Admiral said a few words and bowed deeply. Then he extended his arm and escorted her back to her place at the feast. All seemed to be well, and we dined and talked exuberantly with our banquet partners well into the late afternoon.

Only when we stood to stretch our legs before dessert did we three have the opportunity to talk alone again.

For a moment, we shifted awkwardly, but Nicola got to the point.

"I believe we understand each other, Felipa," she reported.

Then she turned to my husband. "As I told you, my dear Colombo, I've agreed to help you because the idea has merit, it will help my country, and because your wife has convinced me you are a genius. But you must be more discreet. Please, no more discussions involving you or the King's personal situation or any matter of any similar delicacy. Agreed?"

Nicola de Vicosa e de Resende could not have made her case plainer.

The Admiral understood. He peeled a succulent orange, and passed it around in a kind of mock consecration of his promise.

The fruit was cool, sweet and delicious.

"Agreed," my husband declared, savoring the taste.

Chapter Ten

Not Even Jupiter

For awhile, I could not tell if the Admiral appreciated or resented Nicola's candor, for all during the journey back to Lisbon and the following weeks, he did not say a single word about her advice. Yet, he seemed cheerful enough, keeping his same routine of work and visiting the Genoese, though he seemed to spend less time among them.

I did not raise the subject of the spying either for any question might have distastefully mushroomed into an interrogation about his whereabouts and the motives of Esmeraldo's many journeys. These were not days to spoil with black-mooded questions, for we had another more pressing business taking up our time.

Invitations trickled in, then flowed, the result of Nicola's subtle interventions around the city on our behalf. Some weeks we spent not a single evening meal at home, so often did a white-gloved courier knock at our door delivering a stiff parchment note written in silver ink, asking the pleasure of our company at the Palacio de Paiva, or de Oliveira, or de Albufeira, and so forth, all leading Lisbon citizens, usually from Nicola's burgeoning hospital committee, or diplomats returned from abroad, or, bankers, interpreters, shipbuilders, shipowners, highly ranked civil servants, gentry of the land, confidantes of the King—a bevy of important people.

They were all, of course, bricks in the pyramid we needed, but I was not sure whether we were accomplishing anything, for the gatherings had become invariably the same. Wine, fine food, conversation about the grimy Lisbon weather, what, on the other hand, fine weather we must have had on Porto Santo, my father's frustrations, my husband's maps and travels, the developments in Africa, rising food prices, declining food prices, and so forth.

Amazingly, birds lent these evenings their only novelty, lush resplendent parrots, though they themselves were fast becoming routine as well.

Nearly every leading household we visited in the city then amused itself with tropical parrots, the latest domestic import from Africa, some the size of small stuffed pheasants with beaks the size of human thumbs, puffing their chartreuse or cerulean blue feathers at the slightest tinkle of the dinner bell.

"Say Portugal, Portu-gal," a staid aristocrat would instruct his fashionable feathered mascot, gingerly proffering a huge kernel of corn with a long brass tweezer.

"Porhrr, porhrr," the parrot usually croaked, trying to repeat, fanning its brilliant plumage as the merry guests applauded. So that the parrots would not strafe our heads, the owners clipped the birds' flying wings, using the pluckings for quill pens, or fledgy bookmarks. The Duke of Paiva's library was so flecked with feathers it looked as though every other book had slammed shut on a bird.

Some households used the gilded aviaries as decorative furniture. At the Palacio de Caminha, nearly half a dozen brillant red and green parrots strutted in a cage which stood from floor to ceiling, painted gold, and luxuriant with flowering plants and dwarf palms, all African imports to remind the birds perhaps of their foregone equatorial home, plus a small rock garden and a hewned cross-shaped perch of cypress wood, the height of a man.

"Quite a conversation piece," the Admiral observed, on standing before the cage to our host, the Duke of Caminha.

"Brhrhr, Brhrhr," came the screeching chorus of birds. Who couldn't help but feel absurd?

To speak of the Enterprise at such gatherings was delicate, for we tried to avoid the words "western route" at all costs. When asked about his navigational theories, the Admiral gave nothing away, speaking of the size of the globe and the width between longitudinal lines, intimating obliquely that they might have been incorrectly calculated thus far. And since no one but my husband actually understood the mathematics involved, the Admiral might as well have been speaking Japanese as geography.

Still these evenings drained and exhausted us, though I knew that each social foray, each host and hostess to whom we smiled, each aristocrat to whom we were polite might just tip the balance in our being taken seriously. If enough powerful people spoke of the Admiral, the Enterprise would have its hearing in court.

One day, the Admiral and I sat with my mother over tea in the kitchen. My mother shelled peas, sliding them in a row along her finger. Our cook could have done it, but it was my mother's favorite culinary chore, for she liked the sound.

As the peas pattered into the deep wooden bowl, I wrote letters of thanks to our hosts of the week before, and the Admiral thumbed absently through a copy of what he called "one of the most boring books in creation," a treatise by the writer Fernao Lopes on the reign of the present King's great-great grandfather. The Duke of Paiva pressed the volume on my husband, mistaking the Admiral's comment on the quantity of feather bookmarks among the books for an interest in reading Lopes.

I shall never forget the knock at the door. My husband and I looked wearily at each other. I did not want to go to another party any more than he did.

But someone had to answer, for the knock came a second time, impatiently.

I opened the door reluctantly, until I noticed that this courier had not ridden on horseback, but had been driven in a splendid polished black leather coach. He handed me not an envelope sealed with wax, but a beige parchment scroll tied with a wide cardinal-red ribbon. He did not wait for a reply, which meant it was assumed we would accept.

I unrolled the paper, and gasped in disbelief. So this was the means Nicola had found!

To catch the eyes of the Admiral and my mother, I cleared my throat several times, seeking the same official tone my cousin had used when reading from the Toscanelli letter. With my family looking on at first indifferently, and then with widening eyes, I began to recite the words we had been waiting for, adddressed to the Admiral and me:

> "The very high, excellent and powerful prince King, Joao II, of Portugal, on the occasion of the completion of the sacred altarpiece adoring Vincent, the beloved and holy Saint, commissioned by the Sovereign majesty for the Chapel of the Nation, offers a command dinner and festivity to honor the artist and unveil the work before its Sovereign Commissioner."

The dinner would be in just one week's time.

"Long live Nicola," we all shouted at once, astounded that our plans had worked. My mother hugged the Admiral, practically dancing around him, the jubilant Admiral hugged me. I embraced them both, as we tied the King's red ribbon to the handle of our teapot to celebrate and poured ourselves a toast from a new bottle of sparkling Porto Santo wine.

Clever Nicola. Lisbon buzzed indeed with speculation about the St. Vincent altarpiece, for not only had the artist's name been closely guarded, rumor was that important Lisbon citizens would be depicted in the painting and no one knew exactly who.

The next six days dragged along like tired wagon wheels, so much did I anticipate the King's dinner. And there were no further knocks on the door, except a brief note from Nicola through her courier to say she and the Duke would collect us on the night in question and that we would travel to the Palace together.

And so at last on the Saturday evening we set out, rumbling in the Duke's official coach. But this was certainly not the bouncing vessel that had carried us to Sintra.

Even the driver of this magnificent vehicle sat on a throne, an overstuffed seat draped with a red satin quilt. The high slender wheels had spokes flecked with golden leaves, the carriage handles tooled in gold. Bucolic scenes of Sintra billowed around the blue body of the coach—the Moorish parapets, the Palace towers, and maidens and soldiers cavorting knee high in garden foliage.

At the first Palace gatehouse, eight armored knights stood stiffly, their lacquered spears at rest at their sides. A ninth guard raised his palm to stop our coach, looked inside, and on seeing the Duke, signalled crisply to the others to immediately open ranks so we might pass.

The Duke tipped his ermine lined cap to the lieutenant in a single gesture of reply, and I suddenly became aware that now, we had not only crossed into the territory of the King, we had irrevocably crossed the boundary between our dreams and cool reality. Here, matters would be taken seriously. Too many had been implicated.

We rolled past more guards, these dressed in blousy royal blue tunics. They stood at attention next to whinnying, white-hoofed stallions all seemingly sculpted from the same smooth gray marble.

I sensed again the crescendo of the power of the state. In the shadow of the Palace entrance, as we ambled closer and closer, we were now the driftwood, the unidentified, the itinerant, picked up and carried by a great wave and deposited on the shores of the King of the realm. There was no turning back, not for this evening, and not for the Enterprise.

The Duke stepped out first, taking Nicola's hand. I followed, then the Admiral. Two pages immediately fell in behind us, and we walked as a sextet through the antechamber. All around us, adornments of royal lineage and national heritage. Under our feet, taken for granted yet inestimably valuable, the famous Roman mosaics, ancient tile inlays of sinewy black leopards lifted whole from Coimbra and reinstated in the Palace floor.

I thought there would be time to talk with Nicola about how to manage the Enterprise discussion, but just as we entered the royal banquet hall, a special attaché came up to us, snapped his heels together and called for both the Duke and Nicola to join the King in his chambers right away, to attend to a detail related to the unveiling.

Soon, Nicola would swirl out of all reach into an eddy of conviviality and protocol, so I touched her elbow to signal her to try to make a moment for me now. But the omniscient Nicola needed no reminder. She turned away from the waiting lieutenant just long enough to say, "I will try to keep you in sight, but may not be able to speak directly once the full activities are under way. The King has been briefed though, so it remains for you to speak of it." But how?

I ran through mentally what I knew about Joao II. The King drank no wine, preferring water. He disliked gratuitous formality, but appreciated deference. The King believed he had a right and wrong side to his face, so it was best to allow him to favor his flattering angle, but which was it? He had a tendency to speak through his nose, flattening his words, so often the listener had to squelch an urge to laugh at his nasal sound. But the King also had a frigid glance that would instantly indicate if the listener transgressed.

The King had faced a charging bull unflinchingly once in Alcachute; he often dined alone without the Queen; he did not scent his handkerchiefs. What else?

"And don't forget the King had an Italian tutor, Siculo, from Sicily, I think," Nicola added quickly before leaving me, as if reading my frantic mind.

She pressed my hand between both of hers, and then, in a final whoosh of her Sintra-green satin gown, a coterie of Kingly aides whirled around Nicola and floated her away.

But my husband and I were not alone, for as I looked around and slowly drank in the evening, I could see this was no ordinary supper where we would wait politely to be seated. This would be an ongoing feast. We eyed the expansive courtyard, planted with citrus fruit and flowering trees.

Everywhere were long banquet tables, covered with pure white dining cloths, their corners held down against the breezes by cherubic young boys dressed in one-piece scarlet suits.

Here was a cornucopia of Portugal and her colonies—grilled Atlantic sardines blackened with ground African pepper, dried Moroccan dates and pounded sesame pastes, blanched nougat studded with split almonds. In order to meet the King, it seemed we would dine little by little, and little by little, be entertained.

My eyes caught light glinting from the wine table. A regiment of the King's pure silver personal goblets had been set out. The cups were unusual, each a cone resting on a heavy brass base sculpted with a pelican, the King's emblem. The bird stood with wings curled in, head bent down to peck its own breast to feed its lifeblood to its offspring.

The guests had to lift only the silver chalices to sip their wine, leaving all the pelican bases grounded on the table.

"At least they aren't parrots," my husband wryly observed, raising his cup to his lips.

The Admiral and I carried our gleaming glasses to a grassy clearing where a ring of guests surrounded some performers. We heard nothing as we approached, no song, no recitation, only hearty applause.

The performers' faces were covered with glistening white paste and powder. A tall thin woman and a taller thinner man were dressed alike in black tight-fitting silk shirts and trousers gathered at the ankle. Like slippery espadon pulling away from a hook and line, they moved slowly and silently—the lithe and famous mimes of Joao the King.

The woman bent her head close to her chest, the brown mane of her hair falling around her face, her eyes glazed with concentration. She raised one arm, extending one long finger from her forehead, scraping one leg and then another, toes pointing to the ground. Her preening head turned back across her strong and bony back. For all the audience, she had become a prancing unicorn in the garden of the King, dancing with her black-ribbed stag. Then an imaginary culminating kiss of fingers until they finally let their characters drain from their faces, relaxed their haunches, and faced us for the bow.

"Bravo, bravo," the dinner guests cheered.

"A miracle of silence," my husband noted, as delighted as the rest of the crowd with the pantomime.

We moved to another circle that had formed on the clay racing court ahead. Clouds of red dust floated above the heads of the guests, and I thought they must be watching some sort of military tournament. But it was the King's Senegalese horsemen, their muscles bridling under their taut coal black skin.

The earth grumbled underfoot, as each man maneuvered two white horses, standing on their backs and holding one gold braided rope lead to each horse's head, the tails of the horses pluming like scarves snapping in the wind.

Then, as if bending a willowbranch, one of the Africans somersaulted backward off the horses, landing squarely on his feet. His mounts trotted to the sidelines, just short of the crowd.

Several court pages walked across the field, dropping yellow marble egg-shaped stones throughout the field in a deliberate zigzag pattern.

A single horseman began trotting, building to a gallop, steering his horse around the course, bending to the ground to scoop—zig, scoop, gallop, scoop—until the entire field was cleared of stones. He had filled a basket he wore strapped to one hip with the marble eggs, and rode up to the outdoor throne of the Queen who sat alone. He presented the basket to her, and in return, she passed him a brilliant crimson scarf to wrap around his neck. The crowd cheered the African and the Queen seemed to adore it all.

"Do you see the King?" the Admiral asked me anxiously.

I didn't yet. He was undoubtedly still involved with the unveiling.

I did, however, see many people we now knew—the Dukes of Paiva, Caminha, Alfara—an assemblage of the highest citizens of Portugal. No longer strangers from distant places, thanks to Nicola now we were recognized and seemed to belong.

My husband moved fluidly among our newfound acquaintances, conversing, praising a particular Senegalese movement to this or that Duke. He radiated confident good looks, standing a full head above most of the men and wearing an unusual burnt orange colored tunic over chestnut-brown silk breeches. He had had the suit cut especially for the dinner by the wife of one of his Genoese friends, and it fit him perfectly. He carried a cream-colored silk mantle over one arm, and tossed it jauntily over his shoulder like a toga when he applauded.

During a lull in the riding, we chatted with the Duke of Albufeira, who spotted a plump, prematurely balding young man approaching, a guitar inlaid with tiny triangles of ivory cradled in his arms and a smile spreading amiably across his boyish mischievous face.

"Oh look," the Duke announced, "Resende himself."

He was Nicola's cousin, the King's poet and resident troubadour who enjoyed the privileges of the innermost royal circle. Garcia de Resende sang like a morning dove, composing music and words as he went along. He had grown up at Court, worshipping the King as a young man and winning his confidence with his cheerful lyrical ways. Now Joao II had assigned him the rank of page of the writing desk. When the King sent letters or decrees, Resende stood at his side, holding a rack of extra inked pens so that the King need never wait for a replacement.

Resende had all but invented the improvisational verse that had become a celebrated feature of evenings at the Palace.

"And once a maiden in the wood," Resende might, for example, sing, inviting the delighted audience to take part.

"Before a craven hunter stood," an inspired rakish Duke might reply.

A poem would thus travel from guest to guest, embellished at each stop. The maiden might become increasingly rapturous, her plight more dangerous, her rescue more heroic, until she was at last returned safely to her love, who would have in any case been ready and willing to die for her in the woods at the hand of the craven hunter, or anyone else.

The meandering Resende verses eventually involved every guest of the party, I'd heard, and he became the virtuoso hub of the evening. Everyone looked forward to being anointed by his crooning nod.

Approaching us now, Resende enthusiastically greeted the Duke first, with a strum and flourish, but did not begin his improvisations yet. He passed a pink carnation to the Duke's wife, shook hands and hailed his many obvious admirers, then turned to the Admiral and me.

"Good evening, friends," Resende bowed, strumming again. A crowd began to collect, expecting the familiar round, eager to listen and contribute a line. But startling all, singling out my husband, Resende sang a short poem on his own:

"Behold the sailor, fairest, free
An artist sage it is said of thee
A prince of oceans
A dean of charts
A golden man to sow adventure in our hearts."

The Admiral, clearly charmed, led the applause with a broad smile. Nicola had surely planted this.

"The first musical verse anyone has ever written about me," my husband complimented. "But," he asked, "what is the adventure that I sow?"

"Unknowns, lord, unknowns," Resende strummed in response.

"Ah yes," the Admiral nodded, "I do know something about those."

Then Resende himself applauded, and gracefully began herding the guests away from the playing field toward the unveiling of the St. Vincent mural, soon to begin. The King and Queen were nowhere to be seen, but Nicola and the Duke had reappeared and seemed to be in charge.

Nicola, still surrounded by adjuncts and admirers, nevertheless managed to sweep over to me for a moment to say, "It hasn't gone according to plan; the King dislikes the painting and the artist cannot be found. But the King feels obliged to go through with the ceremony, for he did commission the work to venerate the Saint, and he is tired of waiting."

Just as she finished her sentence, three trumpeteers stood up in the musicians' box. Red silk cloths embroidered with crossed lances hung from the horns, and after ten flourishing brassy notes of announcement, the King entered resplendent, with Leonor equally alluring on his arm.

I was transfixed.

"Long live the most serene and mighty King of Portugal," the Duke hailed His Majesty.

"Long live Joao II," we echoed in unison, bowing as one.

Joao II, though, quickly signalled all to rise. Over his gown he wore a long blue silk robe lined with spotted ermine, but soon dispensed with it, loosening the jeweled clasp from his shoulders and passing the robe to a nearby aide.

Underneath, bright red silk flowed to the floor, with red jewels—rubies no doubt—sewn as binding over each shoulder and around the neck.

The Queen wore a shimmering scarlet gown with a scooped neckline, a double lace inlay covering her chest, flecked with embroidered roses. Over her dark black hair, she wore a headdress studded with red and yellow gems—rubies too, as well as topaz—forming three jeweled rows, each dangling slightly over her forehead just above her brow.

"My most loyal and welcome subjects," Joao began, and indeed I did have to suppress an urge to smile at his whinish voice. But his winning manner soon overcame the distracting twang of his words.

"I trust you have been well entertained, and that none of your needs have found my faithful servants wanting. Before our banquet and our further evening, let us now behold this great artwork, the event for which we have all been gathered."

He stood in front of the painting, which was held securely in place by several aides. I could now see it consisted of six panels, forming a fan behind the king.

The King and his aides carefully pulled away the covering cloths. Instead of a formal religious painting, here was a shiny blur of art and reality, rendering the history of Portugal. A crowd of nobles mixed with people of the land and collected at the feet of the Saint.

The guests began to murmur but then the King commanded silence as he explained his commission, saying "Even though the overall result is more somber, more inventive, than I'd hoped, my intention was to depict ourselves and the range of our beliefs."

The King walked in front of the artwork, pointing out various personages with the pride of a father introducing his widely varied family.

"Let us begin at the beginning," he proclaimed, pacing between the audience and the painting.

"Behold here, in the most brilliant red robes with the finest African gold tint, Saint Vincent himself, dispensing holy readings. And bending at his feet, my father, Alfonso, our greatest King and inspiration, while I, a boy, uncomfortable I would say from looking at me in that tight-fitting cap, stand at his elbow. My mother, Queen Isabel, kneels, the rosary draping as you see from her fine and nimble fingers."

So many figures were painted there—rueful Prince Henry; the Archbishop of Lisbon, flanked by two Canons, including my own cousin, Martins, whom the King explained was away at this very moment on court business in Castile. There was a Duke of Braganca—not the traitor but one of his ancestors—and many many knights, fishermen, and sea pilots.

"On this furthest panel," the King explained, "we have the people of Portugal in all walks of life—a Jew, a Moor, an unfortunate beggar."

"And," he added with a cunning eye, "even the artist appears, our dear Nuno de Goncalves who, having chosen to miss our party for reasons we do not know, nevertheless painted himself into our painting."

The crowd laughed uneasily, not knowing if the King meant to be amusing.

With that, the King applauded, all of us following suit. "Now if you wish you may all inspect our commission more closely," he directed, stepping away from the painting, his guards forming a tight phalanx around him as he walked out of our path.

"We will never get near enough to speak to him," my husband bristled with frustration, and indeed the King seemed virtually unassailable now.

We filed past the polytych and examined it more closely. There were over sixty people crowded into the scene, all seeming to wish to brush shoulders with the Saint, who radiated an aloof knowing tranquillity.

My husband gazed into the serious and saddened eyes of Prince Henry, the present King's uncle, the greatest navigator of Portugal so far. But I had to admit, dressed as he was in somber garb, his graying mustache drooping, his skin pallid, he hardly looked like a man sustained by the sun and the widest oceans yet known to civilization.

"When did he die?" my husband asked.

"About 25 years ago at Sagres, alone and poor," I answered.

"Did he gain nothing for all his troubles?" the Admiral wondered, somewhat surprised such a famous man could have so inglorious an end.

"His expeditions did not even earn back their cost," I explained, according to my mother, who had been told it by my father, "though his discoveries were obviously invaluable to Portugal."

My husband looked again at the dire prunish face of Henry.

The King was right; the painting was too solemn. Perhaps word of the King's perturbation had filtered out and may well have explained the artist's absence. The guests now were ill at ease, for to return to the Senegalese riders, or to the ample drink and laughter of the outer court, seemed too indeferential in the shadow of the all-seeing, all-holy Saint Vincent and his retinue.

But luckily Resende, apparently on instructions, emerged again as if from a hole in the floor to reignite the evening.

As the guests milled about, unsure of where to go, Resende's tuneful guitar set a new mood.

"Perhaps," he sang, "the time has come
To let rise among us a mighty sum
Of songs and verses, all to bless
Great Joao the second, and no duress."

The King laughed deeply, appreciating Resende's light relief, and immediately snapped his fingers, commanding his lutes and mandolins to begin. The soldiers obediently redraped the painting and lifted it out of the way against the furthest wall.

The King seized Nicola's hand, holding it high above his head, leading her out onto the floor. He began the impromptu dance, approaching her, retreating, approaching in a swaying ballet in time with the tambour drums. The Duke took the Queen as partner, and one by one, other couples began.

The Admiral and I hesitated, but only momentarily, for I saw the King had already shed Nicola, and moved along to dance, and speak, with the Duchess to her right. He aimed it seemed to partner each woman for awhile. It looked as if we might have no other chance to talk. To capture the necessary time with him, I suddenly knew I too would have to join.

While I danced with the Admiral and then the next man and the next, I kept my eye on the King, whose crown bobbed and glistened like a golden cork on the sea of dancers. He was ten, then eight, then six women from me. How would I begin when he at last arrived?

I took a deep breath, tried not to lose my step, kept my eye on the King and counted the music. Four women away, then two, then too soon, his arching arm reached mine, and he had taken my hand. But I needn't have worried over what to say first, for that I had forgotten was the King's prerogative.

"Welcome, my lady," he spoke, a formality in his voice, as he had said those basic words many times before. "I am delighted for this chance."

"It is I, Your Highness, who am delighted," I replied.

120]

The music took us a step away and back, then into each other's hearing again.

"I have a favorite aunt Felipa, did you know?" the King asked, clearly aware of who I was. "She chose the convent and writes lovely verse peacefully there."

"I am familiar with the instinct for writing, my lord," I answered, still somewhat quaking from the close proximity of the head of State.

"And convent too, I've heard," the King inserted. Nicola did very well what she had chosen to do, I saw. Again, we withdrew, rejoined. How would I bring it up?

"Your husband is Italian?" Joao then inquired, obviously already knowing the answer, glancing over to the Admiral, who now danced with Nicola and wisely refrained from glancing at us.

"Yes, Lord, as was, I understand, Your Grace's teacher." Was I speaking to the side he preferred, I wondered.

"Indeed, though I didn't think Italians considered Sicily to be Italian. But then, I had several tutors from that fractured country, from various districts. They taught me well, a very scholarly group from whom I learned Greek and Latin, and how to consider many many quandaries." The King was proud of his education, and I saw a chance.

"My husband also speaks Latin," I offered tentatively.

"As well as the language of the stars and oceans, if I am properly informed," the King added. Did it seem he danced with me longer than the others?

"But you too speak Latin, surely," the King diverted, "a daughter of Lisbon's finest school and wife of so erudite a man?"

The music seemed to climb as if readying to stop. I searched and wracked my memory, felt myself fumbling for the ancient vocabulary. The flutes took up the melody. Respite. More time. The King still held my hand, stepped back, swung toward me. I saw the All Saints garden, the stiff chairs, the airless rooms. I heard again the endless rote repeating, Latin prayers, Latin proverbs. Then, miraculously, I felt the surfacing of the words I needed.

"Vereor, domine, ut meus Latinus tibi placeat," I said. I had scavenged my brain to compose the phrase—it meant "I am afraid, Sir, my Latin would not please you."

"No, no, no, that is fine, excellent, bravo, and in Latin no less," the King responded. "Contrary to what you say, the quality of your Latin is very very good," he complimented gaily.

"And anyway, dear lady," he added, relishing the linguistic joust, "ni Jupiter omnibus placeat."

He paused, as if to rinse his palate between wines, then resumed his official tone, just as the music seemed to reach its true and last crescendo.

"I must receive the chieftain Cacueta in two weeks' time. Tell your husband he may come and see me too." I was stunned.

And then the King, missing no step, breath or beat, signalled his players not to stop, but to begin the song again. He danced as smoothly as the night had fallen on to his next excited partner.

I blessed my Latin drills again. Ni Jupiter omnibus placeat.

"Not even Jupiter can please everyone," the King of Portugal had declared to me.

Chapter Eleven

The Steam of the Congo

From then on, I thought of him as The King of Jupiter. Had he really agreed in the midst of a light ballet to see us?

"I had no idea you spoke Latin," my husband remarked when I described wide-eyed what had happened as I danced back into his arms.

Nicola reappeared only long enough to command her carriage take us home, and to whisper the words, "The King wishes to see us, so we cannot leave with you." She hugged me and then raced away in a flurry. But what next?

We would see him after Cacueta, Joao II had said.

"He's the emissary of the King of the Congo," Nicola explained to me on the first afternoon she had found to visit after the King's propitious dance. The Admiral was at the port to study the design of the Portuguese ships and to calculate what the Enterprise would require in vessels and provisioning to prepare the proposal for Joao II.

Having Nicola was like having my own eyes and ears at court.

She continued.

After we'd left the Palace, Joao, having summoned his closest aides to the private royal apartments, announced that he deeply disliked his own cameo portrait as a self-righteous boy in the painting he had just unveiled. He ordered Resende to note that unless the painter, de Goncalves, could be found or voluntarily returned to the Court, he would receive neither payment nor reknown, and the painting would be recorded in the royal inventory as an anonymous work.

Resende had been startled at the King's vehement reaction, but the page dutifully took down his master's command, beginning a new crisp page in the King's diary with the Goncalves instruction.

Nicola believed the King was making much of the Goncalves affair to distract himself from diplomatic turmoils, and that Joao did not dislike the painting bitterly enough to discredit the artist forever.

"Our King will mellow on this point," Nicola suggested. "Timing is critical with him."

"As is speaking to his flattering side, I've learned, thanks to you," I replied.

We laughed, and Nicola continued her account of the evening.

Joao sat, still in his scarlet robes, on an enormous cushion on the floor, as was the custom for chieftains in Morocco. He sipped fruit juice and munched split almonds obsessively, swirling his fingers among the nuts in a blue and white bowl that Resende regularly refilled.

Vizinho, a Spanish mathematician I knew by reputation only, had also been among the late night confidantes. A learned Jew, he had come to Portugal several years before, smartly sensing the winds of favor blowing against him in Spain and at the invitation of Joao, who enjoyed maintaining experts at hand to address particular royal problems.

Vizinho had been assigned to the King's navigational advisory group with the express task of providing Portuguese mariners some way to tell their latitude while they groped along the coast of Africa below the point where they might still take bearings from the North Star.

Clearly, Vizinho's meeting the Admiral and endorsement of the Enterprise would be critical to the King's approval.

Nicola went on. That evening the King solicited Vizinho's views on the exploits of Diego Cao, one of the King's most trusted explorers. Cao was so personally close to the King that Joao had often sent him to the Moura castle with a message or gift for the incarcerated young prince.

Now, Cao claimed that he had reached nearly to the Indian Sea on his latest journey to Africa and he had brought the emissary, Cacueta, to Portugal. The King wondered whether Vizinho could accurately recalculate Cao's voyage and verify the distance actually sailed.

Not only did Cao claim to have practically rounded Africa, he had pushed Portuguese marine exploration into the thick vein of the continent, the Congo River. He had shown the region to be more advanced than any African realm the Portuguese had yet discovered—all without fearing the tangled forest canopy, as dark in day as at night, or the enormous rough-scaled crocodile lizards, as long as two men end to end, with teeth like sharp ivory daggers and jaws that clamped as quickly as a blink of their gray-granite eyes.

Cao had believed the river might cut through the vastness of Africa—now an obstacle to Portugal in reaching India, despite the slaves and pepper and glittering trade. If so, the journey to the East would be miraculously shorter.

But after days of nudging ships and men up the inland river, no end came. Cao resolved to backtrack to the sea when his expedition was suddenly surrounded by about ten tall spear-bearing black men, cloaked in palm fern capes, but naked otherwise. They closed in on the Portuguese, and a lesser European might have attacked in fear. But Cao shrewdly waited, gesturing calmly, smiling all the time.

He negotiated to send a small party of his men inland with the Congolese, exchanging them for a handful of African hostages, who joined the Portuguese camp.

Then, Cao ordered a suit of the best embroidered Portuguese finery be given to one of the Congolese, commanded that the guests be served their meals before the Portuguese sailors, and ordered that the Portuguese never take a drink of fresh water before offering the Africans the first sip. This all to ensure good relations with their leader, whose name the Congolese hostages kept repeating— Manicongo, Manicongo—in rich woodwind voices. Cao wanted only good relations with this "Mani," to seal trade and navigation through the Congo.

However, Cao soon tired of waiting and went in search of his men up the Congo River again. After a day or so, the water began to grow more wild and the riverbed drastically narrowed. Suddenly, one morning, the Congolese hostages jumped from the moving ship to shore, taking with them all the rope they could carry. Feverishly they looped the ropes around the pillar trunks of the tropical trees and clambered back on board, tying their ropes to the solid prow of Cao's vessel, keeping it from making any progress upriver. Then Cao, infuriated and perplexed, at last understood—the Congolese were warning him. His ship had entered a gorge, and he signalled the fleet behind to drop anchor immediately.

The Africans had saved his convoy. Above were two twin steep cataracts where the river Congo fell like freshwater smoke against the stones. This was Ilala, as the Congolese called it, the roar that never ends. Had the Africans not acted, Cao's entire expedition would have been crushed at the bottom.

Eventually, Cao's crew members did reappear, with more Africans, including the King of the Congo, the Manicongo himself. The Mani gave Cao a fresh leopard skin, still wet from flight, and Cao returned the gift with a brass candlestick and an ample supply of candles, which the African had never seen.

The Mani assigned an emissary, Cacueta, to carry ambassadorial greetings to the Portuguese King, Joao II.

Cao embarked Cacueta and left the river to continue south along the coast. When Cacueta first saw the limitless rolling waves of the open sea, he shivered and cried out in fear. But Cao sailed on, and forest melted into grasslands and rocky hillsides into desert before he turned around, confident he had gone to the tip of Africa.

He returned to Lisbon and announced proudly that he had reached 22° 10′ S below the Equator, the threshold of India.

"Can it be possible?" the King had asked Vizinho in his chambers, the night of the St. Vincent unveiling.

According to Nicola, Vizinho took some time to form his reply, for he knew that the King, reveling in the first blush of Cao's success, had already sent an announcement letter to the Pope, before soliciting Vizinho's opinion, in the form of an "Oration of Obedience." The King had presented Cao's journey as the definitive discovery of the point at which African seas met the oceans of India. Vizinho thus had either to verify Cao, or contradict a royal message already en route to Rome.

In an age of exploration, ironically, the audacious were often alone, treading on risk with their nerves, eager to prove a new fact or a new distance, yet necessarily eager to please. Vizinho, a scientist, was also an exile grateful for the refuge given him by the Portuguese. And who can say whether kings value sound advice more than blind obedience?

Vizinho replied tactfully that the matter could be settled only when a clear map were available and the voyage had been duplicated by another Portuguese, or by Cao himself.

"For the moment," Vizinho had stalled, rubbing the collar of his doublet, "there is no reason to doubt the words of your Majesty's unquestionably devoted servant, Diego Cao."

"Appreciated, my dear Vizinho," the King replied. "So be it. And until we have this proof, we can busy ourselves with the Congolese emissary Cacueta, whom I must meet."

"And a certain Genoese, I understand," Vizinho added, "with a prominent Portuguese wife."

And then, before Nicola could intervene, the King responded, "Indeed the very one about whom we have heard so much. See the Duke of Viseu about it. He has some information about the gentleman I would like you to review."

Nicola believed her husband would speak no ill of mine, but there was the matter of the dossier, which the Duke was now compelled by royal command to share with Vizinho.

"There can be nothing but insinuation in it," I defended, "and you yourself said no one spoke about the King's private business or family matters in public. Would Vizinho dare?"

Just then, I heard the front door latch lift. The Admiral was home. He warmly embraced me, then Nicola, delighted, it seemed, by his visit to the port.

"Their caravels are ingenious," he exuded, unrolling a small diagram of a hull he had drawn just that morning. "Swift and sharp in design yet also deep in the hold."

"Were you seen drawing the ship?" Nicola quickly probed.

"No one paid the least attention," my husband answered, rolling the drawing closed again. "You women do have a taste for talk and intrigue," he said somewhat crisply.

"You forget," I chided, "that it was women, Isabella and the King's wife, who offered up their children, who really sealed the peace between Spain and Portugal."

"Now who is speaking heresy," my husband chided back lightly. "Do you not credit your perfect prince?"

I reported to him the news of Diego Cao's voyage, not yet public knowledge, that Nicola had just relayed to me. I was startled when he quickly and confidently responded, "Diego Cao's claim may be a state secret, but it is an impossible tale nevertheless."

Nicola and I both eyed him sharply. He seemed so unswervingly convinced.

"Poor Diego. He turned back too soon," my husband declared assuredly. "Anyone who knows navigation would know that the coast of Africa is much longer than that. Cao is lying, or deluded."

With that he dismissed the achievement the King had trumpeted to the Papal court. Nicola cringed. "The King's commissioner, Vizinho, essentially corroborated Cao's report," she said, thinking my husband ought to know.

"He's wrong too," was all the Admiral chose to reply, cutting himself a slab of bread and picking at the grapes in the fruit bowl.

Nicola told us she would be unable to attend the audience when we met the King, as the Duke would likely be sent to Burgundy to collect some documents pertinent to land titles currently in dispute.

"I don't know when we'll be back in Lisbon," she said with the reconciled tone of a woman accustomed to an unpredictable life, "but your appointment with the King is confirmed. I checked with Resende who has it duly marked in the calendar. But note well, in fact, it's a week later than the King had thought. You follow Cacueta, the very same afternoon." It was still ten days away.

Nicola kissed us both. My husband took her hand and said, "My wife's dear friend, you have done a great and lasting service to Portugal on our behalf."

He bowed and Nicola touched his shoulder as he raised his head, peering straight into his face.

"Indeed it is your wife," Nicola replied, ever my advocate "who has done the truly lasting service."

I saw her to the door, and we embraced as tightly as when we had rediscovered each other on that Sunday afternoon in Sintra. In our parting, much more than a confidante took leave. I felt bare and vulnerable. It was the same feeling of irrevocability I had had the night we approached the Palace, but then we were safe in the aura of power that engulfed Nicola and her husband. Now, as she left, I saw our past, our giddiness, vanish too. We were more than wives to our husbands, more than friends to each other. We were women who, wisely or wrongly, had dared manipulate the world of our King.

What lay ahead was no secret elopement, or a stolen night with a fiancé. Nicola and I had together faced affairs of state, as if they were the episodes of girlhood merely grown to a grander scale. With Nicola, I could dally with the Crown, and now, with Nicola, the protective liaisons of youth disappeared down the cobbled street to the sea.

The Admiral was sitting on the sofa, again reviewing his diagram of the ship, when I returned. For awhile, neither of us said anything.

But then he spoke. "It's good that my audience follows Cacueta's, for the King will have expended a lot of energy to receive him well. The Congolese are esteemed these days."

It was true that the Crown felt the Congolese people to be less warlike than other Africans and more interested in commerce. The King therefore hoped to gain their alliance and an emissary would likely be grandly welcomed. But that was not my husband's point.

"The King of Portugal must seem to be respectable. He must redeem himself in African eyes, after what's happened with Bemoin," the Admiral continued, making a second copy of his sketch as he bent over the small footstool.

I wondered what he meant, for I had heard the rather fabulous story of Bemoin at one of the Lisbon parties and remembered nothing untoward. On the contrary.

Bemoin was a black Moslem, a prince of Senegal, who apparently got on very well with the Portuguese sailors by favorably trading them horses and supplies. He hoped in return our King would protect Bemoin's own throne in Africa. But when Bemoin was attacked by another faction that disliked his close relations with the Portuguese, Joao II did not send reinforcements, claiming Portuguese troops ought defend only Christians.

Finally, the besieged Bemoin found shelter in a Portuguese fort, and with a handful of loyal followers sailed to Lisbon on the next available ship. Here he was received warmly by one of the Dukes who had done business with him in Senegal, outfitted splendidly in white fur and red silk, and given a suite of rooms in the Duke's household until the King himself could receive him.

When the day came, Bemoin, now robed like a Portuguese, his camel-toned turban the only hint of his distant religion, bent ceremonially before Joao II, begging for the right to become Christian. The King, startled, agreed, though it meant that should Bemoin ask again for defense, the Portuguese throne would be dutybound to help.

Bemoin remained awhile in a Lisbon monastery to be educated in Christianity, and was baptized and renamed D. Joao Bemoin. Joao II, eager to restore the good trade relations he had once enjoyed in Bemoin's homeland, outfitted a fleet of ships, commanded by Pero Faz da Cunha, and sent Bemoin back to Senegal to recapture his honor.

That was the last I'd heard of it. But the Admiral had additional news.

"Bemoin never reached Senegal. He was stabbed in his sleep by da Cunha, who accused him of treason," the Admiral reported.

"But he was under the King's protection," I blurted out.

"Felipa, that does not always mean what you think it ought to mean," he answered, curling his lips at my surprise.

"The Queen would not even let the black man kiss her hand, I have heard. The story is that da Cunha was authorized by an important figure—perhaps the King himself—to kill Bemoin, for the Senegalese was too openly supplying the Crown with slaves taken from

[129

his own tribe. The King was embarrased and did not want to be implicated in Bemoin's affairs. In fact Bemoin narrowly missed being poisoned in Portugal by one of the Palace's Senegalese riders. They hate performing there, though they bow deeply, and they despised Bemoin for his collaboration.''

The Admiral finished his work and stood up to return to his study. Then he added, ''Obviously if Cacueta were to find out what had happened to Bemoin following his embrace of Christianity, he would denounce the Portuguese to the Congolese King, and undermine any prospects of trade. It means that Cacueta's audience will have to be a splendid affair. That will likely enhance the King's mood on the day he hears of the Enterprise.''

How had he learned all this about Bemoin, I demanded.

''Open your eyes, Felipa,'' my husband remonstrated. ''Nicola is not the only source of information.''

Chapter Twelve

The Perfect Prince

And so the day came. The Admiral and I rode to the Palace in a coach loaned to us by one his Genoese friends, but it looked in every respect like a true Portuguese coach, painted with cherubs floating among billowing white clouds—the celestial scene that had become as fashionable in Lisbon as exotic birds.

We arrived at the gate and gave our names to the guard who passed them to a colleague who leafed through a sheaf of parchment appointment cards to find the one with our name written on it, then nodded to let us through. Without the gay murmur of partygoers, the Palace buildings loomed stark and somber. There were no white plumed headdresses on the stallions, no brilliant scarlet pennants sailing in the breeze, nothing festive in the ambience.

The Admiral and I walked in silence behind a soldier to the waiting room. I still hear my every step against the stone, thinking they seemed like the only noise I had heard in days. For recently, the Admiral and I had barely talked. From dawn to darkness, he shut himself away at his desk, creating grand maps and documents. He emerged once in the morning and once in late afternoon to eat a hurried meal. Most dinners I ate alone, or with my mother, whose health now kept her mostly confined to her rooms.

I felt as if I lived alone, since at night, the Admiral climbed into bed very late, never trying to rouse me. Often I was not asleep. As I've said before, my husband was not at ease with intimate subjects and I had never found a way to broach them. And much between us went unsaid, though certainly these days were times full of things to say between a husband and a wife. There was an enormous surge of expectations, for it seemed now that our entire married life was culminating in the audience with the King. Yet the Admiral did not speak once to me about it.

And since Nicola and the Duke had left Lisbon, we had fewer and fewer, and then no invitations. Nicola and the Duke had been the catalysts of our reception in Lisbon. Since the Admiral was so consumed by the Enterprise and preparing his materials for the King, he refused all distractions and I did not feel free to invite people to our home. And so, the days between my dance with the King and the audience with him seemed an eternity.

Until this point, I confess that the patriotic aspects of the Enterprise had been secondary to me. Save for Nicola, I had no link to politics, and after my marriage, my husband had been my nation.

But now as we headed deeper into the winding halls of state, I could really feel that the Enterprise did present the King a sterling chance to execute a dazzling new vision. A western route would save the King an enormous quantity of time and money, and command the envy of all the thrones of Europe. While other Kings and Queens scrambled to reach India, Joao II would be there first, the Enterprise the golden key to the East.

The Admiral smiled at me, took my arm in his, and for a brief moment or two, our steps fell to the stones as one.

"This way," our herald guided us, down one corridor and up another, smoothly maneuvering us as if we were a liquid running through a maze. We approached the very heart of Portuguese power.

Finally, we entered a corridor that did not turn but instead emptied us out at the foot of a large oak door, studded with brass beads, across which was written the guiding motto of the royal family: War, Justice, Revenue.

The Admiral read the words quickly, and said under his breath, "Let us hope today we don't have to endure the first to have access to the third."

"You are indifferent to the second?" I said.

"That, my dear wife, is an element whose bearing on the meeting is entirely unpredictable."

Our escort put his finger to his lips, motioning us to be silent. The great door opened. With an authoritative nod, a guard took my husband's portfolio stuffed with papers, as well as the several rolls of maps the Admiral carried under his arm. The soldier pressed these, turned them over, pointed the tubes to the floor and shook. Then I realized why—such long scrolls of paper could easily conceal a dagger or a sword.

The guard rifled everything, though not reading anything, and patted each packet to be sure it was flat. The Admiral endured this search without a word, for in this court, in these times, on our mission—no one could protest.

We stood in a large antechamber. Just as the documents were returned to my husband, a door ahead opened, and Resende appeared, still rosy-faced, dressed again in elaborate brocade, followed by a tall black man, also dressed in the Portuguese manner. The men laughed and jostled each other. Surely this was Cacueta, leaving his audience.

"Ah, my Genoese master of the seas," Resende greeted us jovially. "And my lady," he added, kissing my hand.

"You are punctual," Resende continued, "but we are somewhat tardy. Please let me see our African guest out, and then I will return to guide you in." He steered us to a small velvet sofa, still somewhat plush, but fraying with the wear of many who had sat upon it, fidgeting, awaiting a King's good word.

I felt myself tighten. My eyes scanned the gilded ceiling, the walls, the black and white tile patterns of the floor. I gazed at my husband, who looked elsewhere.

Suddenly, I felt invaded by fears, my confidence melting into last-minute misgivings. Were we mad to be there? Only now, like a runner completing a race and at last pausing to let his breathing catch up, did I allow myself to question whether my husband's calculations were right. Only now, when at last he had to prove his beliefs in the only forum that mattered, did I free myself to wonder. Could the distances be as he measured them? Perhaps he was too sure. Perhaps we were not ready. In the face of the massive power of all of Joao's experts, how could we know something they did not?

And a western route? Could it be true that we now sat on the royal waiting sofa because of a few words I had uttered seeking the embrace of my husband on the Porto Santo beach? On this, we would launch a kingly enterprise? Surely we were both fools to have come this far. All of a sudden, I was terrified of our brazenness, terrified I let myself get too carried away.

"His father once already discounted Toscanelli, remember," I whispered to my husband, as if this small reminder could help us now.

"I have no intention of even referring to Toscanelli," the Admiral replied in a voice even more hushed than mine. "And I forbid you to mention him, in the event the King asks you to speak. This will be an entirely new proposal, and if the King is not captivated by it, he ought not be King."

My husband obviously had none of my apprehension, and no intention of crediting the Florentine geographer. Resende returned to the antechamber before I had any chance to comment, still smiling.

"Africans are beautiful and pliable," Resende noted aloud, as he swung open the King's chamber door. "Have you been there?" he asked the Admiral.

"I have been to many many places," the Admiral sidestepped, "as you yourself so harmoniously sung."

Resende bowed at the flattery, though surely aware that the Admiral had not directly answered the question.

In a matter of two more paces, we stood before the throne. I abandoned my worries, for they were but useless weights to me now.

Power finds its sternest voice, in fact its strength, in the wordless quiet that precedes a pending matter, I learned, for at that moment in the crowded chamber, no one spoke because the King, the authority of the hour, had not yet appeared. The space he would soon occupy loomed large, enveloping us even in his absence.

For awhile, no one told us where to stand or sit, and we languished in the center of the room, exposed, as if on exhibit. I sensed the outlines of others, sitting off to the side, but though my eyes were open, I saw nothing, as if the hall had filled with vapor that swirled around my husband and me, obliterating us.

Then, yet another door swung open, an entourage entered, flanking Joao II, who strode into the chamber. It was as if only his presence could give warm blood to our wooden figures. The sitting shadows rose together, driven by the single motor of awe.

The King's words melted protocol and he stepped toward us, saying "I regret the delay, but I had to record my thoughts of my previous audience before they escaped my mind and dissipated into other business. Yours, for example. Have you been introduced to everyone?" The King looked at me, but not yet at my husband.

Resende interrupted. "Allow me, Lord," he said, taking the task in hand.

A carved oaken gallery of seats dominated one side of the room, and four men sat there. I had dreaded the thought of a committee, as had the Admiral, for from all accounts, it would have been better had we met the King alone.

Resende pointed out each one.

"Here, dear guests, you meet the King's counselors on important matters, in particular, navigational business. The first gentleman I present is the Bishop of Cueta, who sits nearest the King, providing as he does valued advice on the divine implications that form the foundation of all decisions by our royal family."

The Bishop wore a brown unshapely ecclesiastical robe, much like that of a monk. He seemed considerably older than the King. I wondered why Martins was not there instead, for surely my cousin was the more eminent advisor. I had been unable to reach Martins for days.

"And next to His Grace, the Bishop," Resende continued, "we have two mathematical men, the Doctors Rodrigo and Vizinho." We had heard only of Vizinho, the key man, through Nicola of course. He was dark-eyed, his black beard came to a point, and he radiated sharp intelligence. Rodrigo seemed less attentive on first reading.

"And our fourth, the great commercial attaché to the King, Senor Fernao Gomes." I would not have expected him, since he had no scientific background that I knew of, though he had been granted the monopoly on the Guinea trade. "Senor Gomes understands business implications and he offered to advise the King on this matter. His words often find direct reception in the King's evaluations." So that explained the merchant; Gomes had invited himself.

These four men now took their seats again, and behind them, I could see several black men stripped to the waist, each holding a tall silver spear close like a third arm. They were no doubt some sort of African guard formed for the visit of Cacueta.

Joao II approached us, speaking to the Admiral for the first time.

"You are the Genoese explorer of whom so many know?"

The King's tone was fraternal, comforting, even welcoming. I felt the Admiral relax at my side somewhat.

"We have not spoken before," the King declared.

"No, Your Grace," my husband agreed, rising from his bent knee having kissed the King's sapphire ring. "At the pageant for the unveiling of the St. Vincent offering, you spoke only to my wife."

Joao smiled at me. "Yes, I remember well," was all he said. "Did I tell you then that my favorite aunt shares your name, Dona Felipa? She has been cloistered most of her life, and she writes verses to pass the time."

"Yes, you told me that, Your Grace," I replied.

"No doubt," the King answered, with the hint of a smile. "Poetry is for women, and politics for men, with the exception of Resende, of course, who seems at home with both."

Resende, as usual sliding freely here and there until summoned, then appearing on perfect cue, took his signal, came up behind me, cupped my elbow, and led me to a seat behind the four gentlemen, just in front of the Africans. I could barely see over the cap of the Bishop, but at least I hadn't been asked to leave the room.

Then, Resende quit the chamber briefly, returning with two aides who carried a long table and a globe which they set before the King. Then Resende bid the men carry out a gilded cage housing an acrobatic tiny brown monkey and another in which a bright red parrot hopped nervously between two perches.

"Bravo Resende," the King complimented, "an apt change of accessories. These animals chortle too loudly and I believe our guest does not wish to speak of Africa."

But only the accoutrements of Africa were leaving the room, for the globe bore witness to the Crown's current tendency, as the African continent bulged on the flanks of the world, painted in brilliant gold. Gomes appeared to be already making notes, trying to look down to the sheaf of paper in his lap, without taking his eyes disrespectfully from the King, who had taken his regal seat.

Now only the Admiral remained standing and he arranged his materials on the table, as if he were a prophet preparing a mystic ritual in a Moroccan bazaar. From a sack of velvet cloth, he produced his own small globe and gently set it on the table, then several of the long brown seed casings we had found, and a number of pieces of beach wood from my collection, including the one carved like a fishhook—all the seaborne clues of Porto Santo now set before the King of Portugal.

No one spoke at first while my husband prepared the table, but Rodrigo and Vizinho kept eyeing each other, as each new bit of wood emerged from the Admiral's sack. Then Gomes said aloud, "Perhaps the gentleman is more merchant than navigator."

"I assure you, Sir," the Admiral replied coolly, continuing to arrange his display, "that would never be the case."

Gomes took his opportunity. "Well then you would be unique among your Genoese compatriots," he retorted, "for they haven't shirked from embracing the commerce of Portugal when Italian business proved less vigorous."

My husband, fortunately, chose not to rise to Gomes' bitter bait, knowing quite well that the Genoese businessmen were resented by the native Portuguese.

Instead, he calmly completed his installation, though not yet unrolling his maps, and turned to await the King's signal.

"If you are ready," the King began, "let us hear from you."

The two were splendid peers, the King's eyes gripping my husband's, his green cloak the same color as the Admiral's. Two men who loved and knew the sea were at last meeting on the common ground of a grand and expansive prospect.

The Admiral began, giving an excellent lucid recitation of the navigational facts known to this day, a kind of lesson of the sea summarizing what was known of the world, walking around the table, occasionally resting his hand on the King's globe as if on the shoulder of a friend, leaving no spaces between his sentences to admit interruption, but giving no appearance of feeling rushed. Clearly, he wished to be sure they were all beginning with the same basic knowledge of geography, and he looked constantly at the King, but carefully acknowledged the advisors, focusing his gaze particularly on Vizinho, avoiding Gomes as much as politeness would allow.

Then he began to build the staircase to the reason for this visit—the Enterprise.

"And though, Your Majesty," he said whirling back to the table and now fingering his own globe, "all this information on navigation has of course been gathered by excellent minds embarked on excellent research, much has been conjecture, and I believe the course of current thinking is incorrect. Quite simply, your majesty, if the goal is to reach the east, I propose to demonstrate an audacious, I admit, original idea—that the best plan to reach the east would be to sail west."

He said it slowly, clearly, and paused for a moment to let the sentence take flight around the room.

The King looked at the four gentlemen, who looked back at him like children without parents, but my husband did not allow time for any opinions to form. He pushed his flowing hair from his eyes and continued.

"With respect, your Grace, allow me to document the theory."

He began then to open the maps, and I heard the crisp rattling as he made an elegant performance of undoing the first large roll tied with golden braid. The King approached the table, and the counselors arched and craned their necks, for they could not see the paper from their vantage point, but could not leave their seats unless invited by the King.

The cartography, brilliantly precise, would no doubt impress Joao, for my husband was the finest mapmaker in Portugal. Each line of coast or longitude or latitude was a dark black unshaking thread of ink, a line of perfect confidence, meant to foster the confidence of others. The King ran his hands over them, reading them in silence.

The Admiral, clearly now in the grip of enthusiasm for his subject, continued his presentation.

He unrolled a second map, and placed it corner to corner over the first, saying, "And that the East is so rich, Lord, why not reach it the fastest way?"

Then the Admiral took the King on a journey of adventure. Pointing out references on his charts, the Admiral toured the magic lands of Cathay and Cipangu, his long nimble fingers tracing each peninsula and bay as he imagined them to be, as if he and Joao II were sailing together along the very coasts, as if the King's gleaming walnut table were the spitpolished deck of his greatest ship.

The King was a born seafarer, and though he was obviously listening intently to the Admiral, he was not one to reveal his thoughts by small gestures or inflections in his voice. When the Admiral spoke of rooftops inlaid with hammered gold, and spices growing on trees, all the King responded was "I see the gentleman has great faith in Marco Polo. But were all that you say true, wouldn't we already know it?"

The assembled advisors chuckled then, and the King looked their way for approval of his challenge.

"Indeed," Gomes nodded. "And anyway, Dutch buyers prefer African pepper to Asian."

I was so madly tempted to interrupt, for now I was fully confident again, restored by the excitement of the moment—the Enterprise *was* right, I was sure. And I yearned to urge the King to recall the letters of the erudite Toscanelli. But the Admiral would have been furious were I to say a word, let alone remind the King of his own father's last rejection of the westerly idea.

I kept my eyes on Vizinho and Rodrigo, at whom the King repeatedly glanced whenever the Admiral advanced his calculations and the theory that via the west, Japan was very, very close.

These were medical men, logical and learned men. Surely the caliber of my husband's calculations could not fail to spur their curiosity. Yet when my husband suggested to the King, "You would be, sire, in the company of Alexander the Great, or Nero, were you to execute the Enterprise," the doctors primly shook their heads in skepticism.

"What are these?" the King asked, picking up the wood and seed pods.

"Proof that the currents flow as I say," the Admiral replied, "and that eastern lands lie close to the west." My husband outlined his theories of how the oceans flow in relation to the distribution of the land masses.

"If Japan were further than I suggest," the Admiral summarized, "these witnesses from the beach would never have landed in Europe, but would have been tugged to the bottom of the sea."

The King passed a piece of driftwood to the Bishop of Cueta who merely rubbed his thumb along the surface, handing it on to the doctors and the merchant, who passed it back to the Bishop. It seemed to carry no significance to them whatsoever.

Then Gomes again took the initiative, asking in full-voiced derision, "Do you really expect the Crown of Portugal to launch a costly expedition based on beach bits and seed casings no donkey would eat?"

"Donkeys do eat them, my lord," the Admiral replied, now too annoyed at Gomes to resist, handing a seed pod to Gomes with the slight bow of a waiter serving a meal. Even the doctors had to smile, but their faces glazed over again when the King caught their eyes.

My husband continued, undaunted, sketching with satin sentences the fortunes to be made ahead, great palaces in the air. Shall I ever forget the sight of him, standing very close to the King, locking eyes, his voice rising slowly, but deliberately, with the words, "Behold the magnificent brocade of your robe, your grace, your Highness, filaments of glittering gold, woven for you by the nimblest fingers of your land. But in the lands I profess to visit," and here the Admiral moved just slightly away from the King, closer to his papers, putting his forefinger down exactly on Cipangu, "not only is the sunlight constantly the same golden color, but there are entire cities, entire palaces, writhing with cupulas and balconies, sheer pastries of gold."

The King was rapt, it seemed, and remarked, "The gentleman does know how to be persuasive. But how can we be sure the roots of this are not merely in the imagination? And let us not forget that we have already reached the end of Africa. India is but a solid steering ship beyond.''

The doctors nodded.

The presentation had already taken a full hour at least, and the King seemed tired, perhaps ready to take the matter under consideration. But then, the counselors came to life.

"Why did you come to Portugal?" Vizinho suddenly probed, diverting the talk from navigation. "We have heard you literally washed up on our shores, like the wood on the table.''

The Admiral was stung, and stung back.

" 'Our shores!' I see. I am surprised, Sir, that you, a visitor yourself, could feel so protectively Portuguese so soon.'' Obviously, Vizinho took the reminder of his exile bitterly.

Vizinho stood. "Your mind is agile, Sir, as is your tongue, but I am surprised you did not mention ten vast bridges of gleaming white marble. That would have been very Italian.'' Obviously Vizinho had read the Toscanelli correspondence. Had he been in Portugal when the King rejected the Florentine plan? Perhaps he, Vizinho, had had a hand in the rejection.

Still, I had the impression that Vizinho, a scientific man, understood the plausibility of the Admiral's claims.

But then Gomes seized the center of attention.

"It seems odd that for selling only sugar, you have done an extraordinary amount of traveling. Is that business so profitable?'' Gomes asked, letting the suspicion in his voice flood into the room like clouded water.

But the Admiral saw a way to maneuver.

"Are you the same Fernao Gomes who has had exclusive trade rights along the Guinea coast?''

"Yes, how did you know of that?''

"It is my business to know these matters,'' the Admiral declared, adding mockingly, "and though you had exclusive rights to all except ivory, you of course never, ever traded any of that smooth white product, despite its beauty and value, never, of course.''

The Admiral had indeed listened well to the captains of the ships at Porto Santo. He had been storing information like seed for the proper field.

"Be careful, my Genoese friend, of what you insinuate,'' Gomes warned defensively.

"I insinuate nothing, Senor Gomes, but I wished only to clarify a point—that for you a successful western route to the east would not spell success, but ruin, your fortunes being dependent on Africa. I merely wanted to remind the King of your commitments which might influence an objective evaluation of what I have been saying.''

''The King knows of my service well,'' Gomes replied.

''Exactly, Senor Gomes, exactly,'' said the Admiral.

Joao II had stood silently by during this rather acrimonious exchange.

''Gentlemen, please,'' he said. A single gesture from the King and Gomes sat down again.

''Tell me, Colombo,'' the King began, ''since you have apparently excellent commercial contacts and sources of information, why do you not make this expedition on your own. Why do you need our help?''

But the Admiral had long since abandoned the prospect of a private enterprise.

''Your majesty, consider the scope,'' he coaxed. ''Private donations are for hospitals and orphanages, ladies' works. Mine is an affair of state in its implications. Surely your majesty can see the importance for his Highness were Portugal to secure the shortest route to the east.''

''We are already on the verge of securing it,'' Vizinho interrupted.

But then, the Admiral replied too quickly, unthinkingly, ''Diego Cao turned back too soon. The true tip of Africa lies much further than his voyages proclaim.''

With this, Gomes muttered ''He *is* mad,'' stupified that my husband could denounce Cao so publicly.

By now Rodrigo was on his feet, reading the Admiral's charts, unhampered by the King, who walked back and forth between his throne and the table.

Rodrigo then spoke up, pointing to a map. ''You have here noted the presence of a strange sea thick with slimy weed, due west of Portugal en route to the east.'' It was a sea noted by Portuguese sailors and documented by my father. ''How would you propose to penetrate what would surely be a vast obstacle?''

''Portuguese ships would have no difficulty in such weeds,'' the Admiral answered. ''They are designed to cut through beautifully.''

But then Rodrigo turned the answer to a question. ''Does the King not wish to know how the gentleman obtained his knowledge of the design of our ships?'' He posed, casting doubt like a shadow.

[141

But the King did not reply. Clearly, already much too much had been said.

The King then broke the silence.

"All of this will require study," he proclaimed. "I am considering appointing a commission to review this proposal, for you ask much support—several ships, a title, more than I have supplied some of my own expeditioners. It is all to be delicately weighed."

The Admiral had hoped that with Joao, man to man, the Enterprise might succeed. But the others—they all had too many reasons not to help. Still, the Admiral tried.

"But your Highness, surely you and I together understand the significance of the matter. If your Highness needs more time . . . "

"Time? But of course, the King requires time," Gomes answered unasked.

"What does the Bishop say," the King wondered, "who has been silent all afternoon?"

The Bishop still held the Porto Santo wood, and remarked only that "The King might wish to know that the Governor of this island where the wood appeared was Perestrello, and he was more than mildly troubled by the Crown's pacification of Morocco."

"He was a navigator, too, I believe, and your father-in-law?" the King said, glancing at my husband.

"I never met the man," the Admiral replied in disassociation.

"And," the Bishop remarked, "I would hope the King has spoken to the Duke of Viseu, for he has much information about our guest."

With this, my husband glared icily at me. I had never told him all that Nicola had confided, and now the Enterprise was falling prey to intrigues I had never taken seriously.

Then Gomes again, with the stealth of a man who sensed the moment to deliver one last dart.

"The Genoese gentleman, of course, leaves a good impression, for he has studied the world and the sea well. Yet is it possible all this knowledge comes, shall we say, from trading widely in goods of which the King would disapprove?"

The weapons insinuation again. I remembered Nicola talking to me in the garden, the rumors, the intimation my husband was being followed. How would he answer now? But the Admiral seemed prepared.

Eyeing Gomes fixedly, he retorted coldly, "Better than to cause the death of loyal subjects! Surely the King knows of the urcas burned in Africa to guard their design, but perhaps not of the several crew burned alive by accident, for no one knew they were on board when the orders came. Poor men, and one of the captains, I have heard, wanders mindlessly through Africa racked with guilt, afraid to return to Portugal for fear he would be killed to keep him silent. Surely, the King would want to know of these things as well, friend Gomes.''

My husband sent a brittle glare toward his accuser, but his strategy was risky, for now he too made daring intimations, tying himself to knowledge of dirty business. He had barely stopped short of implicating the King himself in the murder of a Portuguese crew.

He must have heard about men dying in the burning of the urcas from the Genoese, for this part had never been told to us at Porto Santo.

"I see you have ears on all the continents," the King noted dryly.

"As I have said, sire, it is by necessity," the Admiral answered. "I do not dally with my aspirations, nor do I cloak the fat of poor ideas beneath loose-fitting garments. The plan I propose is serious, your Highness." The Admiral began to collect his papers.

"I deeply understand, which is why I will refer the matter for further study." Obviously, the King did not wish to publicly take the responsibility for the decision.

"As you wish, my Lord," my husband said, angry, disappointed, resentful, bowing respectfully but without conviction.

The King began to leave, but then stopped, walking over to my husband, as if to comfort him, as if to flatter him and show appreciation for the vast extent of his effort. Placing a hand on the Admiral's arm, Joao softly said, "No matter the outcome, my friend of grand ideas, I have enjoyed our discussion, and perhaps you can come to talk among us again." Then the King walked away.

But despite the graceful exit, the case was lost. We had only to wait to be told.

"Damn the fool!" the Admiral bellowed, when the King's courier finally came to tersely announce the King's regret.

"He never intended to agree. His eyes and ears were shut from the start," my husband stormed. "Who could expect reason to prevail in such a worn out, unreasonable and musty place. Damn the King and this country!"

On and on he went, blaming every shred of earth and stone in Portugal. "I am tired of parrots and mindless parties, of weighing what I say, of being watched and followed, suspected," he blared, disgust and condescension wrapping every word.

For weeks, there was no approaching my husband, no comforting him, no speaking to him at all. When I once suggested that perhaps the King would reconsider if the costs were lower—one less ship, a lesser title on success—my husband only flew into further rage. He addressed me as if I were a stranger, saying "I shall not reduce myself before those who are already beneath me. I offered him a share in greatness. Never speak to me about such a compromise again."

I was lost, with no means to soothe his desperation in those days, or my own. My mother was too ill and frail to be my confidante, and my cousin Martins, from whom I at last received a note, gave little sympathy, expecting as he had the King's rejection from the beginning. And my friends at court—Nicola and the Duke had not returned from Burgundy. We were utterly alone.

I chose a moment in those days to remind the Admiral that we had once thought of perhaps mounting the Enterprise ourselves, and had some funds aside expressly for that purpose. I had thought that since we had cultivated some Lisbon contacts, with a little more work, perhaps these people too might contribute.

"Give money to what the King has kicked aside? Not likely," the Admiral bristled, hating my solution but having none to offer himself.

He would have nothing less than royal partnership now, having tasted the sweetness of power and potential at Court. "It must be done in a manner that will escape no one's notice," he declared, "least of all the weak-kneed King of Portugal."

One afternoon not long after, I passed the Admiral's table on the way to my dressing room. It was as usual piled with loose folders and drawings of island continents in the west. I reached over to fondle one of the small globes the Admiral had built, for I loved his engineering models. By chance, I glanced beyond it, across the table and saw two letters written in a beautiful hand. I quickly read the heading, "Paolo the Physician, to Cristobal Colon, Greetings." Why did the writer use the Spanish form of my husband's name, I wondered.

My eyes continued down the page, now crackling in my hands. "I perceive your noble and grand desire to go to the places where the spices grow and in reply I send you a copy of another letter which sometime since I sent to a friend of mine, a gentleman of the household of the most serene King of Portugal . . . '' Surely this was a recent letter from the great Toscanelli to my own husband!

The script was elaborate, the parchment the color of eggshell, and I could visualize the writer, bent and busy, streams of Tuscan sunlight in his geographer's room as packed with books and papers as the Admiral's. If my husband had a correspondence with Toscanelli, perhaps we could go to Italy and join . . .

My husband saw me reading, and approached.

"Darling," I said looking up at him. "I had no idea you had been writing Dr. Toscanelli."

The Admiral quickly took the letters from my hands and folded them. "There was no need to tell you," he answered.

"When did he write?" I persisted curiously, for the letters were oddly undated.

"I don't remember now," was all he said.

I would have loved to meet the famous doctor, after all we had been through to find his letter, and mentioned the thought that we might go to Italy and combine forces to launch the Enterprise. But the Admiral interjected.

"Toscanelli has recently died, and the dates of the letters are no longer important. I wrote him myself, for I suspected it would be wise to have my own letters, for I shall need more proof and documents to present my idea."

"My idea." The last words echoed in my mind. "But," I began, barely speaking my thought before his gaze prevented me. In an instant I understood. It would never again be *our* plan, or even *the* plan. Now the Enterprise bore the dimensions of Empire, and I would have to abandon all claims to it if I wanted to keep my husband. Now the Enterprise was his.

"Your King has played with me," my husband bitterly complained.

On he rambled. "And what if the Genoese are trading arms to infidels against the Pope's decree? Surely they are not alone, nor suffering from lack of good example. I think your King stands at the top of this mountain they accuse me of. Surely others would be interested in knowing that! Your King rejects me because I know too much about his real business."

Now his words were treasonous. Now we flirted with danger.

But the Admiral was ahead of me. "I am going to Spain. They say the King's cousin, Isabella, has all the attributes of a man, which means she makes decisions on her own, independently, without counselors or commissions. Now that I have seen one throne, I can easily see another. I ought to have gone to the Spanish crown in the first place. I am through with the fading star of Portugal."

He closed the door of his study behind him, leaving me alone to ponder this new intention. It was the first I had heard of it. He had said he didn't need Portugal anymore. The thought hung in the room like a suspended stone.

Chapter Thirteen

The End of Portugal

At times, giving voice to one's fears diffuses them, like finding out that the shadow on a window is not an intruder, but just a branch shifting in the wind. Yet at other times, speaking of fears gives them life and authority. Then retreat is very difficult. I therefore remained silent about the Enterprise idea, and who had had it first.

I had no thought of going to Spain, certainly not then. And since most of what happened there to my husband is by now well known, I shall recount only those events that pertain to me.

Armed with his correspondence from Toscanelli, the Admiral left for Seville, stopping en route to visit with several of my cousins who had left Portugal when insinuations against my family's loyalty were at their peak. I wrote the Admiral letters of introduction, and he slipped them into his black velvet portfolio without reading them. He would live in Spain on the money we had put aside to defray the costs of the Enterprise. And he promised he would let me know as soon as he received sovereign backing, and that we would sail.

"I'm sorry you won't be coming with me," he whispered the night before he left, as we lay in bed.

"If mother were feeling more well," I began, but then the Admiral kissed me full on the lips. And for the first time in as long as I could remember, he filled with wanting. He rolled his body on mine, and exhausted all his power inside me in a gasp of final pleasure.

I had long since given up discussing children with my husband. He had seemed so adamantly opposed, and all the preparations for meeting the King had deterred me as well, drowning my womanly yearning in the splendor of the Enterprise and the notion that fulfillment could be found in something else.

But now if the idea was no longer mine, if now the Enterprise was a moribund matter in Portugal?

"Perhaps I'll join you in Spain," I had said to the Admiral, the morning he was to leave.

"Perhaps you'll have reasons not to travel," he answered giving me a long tender kiss on the lips. I remembered the night before.

Did he now want a child?

When the Admiral left Lisbon, we both understood that he might be gone for a very long time. But, there was little choice for me, for love is the most complex of human emotions and I loved the Admiral with all of my heart. He embraced me one last time and stepped into the round rocky carriage that would carry him across the brown-gold fields of my country to Spain.

I had not been alone in Lisbon since my days in the convent, when the city sat beyond the stone and ivy walls, within sight but beyond reach, and it was an odd experience to be without my husband, whose ambitions had been my compass for so long.

When Nicola returned to Lisbon, not long after he left, I asked her to accompany me to a physician for it seemed to me, after the last time the Admiral and I had slept together, I could very well, at last, be expecting a child.

But my body signs were false, according to the physician and he doubted I would ever be pregnant, after all this time, due to what he called a structural defect. He seemed quite sure, said I was otherwise in good health, and would not answer any questions when I asked for more details.

Nicola expected me to be sad, for she and I had talked often about my fears and frustrations at not conceiving. She and the Duke had begun a family early, and Nicola's busy life included three small children and constant discourse on governesses and whether they could be sufficient substitute for a mother off in Burgundy or other diplomatic ports of call.

I was more numbed than distressed by the physician's news. In the time since the Admiral left, I had allowed myself to dream a little and recall that warm desire for a baby. But if I would not be a mother, what then would I be?

I did not have news of the Admiral's activities. And no means to write him, for he had no address in mind when he left.

For her part, Nicola only once voiced direct feelings about the King's rejection of my husband. One afternoon, after she had stopped by to visit my mother, she told me as she stirred sugar into her tea that the decision to reject our proposition had not been made all at once.

"The King saw merit in the Enterprise," she recounted, "but his advisors did not. It's small consolation that the King might have been convinced, I know."

I put my finger to her lips. "Might have been is insufficient," I said. I did not want to dwell on missed possibilities.

Portugal is over, I kept reminding myself, and I did not want to have my hopes dashed again.

Not long after that, however, I received an untoward letter from the Admiral. I had expected my husband to give me news of his whereabouts at least, and speak of missing me, for this had been a long separation, but it was instead a staccato message of some urgency.

He had heard that the Portuguese King, having rejected the Enterprise, had nevertheless dispatched a well known sailor, Ulmo, to sea to explore the merit of the western route! It was shocking news, though it conformed to what Nicola had intimated, although she had not mentioned Ulmo. Surely she would have had she known.

The Admiral asked that I verify the report at once, but he wrote "Do not ask Nicola's intervention," underscoring "not." What now did this mean, for how else to verify such news, except through Nicola?

I thought of trying to see Martins, but before I had even written him for an appointment, another startling turn of events—the Admiral returned to Lisbon, unannounced!

He rushed into the house and hastily explained that he had received news through his Genoese friends that Joao II might see him again, might indeed reconsider the Enterprise.

"The project moves very slowly in Spain," he confessed, after he kissed me lightly, looked in on my mother, and now sat at the edge of our bed.

"Have you established any point of entry at all?" I asked gently, doubting that he had, without well-positioned contacts.

He did not answer directly, saying just that the discussions were taking time.

Then he added that he had lost faith in the Duke and Nicola— he would not be more specific—and that I should no longer give them my confidence. Before I could protest, he was up again and gone to the Genoese quarter.

[149

He stayed in Lisbon only briefly, for though it was true that the King had dispatched Ulmo, Ulmo had returned to Lisbon after a few days' western sailing, reporting that he had found no coasts, no land and certainly no Japan. And amazingly, my husband was indeed summoned again by the King. But the actual meeting proved perfunctory, a stiff, formal encounter of no substance at all. The King stayed with the Admiral—I did not attend—only long enough to make idle chatter about what effect the Admiral thought the current dry weather was having on the Spanish orange crop. For my husband, the return to Lisbon had been entirely useless.

Needless to say, my husband bellowed again, furious at having been duped, furious that he had allowed himself to raise his hopes and obey a kingly whim for nothing.

Soon thereafter, though, we understood what the second audience with the King of Portugal had been about. I had asked the Admiral to walk with me to All Saints, for this seemed the only chance to tell him about my visit to the physician and speak to him about our prospects for a family. But I hadn't had time to bring the matter up, in the face of the sudden rekindling of the Enterprise.

We stood on the outskirts of the convent garden where we had first met so many years ago, and I fumbled for a way to explain what the physician had said about my body.

"I assumed you were not pregnant when I did not hear about it," the Admiral acknowledged.

"How could I let you know," I replied, "for I had no idea where to write you in Seville."

"I've gone to Cordoba now," he offered.

There was little to say to that.

We stayed at All Saints for most of the afternoon, and the Admiral poured out his frustrations at the Spanish court.

"There they have little appreciation for mathematics," he reported. "No one I've met has ever heard of Toscanelli, let alone his letter. My correspondence is meaningless there. I ought not have bothered."

He sounded hopelessly bitter. I offered to accompany my husband to Spain this time, but though he said my presence would soothe him, he also said he did not wish to subject me to the daily ebb and flow of waiting and hoping to see the Queen. He said he was living in a small single room, rented to him by the friend of a Genoese merchant, quarters being difficult to come by in the city of the Spanish throne.

"But aren't you lonely there?" I wondered, "It all sounds so grim and unencouraging."

He held my hand to his chest.

"Yes and no," he replied, "for my days are too busy to allow me to miss my wife, and at night, I usually dine with the de Haranas and I'm always recounting the events of my progress. This family has proven to be wonderful allies and friends. They have a thriving apothecary shop and through them I have met many Spaniards." I hadn't known that my husband had established any liaison interesting enough to command most of his evenings.

"Will you send for me when the matter is settled?" I insisted.

"The moment it is feasible," the Admiral replied, now distracted by the scores of people that had begun lining the riverbank.

"Dias," they murmured one to the other. It was the famous Portuguese captain, triumphant, having apparently just accomplished the greatest feat in navigation. Building on Cao and the others, Dias claimed to have rounded the Cape of Africa at last. With the nation's new hero returning before our eyes, no route other than the southern one could ever be the shortest and most preferable. With decades of Portuguese audacity and intrigue having at last borne success, the door slammed on the Enterprise in Portugal once and for all.

The Admiral roared with anger, "Why did this damnable Portuguese King send for me, when surely he knew the Dias news? Did he merely wish to rub my face in it?"

Indeed. But when I later consulted with Nicola, against the Admiral's wishes, the situation became crystal clear. My husband had served neatly as a pawn between the powers of Spain and Portugal. Even Nicola seemed embarrassed that our King would summon the Admiral for no apparent reason, other than to keep him away from Spain.

"Was it just to annoy Isabella?" I asked my friend.

"Not annoy, but disorient. Until he was absolutely sure of the actual results of the Dias voyage, our King did not want Spain to think him uninterested in the western route. If one king is interested, another sovereign must be interested too, lest one side or another get some advantage. And perhaps he hoped Isabella would spend some energies on exploring the western idea to sap some of her strength and treasury." Nicola seemed to agree with this reasoning.

"But anyway, now the matter is surely settled," she summed up, "Africa is the proven route to the East."

To hear my dearest friend also now dismiss the Enterprise angered me. I disliked the idea of the Enterprise reduced to a tug of war on the gaming field of royalty.

I needed to know who had Isabella's ear.

"But how would the Queen even know that the Admiral had returned to Lisbon?" I asked, "The Admiral has not come the least bit close to her yet. Might the King not have been wasting his efforts, if Isabella did not hear?"

Nicola rose to the question. "She would not have learned of it from Ferdinand, I'd wager, for apparently he does not sway her much," Nicola replied, ever knowledgeable. "More likely, her source was the accountant, Santander. He is the Spanish counterpart to Resende, I've been told. He gave her good advice about how to extricate herself from the Moroccan War. And he is also the source, they say, of the idea of expelling the Spanish Jews. When our King wishes to buzz in the mind of his cousin, the Queen, I gather he passes his news somehow through her bookkeeper."

I had what I wanted.

By then my husband had been giving some thought to approaching the throne of France, but here too, Nicola was an inadvertent ally. After her long stay in Burgundy, my friend had gleaned that the French throne suffered extraordinary debt and was scrambling for its life. It would be an inauspicious moment for an overture on the Enterprise to the sovereigns of France. No, I believed the only hope lay dormant in Spain alone.

So as my husband prepared to leave Lisbon once again, intending to make one last attempt to see Isabella and then, if unsuccessful, cross the border to France, I suggested that he abandon direct entreaties to see the Sovereign herself, but seek to see Santander instead. By my calculations, and the budget the Admiral and I had prepared for Joao II, costs of the Enterprise amounted to not more than a week's entertainment for the lavish Spanish court, and certainly not more than a week's cost of the Spanish army during the Morocco campaign.

"It is a tactic worth trying," I urged the Admiral, proud of my strategy, "Accountants wielding figures can be very convincing."

My husband was skeptical, but agreed that his new Cordoba acquaintances, the de Haranas, had indeed mentioned Santander and the confidence invested in him by the Queen.

"All right, I'll take it up with him," the Admiral agreed, "but why would the Queen care now about the Enterprise, and not before?" he wondered.

"Because Portugal is now doing something else," I replied matter-of-factly, as I tied his sack of belongings, never revealing the source of my interpretation. The Admiral left Lisbon again.

The time I spent without him was yawning and empty, and again I heard little from him.

Compounding my loneliness and plunging me into profound sadness, during this period my mother died. Nicola and the Duke were gone again on Kingly business and news could not reach my brother before the mass Martins, the Canon, offered in my mother's memory as an expression of royal respect for the Moniz family. I had hesitated to write the Admiral, and so I was a lone figure in the dark wood pews reserved for family, a prominence that only exaggerated my solitude.

I had not prepared myself well for my mother's death.

She, however, had had more courage, one day having gone so far as to feebly wonder to me, as time ran out, if there were not "things" we ought to be saying, between each other, a daughter and her mother.

But I deflected. There would be time to speak of "those things," I said, for now we should talk only of her getting well. She smiled at my optimism, not believing in it, but probably not wishing to force me to face the matter at hand.

She had become so wan and small, that at times when I looked in on her, the bed seemed to have been abandoned. Some days she slept from daylight to twilight, and woke at night, as if afraid of the darkness in which the hissing grasp of death might go to work. On those nights, I too would awake abruptly, feeling her wakefulness through the shelter of my own sleep. I would then open her room to check. My mother lay there, eyes open, waiting for the morning. I sat with her.

At these times, she tried to speak, seeking to be good company, still, in dying, a woman of good graces.

Often, she referred to her mother, Madeira, the past.

"Your father loved us all," she whispered one night, as we sat together awake in a sleeping city. "He would be here with me, waiting, as you are."

"Yes, mother," I answered, "I believe he would."

She paused, then slowly pushed the words into the air.

"He wanted to explore, rather than discover," she said, "they were different to him." Then she slipped into sleep.

At these times, she held fast to my hand across her chest, and I barely felt the weak pace of her heart, as if she were a child not yet fully formed. I could almost believe she was just beginning life, so similar were its first stages and its last.

It seemed natural for her to recall my father at these moments, reaching back to the time when youth was the blood of their island outpost and the liquor that held off despair. Yet the days we might have really spoken of his journeys and their meaning had been forever lost to me, so overtaken by my own preoccupations had I been.

Unable to speak to my mother of what she meant to me, I let myself believe that these nights and days with her would not yet end.

But I stood in the massive do Carmo Cathedral where I had been married to lay my mother to rest. All my excuses, all my tormented sense of opportunities lost, all of what I wished to say but had not, collected in slow small tears. I had taken my mother's presence in my life entirely for granted, and now, alone in the group of mourners called by protocol and loose connection to share my grief, I realized I had lost the last guaranteed love, indeed the only guaranteed love in my life.

With the rites of her death, came the true passing of Portugal for me.

Shortly thereafter, I received a note from my husband, who did not yet know about my mother, reporting that my suggestion had worked and the accountant Santander had indeed taken up the cause. I had been preparing to travel to Cordoba when I received the second letter and the jubilant news that, at long last, Isabella herself had agreed to support the Enterprise with three ships, sufficient funds, and a title of Admiral for my husband.

Not waiting for instructions from him, I went eagerly straight to Palos instead, and of what happened there and since, I have already written.

Chapter Fourteen

The Admiral's Logbook

I did not take up my journal again until we were far away from Gomera, and the Governor Beatriz de Bobadilla, for I wanted time to let settle the disquieting events that had made for our false start.

Now the sun travelled across the page as shafts of white light through the tiny cabin window. The sea outside was quiet; we had been sailing approximately three weeks.

During this ripening time, rituals of shipboard had become second nature. The men adjusted well to my presence, seeming at times to good-naturedly enjoy the sight of me in my Porto Santo trousers, trying to keep from slipping overboard.

Bathing was the hardest task to which I had to accustom myself. The men, at least, had what they called "the garden," nothing more than a board seat tied to ropes and lowered to the ocean. They would hoist one another overboard, then sit in the sea and let the waves wash over them. Once de Terreros lost his flute in the ocean while visiting the garden and never did so again.

The sticky black-blue sea served for universal washing, and we conserved all freshwater exclusively for drinking. The Admiral and I bathed in our cabin, of course, first he, then I, using buckets of seawater Juan supplied us.

In the morning, he also brought our breakfast—usually bread in the form of ship's biscuit, warm water, cheese and salted fish.

I had never been expected to cook, fortunately, for it had never been a favorite activity of mine. But here in any case, the kitchen was nothing more than a darkened tin box filled with coals, smudged from many fires, smoldering all day under various watchful eyes, and the great black orb of a single pot, hanging always in place.

There was one large water barrel in the middle of the *Santa Maria*'s main deck, and otherwise the central deck was bare, save for two cannons drooping like the lifeless snouts of pigs.

The men rotate the cooking tasks among themselves when de Terreros is otherwise engaged, but it is Chachu who busies himself each morning assigning the task to someone if no one has volunteered. Somehow Chachu has assumed the unofficial role of leader, as he is so multi-talented the men seem to look to him instead of Diego de Harana or even de la Cosa himself.

Fifteen massive timbers hold up the main deck, painted black, and one can see the knots where branches used to be. In the center of these, the towering main mast casts a long shadow, its basket lookout station above hanging like an arrow quiver in the sky. We've tied spare planking and spars to the sides of the ship as well as extra oars. We carry as much outside as inside the ship, and sometimes we seem like a travelling general store.

All day long, the men perform their chores, cleaning, caulking, mending sails, scrubbing, then cleaning and caulking again—the critical drudge of the deck.

Our cabin is the only private place on the entire ship, so each of the crew has only the privacy of his mind, for the sailor's wordly possessions amount to a twist of bedding and a bowl.

I cannot help but admire the men who sleep below, most of lower social station and not much of a notch above poor. Between the pitching of the seas and the slope of the ship, I don't know why they don't all roll helplessly to the centerhold like stones rolling down a hill. But, I assume, they make themselves stable somehow and get their rest.

There is a foredeck outside of our cabin—in my mind a spacious patio though it is barely big enough for a gathering of a large family—and afternoons when the ocean is calm, I often take the bedside chair from our cabin, and sit in the fresh air, not writing, but thinking of what I will write, or just listening to the steady, whispering sound of the sea falling away from our bow. *Pinta* and *Nina* generally sail within our sight, but I have not seen Pinzon since our awkward conversation on the quay at Gomera.

We planned a rendezvous of the fleet once, according to the system established by the Admiral, namely that a cannon shot would be fired from *Santa Maria* to signal the other ships to sail close enough for a tender to travel between them. But the winds by then were too strong to waste. Since there was no special need for a conference, the Admiral did not pursue the meeting, preferring to sail on.

I've noticed too that Luis Torres, our translator, who seemed rather timid during the preparations in Spain and during the festivities of our leaving, appears to have blossomed in the special society of our small boat.

It is as if here, free of the conventions of Iberia, he is also free of being labelled a Jew. He easily mixes with the crew, who reciprocate his goodwill, especially as he hauls up the bathing buckets for his own bath, for he does not use the garden apparatus, claiming that he cannot swim.

He too sits on deck often, enjoying the warm breezes, reading. He seems to be about Diego de Harana's age, though more boyish, and his long brown hair flies wildly in the wind.

I don't know where Torres was born, but the Admiral says he converted to Christianity as a very young man, against the wishes of his parents. He speaks Hebrew as well as Arabic and a smattering of African languages, but I never heard him speaking other than Spanish.

Usually the Admiral and I dined alone in our cabin. Torres, de Harana and de la Cosa took their turn dining with the crew.

However, one evening I suggested to my husband that we invite these officers to dine with us. I wanted to get to know them better and after so much sailing, I felt we might benefit from their view of our progress. At first the Admiral did not see the point, having utter confidence in his own view of the matter, but he accepted the idea, saying "My dear wife, we perhaps would both enjoy the change."

The Admiral's worktable was the only table in our cabin, and cleared of all papers and books, would tightly seat the officers, the Admiral sitting at one head and me the other.

Mostly, the evening meal consisted of a warmer version of breakfast, with the addition of potatoes boiled in seawater and salted beef which we had loaded in the greatest quantities possible. Serving the dinners was no simple matter for Juan, the cabin boy. He had to carry one tray at a time, place it above his head on the "patio," climb up the small ladder, then pick up the tray and walk across to our cabin door.

But de Harana knocked first, bending his head when he entered, being a very tall man. He appeared fully and comfortably extended only when he was sitting down.

The Admiral poured him a glass of ruby red Andalucian wine, and de Harana sipped it slowly.

"You were very kind to welcome my husband to Cordoba," I said, while we sat waiting for the others.

"My family is by nature friendly," de Harana replied warmly.

"Have you a large family?" I asked.

"My brother, my mother and several cousins," he replied.

"In fact, it was my youngest cousin, Beatriz, whose own parents have died, and who came to Cordoba to live in our care, who introduced the Admiral to us."

"She worked in the apothecary shop," the Admiral added, as he passed me a glass of wine.

"Indeed, my family's shop, madame," our guest continued, "and your husband was very kind to her."

"No more than any stranger would be who had received such kindness," my husband interjected. "Through the entreaties of Beatriz, the de Haranas spared me many dinners alone."

"We would have liked to have done more," de Harana apologized, "and it is a pity you, Dona Felipa, who speak such fine Spanish, could not join your husband in becoming acquainted with Spain."

"I would have enjoyed that," I replied, standing up to admit our next visitor, who had just tapped the leaded glass window of our door. It was Torres and de la Cosa together.

The Admiral again did the honors, and we toasted the expedition and the glory of Spain. From the moment we had sailed, as Spaniards tossed us roses scattering on the Spanish seas, Portugal had ceased to be my country, for it had too brutally refused both the idea and the man in whom I so much believed. Yet I did not feel Spanish either.

The longer we sailed away from nations, the more I felt nationless. And in the borderless ocean at our feet, I could no longer picture borders at all. The division of Europe here seemed so meaningless, unenforceable, perhaps even unnatural. Had Kings set sail, how could they have determined the limits of their ocean kingdoms? The sea would flow under any fence, or smash it in the whim of a storm.

No, away from our familiar delineations, the common language we spoke formed our only unity other than the destination that was our common goal.

Torres began to explain to de la Cosa the importance for Spaniards to know Arabic.

"One cannot enter the Moorish mind without language," he said, "for language is the window, the key, the portal to all peoples, if you will."

"Perhaps speaking the language would be a crucial merchant's tool, and the only true means to maintain a Sovereign's dominion," de la Cosa added, "if you see it as so important."

"Yes," Torres agreed half-heartedly, "but I was not speaking of mercantile control as much as a basis for cultural . . ."

"No," de la Cosa interrupted, "business was not what you meant. On the other hand, sometimes one need only speak in terms of money. Santander's wily calculations did open Isabella's ears, we must all admit. Using the accountant was a brilliant tactic on your husband's part, madame. He was so shrewd to think of it."

"Indeed he was," I agreed, letting it pass.

De la Cosa was the eldest of the group, a burly figure who had become quite rich in shipping between Spain, Italy, the Canaries and Africa. He still had a proprietor's bearing, even though here he was merely second-in-command.

Steam rose from my plate, and the tangy if salty taste of the stringy beef was welcome.

"Tell me, Luis, how do you plan to adapt your tongue to the matter at hand, for you speak no Oriental languages do you?" de la Cosa asked, intent on a discussion with our translator.

Here, the Admiral interrupted.

"I agree with Luis that language will be critical, but I am confident that the people we meet will respond to our impressive splendor, which needs no language to introduce it, of course."

"Of course, Admiral, and they will respond to our faith. You were wise to help the Queen see the importance of our trip for Christianity," de la Cosa complimented.

Here I was surprised. "What do you mean?," I asked.

"Surely, Madame, the Admiral's promise to convert our new-found partners ahead to the Christian faith had much to do with her decision."

Luis Torres shifted in his seat, as did de Harana, who avoided my glance. It was clear that I was the only one who hadn't known about the conversion aspect of our mission.

"We did not speak of that in Portugal," I said quietly.

"And we do not speak of Portugal anymore," the Admiral answered, by way of sealing the subject.

"It just seems to me that establishing a western route is navigational business and gathering souls is the work of the Church," I insisted, for while I surely believed in God, I was hard-pressed to see why and how our fleet could properly install Christian teachings—we simply intended to come and go.

What empowered mere sailors to prove the word of Christ, I asked myself. The truth was we had set sail on science, not the hand of God, but this I would never say in public.

"My dear wife," the Admiral began directly, looking straight at me, again clearly signalling that he did not want this line of talk to continue, "do not concern yourself too much about these matters. We sail with the Sovereign flag. The Sovereigns are blessed by the Pope, and therefore indirectly so are we. We will command faith by the goodwill we carry."

"And besides, madame," de la Cosa picked up the theme, "we have with us a living example of the wisdom of conversion in Luis here at our table, who was once after all a Jew and perhaps further from Christ than any Japanese. He can expound even in an expedient language on the potency of our Lord."

I felt Luis tighten uncomfortably and was glad when he countered crisply, "As long as I am not expected to count souls like beans." De la Cosa attempted no reply.

Diego de Harana deftly turned the talk away from this unexpected sore spot.

"Come, gentlemen," he interceded, "all we need to be counting are the leagues we sail. Let us listen to the Admiral's progress report."

Here, at last, was my husband's natural element.

"Thank you, Diego, for indeed this report was the reason I summoned you here tonight." The Admiral of the Ocean Sea was about to blossom, and soon all eyes riveted on him as he spoke.

"By my calculations, we have thus far sailed 500 leagues, which means half of our journey," he announced, "in that a degree is precisely fifty-six and a sixth miles, and given the movement of the sun across the sky, if we keep a current speed."

"But, Admiral," de la Cosa interjected, "speak in terms I can understand and convey to the men, please, for lately they have been pressing me about when we would arrive at land."

"You ought to have told me that before, Juan," the Admiral shot back sharply, "I thought we had buried their niggling fears at Gomera."

"Excuse me, Admiral, I meant to confer with you," de la Cosa justified, and added "do not fear because I always calm them, but what, after all, may I tell them?"

"Tell them we have completed half our journey," the Admiral sharply repeated.

"Are you sure he should be that precise?" I questioned.

My husband did not reply and I did not repeat my question.

"You may also tell the men," the Admiral added, once he was sure I would not persist, "that this is a glorious historic trip, and that I believe we have several weeks more sailing ahead, depending on the wind."

"Very well, Admiral. Shall I signal Pinzon to give him this report?" de la Cosa wanted to know, Pinzon, a captain, needing as much as anyone to be well informed.

"Pinzon seems to enjoy striking out on his own sometimes in our sight and sometimes not," my husband answered, now spooning to each visitor a dessert of ground biscuit sweetened with honey.

"When Pinzon requires a report, I feel sure he will signal us," the Admiral added icily, licking a dot of honey off his lower lip.

"Indeed there is no point risking a difficult maneuver if it is unnecessary," de la Cosa hastily agreed.

Our dinner then adjourned, after one more glass of wine, and after the Admiral, in a gesture that surprised me, cleared the table himself. He unrolled his beautiful map of our route, laying his recordbook at the top to keep back the curl, spreading the chart out flat to show Torres and the others. The precision of the drawing reduced them all to murmuring approval, and they retired feeling well-supped and well-informed, I felt sure.

De la Cosa, though, bumped his head when he stood to take his leave and Torres and I smiled to each other.

As Luis left, he agreed to teach me the Arabic alphabet, for it seemed like a productive activity that would help us fill our time, and he had no Japanese texts aboard with which to work.

After the cabin boy had made his trips to take away the plates, I began to undress for bed, as did my husband. The candle had dimmed, and his shadowy outline moved from table to cupboard to bed.

He was such a handsome mysterious man to me still. I did understand how bitter Portugal had been for him, and now that I was seeing what such an expedition required, I realized that my own family means could never have been sufficient. Only Sovereign backing made the voyage possible, and perhaps indeed the Sovereigns would only give their backing to a mission that would hold them in good stead with the Pope.

My husband lay in bed, saying nothing, but still awake. I asked him what was on his mind.

"I wish that you not speak in front of others about matters that are mine," he replied, in a distant authoritative tone odd to hear from the man with whom one shares a bed.

I was greatly taken aback and said, "Sometimes, my husband, it is not easy to know where our matters cease to mix."

"As you were not in Spain, you ought not judge what transpired there."

"As you wish, but I do not like the conversion aspects of our . . . " At this, he interrupted firmly.

"Felipa, it is simply not acceptable to have my wife question me in public."

"We are not in public now," I murmured, curling into his warm body for the first time in many weeks. With the worries of Gomera behind, I wanted to dispel his tension with affection, indulge our love again.

He kissed my throat, soon aroused, and whispered that, after all, he had a right to be annoyed.

"Given our role, even in our private cabin, all we do is public business," he continued, as he kissed me.

"Not everything, darling," I said. It was not often that I could melt my husband's resolve.

"Some things can be done very quietly," I continued, whispering.

He lifted my nightdress and his own, and we barely moved, trying to still the creaking of our bed and yet be together, for the night was silent and the man on watch stood just above us. We were very very quiet, and then it was over, and I dozed.

But I awoke abruptly when I felt the Admiral's weight move away from me. He slowly left our bed, lit a stub of a candle and walked to the cupboard. He removed some papers, this time a folded map, not a rolled one, and a sheaf of papers in a leather folder, not a bound leather book.

I could see that he was entering calculations again, but this was not the map, nor the book, he had just shown the crew. He seemed to be making some kind of separate record.

When he was finished, he opened one of the windows, letting in the sound of the sea. Though I did not sleep well again that night, when he rejoined me in bed, the Admiral slept calmly through to morning.

162]

Chapter Fifteen

The Seaman's Lights

The next day a warm rain fell, the first in many weeks, but the sea lay flat and no storm breeze blew. My husband again summoned de la Cosa, and the two discussed a shift of duty for the crew, thinking that it would now be best to change the watchman every three hours, instead of four, to be sure that as we came closer to land, fresh eyes were always ready. De la Cosa also felt the reduced watch duty would give men looking for land less time to worry about the fact that they weren't seeing any.

Though we were seeing signs. That very morning we floated through dense sheets of green-brown weed, bound together almost as if woven on a loom. For awhile they slowed our progress and Caro, the goldsmith, who happened to be on watch, suddenly appeared at our cabin, urgently asking the Admiral and de la Cosa to come and look.

True enough, we had met a seaweed wall, but my husband had read of these weedy waters in my father's papers, and had spoken of them to the King of Portugal. The *Santa Maria* slowed down, mired like a corn wagon in mud. The men seemed uneasy as the Admiral, though, spoke calmly about it, explaining that he had expected to meet this obstacle at just this time so surely we were on course.

Chachu lowered a bucket and pulled it aboard. My husband filled his palm with the weed, rubbed his fingers through it, and dropped the wet shredding straw to the deck.

"Give this flowing barrier no further thought, my comrades, for it surely is an indicator of land." He returned with de la Cosa to our cabin.

By then it had stopped raining, and I lingered on deck.

Caro hauled up more seaweed to examine it more closely.

I poked through several clumps. Little balls of red fruit, berries as hard as beads, hung on twigs caught among the roughage. De Harana joined me, also fingering the grass.

Caro suddenly whooped with joy, for he had come upon a tiny live crab, the size of a baby's fingernail and began shouting to all to look. The crab twittered among the weeds, a minute pinkish translucent shell struggling across what for it were colossal slopes. It looked nascent, perhaps not even yet fully formed—certainly a crab in its most original form.

"The tiny crab is a large distraction," de Harana observed with a paternal smile, "and they assume it means land is near."

"And it probably does, at least my father's papers suggest that such clumps of weed do not form outside of currents shaped by the land," I answered.

"Your father?" de Harana asked with a surprised tone.

"Yes, Perestrello, a navigator like my husband," I replied.

"Oh, I thought your family were merchants like mine," de Harana answered.

"Who told you that, I wonder. My father's name is very well known even outside Portugal."

"My cousin, Beatriz. I suppose the Admiral told her, but then she must have got it wrong."

Diego seemed embarrassed.

"Beatriz is not the most reliable these days," he observed. He spoke like an older brother speaks of a younger sister endangered by her innocence. He seemed quite worried and said he feared she had fallen in love with someone who would never marry her because of differences in their social position, she being the orphan daughter of country parents, and the suitor of some sort of noble birth.

"She will not introduce any of us to him and I am sure she lies to us to be with him. She has become uncontrollable," he lamented, concern vivid in his voice.

"Love will do that to a woman," I replied, "It is only love that brought me to this ocean." I was surprised to hear myself say that to a member of the crew.

It was odd to be crouching over a tiny crab on the deck of a ship at sea, talking of love and the love affair of a woman I did not know. But love is a warming subject and Diego seemed to feel the need to speak of his family.

I remembered then the caramel-colored face of a woman at Palos, who had passed a rose to Caro just before we sailed—his wife.

164]

I was quite impatient with her crying and it seemed a sentimental gesture to me then, as I was eager to be underway. To me, Caro would simply be our goldsmith, but to her, he was her husband going away on a mission whose consequences or safety no one could predict. She looked afraid, the portrait of a wife whose own essence and reason for living was sailing away before her eyes. On such a mission, it was so easy to think of each crew member as the embodiment of the job he performed, a goldsmith stripped of family, a caulker with no past, a carpenter with no home town. But that was absurd.

Each of them was the sum of his history, connected to others, depending on others, needed by others—somebody's husband or lover or father or son.

It was easy for me to forget this, since the Admiral was my family, and I was here with him. For so long, he had been my only meaningful connection to other people. There was my brother, of course, but he was so long out of touch as to be an absentee in my life. Listening to Diego speak of family feelings reminded me that we had not set sail autonomously, but each with our personal set of emotions and experiences, not all of which could be left behind with the untying of a rope and the raising of an anchor.

Chachu had had the foresight to set out barrels while it had been raining. He had heated some of the rainwater in a clean stew pot, and was now delivering it to our cabin. He held the pot of hot water with one hand and a small half barrel of cold water cradled against his chest, while he tried to tap on our door with his knee.

"Chachu, I am here," I called to him from the foredeck where he hadn't seen me. Oh for a glorious bath ahead!

I quickly relieved Chachu of the steaming stew pot, and returned to my cabin. De la Cosa and the Admiral had adjourned their meeting and headed below to examine the condition of the ropes, for our main anchor seemed to have slipped lower in its socket.

I told my husband I would be latching the cabin, until I finished my bath, as he stepped out.

I put the water barrel on the floor next to my bed, wedging it between two beams, moved the Admiral's table back to the wall, and let my clothes drop.

I poured a little hot water into the rain barrel and dipped my cloth, even letting some water drip and spill. This was an occasion to relish.

I poked the cloth into my ears, then pulled it around the back of my neck like a fine evening scarf, water drops sliding down my spine, tickling me, sweet welcome precious drops—oh the excitement of feeling clean and not sticky with endless salt.

I even washed between each toe, so blessed did it feel. The newly bright sun spread in shafts at my feet and along the surface of my bath water. I stood nude for a moment, and let the warm cabin air dry me, then wiped the last of the water away.

I dressed again, but what now to do with this lovely gift of water? I couldn't bare to dump a bucket of fresh water into the sea.

I plunged my nightdress into the barrel and swirled it around like a spatula in soup. It was so long since I'd washed my clothes— in the fresh scoured feeling of my skin, I was suddenly aware of how much time we had been away. How long it had been since I'd seen any color but ocean blue and stormcloud gray. How quickly I had come to do without the comforts of the city and how quickly, with the quickness of a single barrel bath, I could come to miss them again.

I rinsed several blouses, and only when the water had given its full service, did I toss it out.

Putting the furniture back as it was, I opened the top drawer of the Admiral's desk slightly to get a better grip on the heavy slab of oak. I felt some papers and remembered last night and the double set of journals.

Why was he keeping two records? I supposed he wanted to have a security copy, so why not simply ask him, but then he'd know I'd seen him writing separate logs. No, I resolved to keep this issue to myself, until the right occasion presented itself. And anyway, I thought, soon we would be reaching land.

But, we did not. On we sailed for several more weeks, with more weed, more supposed signs of shore. The decks of the *Santa Maria* were becoming like the Porto Santo beach, a catchall of signs of land that never came into sight.

And more and more birds. Once a very large black and white tern, with staring, darting eyes, visited the ship and did not take off again even when various crew members brusquely walked right by it. The bird hopped from deck to barrel to cannon pipe to rope, perching at random, as if staying obligingly out of the way of work yet monitoring who and what we were.

Then the Admiral said he spied a frigate, which according to him, is never found more than 60 miles from shore. It never lands on water, eating by attacking other birds in flight, which by reflex or fear regurgitate what they've eaten. The opportunistic frigate then simply catches the meal mid-air.

I personally never saw these skybound acrobatics, but I saw something equally astonishing. One day, a pair of gray mammoth whales jumped high into the air.

Falguero on watch yelled their sighting, and soon we were all at the ledge, speechless at their power. According to Chachu, the Basques harpooned such creatures from long galley boats, and reported the animals could tip any boat with a touch of a fluke. Yet they seemed so peaceful, their bodies rolling as they surfaced at regular intervals, sloping, diving, returning, breathing through a hole in their skulls—a whoosh of air and water. They slid through the surface like a hand into silken gloves.

How different from the sea monsters of landbound legends, raising havoc with clenching teeth and grasping fangs. Ours was not a ferocious Sea of Darkness, but a shimmering treasury of creatures thriving in the limitless realm that gives them life. In this way, the ocean teased us with its mysteries, but not, alas, with land.

And not only was there no land, but there began to be less wind. *Santa Maria*'s progress dropped to practically nothing.

A resigned silence descended on the ship. As at Gomera, morale was slipping.

One afternoon, since it was so calm, I decided there would be little risk in my climbing a short distance up the foremast. I hadn't ever done this before, and I thought I might again see whales from such a vantage point.

It was, for the *Santa Maria*, the longest journey possible, thirteen steps from our cabin door across the mid-deck to the first ladder. Down and across a few more feet, then under the foredeck. Here was a black niche, empty but for the giant ropes holding our forward anchor tautly out of water, an anchor in waiting.

I stepped toward the ladder timidly, for it cut right through the ship up from its belly to the upper deck, strictly vertical. The rough ropes were very thick and I could barely grip them all around. One step, two, several, then I broke through to the sky. The calm sea under our keel roared softly. I had intended to continue to the crossbeam, another four or five steps, but I was suddenly terrified of the height.

I contented myself with standing on the foredeck alone, not looking down the ladder I had just climbed. And no one called to me, for my foray escaped all notice.

Which is how I overheard Falguero and Peralonso Nino, a pilot, who apparently stood in the niche that I had vacated. Their voices rose through the anchor hatch to my ears, Peralonso's first, speaking of the Admiral.

"His compass dropped to the northwest a few nights ago," Nino asserted to Falguero, "so he ordered me to fix it to north again at sunrise. He says the needles were true because the North Star moves, not the compass."

"Do you believe him?" Falguero wanted to know.

"If I'm like the others, I am getting tired of believing him," Nino answered acidly. "I am not as easily convinced as our soft-eyed King and Queen."

"Does everyone know about this compass matter?"

"I've decided to make sure they do," Nino answered, "we've sailed too long to be on a true course. Our progress cannot be what he says, for several men believe they've seen land and we've sailed beyond it by many days."

Their voices broke off suddenly, as if they had been unexpectedly come upon, and they shuffled back to their posts. I hid further into the prow and waited a good ten minutes more to be sure they would not come back, then climbed down. Neither of the men were on deck.

My husband was at work in our cabin and I had to decide how to put my new information to him. He barely looked up.

"It is still awfully calm," I began.

"Yes it is," he answered, smoothing out the map before him, dipping his quill in his inkwell that easily stayed in place on the top of his desk on such a flat, innocuous sea.

"You remember the problem of the Greeks," I jostled.

"And you, of course, remember the solution," he replied. "Since we have no young lady virgins aboard to sacrifice, perhaps we'll have to offer up Chachu to raise a wind."

"Darling," I probed, "are you not taking the situation seriously?"

Then, challenged, he came to life.

"What would you have me do? We are on course and we will arrive." The memory of his double record entry nagged at me.

"How far have we come?" I inquired.

"I haven't calculated today's progress yet," he said, evasively, so I had to be more direct.

"The men are nervous with rumor," I informed him.

Now, he stood.

"Felipa, I've asked you to stay out of navigational matters! You do not heed me."

"I am not your daughter," I replied, my defiance startling even me, but I went on.

"On such a small ship, it is impossible to stay out of matters— we are all on top of each other, the crew rubs against itself, they want to go home . . . "

He cut me off sharply. "You sound like you speak for yourself, not them."

I told him of what I had overheard, and he dismissed the insinuations with a single word: "Ignorants."

I asked him to speak to the men, as he had at Gomera, for they craved to be fed confidence as only he could serve it.

"It is de la Cosa's job, or Diego's, not mine, to work among the men," he deflected. But he did promise to consider calling a meeting. However, events began to move more rapidly.

That afternoon, a single smoke cloud rose from *Pinta*'s deck, the prearranged signal that Pinzon wished to speak to the Admiral. There had been no contact between the two since Gomera.

As the seas were calm, he sailed *Pinta* closer than she had ever been to *Santa Maria* and thus had a very small distance to row. *Nina* bobbed beyond.

Pinta maneuvered like a well-trained parade horse, and it was obvious that if Pinzon had really wanted to stay with us, he easily could have. He sailed alone because it was his preference.

And now here he was—as tall and confident as ever, his head bare, his cape deftly draped on his shoulder as if he had just stepped from a tailoring shop.

He kissed my hand when he reached the main deck, where I stood with the Admiral to greet him.

"Too long without the sight of a woman," he said boldly, as he straightened up from his bow, looking directly into my eyes.

"You'd not have that problem, Pinzon, if you'd stayed closer in the convoy," my husband quipped, stinging the Captain in front of all assembled.

Pinzon said nothing, but followed the Admiral to our cabin and the two conferred alone. None of us spoke, and we all kept our eyes on the door. Undeniably land fever had gripped our fleet.

When the meeting broke up, the Admiral crisply announced that he and Pinzon had conferred on our progress and that he, the

Admiral, was going to confer with Yanez on *Nina*. The three ships would continue on their way, the course unchanged.

Murmurs spread again. Falguero tossed a stone at a flock of terns that flew around us.

Diego rowed the Admiral to the *Nina* and the tender slipped through the water without resistance, Diego's oars barely touching the sea.

Pinzon, however, rather than return immediately to *Pinta*, lingered on the flagship, first chatting with de la Cosa, then Luis, then Chachu, dipping a bowl into the barrel where some rainwater remained and taking a long refreshing drink, letting the water run through his beard, savoring the cool moisture.

I stood just in front of my cabin, ready to go in, but not quite stepping inside. I did not want to shut myself off from the activity of the deck, but I did not wish to speak to Pinzon.

However, he spoke to me, pointing out the school of porpoises that had all of a sudden surrounded *Nina*. The gray sleek fingers approached *Santa Maria*, twenty or so, high-jumping like the Senegalese riders of land.

"Joyous, aren't they," Pinzon observed now standing close by, "I think they like the sound of the oars."

"Why do you say that?"

"Because almost each time I've put a tender out, they surround it, and at times they swim along with the nose of the ships, as if to race."

"We've seen whales," I reported.

"As have we—these porpoises seem to be the same species, breathing the air as well as the water."

Pinzon remained as enraptured as anyone by the splendid sights thus far.

Then he turned somber. "May I speak freely, Madame?"

"You've never hesitated before."

"You know you are perhaps the only one who can convince your husband to change course."

I was startled at this, but Pinzon continued before I had a chance to say a word.

"I've just tried to tell him I saw land two days ago, to the north, not the west. He refused to believe me and said he was tired of false sightings—others too have told him of this, but he says we've only seen squalls of clouds or shadows. All the men now believe we've sailed past Japan."

170]

"And you?" I pressed him, for Pinzon always guarded his own opinion for the last.

"I confess I believe that as well. Madame, we must convince him for the good of us all. The expedition is lost otherwise."

And on he went, urging me to convince the Admiral lest we fail utterly to carry out our promises to the Queen.

"Your husband is a genius, but headstrong," Pinzon pronounced, "if you permit me."

"Why don't you stay with our ships?" I challenged him, remembering that he had all but ignored us since Gomera.

"Madame, we've known since the outset that *Pinta* was the faster ship. I simply cannot reign her in like a cart when she yearns to pull ahead. The slightest breeze in her skirts and she flies. I refuse to deny my ship her strength; she is so beautiful. And, truth be told, I've been trying to scout for the Admiral, intending to report to him my sightings so that he might announce them."

"Yet you did not report your sighting of two days ago?"

"Madame, that was so obvious that I thought he would surely see it himself," Pinzon replied dryly.

"He cannot see everything," I defended.

"Precisely, Madame, which is why we all must help him. He is only one man and we are the many on which he counts. If you love him, you'll join me . . . "

I broke his sentence with my own.

"I need no reminder of my love for the Admiral," I interjected. Pinzon lowered his head like a chastised boy.

"I apologize. I spoke out of turn."

"Yes, and anyway, you did think enough of the western route to let the people of Palos think it your idea." Perhaps for once I had put him off balance, but Pinzon held his own.

"Madame, you have obviously misunderstood some third party," he explained, "for I merely used my reputation to enhance the situation, and otherwise, we'd have no crew at all. And then, even you and I would not have ever met."

His smile broadened as he added, "a turn of events I for one would have deeply regretted." He gave me a mock bow, and I flushed with embarrassment.

I hadn't seen the Admiral's boat returning. When he spotted me talking with Pinzon, his eyes turned cold as rocks in winter.

With this, Pinzon stepped away. I had made no promise to him about the course, each captain returned to his respective vessel, and our fleet sailed on.

[171

The winds picked up for several days, and we seemed to glide through the water. But our progress did not seem to calm the crew. Rather, if Pinzon was right, our speed only carried us further beyond our goal.

Still each day at sea was different, each day varied birds, a blushed sunset, an opera-rose sunrise, each day changing light on the water. Yet in the fatigue of sailing and the fear of sailing in vain, it became more difficult to take joy in the journey.

Our objective seemed lost in the voyage—now the obsession was with proof, rather than discovery—who would be proven right.

Why had we come indeed? Japan had begun to feel like a grand illusion, even to me. Could land really be ahead after so much sailing? Yet it was unthinkable that we had come this far only to establish a grandiose and costly mistake.

The thought that we were wrong darted in and out of my mind but I did not dare share the worry with my husband, nor surely any other member of the crew.

The Admiral was right, of course, to hold fast his views—he had no choice. But I, could I bridge his vision and the reality of these days at sea? One day my choice was served to me as if on a plate.

Juan de la Cosa, Chachu, Torres, and Diego stood in a group one morning, each taking breakfast from de Terrero's large pot of broth. I was up early, and I had left the Admiral at work in the cabin.

De la Cosa was speaking to the group, but abruptly stopped on seeing me. I felt like a blanket smothering a flame. Chachu filled my bowl and then I turned to de la Cosa.

"Juan, I am neither blind nor deaf. If you have secrets from me, I must assume they are secrets from the Admiral."

De la Cosa seemed always to have the look of a man who, if asked to swallow his shoe would do so, even say it was tasty, if he thought there were some advantage to gain.

"Madame, surely you must know we speak of our dilemma— we have long since passed land and I am hard pressed to keep the men from refusing to service the sails."

"It is as blunt as that?"

"Yes, and as these men know me far better than your husband, they look to me to decide, and I confess I too have grave doubts about this course."

Chachu shifted his weight from one bare foot to the other, clearly uncomfortable. I asked him if de la Cosa's assessment of the men's mood was correct.

"You know, dear lady, how loyal I am, and yet I fear we are all becoming ready to follow Senor de la Cosa."

"He says he is following you," I noted.

De la Cosa too shifted in place. He knew my point, and said "Madame, though you have good relations with the crew, surely you cannot expect someone of Chachu's rank to speak directly what is in his mind?"

"Juan, rank means nothing in this matter. Mutiny . . . "

"Not that, Madame," de la Cosa quickly interrupted, knowing that the mere mention of mutiny on a Sovereign mission was tantamount to treason.

"What would you call it then?"

"A reconsideration of our course, now, before it is too late. And no one would be the wiser in Spain. The Admiral would still have his accolades, and we would have land."

"And you, Diego, do you agree?" I asked the young de Harana.

"I fear, Madame, there is little to choose in such bleak circumstances," Diego said, free will evaporating in our distance from land.

"So what are your plans?" I pressed the group, for the matter had clearly boiled like seaman's soup to overflowing. De la Cosa had tasted the crew's loyalty.

"Tonight we will pull down the sails if the Admiral does not change direction," de la Cosa advised me.

"You understand the consequences of that remark?"

"Indeed, Madame, do not forget I own this ship, despite its charter to the Admiral. I make no statement lightly."

I asked again if Chachu were ready to follow this new leader and again he teetered between fear and fidelty. He did not reply.

"Give me time, Juan, to speak with my husband. Another day."

"Madame, your role is not to stay judgment. The men will not wait."

"It is hardly for you, Juan, to define my role."

I spoke directly to Chachu then.

"Are you not willing," I entreated, "to give me one more day? Surely a Basque can see the value of one more day after the great distances we've come. Search in your heart and you'll find your own belief that my husband is a fair man."

"This is not my choice, Madame," Chachu replied, nervously "but the other men are difficult to convince." I changed my argument. For suddenly, in the challenge of all the eyes before me, I could not bear to have the Porto Santo idea, and the career of my husband, smashed on the jagged rocks of pride and worry. I felt designer of the Enterprise again, in rising to defend it.

"Please gentlemen, I ask you as a lady, and one who has heard the greatest mathematical minds of Europe debate the merits of this route. If Mr. de la Cosa's words are not undertaken lightly, can you imagine that such an important voyage with all it entails received any less serious consideration?" I had their attention and capitalized on it.

"This voyage has been years in the planning," I explained, "and the thrones of Europe were vying for the honor of supporting it. No, this quest is honorable, and well thought out. Give me the time to speak to my husband."

Chachu, at least, had been reached.

"Our Admiral's wife has more backbone than the crew, Master Juan. I for one could not refuse her," he said with assurance.

De la Cosa had to give in, for without Chachu, whose uncanny instincts about the sea held him in high regard among unranked crew and officers alike, the revolt lost cohesiveness. And without Chachu, de la Cosa would never make it back to Spain.

I dreaded the task now before me, for I could predict my husband's rage. But now he would have no time to think about the matter. He would have to act, pushed into a pitiful corner.

I knocked on the cabin door, and stepped inside.

My husband was washing his face, bent over the porcelain bowl, his hair cascading over the shoulders of his white silk shirt. He patted both cheeks, then slung the towel over his shoulder and smiled, joking that he would have wondered where I had gone for such a long time, except that everyone's whereabouts on the *Santa Maria* were so self-evident.

He slipped his leather doublet over his head and was making ready for the day. His confidence in his personal lens was his most inspirational quality, yet now that singular view of the world would perhaps spell the end of his dreams.

"Darling, not everything on our ship is as apparent as you believe."

He stopped and looked very seriously at me, recognizing that I had never used this demanding tone before.

"The men again, I cannot, they are very . . . " I was trembling. I had to come to the point or explode.

"The men are eager for a change of course," I declared in a low voice, using the most straightforward words for perhaps the most traumatic idea I could ever utter to him. His eyes filled with rage.

"You conspire against me? You are no better than Pinzon!" he accused. "Did I not refuse him a similar idiotic request?"

He hurled his words like daggers, and I felt reduced to the level of the lowest gromet of the deck.

But somehow, against his derision, I had to make him understand that matters had reached a crisis point surpassing both of us. I hadn't known Pinzon had already been over this ground, but now I had to convince my husband the problem was more than any one captain. I was about to begin my recitation when he lashed out again.

"Felipa, I have more than once asked you to keep out of these matters! You will not understand. I watch you among the men, smiling, talking, asking little questions about their little tasks. They are using your goodwill, and your naiveté, my wife. They want a course correction, of course, because they want land. So do I. But they want it for money, for the Queen's prize that goes to the first to sight Japan. Don't you have the depth of mind to understand that simple unvarnished fact?" His face was dark red with anger.

I had never heard of this prize.

My husband flushed with fury, his voice infused with condescension and disgust.

"Our trip is a journey of destiny, discovery. I thought you were above the common thoughts of the common crew, a Perestrello, a fine Portuguese lady. I thought you could understand things." He began pacing the cramped cabin.

He mocked me, but he was right that I was truly an innocent. A prize. Of course. A purse of money for de la Cosa, de Harana, Pinzon. Money.

"I conceived the prize to keep the men focused on the point ahead," my husband ranted, "I hardly expected my own wife to undermine me."

He looked out the windows, turning his back on me.

It was the most wretched moment of our marriage. I felt small, stupid, exposed.

I tried to recover.

"Surely I am entitled to my opinion. You cannot expect me not to think at all about what has consumed my life since our meeting. All our life together . . . ''

He interrupted in a voice as sharp as the tip of the knife in his belt.

"Yes, Felipa, every moment has led to this one, every word has brought us to this mission, every promise, every month, every idle conversation with people who could help in two countries. Indeed. So if it is not all to be wasted, never ever question my authority again. I do not need you to save my plans. I do not need a woman to . . . ''

A cheer rose on deck, suddenly. Then a second.

My husband raced outside to find Diego de Harana making his way through an assembly of the crew, holding a note. It was from Pinzon on *Pinta*, sent over by tender.

A crew member on *Pinta* had picked up what appeared to be a plank from a building, and a strip of wood apparently carved by a human hand. Pinzon asserted these were blowing from the north, a sure sign of land.

But my husband had had enough of other people interpreting and giving orders. He climbed a few steps to the deck above our cabin and raised both arms to demand attention. Then he spoke, not as at Gomera, when he identified with the crew. Now he used a more exalted, commanding tone.

He began. "Now hear me well, my comrades. No one wishes to reach land more than I. For days we have sighted such debris, and I myself have seen more than I have told you. I have kept many sightings to myself, not to raise false hopes. These are all signs of land. But the land is to the west, not the north. We will stay on course, despite Pinzon, despite the erratic winds, despite your fears. For I am right. We will reach the East, and I am so convinced that your complaints are useless, that I will promise you, in the name of the Queen and my God, that if we do not spot Japan in three days, we will turn back."

I was stunned, as was every other person on deck. This was his crowning audacity. But he wasn't finished.

"In return, you will double the number of lookouts on each watch, and the first to see land will not only receive the Sovereign's prize, but a personal prize from me, my leather and silk doublet that is my most precious garment, that will in the future bring its owner much reknown."

De la Cosa had no choice but to disperse the men, and carry out these new orders, for to refuse now would be a criminal act. Mutiny had been blunted.

But the next day, *Santa Maria* was still fraught with rumblings, each moment seemingly to foresignal a great final explosion of human tension. That night, the Admiral ordered all on deck for special prayers, and he himself stayed up on deck very late into the night. I felt every single mind on board counting out the three days.

It was now October 10, 1492.

Between the Admiral and me, no unnecessary words were spoken. He had not yet forgiven me.

But I did not realize how far he felt from me until the next night, when our sleep was broken by the page banging on our cabin door yelling, "Almighty god. Yzquierdo, the seaman, has seen lights flickering on the horizon."

The Admiral rose calmly, told the page to tell Yzquierdo and the others he was grateful for the report, but that he, the Admiral, had seen such lights the night before. Being already well aware of lights moving on the horizon, the Admiral still was owed the prize and the men should return to watch.

"You never told me about the lights," I whispered.

"How can I share anything with you after all that's happened? I feel entirely by myself, Felipa."

How could I swim out of the guilt he heaped on me?

I tried to justify my feelings.

"But my husband, please understand. I too have a stake in this affair. I only wished to help you. For all of these years that is all I have tried to do."

He wiped my tears with his forefingers.

"I know, my wife. I know. But these matters are too great for you. I could have let Yzquierdo take the credit—probably you are thinking that. But I must remain in charge. I must."

We slept again until finally destiny overtook us. A single cannon volley from *Pinta* studded the night, the pre-agreed signal. Again the page knocked with the news that de Triana, the Pinta's lookout, had seen a white glistening cliff.

We scrambled to the deck.

Indeed there was a shadow there that had to be land, and a yellow light rose and fell, a soft beckoning flicker when the waves stopped, riding the most distant swell of the rolling dark water.

None of us knew its origin. But all of us understood that the many hopes of our journey now were flowing to this tiny, fleeting glimmer, a sign of arrival at the end of the long, empty night of ocean behind us.

Each man's face glowed amber in the torchlight. A few dropped to their knees.

My husband ordered all three ships to lower sail and anchor, lest we drift beyond the land in the dark.

De Triana had seen it. There could be no debate. But as the sea flickered, far away, as far as anyone had ever sailed, the prize was the vast new reach of possibility that gathered before us.

We had only to wait for daylight to reap what we had been the first to accomplish.

None slept, but we all stayed on deck, as the day slowly lit the night and the horizon became gold with morning. As the darkness lifted, we recited the "Ave Maria" together, each voice blending with the next.

As one, we beheld the great green cathedral of an entirely new world.

Chapter Sixteen

October 12, 1492

My eyes trembled with awe. No master artist of Europe could add to this masterpiece, a green-blue illusion like an aquamarine tray heaped with emeralds. It was as if there were no air around us and our three ships floated on a sea so clear there seemed to be no sea at all. The still waters were crowded with fish, brilliant and shimmering blues, reds, yellows, fish darting everywhere, all lit by a blinding sun that glittered on the surface, as if showering itself on crushed crystal. The merest waves rippled lightly on a beach of powdery sand, soft as sugar, a graded slope falling away from a wall of green sunlit forest.

Surely this land was still mirage, still a false sighting, for if the human mind had ever conjured such serenity, surely it could disappear like vapor at the touch of a human hand.

We stood together on the deck of the ship, stunned, and it suddenly felt not that we had sailed for three long months, but that we had been carried here overnight by a divine fingertip, put down to kneel before this sacrament of place.

A white perfect cloud crowned the summit of a small mountain at the center of what seemed to be an island.

The Admiral too for awhile could only accept the sight in silence. Though he had never faltered in his argument that we would reach the East, now that we had arrived, even he could not formulate the moment in mere words. We had no ready portal to this world, despite all our estimates and plans. For the unsullied spectacular beauty of this place, we were all totally unprepared.

The Admiral ordered the tender to take him and the captains to shore, for there seemed to be people collecting there. Excitement swept our convoy like wildfire. But when I moved to step toward the Admiral's boat, he raised his palm immediately to stop me.

[179

"Not yet," he ordered, "I expect peace but I cannot be sure." He promised he would send for me as soon as he had judged the prevailing mood.

An hour passed. I felt like a corked bottle until I heard the shallow dip of oars as Pinzon's pilot, Xalmiento, rowed to *Santa Maria*.

"The Admiral sent me for you, Madame," he said. "You must come now as it seems we might be moving inland."

And so I stepped down into the small boat, never taking my eyes from the jewel of the shore. I could see that the royal banners were unfurled, the huge "F" and "Y" for the King and Queen, for the first time flying over these gleaming beaches, and a large cross planted in the sand.

"The Admiral has already taken possession," the oarsman remarked, "and explained that to the people here."

"But does Luis speak their language, for how will they understand?"

"That I cannot say, Madame, I was not close enough to hear everything that took place."

The sea abruptly became too shallow for the oars, and we waded to shore.

It was magnificent—warm lush sea, warmer embracing air. The steamy dark forests dripped with an anarchy of plants and flowers; deep green moss tumbled from the tops of trees like capes tossed by a giant hand, and all more alive with the songs of birds than any woods of the most wooded parts of Madeira. Surely here was paradise.

But we were not first. People were gathering on the beach, emerging from the forest. They had perfect posture, their skin the rich color of dark wine grapes. Some women wore very short apron-like skirts tied to their waists, but most, men and women, were entirely naked.

No human being, including the Admiral, had ever stood before me totally without clothes. But for my own body, human nudity was largely outside my experience, and I confess I was transfixed by the strong private features of the men, the bare brown breasts of the women. The people stood utterly without shame.

My husband gave me a somewhat perturbed glance, but in the honesty of these new surroundings, European modesty seemed absurdly out of place. The Admiral continued reading a declaration of possession, claiming the lands—whatever they were—for the

Spanish, all dutifully recorded by de la Cosa, while the people on the beach stood in a loose huddle, staring, and making absolutely no sound. Their deep brown eyes brimmed with welcome and inquiry.

All were handsomely built and lean. In fact in well-indulged Lisbon, these people would be considered excessively thin. They had black hair that fell straight to their shoulders. Though no man wore a beard, almost all the people decorated themselves with streaks of paint, zigzag orange and red lines or swirls down the nose, across the cheek or the arms, chest, legs or ankles. Against naked skin, the shiny colors glistened.

I stood behind the Admiral and the men, taking in the scene. But as I looked, a woman broke away from the group and headed straight for me. Her face was somber until her nose was almost touching mine. At first I flushed with fear thinking she meant to shove me back into the sea from whence I'd come, but in seconds, she was embracing me warmly, leaving streaks of her body paint on my white linen blouse, and then bursting into laughter when she saw the pasty lines from her face recreated on my clothing. She giggled and rubbed her index finger into the painted circle winding like a bracelet around her wrist, then took her reddened fingertip and streaked the bridge of my nose and my cheeks. When she was satisfied I was properly decorated, she clasped me again, and returned to her place in the crowd.

I had been initiated, I guessed, and one by one the crew turned their heads to me and smiled deferentially. The Admiral too took good note of the welcome I had received and nodded approvingly. My benefactress stood still among her people, happily smiling, as if proud to have been the first of her race to touch one of the foreigners. If these people had any fear of us, they hid it well.

They also had an innate sense of good manners. My husband had read his statements and laid claim to the homeland of these natives without once being interrupted.

Only when the Admiral seemed to have nothing further to say, did one of them step forward to speak. He wore a strand of yellowish cotton holding his shining black hair in a knot at the top of his head, and a single thin loop earring that might have been gold.

He began speaking in a rich-toned voice, but in a language none of us could grasp, full of short clicks. He paused often, as between thoughts, though I could glean no meaning, for there was no familiar sound at all, no word resembling any of our own. We all eyed Luis Torres, of course, to see if any of what was said made sense to him, but his face was as blank as the Admiral's.

The speaker carried no weapon, and naked in the brilliant sun, he embodied vulnerability. Yet his people revered him, for a respectful hush fell over them as he spoke. Here, without weapons or clothes, he was obviously nevertheless King.

When he finished, even the Admiral recognized that he faced some sort of peer, and gave orders that the men drop all muskets to the sand.

With this, and the first speeches between old world and new completed though neither side had understood the other, our men whooped with satisfaction. Some even kissed the soil, which amused the local people who laughed heartily, thus shattering any lingering tensions among us.

How extraordinary to think how far we'd sailed across unknowns, then to arrive in this warm, moist Eden and meet a people totally alien to us and yet, in a few moments of contact, have the experience defused of all fear, rendered festive, even normal, dare I say. Having been so obsessed with the journey itself, it was as if there were now little room left in the mind for worry. I felt enchanted and exceedingly safe.

In the next few minutes, the beach became a bazaar. The Admiral offered a handful of glass beads to the chief, who rolled them in his palm with his index finger, examining them.

They were worth nothing to us, but they seemed to please the leader and he passed them among his people.

I watched the simplicity of the scene. How odd that the entire culture of Europe, and the power of the Sovereigns of Spain, were represented to these, our hosts, by a few glass beads. By these gifts, we ought to be judged poor, I thought, but these people appeared greatly impressed.

No sooner had the beads been passed one to the other than more natives emerged from the woods—if they had been there all along, one could never know, for these dark woods could easily swallow whole groups of men. These new arrivals carried all manner of gifts for us. A man bent before Pinzon, and laid a pile of large brown leaves at his feet, as well as a long bamboo stick carved to a point, probably a spear. They also brought spools of what looked like sewing thread.

Pinzon motioned for me to come and inspect it.

"It has the feel of a slightly damp silk or cotton," I pronounced. The strands were as refined as any I knew in the weaving shops of Lisbon.

Then, a veritable parade. The people would slip from the beach disappearing in a rustle among the branches, then emerge with more presents, as if the green wall were a splendid warehouse overflowing with extra items they wished to give away.

One tall man carried a blue parrot the size of a chicken on his shoulder. The bird's beak was nearly the size of the native's own nose. Was this what the jungles of Africa were like, I thought, lush with parrots?

In exchange for the first wave of gifts, our group offered some red woolen sailor's caps and more beads. I saw Caro offer a young woman a piece of a chipped yellow porcelain plate. Its luster seemed to please her, but I knew Caro would never make the gift of a broken plate at home. Still none of us had come to shore prepared for all this interchange. I moved closer to the Admiral and said, "Perhaps we ought to instruct the men not to trade useless items?"

"Now is not the moment to forbid what seems entirely natural, Felipa. We'll speak of it later. And anyway I've already told them always to return any offering with an offering and I have forbidden them to give away items of value until we have the information we need. Caro is only following orders." With that, the Admiral stepped over to Luis and the two began to try to make sense of the language.

Pinzon, at least, had had the foresight to bring a tiny round brass bell along with him, and he was ringing it slowly in the ear of the dark man with the parrot. The light chink, clink, chink, charmed everyone. The people passed the little brass ornament hand to hand approving the sound as we would a palace concert, each taking turns ringing and giggling in a delightful duet of babble and bell.

They seemed also intrigued by the bell's metallic surface. I noticed that, except for an earring or two, they wore no ornaments of metal, and that all the bowls and utensils they offered were of scooped-out gourd or wood.

And then something very unfortunate happened. One of the men had been fingering the hammered brass sheaf of the Admiral's sword. Innocently, the Admiral removed the sword from the case to show that off as well. But before the Admiral could prevent it, the man grabbed the blade, instantly slashing his own fingers. It was not a serious wound, but he was horrified to see he had drawn his own blood, and raced away from my husband screaming toward the water.

[183

The gathering took on a stunned silence, until one woman began to wail loudly as if she expected the man to die. The Admiral too looked shocked and full of regret.

I myself was paralyzed, so quickly had the event occurred—but Chachu sprung into action, the surgeon, Sanchez, not thinking fast enough. Chachu tore the red bandanna from his neck and followed the man to the sea. He gently took the man's hand, and plunged it into the water. Though the saltwater obviously stung the man's cut, for he flinched, he let Chachu try to soothe him. Chachu then wrapped his bandanna around the man's outstretched palm, tying it tightly, gesturing that the scarf was a gift that could be kept.

The local man did not smile, but he did not reject the bandage. He walked slowly back to his people, spoke to them, and then one by one, they walked into the forests, leaving all the gifts they meant to offer scattered in the sand, dropping everything we had given them as if they were hot coals. Even the bell landed in the sand with a flat, sad untinkling thud.

In moments, it was as if every one of them had vanished into another zone of time separated from ours by the extravagant green line of forest, as if they had never been there at all.

Chachu began walking up the slope of the beach to follow the people, but the Admiral stopped him, shouting "No, do not. Let us leave. We must establish now that we have no need of them if we wish to make use of them."

He ordered us all to the tenders, and to row away without looking back. He did take care, though, to leave all our offerings so far— the caps, the beads, the broken plate, the tiny bell—piled neatly on the beach.

I felt deeply sad, not only by the abruptness of the events, but because it had all been so inadvertent. Before we had even spent a full day here, we had brought harm to this place.

The Admiral called all the officers to join him on *Santa Maria* for a meeting in our cabin. I stood on the deck and looked back at the green, white and blue horizon we had just left. Had I really just walked there? Had any of it happened at all?

I kept staring at the beach but nothing stirred. I could still feel the penetration of the Madonna-like eyes of the woman who had embraced me, still smell the forest, its wild perfumes travelling across the shallow waters. Had we so easily lost this unexpected purity among people who knew neither of our banality nor our glories, people who had accepted us without the least knowledge of who we were, people who had become phantoms at the first hint of danger?

I desperately wished to retrieve that first mesmerizing moment and did not take my eyes from the beach until I heard Pinzon's voice behind me.

"They'll come back," he said over my shoulder, "I am sure of it."

I turned and found myself face to face with him. Only then did I notice that Pinzon had acquired the huge blue parrot from the beach. The plush bird squawked mightily, but stayed perched, its claws like eagle talons gripping the full breadth of Pinzon's shoulder. It was the largest parrot I had ever seen.

"The bird hasn't budged since he was given to me on the beach," Pinzon explained, feeding the parrot a fat red berry.

"I didn't see the transaction," I said.

"So many goods being transferred, it's not odd you missed it," he answered, inserting another berry into the parrot's beak. Unlike the parrots kept as pets in Lisbon, this new world parrot had not had its plumage clipped at all. Apparently it simply was too tame to fly away.

Juan, the cabin boy, then stepped up and said to Pinzon, "The Admiral doesn't wish to continue his meeting without you."

Martin Alonso, as usual, took events in stride. He casually placed the parrot on Juan's shoulder for safekeeping, and remarked, "Well, he did not let me know he had begun."

I followed Pinzon into our cabin. The morning's events had been so exciting, so exotic and so unexpected, it was only now that we began to be concerned with the fact that we did not know exactly where we were.

Chapter Seventeen

Which Glorious Island?

I stepped into a room full of elation, celebration and confusion.

The Admiral had already poured each man—de la Cosa, de Harana, Yanez, Caro—a large glass of his finest Madeira wine. He passed one to me and Pinzon, and we stood elbow to elbow, glasses tinkling like the brass bell on the beach.

The men relived the incidents of the morning, for the first time letting themselves express openly their bewilderment at the extraordinary contact we had just had.

Even de la Cosa with his normally narrow merchant's view had to admit the place was inestimably beautiful.

"Admiral," he said, well into his second glass of wine, "I could never have ever guessed we'd come upon such utter virgin bliss."

"Indeed," the Admiral acknowledged coolly, feeling utterly vindicated.

"Nor could I ever have anticipated how docile the inhabitants would be," Caro noted, now too holding out his glass for a second time.

"Or how naked," de la Cosa quipped.

"Oh, excuse us, Madame," Caro noticed, nudging Juan who had not realized I had come into the room.

"Not at all, gentlemen," I said. "Just as the people here, these matters need not be shielded. We have no doubt only begun to experience the new ways of this land."

"Here—here, drink to that," they muttered together as the Admiral poured Madeira again for us all. The men broke into smaller conversations and soon the atmosphere was more of a party than a conference. The near mutiny was not spoken of at all. It was now as if that crackling near-disaster had never taken place.

The Admiral tapped his dagger lightly on his white porcelain facebowl to signal that he wished to begin the meeting.

"Gentlemen and friends. I wish to take this historic moment to pronounce that, despite the concerns expressed on this very ship several days ago, we have, as I fully expected, by the Grace of God and our own courage, reached the Indies, the east lands of Asia."

"Amen, Amen," de la Cosa declared and we all gave a rousing toast to the Admiral.

"Now as to our location," my husband continued, when the cheering died down.

"Perhaps you have not made the same detailed study as I have of the works of the great explorer from my native land, Marco Polo. But, as he recorded that there were approximately 7,440 islands scattered like bird droppings off the coasts of Asia and Cipangu, you will not, I trust, hold me immediately responsible if I cannot say yet exactly at which of these islands we have arrived."

My husband—how he could handle an audience. He was ingeniously addressing what was on the minds of all in the little room, blunting their opportunity to ask, but still wholly evading commitment.

"I promise you," he continued, "that soon the Asian mainland will be ours. So I propose we anchor here for several days in order to let the men rest, and to discover the gold mines that surely cannot be far."

Here, the assembly cheered again, for they had certainly hoped we would not be raising anchor right away.

"I trust these wonderful paintbox fish will be safe to eat," Pinzon remarked, using the bottom of his wine glass to smooth the wrinkles in his trousers across his kneecap.

"Fear not, Captain of the fleet-sailed *Pinta*. We will not have to resort to eating your parrot," my husband joked.

"Your plan of resting here awhile sounds excellent to me, Admiral, perfectly excellent," Pinzon replied. "I for one shall certainly want to understand more about this place. Tell me, does the Admiral have any idea why these people, Indians, as I suppose you'd have us call them, dropped the bale of leaves before me?"

"No doubt these are mysteries that the future shall make clear to us, dear and faithful Captain Pinzon."

But Martin Alonso had more than leaves to discuss.

"If we agree on your pronouncement, Admiral, that we are at our landfall, do we not also agree that my sailor, de Triana, spied this coast first and therefore *Pinta* deserves the Queen's reward?"

The other men nervously cleared their throats and waited to see who would be the first to speak. The Admiral was undaunted.

"As I told the cabin boy at the time, I had seen the lights and land before. Until I determine which land we have seen when, in relation to the land before us now, I cannot agree that the prize belongs to anyone at all."

Pinzon, though, persisted, and all eyes held to him.

"With respect, Admiral, do you deny the land the men saw several days before our arrival here was not also land on which we might have called?"

"I deny nothing, for everything on this subject is premature," the Admiral insisted heatedly.

"Very well," Pinzon said, sensing he did not have the support of the group in his line of argument, "but then could I, as a Captain, be told the number of leagues we've sailed to reach this very bay?"

The meeting had become a stand-off between the two.

With that last challenge, the Admiral took offense.

"Our navigation is no secret, Pinzon. Here." The Admiral took a step toward his cupboard, opening the door. "If you wish to have calculations, I have kept the most precise navigational record made of perhaps any voyage in history."

He took out his bound notebook, and slammed it on the table in front of Pinzon.

"Here it is," the Admiral announced, "the only inarguable, my daily log. Go ahead, avail yourself."

The men hung still, backdrop figures in a passion play.

Pinzon reached for the record, but then pulled back. He put his glass down on the table, resting his hand on top of it as one does to signal a barman one does not wish to drink anymore.

"Gentlemen, gentlemen," interceded an anxious de la Cosa, "let us not mar this historic day with administrative debate."

Pinzon pushed the record book back in the Admiral's direction. He looked squarely at him and said, "You have misunderstood, dear Admiral, for I have no wish to probe your private records. I simply wished an estimate, for interest's sake. Who was first may indeed prove to be a relative matter and there will be time to . . . "

A loud commotion on deck interrupted him. The Admiral raced to the window.

"Here they are," he declared with satisfaction looking out at the scene, "I knew they would be far too curious to stay away." He walked right by Pinzon out to the open deck, leaving us to follow him.

Outside on the sea, about 40 men from the land paddled in a single enormous boat toward the *Santa Maria*, their rowing sounding like a waterfall.

Though the Indians shrieked at us, this was no attack for they were all smiling and laughing. In fact, at one point the approaching craft tipped over, throwing some men into the sea, and soon the Indians were swimming around happily as if they had forgotten they had a destination in mind.

Their vessel was extraordinary.

"My god, it must be carved from a single tree," Pinzon observed. Indeed the boat looked like a whole trunk had been scooped out to make space for an army of rowers.

In minutes a second vessel set out from shore, this one smaller, fitted with about 10 men, also paddling madly. But once they got closer I could see that this boat was overflowing with more gifts— more spools of thread, leaves, round green fruits I could not recognize, and amazingly, several more large parrots.

By then, the Indians had righted the first boat, bailing it out with large split gourds. The oarsmen held the larger ship steady until the offering vessel came up behind, and then the two approached together, their dignity recovered.

But the Admiral moved quickly, calling all captains to their tenders right away.

"Quick," he yelled, "this ship must not become a common thing to them." Apparently he wished to head off their boarding *Santa Maria*.

"Juan, let Caro help you fill a sack with trinkets and several tins of molasses," he ordered the cabin boy, "and follow me to shore with it."

Juan hopped to his duty, and our men raced madly back to shore in a small fleet of boats, as if suffering rowing fever, the Indian convoy now following them. I laughed out loud, for we had gone from the stiff tense decorum of an officers' meeting to outright sailors' anarchy. Still, all of this was new, so who could say how things ought to go.

I waited for Juan and took with him the last dinghy left and, once again, made my way to land.

This time, Indians had convened further along the beach, in a tiny cove where a greenish stream gave out into the sea. A small lagoon formed behind a tiny sand bar and we all realized instantly that the people here were about to share the greatest gift of all—fresh water.

Women and children were bathing, and tall green rushes grew up from the lagoon edge. A lone woman carefully broke off a few, picked the soft yellowish fronds off, and then began braiding them into her daughter's hair. The child squirmed in the sand, like children everywhere, but the woman spoke soothingly to her and the little girl sat still.

I swallowed a lump in my throat and thought of my own mother, and how much I wished I could tell her of these fantastic events.

How I wished to tell Nicola and the Duke and all the skeptics, to see the King's face as I described the luscious sweet taste of the water. I watched the woman from a distance as I sipped.

Our crew was again busy bartering, and again the tall leader from this morning spoke to Luis, the Admiral and Caro, though all three showed no more understanding of the language than before.

My eyes scanned the tableau of forest and sea, trading and talking, and then, I saw the tree.

How could I not have seen it this morning! Long brown seed pods hung by a tough fiber stem, some as long as machetes.

Evidence! We had been right! I ran under the gnarled parasol and saw the casings were exactly the same as what we'd found on the Porto Santo beach!

"Darling, darling," I called to the Admiral, "look at these wonderful pieces of proof." I jumped up to tug one down but it held fast. An Indian man swooped over, easily reaching a pod, handing it to me ceremoniously. Not waterlogged from an ocean journey like the ones we saw at home, here in the sun the casing had dried to the toughness of wood. It fit the hand like a sword, but the Indian took it back, tapping it on his palm so I could hear the rattling sound of all the seeds inside. So these were the islands where they came from!

"Darling," I called to my husband again, "the clues on our beach were absolutely right!"

My husband walked slowly over to me, took the pod, smiled and tapped it on his knee. "Indeed, a nice rhythm maker should these people wish to dance," he said rather flatly.

"But don't you remember the driftwood and these very pods and . . . " I insisted, so excited by the find.

"Of course I do, of course," he said, soothingly, slipping the seed pod through his belt. "But come here and see what you make of this."

It was both uncanny and amusing. Our dedicated translator would speak, but the Indian leader would say nothing. Luis repeated his phrase, poised with pen and ink to attempt to write down the man's response phonetically. But instead of speaking his own language, the chieftain proudly made an effort to repeat Luis' words, trying to imitate Spanish!

I laughed out loud, as did the chieftain. I tried to be serious for Luis' sake, but to his credit, he also saw the humor in the situation.

"Come Madame," Torres said lightly, "do not distress my class."

Again he tried, saying slowly to the Indian, "Do not repeat my words but say your own." He held his pen ready.

"Daw noit repet oyn," came something like the response.

"They will be very easy to convert," de la Cosa observed, "for they seem to enjoy a tendency to repetition."

"I would not assume they will embrace religion just because they can mouth our words," Torres replied, resenting this unsolicited commentary on his particular profession.

Giving up for now, Luis began rolling up his still-blank paper, but when his would-be pupil gazed at it longingly, Luis handed the empty sheet over. In return, he was given a long tube of reed fitted with a large white hook, presumably for spearing animals and apparently made of bone. The polished point was nothing to trifle with.

The Admiral ordered several crew members to return to the ships to gather all empty water barrels so they could be refilled here. Then, he motioned upstream to the speechmaker, the man we assumed to be in charge, and all of the local people including the women and children walked up the stream into the woods, ourselves following.

The little river was the only path, and our men, including the Admiral, rolled their trousers to the knee, some kicking off their heavy boots into the sand and proceeding barefoot in the water. I was the last in the group.

The forest above loomed like a maze against the sky, alive with the screeching of birds and tangled with vines. I felt I was being swallowed by a great moist green mouth, and negotiating a sinewy trail into the heart of a great green lizard. All around were dense dark woods, and trees taller than the pillars of Sintra, grayish brown trunks fatter around than wagon wheels.

I lost my footing while I gazed at a huge lemon yellow butterfly as large as my hand, fluttering like a leaf that would not settle on the ground. Though I didn't fall, my slight gasp was heard by one of the women from the lagoon who was marching ahead. She stepped out of line, waited for me to pass her, then stepped behind me, as if to protect me from what might lurk at my back, or should I slip again.

It was only a few minutes walk farther, however, until we reached a clearing off the stream, obviously a village. There were seven round huts, one a stockade-like affair with wood pillars and a single raised floor. Each building, if one could call them that, had a roof made of woven palm fronds.

One or two huts had mud walls but for the most part these were open-air constructions. A few village elders sat regally on the ground. One woman wore a hammered gold bracelet roughly four fingers wide, and little else.

I watched the Admiral's eyes scan the entire scene, giving orders to the men to make a mental inventory of what items we might add in barter to these households. The Admiral walked from house to house, as if he were a purchasing agent. None of the local people raised any form of objection.

A single branch above my head began swaying wildly, and I caught a glimpse of a large brown rodent with a long emaciated tail, gnawing at the hard branch. Then before my eyes, the animal fell to the ground, knocked dead by a stone pitched with perfect accuracy by one of the younger men. He picked up the furry creature by its tail, and handed it to the woman who had seemed to take an interest in my welfare as we had walked.

I followed her into an open cooking area where I watched her force a sharpened reed into the animal's mouth, right through the animal's length. The rod was set between two notched sticks set in the ground, and the impaled animal left to be cooked later over an open flame.

"*Boucan*," the woman said to me, smiling at the sight of what I guessed would be a hearty meal.

"*Boucan*," I repeated. I've learned the name of an animal, I thought, but before I could pass this information along to Luis, the Admiral declared there was too little daylight remaining, and for safety's sake we should return to the ships.

192]

I smiled at the woman, and hoped she would understand I meant I hoped we would see each other again.

I walked back out of the giant lizard mouth. In the twilight, the sea shimmered almost golden, and the fragrant evening air was invigorating.

Once back on the ship, though, I lost this burst of energy. I realized I had not slept in almost 24 hours, and though I longed to watch the first sunset in this place, my body ached for rest. The Admiral had stopped his tender at the *Nina*, and so Juan and I were first to reach the flagship.

"I'll not have dinner tonight, Juan," I instructed "Please tell the Admiral."

I stepped into the cabin and listened as the oars of the men broke the sea in regular gentle splashes, men saying "goodnight, good appetite," the farthest they'd been from home in their lives.

Again I was unsure if this day had actually happened to me, if in crossing an ocean we had not crossed a line where mind and imagination mix, where all our words were tools for dreaming.

The Admiral's record book still lay on the table where he had thrust it at Pinzon.

I wished that this book was, as my husband had said, the only record, the one inarguable. But I knew it was not.

I slipped into the sheets gone limp in this new humidity and slept until dawn, never hearing or feeling my husband, until next morning, when he passed his hand through my hair on waking and leaving our bed. The record book had been put away.

Chapter Eighteen

Papaya, Coana, Iguana

Next day it was another gorgeous morning, and as soon as breakfast was done, everyone headed to shore. I rode with the Admiral, who now adopted Caro, the goldsmith, as his aide de camp, so to speak, and the two conferred en route about the quality and quantity of the gold here and how to get it.

Our tender beached with a whoosh, and no sooner had we pulled all the boats to shore, than the Indians again stood before us, as if conjured from thin air.

We walked under the lush translucent canopy to the clearing once more, but unlike the quiet afternoon of yesterday, the morning bustled with activities. Various Indians, mostly women, gathered fruits of every description: huge green lemons—the only fruit I recognized—plus coarse brownish fruits with briar-pocked skins, tiny fruits with fiber crowns, and clumps of beautifully curved, long yellow-green melons, still attached to their branches.

They piled this cornucopia at the foot of a giant fern, as if making offerings, and seemed to have no other mission for the morning. The *boucan* of the night before had been devoured, the firewood now a pile of exhausted dust.

The Admiral and Caro paid a good deal of attention to the jewelry of the elders, and attempted through Luis to determine the source of the wealth.

I spotted the woman who had embraced me so suddenly on the beach. She had slit one of the yellow melons with a stone, and seeing me, passed me an arc of it trickling with juice. It was exquisite, sweet and sugary, melting on my tongue. The center nest of the fruit was packed with shining black seeds, which the woman very gracefully let drop from her mouth into her hand and then tossed over her shoulder.

"Papaya," the woman suddenly said. Her name or the plant, I wondered.

"Papaya?" I inquired, pointing my forefinger to the woman herself. But she burst out laughing.

"Papaya?" I asked again, this time pointing to me.

She giggled anew, gathering the other women around us with the luster of her laugh.

"Papaya?" I questioned a third time, now pointing to the clump of yellow fruits on the floor.

"Papaya," they said in approving unison.

Eager to learn more words, I pointed to myself and said, "Felipa."

"Felipa," they all repeated.

I pointed to my hostess. "Felipa?" I asked.

"Coana," they said together. Perhaps that was her name.

"Coana?" I repeated, pointing around the circle to us all.

Then came a chorus—*Coana, Amaru, Ozama*—each woman in turn.

Then onto the pile of fruit—each one fingered and named by Coana—*mamey, guanabana, guava*. Names that sounded like they could be tapped out on a drum. New names in an ecstatic new world. I glanced around for Luis but did not see him.

Elated at my progress, I lost track of what the rest of our party was doing.

Coana and her friends then led me into one of the houses and began pounding a grainy powder between two stones, dripping water into the mixture until it became a mealy paste—*"casaba,"* they said. Did it mean bread, stone, grain?

I watched the women intently, for they were quite beautiful, coal-eyed, with burnt siena skin. I had practically ceased to notice their nudity, nature now seeming as fitting as any dress. Occasionally, one of them would finger my garments and giggle, but by and large, my lack of nudity did not seem to disturb them in the slightest. I noticed too that their foreheads were unusually flat, giving them an odd appearance at first glance, but their rich coloring and elegant bearing made them lovely to look at nevertheless.

Clearly while the men went about other business, the women tended house—the same division of labor the world over. Yet these women had also no fear of the forest. In command of their surroundings, they were equal to any of their men.

I could not discern who might be sisters, mothers or daughters. Bonded in a community of womanly chores, they all seemed to enjoy the familiarity of family.

When I emerged from the hut, I noticed the great pile of fruit was entirely gone. Coana took a step toward the forest, then glanced at me with an inviting look.

We walked into the density together. The dew of the morning sat in drops on impenetrable leaves, resistant crystal bubbles that in a few hours would be drawn up into nothingness by the searing sun.

Coana slithered ahead, never actually gone from my sight. There were countless butterflies—ocean blue and sun yellow and the palest green—fluttering among the wealth of blossoms. There were plants that seemed to grow in thin air, shooting off flowers not rooted anywhere that I could see.

But as I watched the butterflies judiciously selecting the most tempting site, I was beset upon by minute flying insects that had no problem at all in choosing where to land—me. In moments I was being pricked everywhere I was bare—arms, legs, even through my blouse. In this banquet of a forest, I was the most wanted morsel.

Loud buzzing sounded in my ears as if I had walked into a cloud of biting air. I wildly slapped myself, swatting my own scalp for they were attacking my head as well. Coana understood at once, and grabbed my arm, pulling me back to the clearing.

I had become a relief map of bumps. And perched there still on my arms were three of the largest mosquitoes I had ever seen, their needle noses like pencil points poised to stick. Surely they are not going to bite me again, I thought.

But I was amazed by their unwordly size and so I watched them do their work, for what difference could one bite more make now! First, they were immobile as if each were waiting to see what the other would do. Then, I felt the prick and watched a slight pinpoint of blood rise on my skin. I don't know why this fascinated me but soon I smashed the annoying flying cannibal, as well as the other two before they had a chance to bite.

Coana had watched me, making no move to intervene. Then she found among a collection of gourds lying on the ground, one particular brown one carved with a series of double spiral lines that contained a thick brown paste. She dipped her finger into it, then smeared the oily substance across her chest and down her arms. She held out the gourd to me.

"*Casaba,?*", I asked, thinking this was the substance I'd seen her pounding out earlier.

She said nothing, but smeared her arms again. I looked more closely at the substance. It was definitely made from plants, for there were still some crushed leaves in the otherwise smooth paste. No, this paste was not what I had seen before.

Could this substance soothe my insect bites, I wondered, for why else would she bring it to me now. I dipped my own finger into the gourd and tentatively smeared my arms. Coana nodded that I should continue. Brown in the gourd, the ointment was colorless on the skin.

I smeared it everywhere I had been bitten. Then Coana started toward the forest again. When I hesitated, she smiled and took my arm gently, urging me forward. We slipped into the green, but this time I was invulnerable. I even watched mosquitoes hovering over my skin like butterflies over the flowers, but never landing on my body. So, this was not necesarily a medicine to cure mosquito bites, but a repellent to prevent them in the first place. Amazing!

We gathered a host of fruits and came back to the clearing. I hadn't had a single new bite.

Pinzon was there among the woman as they wove palm fronds and pounded the various pastes that I now knew were likely of a great variety of uses.

"What have we here—a European woman bearing native fruit?"

I laughed and proudly said, "I've had an exquisitely full morning, Mr. Pinzon. I've eaten what is called 'papaya' and outsmarted the insects with this marvelous paste."

Having a foreign man around them did not appear to disturb the women. This ease of the sexes—it flouted every convention of my upbringing. How did they master it, with nudity as commonplace as the weather.

"I see that they have not yet donned the brocade robes of Cipangu," Pinzon observed wryly.

"No, indeed, but they do know every fruit and plant in this forest. Nothing bites through this paste, and look, you cannot even see it on my arm. I'm sure it comes from one bush or another."

Pinzon looked at my forearm more closely. "Absolutely perfect unmarred skin," he said, affecting the tone of a mock inspector.

"Not a thing is visible of your miracle cream," he continued. "Very interesting. But come along with me over here. De la Cosa and I have solved the riddle of those other plants."

"Wait," I said, just as Pinzon had turned his back. I took Coana's hand and brought her next to me.

"I believe her name is Coana," I said, introducing her to Pinzon.

"Martin Alonso," he replied gallantly to her. She looked at him warmly with her dark coal eyes focused straight on his. Perhaps looking in her eyes like that will keep him from glancing over her body, I heard myself think.

"*Papaya*," Coana then said to Pinzon, offering him the long fruit she held in her arms.

"Thank you, my sweet lady of the forest," he replied, taking the fruit in both hands as if receiving it it on a silver tray and smiling broadly at Coana, who did not look away.

Putting the fruits I had collected on the ground, I thanked the women with a smile. Coana knelt on the ground with the others to begin sorting the harvest.

"You've made a friend, I see," Pinzon noted, as we walked toward a gathering of men. "The women obviously gravitate to you."

"Oh they are so absolutely gentle," I replied, "and they know these woods like you and I know our ships."

"I daresay," Pinzon agreed.

"Where is the Admiral?" I wondered aloud.

"He's gone with Luis, Caro and one of the leaders farther inland."

"Have they learned something about gold?" I asked.

"It is very hard to gauge what they are learning. Caro just seems to be biting every piece of jewelry presented to him, and Luis has yet even to begin to crack the local language."

"I thought gold was gold, and that they'd be glad for any at all."

"No Madame, there are differences in grade. It's a fickle metal," Pinzon said.

"Well I'm sure they'll be satisfied since gold is, after all, only a secondary object of this journey."

"So we'd been led to think, but your husband seems bent on it, if you pardon me," Pinzon said impatiently.

"My husband, no doubt, regards the presence of gold as a confirmation of our whereabouts. He must seek it out as part of his duty to the Sovereigns."

"Yes, I suppose that is one way to look at it, to take a defense of him."

Pinzon abruptly changed the subject, and stepped briskly ahead. This man—what *did* he think of my husband?

"Hurry, Madame," Pinzon admonished, "or else they will have stopped."

In the center of one of the largest buildings, several men had gathered, and a collection of the dark brown leaves we had been offered was lying on the ground. No women sat in the group.

A muscular young man with his hair tied back off his face bent over the leaves and selected a few, seemingly based on length, quality and color, taking great pains to achieve an acceptable assortment. Then, by means of rubbing two pointed twigs swiftly together, spinning them between his palms, he ignited the leaves, not burning them, but getting them to smolder.

When there was a constant stream of smoke, the Indian pointed one end of a hollowed reed into the pile, the other into one of his nostrils, and inhaled the vapors up into his head. He closed his eyes and seemed to drift into a calm reverie, passing the reed to another man, who in turn inhaled.

Other men followed suit.

It was hard to tell the purpose of this ritual, but there was no laughing or smiling associated with it. And these leaves surely meant something, for they had offered them as gifts to us.

After all the Indians had taken in some smoke, they pushed the leaves apart with sticks and put the fire out. Then the men picked out the uncharred remnants, cleaned them of ash, and put them carefully between two sheets of bark, presumably to await next use. They did not offer us any leaves to smoke, but neither did they in any way hide their activities.

"What says the prosperous apothecary about these leaves?" Pinzon chided de Harana, who had also witnessed the odd event. "Medicinal perhaps?"

De Harana was as befuddled as the rest of us. "I dare say not, for healing smoke would clear the head, not fog it."

"You know I doubt a European would ever plug his nose with burning leaves," observed de la Cosa to Martin Alonso and the rest of us, "but if there were some taste involved, we ought to be able to interest our compatriots in this."

Pinzon stepped up to the Indian who had first begun the inhaling, and gestured diplomatically to the bark sheets. When no one stopped him, he removed one brown leaf, and drew it to his nose.

"It is certainly aromatic enough," he announced.

"*Cohiba*," said the Indian.

"Do you think that is his name?" Martin Alonso asked me.

"You ask a novice. I've had only one haphazard lesson. But I thought I heard one of the men call the leaves '*tabac*.' "

"I suppose the context will come eventually," Pinzon resignedly said. He put the leaf carefully in his doublet pocket.

The Admiral and Caro returned.

"They say that gold is on the next island called *Bohio*," Caro reported.

"But how did you extract that name?" I asked, curious.

"There is a smaller settlement inland, and the people there told us." Caro explained.

Luis then said, "but Admiral, I believe, from my conversations here, that *bohio* is their word for 'house.' "

"No, Luis, I beg to differ," the Admiral replied without a single hesitation, "I am sure they understood my question and gave me the name of a place."

"Perhaps I ought to accompany you the next time," Luis suggested, "for I have been learning things, as has Madame."

"We've seen it is very easy to be confused with meanings," I offered. "Just here, there seem to be two words for these leaves, *cohiba* and *tabac*."

"Maybe that means there is more than one type of leaf in the pile," the Admiral observed.

Then he declared we would stay on here awhile more, until we had explored the island fully and gotten our bearings.

And so we came freely to the village, which was full of fascination. When we came ashore, I always saw something new and began to wonder whether I was indeed sharpening my skills of observation, or whether each day the Indians chose to unveil some new aspect of their lives.

They were a people that knew no metal, no wheels, no gunpowder, no fire other than what they could start by their stick-spinning method. They hunted or fished every day for fresh food, and seemed to live exclusively from the forest and the sea. Their implements were either stone or shell. Yet, for all their nudity and wilderness ways, they were not savage in any sense. On the contrary, they exuded civility.

I could never have anticipated, in all our time of preparation in Europe, the joy I would find in being here. To encounter such a placid and welcoming society had never entered my thoughts.

Here every question met a question. There was no Toscanelli letter to study, no previous reports to digest. There was nothing to read anywhere on the subject, no one to consult, no reference book, no reference at all.

I could now understand my father's burning drive to explore, and why my mother endured the solitude of Porto Santo, so that they could remain at the portal of the unknown world.

And in the excitement of stalking details such as learning the correct name of a fruit, much more basic questions rushed into my mind—like where did these people come from and how did they arrive? Did they row their huge log boats from Asia and sprinkle themselves along its coast among Marco Polo's countless islands? Why didn't Toscanelli refer to them? Did they too build great churches we hadn't yet seen and who indeed did they worship in the absence of Christ?

On our third afternoon on this island that my husband had christened San Salvador, I was ashore with Chachu who had himself frequently gone fishing with the Indians. Gone were our meals of salted beef, so indulged were our palates now in the freshest of food from the sea, all of which so far had proven delightfully edible.

Chachu and I watched as a group of Indian men and women stood in the shallows in a circle. Then they pulled us into the water with them good-naturedly. We stood and copied their flailing of the surface, the intent of which was to herd swimming fish within the corral we had formed. But they were not at all interested in the quantity they were gathering. They were instead after a particular fish, the one they called *guaicano*, which had a rather long tail and a sucker on its back.

At last an Indian woman caught one with her bare hands. Chachu and I were amazed. While she held her prize just under the surface of the water, another woman tied a long raw yarn to the *guaicano's* tail, no easy feat for the slippery creature wiggled mightily.

Then they released the tethered fish. Like cannonshot, the *guaicano* fled through the sea until it found a plump large fish to which it could affix itself, affixing seeming to be its only business in life. Thus, the Indians needed only to rein in the guaicano, their living hook, and the usually very succulent fish to which the guaicano had chosen to cling.

Pinzon, who happened upon me with Chachu as we sat drying off on the beach after the episode, called it a kingly method, ''for surely a king could fish from shore and never get the least bit wet.''

"Or a queen," I teased back, "for the women do well at getting these fish, you see.''

"Or a queen, of course, Madame, if you like.'' He chuckled.

Another time I watched the men spit a huge lizard with plates of skin like armor. None of us had ever seen such a creature.

"*Boucan*," Coana had pronounced as she prepared to skewer the animal.

I had thought *boucan* meant the rabbit-sized rodent they had cooked a few nights back. But with the passing of time, I gleaned that any creature cooked on a spit was called "*boucan*"—a way of cooking not what was being cooked.

From Coana, I acquired other words gradually. The rodent was in fact a *jutia;* the giant lizard, *iguana,* and the swift carved boats were known as *canoas.*

And, waving her arms over the beaches and the hills and embracing all the trees in a wide arc, one day Coana said "*Guanahani.*" I assumed it was their name for the place, and when I told the Admiral, he wrote the local word in parentheses next to the name he had bestowed on his map.

Indeed, the Admiral spent most of his time charting the coast line and inquiring, over and over, about gold. He to his occupations and me to mine, our time passed, and as much as it was possible in such a new and unusual place to establish a routine, we did. At night we chatted generally about our day's observations but I did not probe him anymore about what he intended next.

We slept together without much intimacy, for both of us fell asleep almost at once from all our walking and the heavy air.

It was only after we'd been in the bay several days that I began to suspect that Pinzon was spending his nights on land.

Chapter Nineteen

The Flickering Fireworms

It bothered me that Pinzon seemed to come and go from our fold at will. At the end of our daytime visits when the rest of us prepared to return to the ships, he would linger. I had assumed he eventually made his way to *Pinta*, but invariably, when we came ashore in the morning, he was already there, happily peeling fruit, passing it among the Indian men and women who just as happily surrounded him. He always had that pleased look of a man who had slept well through the night.

Yet who could hold it against him if he preferred to stay among the aromatic woods on terra firma, and learn the ways of the Indians in far more detail than the Admiral or I, or any of the other crew?

But clearly, this first landfall was not Cipangu. And though the Admiral himself admitted its beauty exceeded the loveliest part of Andalucia, he wanted to move on.

The morning he had decreed we would sail, I went ashore with Luis, whom my husband had charged with selecting the Indians to travel with us. I went along because I wanted to say goodbye to Coana, at least, and to return to her a bowl she had loaned me to carry some papayas to the ship.

I felt ambivalent about the idea of Indian guides. Perhaps they would be useful as we proceeded, but I couldn't ignore the stories I knew about Africans who feared the ocean and who came to the court of Portugal against their will. One after the other, princes like Caramansa had given in, and soon the African continent had become a peeled Portuguese plum.

But here, I believed, we were not interested in conquest, these lands merely lying between us and our destination. And so I convinced myself that with Indians travelling with us, we could learn more about these places. Then the Admiral would release them on our homeward journey, once we had met with the great Khan.

So Luis and I set out, while the Admiral and de la Cosa planned the next few days of watch and duty, the men now thoroughly spoiled by the proximity of land, and each having in varying degrees of intensity taken Pinzon's approach to island life. Only the Admiral seemed content on the ship.

Pinzon, as usual, sat barechested on the beach, the juice of an orange fruit glistening in his beard. Two Indian men sat next to him fingering his dagger case, but taking pains not to touch the dagger itself, for by now everyone on the island knew that the metal that glinted did no good when touched by fingers. A few other men cleared a fallen tree trunk of the ash that remained after it had been burned hollow, apparently in the last stages of preparing one of their splendid canoes.

Luis began his bargaining, after taking a drink of welcome as well as removing his shirt, following Pinzon's example. Pinzon was now shirtless almost all the time among the Indians and his chest had become a dark red-brown from the sun that hung like a yellow globe overhead here all day long.

The Indian men never made any attempt to shield their nakedness from me, and I, though becoming rather used to it, still had an instinct to avert my eyes, or to sit in such a way that I did not see their private parts. I became rather expert at shifting my position in relationship to their movements, so much so that Luis, apparently distracted by my fidgeting said, "Madame are you uncomfortable in some way?"

Since it was too embarrassing to explain, I simply said I could not get used to sitting on sand, and excused myself to walk alone down the beach.

In the early morning there was no heat yet, and the cool breezes of the night before were fading, so the temperature was always perfect. The lushness made Porto Santo, even Madeira, seem deprived—blazing pink orchids, fiery crimson fuscia, even blushing orange tropical roses as wild as weed—many lovely plants we could recognize and many we didn't. Being here made me wonder if I could ever take any pleasure in my own home islands again, for these gave new meaning to the island ideal.

Two red parrots flashed across the woods—they seemed to always fly in pairs—and I watched them until they settled comfortably on the same branch, their combined weight barely bending it.

"Aren't they brilliant?" I heard a voice exclaim. It was Pinzon. He said he thought he'd follow me and give Luis privacy in which to stumble with linguistics.

Pinzon had rolled his trousers to his knees, and walked alongside me in the water, wet sand sucking at his ankles as he strode, the imprints of his feet instantly washed away by the lapping waves.

"How is Luis getting on?" I wanted to know.

"Who can say? All that is happening now is that he is eating a lot of fruit. Poor man. His best efforts have yet to add up to a working knowledge of this language." Pinzon laughed heartily at the thought of the likeable Luis trying to coax the Indians.

We walked along for a few minutes, until Pinzon said suddenly, "Shall I show you my camp? I've got to clear it out anyway as we are sailing." So he *had* been sleeping here!

Only minutes from the sea, there was a simple hut, a *bohio* for one—that having proven to be the word for "house" and not the name of an island, I had learned one day from Coana.

"My goodness, did you build this so fast?" I asked.

"No, I found it in one of my wanderings," Pinzon answered "No one seemed to be living here. Step inside."

It was empty, save for the net bedding the Indians used, a brightly striped cotton sling, what they called *hamaca.*

"They are wonderful for sleeping in," Pinzon remarked.

The fabric looked familiar to me, but before I asked, he said, "One of them fixed it up for me with a bolt of cloth I brought out from Spain."

All materials on the ships belonged to the Enterprise, but I could not begrudge Pinzon his splendid hammock. Then I realized—this was practically the same fabric pattern I had used on the pillows and sofa of Porto Santo. The hammock rocked like a crescent moon.

Pinzon tossed himself in it. I couldn't imagine its being comfortable, but he showed me how one could lie flat and swing the wide cut part under one's body, then stretch it diagonally across. In this way, the body was almost in the same position as in an ordinary bed.

Pinzon had put a few books around, and had a spray of dark orange orchids sitting on the ground in the corner in an empty wine cask.

"I change the flowers each day, read by candlelight and allow the birds to sing me to sleep. What more could a man want?" he said contentedly.

I had no ready answer, for this indeed seemed existence reduced to the perfect minimum, all satisfactions literally within a finger-tip's reach.

"I thought they all lived together in the villages," I said, wondering why this one house would be off alone.

"So did I," Pinzon replied, "but perhaps this was built for someone sick or dying."

"These slings would be useful for the sailors," I noted as I watched Pinzon asway. "They would be immune to the pitching of the ocean."

"What a splendid idea," he replied, "I'll bring this one to the Admiral and maybe we can have some others made, though I doubt we'll convince your husband to trade away all the cloth of his mission for hammocks for the crew!"

"You did not hesitate, I see," I teased mildly.

"That is our little secret, I trust," Pinzon replied good-natured-ly, "not that a woman should have secrets from her husband, of course."

I turned to face him, suddenly aware that in fact, I probably ought not even be here alone with him. Still I could not deny how much I liked his company.

"I have no secrets from the Admiral," I replied, "but I will keep your confidence on the cloth this time."

"A good woman indeed," Pinzon responded gaily. He looked like he had been born in his hammock under this green-hazed sky.

"You'd rather not be leaving here, I venture," he said, almost reading my thoughts.

"And who," I replied, "does wish to leave such a mesmerizing place behind?"

"Your husband does not seem to mind."

"My husband has other business," I said, by way of reminding both of us that Japan had not yet been reached.

"Yet, you seem to feel the pull of this island as I do."

I admitted that I too would prefer to stay on, and that I longed to travel the island's folds and valleys, to go inland. But this was not what we'd come for, and we had, after all, a purpose.

"Purpose, yes, of course," Pinzon agreed, now flipping himself out of the hammock and pacing from one side of the small hut to the other.

"But what of this? These are riches too, I'd say." He unrolled a pelt from his sack of personal belongings, showing me a collection of various woods, each twig shaved to reveal a stunning variety of grains.

I could not disagree, and we fell into an animated talk about plants and flowers we had both been collecting. Pinzon's eyes sparkled as he spoke of the soothing properties of aloe, of cracking wild cinnamon seeds with his teeth, of the resins that colored the skin that grew in certain prickly pears. These thin-skinned burrs were uncannily similar to the "dragon's blood" seeds that Seixas brought me on Porto Santo. Pinzon handed me one and I crushed my finger into it as if through eggshell, releasing a waxy orange dye.

A pair of red parrots landed on the side of the bohio, perhaps the same two as before. Pinzon imitated their chirp and seemed to be in a dialogue with them. He had returned the blue parrot to its original owner in anticipation of our leaving.

"These birds are almost tame." He said, "in fact this place is a domain of the tame."

"Perhaps too tame," I observed, for here indeed all seemed ours as freely as the fruit.

"Your husband does not refuse the ease of surrender in this region," Pinzon remarked abruptly.

I was annoyed.

"My husband again. You seem to find any way you can to bring him up!"

"Oh, should I not?" Pinzon threw back, his eyes glinting with self-assurance. He let a few seconds pass, then changed the subject.

"By the way, I've solved the riddle of the lights we saw at landfall," he announced. By now all had agreed they had been the torches of the Indians out in their canoes, and so I didn't know of any riddle.

"You simply will not conform, will you, Pinzon," I quipped.

"Conformity, Madame, did not carry me to this paradise on Earth. Nor you. Let yourself breathe this fragrant air, dear Madame, for no one but us has ever smelled this sweetness. Do you wish to hear my theory or not?"

"Who could say 'no' to such a challenge," was all I could think to reply. Of course I wished to hear his tale.

And then he relayed a rather fantastic story that he said he learned from the Indians.

"You remember, dear Madame, that we arrived here beneath a moon that had almost perfectly reached third quarter.

"There exists in these lands a certain fireworm that lives in shallow waters. They are, amazingly, luminescent, candelit we

[207

might say. The females come to the surface, only at this phase of the moon, and glow there to attract a mate. The males, duly attracted, then swim to the surface as well, flickering their own lights so that for miles and miles the sea is full of flashing fireworms, lost in their own universe. What we saw was the beacon of their mating ritual, so to speak.'' Pinzon said with relish.

''It is too incredible,'' I said.

''It is perfectly credible,'' Pinzon defended, ''if you only open your mind to the idea. I've seen several of these worms and can well imagine what masses of them would look like.''

''It has no basis in science,'' I insisted.

''No science that we know of, but I believe it's true. Will you not at least agree mine is by far the more romantic explanation?''

''All your explanations, dear Pinzon, are the more romantic ones,'' I let myself say.

''I am glad you noticed,'' he replied playfully ''And can this wonderful tale of the fireworms be another of our secrets then?'' he whispered.

I nodded, avoiding his searing gaze.

Pinzon gathered his belongings, untied the vine ropes of his hammock and put it under his arm. He left the *bohio* just as he found it, glanced back and threw it the kiss of a man who knew he would never return.

''You don't seem so reluctant to leave it behind, after all,'' I commented.

''In this fabulous garden, madame, the next blossom will surely be as beautiful,'' he replied.

We stepped back through the bush and made our way to the beach where we had left Luis.

When we arrived, we saw that Indians surrounded the beleaguered translator. Coana too was there, observing. Luis was perfectly safe, but he didn't seem to have succeeded in separating any of the men from their island. When we arrived, he said he thought two had agreed to come along, but all of a sudden, when he gestured to the tender, they had run back to the bush. He was now in the stage of renegotiation.

Luis simply did not have the vocabulary he needed. The Indians gave no sign of being willing to move and the new canoe was lying untried in the sand.

A pistol shot was fired from *Santa Maria* and a wisp of smoke rose into the sky. The Admiral wanted us.

"I've got to give up," Luis admitted, "I just do not understand why they suddenly ran off. We'll have to do without them," he said dejectedly.

I had a thought, for I knew what pride these people took in their craft.

"*Santa Maria*," I pronounced as grandly as I could to the group.

They stood by silently.

I took Pinzon's dagger from its sheath, and the Indians stepped back quickly. To reassure them, I plunged the blade into the sand to show that I did not intend to use it, waiting a moment or so.

I took the knife again and pointed it first to the canoe they had just completed, then toward the flagship. When the Indians made no move to stop me, I cut a small hole into the bow of the canoe, well above the water line. I slashed a dangling rope off the startled Pinzon's hammock.

I tied the line to the canoe, and made a gesture of pulling it, pointing again with the dagger out to sea.

With this, the Indians pushed off the boat and jumped aboard, paddling energetically toward our ship. Coana and the women eyed the spectacle, unsure what to make of it. I handed the bowl I had borrowed to Coana, who received it without a word.

On a voyage of discovery, there was no etiquette of goodbye and so I took one of Coana's hands between both of mine, embracing her as she had me on our very first day here, a farewell that seemed ludicrously inadequate in the face of the unremitting pleasure I had taken in her company and her world.

Then, Pinzon, Luis and I embarked the tender and left the ravishing island behind.

The canoe had already reached *Santa Maria*. We three stepped aboard and one of the Indians handed the rope on his craft to Chachu, who tied their vessel alongside ours.

Throughout this operation, Luis and Pinzon had said nothing, though Luis admitted he should have guessed that the men would not wish to leave behind a canoe they had just finished making.

My husband scowled, however, when he saw the additional encumbrance of their rather heavy boat. Luis explained that without it, the Indians would not have come along.

Then Pinzon interjected. "It was your wife's idea, Admiral. You ought to have seen her reason it out with them, then take my dagger and take command. It was absolutely brilliant, my Admiral, a brilliant performance. Just what we needed."

My husband made no comment but gave orders that the Indians be fed and cared for and our anchors be pulled, at last, to sail.

"Not everything need be a secret," Pinzon whispered to me, just before the *Pinta*'s tender came alongside to take him back to his ship.

I could not tell if the Admiral had overheard.

Chapter Twenty

The Greenlit Beach

We sailed through narrow channels, passing small cay after small island, as if threading a needle, but my husband did not wish to stop everywhere, aching as he was for Japan. He did name each place, adding the new points to the maps he hadn't stopped drawing since our landfall now several weeks ago. We always anchored at night, though, for the Admiral feared grounding, the many shoals terrifyingly visible in these clear waters.

And as usual Pinzon kept to his own pace, weaving in and out of our sight, staying mostly ahead. Rumors flew that he was making stops that we were not, but the Admiral could not corroborate this without also stopping and losing more time.

But though we sailed rather nonchalantly through this region as if we'd seen it all before, it was, we had to remember, entirely alien to us. Despite the Admiral's being in command, events outside his control were bound to happen.

For example, the morning after we had left San Salvador, there was no sign of the Indians we had taken along—they were gone with their canoe.

The Admiral at first fumed, railing at the watchman for not stopping their escape, but he also did not wish the Indians' leaving to be perceived as a failure on his part. So he simply said that, on second thought, the Indians had made too many extra people on board, especially since they did not seem to know a thing about Japan.

"In any case, their canoe was too heavy to tow," he remarked to de Harana, adding "it was not a good idea to have it along," perhaps thinking I could not hear him.

Good idea or not, I was privately rather glad the Indians had gone home.

So far, we had seen little gold, but the trading with the Indians we met continued unabated. And here the men, even the merest gromet who in Spain probably would never even be able to afford a horse, availed themselves of Indian bearers and carriers, enjoying the innocence and inexperience of people who would exchange their very best for a chipped Spanish glass, carrying the purveyor of such trinkets anywhere he wished on a hammock slung between two sticks. If the ship blurred social classes, this new land propelled the simplest men to grand delusions.

But of all this I did not speak to my husband. I drew more and more into my own thoughts—thank goodness I could write them. And often when I shared an observation with the Admiral, he discounted the pleasures of what we held in our hand in favor of what might lie ahead. He had no thoughts for anything except Cipangu and where it might be.

He brightened, at last, one day when land again came into view and we sailed several hours without seeing its end. A long reef guarded the coast, and we maneuvered easily for the seas were perfectly calm. The other ships soon followed, having been well within earshot of our signal cannon blast.

The Admiral ordered we anchor and sent an exploratory party ashore. They returned saying they'd seen no people, but that the woods were denser than any woods yet, and fresh water was abundant. The Admiral decided to take stock himself, and see whether to launch a more extensive party inland to the Great Khan, for surely, he thought, this was the largest island so far and probably our destination.

It was another beguiling place. The trees came to the shore like soldiers, giant tall palms, straight as spears.

Landings had their ritual. The Admiral stepped ashore first, planted a cross or unfurled the Sovereign flag. We weren't met by people here, but when we were, the Admiral also made the first exchange of goods and words, putting down his sword to show peaceful intentions when he felt sure we were subject to no attack. Then the men cut down as many trees as there was time, for as much cooking wood as we could carry. They seemed to always overestimate, leaving much cut wood behind like the bones of a half-eaten beast. They always resupplied with water, and then, tasks done, every man took to land, breathing the Indies perfume.

So now the same rhythm began, and the Admiral and his officers met in our cabin to discuss how to make the necessary overtures to the Emperor of Japan. That we might not be at the Emperor's doorstep did not deter the meeting.

At moments like this, everyone had a job to do but me. I decided to explore the cove a little further and went ashore as soon as there was a tender free.

The woods, though dense, were by no means impenetrable, and so I stepped up from the sand, and began walking.

Here it seemed as if the plants had become intoxicated on their own hallucinogenic properties, each plant trying to outdo the other in the shapes and metamorphoses it could make.

I stopped for the sheer pleasure of watching a bright scarlet butterfly hover at the mouth of a scarlet flower, a living wisp of color bouncing above the plant, as if it were a petal dislodged and given wings, seeking and teasing its grounded twin to take to the air.

I walked into a clump of towering papaya trees, their thick tough petals like ungrained muslin. And there was not a single bird, or even a handful, but an orchestra of whistlers and nightingales, and small red birds whose hollow reedy calls sounded like the King's flutes being played through water.

I crossed a very narrow neck of land, with sea easily visible behind and ahead. When I came to the end of the woods and emerged at the ocean again, I felt I had been passed between the elements—water to wood to water.

I stood between two ridges of black stone, crumbly to the touch and scarred like an aging face. These pocked ledges gave out on a rounded wedge of golden sand, as if the sea had felt along the rocky shore until it found a single unobstructed opening on which to leave an amber kiss.

Shaded by the stones, the sand was cool to the feet. In this vault between sun and shadow, a single lime green hummingbird hovered, taking pollen from the flowers that grew from cracks in the rocks in seams of fertile moist soil.

I walked out to the shore and contemplated the flawlessness I'd found. The sea poured into the cove, channeled by the rocky coast into waves, each flowing in from a different direction to splash together like cymbals. White lace foam broke where the waves met, spreading, and then flowing to shore, fizzling into the sand in bubbles.

From here I could see more land ahead of me, a long neck outcropping that ran along the horizon, wispy white clouds veiling the highest hill. Perhaps the peak was the court of Japan, I mused.

[213

The walk had made me very hot, so I stepped into the water. It hissed gently around my ankles, then my knees. I bent into the next wave and cooled myself to the waist before returning to rest on the sand.

There were many sea bean trees, the black seed pods of Porto Santo, once odd messengers, now so common they littered the ground. It was easy to see how a wind could snap at one of them and flip it into these converging waves, sink it to the bottom, lift it up again, toss it into larger waves beyond the reefs and set it drifting far away.

Seeds and flowers were the essence of this place, the clues of the sea, this too full bowl of ocean that tipped in all directions but never spilled, pouring itself to the east, only to be carried west again.

I lay down on the beach and it spread warmth through my body just as at home. I listened as the sea still hit the sharp black crumbling rocks around me, breaking like distant cannon fire, and fell asleep.

When I awoke, nothing had changed and I realized that this was the first time in my entire life that I had been anywhere without family or friends, with no scaffold of society—no chaperones, no husband, no courtly contacts, no crew, no one.

On this beach, as never before, I realized a world of my own discovery. In its unutterable peace, I felt a second soul had come to dwell inside me, having tried with each succeeding wave to gain entry, finally winning, filling the space of my having left everything familiar so very far behind.

Chapter Twenty One

The Seductive Shore

I returned to this private place each day we were at anchor. The three ships stayed on the other side of the isthmus. No one asked me where I was going, or apparently missed my presence, for I slipped away while most of the men were busy with shipboard activity and returned before the cooks were beginning dinner.

Nor did the Admiral ask for me, engrossed as he was in keeping his journal, plotting our progress, and planning with his lieutenants, particularly de la Cosa, how this land could return profit to the Sovereigns, even though it was demonstrably not yet Japan, the inland excursions having thus far turned up nothing.

At the greenwater cove, I felt I had at least one concrete function—to enjoy being there. I bundled my swimming clothes—short cut trousers and a muslin blouse—and found a place to change and stash my shipboard clothes between the rocks. Then I stepped onto the beach and dipped my body into the sea, so clear I could see each slight hair on my toes.

Here I kept my notes and wrote up the plants I had collected. Here too I could sit quietly, uninterrupted, and consider my place in the whole of what we were doing. I was not only without skill for these lands, I was largely without skill for our journey. Unlike the women I had seen here, I had not a single talent for managing without the daily support of our ship.

True, I had suggested the western route—a truth, however, I had so buried from public view, I was its only keeper.

And because these lands throbbed with natural riches beyond what I had ever seen in my life, or beyond what either my husband or I could have ever planned for, my purposeless seemed even more profound to me.

At the cove, I could give vent to these thoughts. If there was a difference between exploration and discovery, it was perhaps that only exploration could be kept private.

In the empty universe I alone had found, I could explore the company of myself.

Which was why I was disconcerted, one afternoon, to see as I stepped onto the beach, that somebody else was swimming in the water, about 10 feet from shore.

I could not make out the face at first, but when I stepped closer, the man raised his hand, and so I guessed that it must have been someone from the ship who had, just as I had, wandered through the woods. I was very disappointed that someone else could have also easily come here, so readily traced my path.

I sat down on the sand and waited but the man stayed in the water. He seemed to have no problem swimming freely despite the pull of the sea. I watched him, still unsure who it was.

But then he began waving to attract my attention. And I knew. Of course. Who else. The bobbing beard was Pinzon's. He yelled, "Madame, it's me Martin Alonso. Hello!"

I signaled back. This man would naturally be the one to seek out and find a niche of beach lost to the eyes of everybody else. I watched him move to and fro until I began to become alarmed that perhaps the currents had become too much for him.

"Pinzon!" I yelled, "Are you all right?"

No answer.

"Martin Alonso," I called again, "can you not reach the shore?"

No answer still, though he continued swimming, moving neither closer nor farther out to sea.

Then, he shouted "I would love to come to shore but I cannot, for I am bathing in the original sense of the word and I am not a fit sight!"

What? Now it was I who could not quite hear. The waves slammed against the rocks, taking up every word.

"I said I have left my garments on the shore. I cannot come to land if you remain there," Pinzon repeated loudly.

Now I noticed a pile of clothing neatly stacked a few yards away. Pinzon indeed—naked in the ocean.

"I'll avert my eyes," I offered, for I did not wish to be driven from my beach by the brazen nudity of this Spaniard. I turned my back.

I could hear him reaching shallower water, huffing as he dragged his legs against the light surf, slashing into the breaking waves. Then he stepped ashore and a moment later announced, "All-clear."

I turned around again, and there he sat on the sand, his shirt draped across his legs, covering himself as the Indians cover themselves with leaves. He did not appear to have any intention of getting dressed.

I sat down, although not close to him. We watched the transparent waves, the sun shining through them as they broke.

"It's rather wild compared to other beaches we've seen," I commented, a bit unsure what to make of the odd situation. Though I knew at home I could never have endured the awkwardness, here I did not wish to rush away.

Pinzon squinted, drawing up the skin around his eyes. Salt dried in his beard, and his eyes seemed to burn him.

"And terribly salty," he said, licking his lips fresh, as then he said, "but very wonderful."

"I know," I answered, then regretting it for I did not particularly want anyone to know I'd been swimming at this place.

"Indeed, I've watched you sometimes enjoying this sea like a child in a bath."

"You've been following me?" I charged, suddenly warm with embarrassment.

"Not exactly. I've gone back to the ships when I've seen you here. I came ahead today only because the beach seemed empty."

I had never seen or sensed him. Had he watched me change my clothes, I wondered? He seemed so nonchalant and yet I flushed at the thought that he had been there when I slipped among the rocks and stood naked studying the hummingbirds.

I commented again on the power of the sea before us.

"Yes it's hard to believe the sea turtles use this place to nest. One would think they are too lumbering to resist the power and reach the shore," he remarked.

"How do you know about that?" I questioned, again surprised by this man who seemed to have been everywhere already. He described how giant turtles as big as water barrels haul up onto the shore, dig madly into the sand, and lay a bundle of eggs, there to be hatched by the warmth of the beach.

"You have seen this?" I asked.

"Indians told me, or at least I believe that is what they said, as we all must intuit rather than know what they actually say."

"There are Indians here?" I said, suddenly looking all around us.

"I imagine, Madame, that there are Indians everywhere we go, though we would never know it." He spoke matter-of-factly, then continued.

"Haven't you noticed the blackened rocks where you hang your clothes? I am sure they camp here to trap the turtles and take their eggs."

"Have you told my husband?" I pressed.

"I am the captain of one of his ships, madame, and not responsible for news. He could be here himself if he wished."

"You are arrogant," I replied, though I was unable to truly fill my voice with anger.

"Arrogance, like beauty, madame, is in the eyes of the beholder. Surely you do not believe me truly arrogant."

He had, as usual, scattered my displeasure and let it sputter out, like the last flames of a cooking fire.

We talked again about the Indians, and what we each had noticed. Pinzon had made keen observations, there was no doubt, and had in fact learned more of their language than anyone else.

"The Indians appear to worship the stones and trees, for I've seen many rituals of smoking before idols depicting the forest, snakes, birds, and so forth," Pinzon related. His eyes brimmed with appreciation for their knowledge and their courage.

"It took real sailor's strength to row away from the flagship, for the seas were very choppy," he said of the flight of the other night, "and to be indifferent to whether we would take retribution."

He had obviously seen the Indians go and done nothing to stop them.

"We'd not have followed them anyway, I'm sure," I replied, "for my husband did not want to be encumbered by the canoe. He plans to take along some other people, later, for these islands are much the same to him."

"That is why your husband keeps such constant record, presumably," Pinzon replied, "so he can somehow tell one from the other, though otherwise he seems not to reflect at all on what is happening around him."

"And you do, I suppose," I defied.

"Would you be sitting here having this conversation if you believed I did not?"

No, of course I would not have been. I curled my toes deeper into the sand.

Pinzon too dug with his feet, using his arches to form the sand into a damp pointy mound.

Then he broke the silence.

"Do you see the Indian face in the mountain across there?"

There was a notched hill on the arm of land that reached around the cove just across from where we sat, but I said I could discern no figure.

"Can't you read the flattened forehead and the open mouth?" Pinzon questioned, surprised I did not see what he did.

"No, I cannot make it out, really," I admitted with frustration.

"Perhaps we'll learn someday that Indians found the flattened head attractive. Perhaps the women even use a board to flatten their newborns' heads. Only such a trauma could explain why they all look that way," Pinzon said, still staring straight ahead.

But I dissented strongly.

"No mother would deliberately deform a child," I disagreed, standing up now to get a better view.

"Madame, deformity too is relative. Can't you see the outline now? Stand and bend your head to the side."

I did, and squinted and finally saw the profile of an Indian across the bay, with fully flattened forehead, mouth agape, as if dropped open in sleep or in crying out with pain or pleasure.

Pinzon was right. But I had now bent over to the point of dizziness. I lost my balance and fell over in the sand, sprawling like flatbread. I began laughing uncontrollably for it seemed such an absurd, ungraceful thing to have happened.

Pinzon laughed too, adding "Aha, I toppled you with the legend of the rock."

"What legend?" I asked, still giggling and trying to right myself.

"The one that says whoever fails to see the Indian face on first glance is doomed to die of amusement, the one I just made up to make you laugh," he said, smiling broadly. Then, in a split second, the meaning turned.

Suddenly the hiss of the sea seemed to travel along my spine. It was as if the thick bark of years of hoping for these sensations had fallen away, leaving them bare to grasp like polished beach stones suddenly uncovered in the sand. There was a knowing instant between us.

His eyes read my willingness. They held mine long enough to be sure, and then Pinzon moved closer, letting his nimble fingers trace my eyes and lips. He took my face between his hands, closer, and pressed his seawarmed mouth on mine. I swallowed his kiss and kissed him back. He murmured my name over and over as no man had ever done.

I was mad to be doing it, yet mad not to, for I pulsed with longing for Pinzon after months of not knowing what to call my confused and swelling feelings for him.

In seconds, his shirt fell away from his legs, and he sat as naked as an Indian with me in his arms. Now, I did not look away, for I wanted to see his entire body, the first time I had seen a nude man so close, so erect, so present.

Soon he reached under my blouse. I gasped, for my whole bare breasts had never been held in a man's hands before. They had never been cupped, nor stroked as Martin Alonso stroked them, travelling their rises. He was the first to summon the deep lying want that flowed now so potently, so easily, within me. I was powerless to resist him, naked now as well.

He gently lay me down and lay himself on top of me, but he did not rush, and there was no need to. Nor was there here any need to be silent, to think of others listening. His hands found every place my own husband had never touched, taking my breasts now full in his mouth, swilling them with his tongue as if to draw all the wine from a swollen wineskin.

And when he entered me at last, I craved him, and held onto him, until the very end, until we both cried out in satisfied desire. At long last, I held a man inside me well beyond the very end, until I was sure there was nothing of ourselves left.

We washed in the greenlit water, but did not talk of what had happened, for there was no need yet to define or name our feelings like another island we had found.

We returned to the ships separately, but met again the very next day. Soon I was seeing Pinzon every afternoon, while the Admiral remained unnoticing.

For my part, I lost all interest in the East; my lover was my new ambition.

He whispered that the sun shone through the lucid lightness of my nipples, that the sea's strength was feeble in the face of his love for me—sweet, romantic, wondrous words.

While reaching Japan remained the Admiral's haunting obsession, mine was to stop at as many islands as possible, so I could meet Pinzon.

Chapter Twenty Two

The Rapids of Fruit and Flower

I know I have written much of my love for the Admiral, and my first years with my husband were full of the brimming power of my feelings for him. But what was happening between me and Pinzon was so profoundly different, that if love was what I had given my husband, then my lover and I had invented a new feeling for which perhaps only the Indians of this place have a word, a word we would not recognize if we heard it, a word that nevertheless captures the feelings as our language cannot for what passes between people whose souls share the same fire, whose minds share the same thoughts, whose bodies meet like streams, then travel and grow wild as river rapids, always the same water.

It is the sort of passion that should be poured only into golden cups.

And because my cascading thoughts for Pinzon were so new to me, yet so comfortable, and so foreign from what my marriage had come to be, I at first felt no conflict between my actions and my marriage vows. In fact all the vows of my life were shattered the first time I kissed Martin Alonso Pinzon.

The island had proven to be the largest so far, but not, the Admiral finally declared, Japan. That still lay ahead. We set sail.

I, however, sailed with my own trials, as I could not rekindle the affection I had for the Admiral when we married and were at Porto Santo, when the Enterprise was born, the days when, seeing Kings, my husband was the sovereign to me.

Against the power of my life with Pinzon, my marriage seemed to have involved someone other than me.

Here in my arms was a man who wanted me, who was unafraid to cede himself, who took pleasure in this place for what it was, and could not have enough.

Since Pinzon had the habit of taking his ship out of the sight of the fleet, often even I did not know where he had gone, and my heart would pound with excitement when the *Pinta* at last reappeared, and Pinzon waved to the flagship, his tunic billowing, bleach-white against his Indian-toned skin.

And then, once we anchored and the supply chores began, I slipped away, now ready to explain my movements with lies if necessary.

The Admiral and I had ceased even attempting the rituals of man and wife, since he refused to sleep on shore, and lovemaking in our cabin seemed out of the question to him now, since he felt sure the men would hear us when the ship was at anchor. At sea, though, once he did reach for me, and I let him, for he seemed so much in need of tenderness that I tried to be woman to his man, but my heart seemed now severed from my body, so much an art without passion had our union become. Still he was my husband, and I cradled his head on my chest when he had been satisfied, weeping for how little I was able to feel for him.

As for Pinzon and me, few of the crew enjoyed the brambled paths that we did and we felt confident no one would follow us when we looked for sheltered meeting points. He or I would scout a spot, then find a ruse to whisper each other a message. We were very cautious not to change our behavior, but still we were taking risks.

Once we met on a small inlet. I had gone out first, then Pinzon joined me. We always made love right away, while we felt safe and wild with the success of having managed yet another encounter, lest someone were to come upon us later. I had still not become accustomed to Pinzon's limitless touch, for he found no parts of me undesirable to caress or kiss. And I learned the map and feel of his body as vividly as if it were of my creation.

Once at the inlet I asked him why he loved me.

"Because you were woman enough to make this journey," he said, without hesitation.

"You mean woman enough to be manly," I said, wanting a more emotional romantic reason.

"If you wish to call it that," he replied, stroking my naked breasts, "but you are obviously far from manly."

And, I had wanted to know, how long he had had in mind to kiss me.

"I'd have kissed you at Gomera," he replied, "when you seemed so confused by Beatriz the Governor, or when you visited my camp at Guanahani, the day I gave it up."

Gomera. I hardly thought of it at all now, but he was right. My heart had indeed stirred for him then, and he had sensed it even as I tried to find his frankness unattractive. The truth was, I now saw, I had been drawn to him since we first met at Palos. But when I told him that, he resisted.

"You were too deeply devoted to your husband when we left Spain to have had a thought of me," he protested.

"How deep is that?" I said, taking one of his earlobes in my mouth and tickling it with my tongue.

"You are becoming quite unmanageable, my dear," he said lightly, kissing me without answering. We got up and walked to the water.

Only once did we dare risk swimming nude. At first I hesitated. But Martin Alonso teased me, saying, "You needn't worry about the sailors, for they do not enjoy places like this. And you certainly would not shock the Indians."

I laughed and said, "But there aren't any Indians here now."

"Not now, perhaps, but as I've told you, we would not ever know for certain."

It was an irresistible sensation, to feel the warm moist air blow across my body, places that had never before been exposed, as if I had been under glass for most of my life.

Pinzon swam around me like a snake, fondling me underwater. I swam into his arms to be caressed, also caressing him until perhaps we might have made love again right there in the sea, but we never did.

Martin enjoyed holding his breath underwater like the Indians, and I could see him in the clear water gliding like an arrow shot from a quiver.

Gradually I too learned to open my eyes under the sea. I watched the fish fluttering lightly in the currents. As the water washed, the contours of the seafloor seemed alive. I held my breath and floated on my stomach, as if hanging in air, and looked down as the waves churned the bits of broken shell and stone, lifting clouds of sand, all the time the sun showering the bottom, a solid becoming liquid light melting through the ocean.

Once I saw an odd triangular creature skate out from under its cover of seafloor, and flutter away, like a sandy leaf in a breeze.

I wanted to share the sight with Pinzon. But he had swum out into the ocean, and out of my reach.

In this way, our days together, measured in hours, were idyllic, each of us discovering the elements of these lands, and embracing them as we embraced each other.

One afternoon, we were both thirsty from the heat and had forgotten to bring a water flask. But Pinzon was ever ready, and produced a thick tube-like stick announcing, "we'll drink from this."

I said nothing, having begun to learn that with this man, explanations often appeared after the words were said. He cut the vine diagonally, then began sucking from one end, and soon water trickled out, giving us each a mouthful of sweet liquid flavored by the plant.

"The Indians taught me this," he explained, as he shook the liquid into my mouth. The plant trapped and stored moisture as if in a cask or barrel. I licked each drop. It was as if we would be granted this sweet nectar only once in our lives, so precious did the water seem on a hot day.

But we both knew our meetings were in constant jeopardy and the voyage was obviously reaching a turning point, for we had come no closer to our destination. The Admiral remained outwardly confident, but his resolve seemed tested.

I myself did not know what to think, for I had ceased giving thought to our destination, in favor of my own journey with Pinzon. For the Admiral, each stop was a new land to be named, assessed, put behind. But for me, each cove or inlet, each half a day, was an opportunity to sneak away, a reason to continue.

Yet when I was alone again on the *Santa Maria*, the scope of the Enterprise returned in cold reality. Much more was at stake than the exploits of my heart and I knew that as well as I knew the danger and delight of my secret liaison.

Diego de Harana confided in me one day that the men were again losing faith, tiring of leaving one land after another behind. Again Chachu scampered around the ship, being agent both of fidelity and mutiny.

Luis Torres, of course, had proven no better than any of us as a linguist here, but now he had learned enough to compile a dictionary of words that would serve others who might someday follow us, as others almost surely would. However, the Sovereigns had not paid for a journey that would bring new languages to Europe. There were Christians to gather, and gold, and Japan.

De la Cosa continued to question the Admiral's decisions, though the Admiral tolerated him better than before because de la Cosa made shrewd suggestions about how trade with the Indians might better be accomplished. While the Admiral wasn't interested in trade per se, de la Cosa had convinced him that the Sovereigns might be easily placated if they could be convinced that these lands were valuable in themselves, as well as stepping stones to the East. Of course my husband clung to the conviction we were well en route, only one tranquil island away from the court of the Great Khan about whom Toscanelli had spoken.

One evening at sea, de la Cosa stayed in our cabin late into the night discussing how to quantify the value of these islands for the Sovereigns, and how difficult it was to conceive of the price of land that was so abundantly fertile and yet uncultivatable in the European sense. There were no wide fields, no expansive hills, and so far, not much precious metal.

Caro had satisfied himself that the gold the Indians wore was of fairly high quality. But he conceded that unless the Indians were to cooperate and describe the location of their mines, we would never find great wealth haphazardly.

I meanwhile stayed outside with Diego and Torres.

We stood on deck and marvelled at the thousands of twinkling stars against the blue-black sky.

Diego said softly, "It is beautiful, Madame, but how beautiful to share the news of it."

"That will come, Diego, soon enough," I soothed, "accolades enough for all."

"I don't mean that necessarily," he said, "though we will all welcome the honor of this voyage, but I mean to share this with one's family, one's intimates—all this can never be truly explained from memory."

True enough, I thought, grateful again for the exquisite company of Pinzon, for otherwise, how to experience the sensuality of this land? It would be lost in one's loneliness. And only when I contemplated my existence with Martin Alonso did I realize how lonely I had become with my husband.

Now, our cabin seemed oppressively small and whereas before I took great interest in the Admiral's doings, and remained for most meetings, this time I had simply not wished to hear the discussion.

De la Cosa at last left our cabin and we said a quick good-night as we brushed shoulders.

My husband sat at his table, but stood when I entered.

"Odd that you weren't here for that talk," he said, pressing both thumbs on the table.

"It was a beautiful evening and I enjoyed the air," I said, letting my hair fall out of the hairpin and beginning to dress for bed. The Admiral glanced at me as I loosened my clothes, and I felt a wave of shame before him.

"An interesting man, de la Cosa," the Admiral continued, "In fact you would have been stimulated by our conversation."

"I see. What was the substance?"

It seems that the two had decided to suggest the Sovereigns plant sugar here. I was startled.

"That seems a rather premature decision," I retorted, "given that we do not yet know how all these lands lie in relation to the East."

"I see that of no consequence at all," my husband replied, folding out his night shirt and pouring some water into the basin to freshen himself for bed.

"You would have to level the land," I announced, knowing he must have counted on that.

"It could be done," he stated.

"But who would cultivate it?" I insisted, not seeing the picture clearly yet.

"De la Cosa has a thought about employing the Indians."

The idea chilled me, but I gave it no serious consideration for I was convinced these people would never prefer cane-cutting to their own independence. De la Cosa, I was sure, was wrong.

"And we'd profit from my experiences with Esmeraldo to secure the best varieties for the climate."

The thought of Esmeraldo made me groan aloud, and the Admiral laughed playfully.

"Poor Esmeraldo. He suffers your wrath even though we are miles away from him."

"The idea that hundreds of Esmeraldos would populate these places makes me cringe."

"You do love it, don't you," he said, a tenderness creeping into his voice.

"Yes, for it has all been such a magnificent surprise."

"We could speak to the Indians eventually and convince them of the profit they'll earn."

"Have you not remembered the problems at Porto Santo?" I countered, "everything does not grow everywhere. Who is to say sugar will grow here?"

"My dear sentimental wife," he murmured, approaching me, "you do feel protective for your island at home, don't you? Perhaps I should bring Seixas across the ocean to give me lessons in the transfer of plants."

"But we did learn something there, didn't we?" I replied, now in my nightgown and sitting on the edge of our bed.

Since my affair with Pinzon, I had begun changing into my bedclothes behind the open cupboard door, a modesty that my husband took in stride, suspecting nothing.

"Not every lesson is transportable, my dear," he said, also ready for sleep, though he sat back down at his table to scribble a quick note.

"I know, but these islands are already the most profuse of gardens. What would sugar add?" I asked.

"Revenue for all, my dear," he explained patiently, as if sincerely wanting me to see it his way, "and justification."

Then he undressed in the dark and came to bed.

"You have had ample time to explore our surroundings, haven't you," he said, his fingers curling through my hair. "One hardly sees you anymore on board. I hope my being so busy hasn't driven you off." He was being unusually affectionate, moving toward me.

"No," I said, "I haven't been chased." trying not to give my lie away. He seemed so very alone.

"Felipa, we are on the verge of the East, I feel it," he confided with the same combination of vulnerability and confidence he confessed after our first great storm at sea, "but it is becoming so difficult to prove this to the men."

I too had developed doubts, but what to say now, when he needed the assuring words of a wife. Who better than I knew what establishing the western route had come to mean?

"If you can prove it to yourself, you can prove it to the others," I mustered.

I could no longer tell whether I had believed in the Enterprise because the idea had saved my marriage, or because the western route had merit on its own.

"You are the only one who knows everything about all these matters, all the truth of the past," he whispered, cornering me in our history. "You do not doubt me, do you?"

[227

He kissed me full on the mouth, but little stirred within me except the self-conscious taint that must dwell in the heart of all who betray someone, surely of all women who one day open to the fact that they no longer love their husbands.

"You will help me, won't you?" he asked, now fondling my fingers, one at a time.

"I am with you," was all I could reply, victimized by loyalty and nostalgia.

But he did not perceive my evasions. He was bent on intimacy that in another time I would have welcomed with all my being. But as he took his satisfaction, my closed eyes saw the dreams of Porto Santo lost like seabeans on the coves of these new islands. I believed those moments of our early life happened to another body, another woman with my name.

With this night, I had succeeded in lying to him in every way.

I felt desperately guilty the next morning. What was I becoming, able to sleep with the man I had married, and wake to craving my lover?

But now I was a prisoner. For according to the watchmen, we had sailed all night along a long uninterrupted coast. The Admiral was elated. All through the day too, the coast ran on and on ahead. There would be no Pinzon rendezvous for now since the Admiral had no intention of stopping until he had determined the extent of this coast, and whether it was, in fact, a peninsula of Asia at last.

I would be remaining on the ship, trapped in the knowledge that I had been taking wild forbidden pleasure in the Enterprise being wrong so far.

Chapter Twenty Three

Neither Land Nor Lover

For three days the cage endured, and I grew shaky with lack of land or lover.

Our ships groped along the coast, and the *Santa Maria* sometimes led, sometimes followed.

The Admiral had signalled Martin Alonso with a musket shot that no stops would be taken until ordered by my husband. Contrary to his previous habit, Martin Alonso did stay in sight, and I hoped it was because he wished to feel at least at a distance my eyes and my presence.

I watched his ship maneuvering through the sea, as if the beams and planks were the muscles of his back, and I thought of holding him as the ships passed white pearl after white pearl of beach, knowing that were we to stop sailing, we would be on one of them. A cauldron within me smoked with the battling forces of past and present, but my love for Pinzon burned through the days and nights, the candle lighting my confusion.

Previously, the *Santa Maria* had seemed sufficient and swift. Now she suffocated me with her slowness and lack of private places. I moved from cabin to foredeck to cooking area, filling the hours with chat with Chachu or Luis or Diego, keeping one eye on the *Pinta*. When the Admiral came to bed at night, I was always there first, my eyes closed, my body feigning sleep.

As one dawn after the other broke along the coast, the Admiral beamed, convinced that at last he had found what he had come for. He seemed to have no wish of stopping, as if that decisive and real act would shatter the joy he took in freely imagining that he was finally sailing the rim of Asia.

On the third anxious day, while standing on the foredeck with the Admiral who was amusing himself by tossing bits of papaya to the gulls, I blurted "I don't see why you will not stop if you want to prove your point."

My husband was somewhat taken aback.

"Haven't you had enough of the sameness of these places," he replied, pitching a chunk of fruit upward to a gull in mid-air.

"But if it is Asia, it will not be the same," I persisted.

"It will be Asia," he declared confidently, "but not yet."

I dared not insist.

That night, he sketched out the coast so far and entered new calculations on his chart. I had ceased paying attention to which set of records he used, now convinced that he had been altering reports of our progress to cover any errors he might be making. But anyway, navigational accuracy held no interest for me at all in these days, other than to dictate where and when we put to land. My final thought before sleeping was oh please let him anchor at last.

Finally, just as our movement through the sea always lulled me to sleep, what woke me on the 4th day was the lack of any forward motion.

The Admiral was not in the cabin and I tossed the bedcovers in drifts to the floor, racing to the window. Land. We seemed close enough to touch it and indeed we had stopped moving.

My fingers fumbled and I could barely do the fastens on my bodice, so much was I trembling at the thought of seeing Martin.

All three ships were anchored in a perfect half-moon bay ringed partly by beach. The trees came marching right to the shoreline and indeed the bow of *Santa Maria* pushed into the woods, like the nose of a courtesan exploring a bouquet of green blossoms.

Juan rowed me the few strokes to shore over unusually deep water for so close an anchorage.

The men were already busy, some cutting trees for firewood and repairing planks, some mending sails they'd spread out across the beach. I jumped to shore, sinking halfway to my knees in the particularly soft sand.

I heard Juan say "Careful, Madame," as he steadied the craft, but I was by then two steps up the beach.

I searched and searched for him, my eyes scanning the whole panorama. He wasn't here! Behind me *Pinta* lay at anchor. Was he still aboard?

The Admiral, Diego and de la Cosa stood in a huddle, a large piece of yellow parchment unfolded between them.

"I told you to give him this letter," the Admiral sharply reprimanded Diego.

"He left before I could, sir," Diego defended himself, "He and Mr. de la Cosa were talking and then . . . "

"No matter. You might have followed him when you realized," the Admiral declared reproachfully.

"He moved too fast, Admiral, and these woods . . . you see how dense they are. I'd have never found him."

"Who?" I had to ask, never expecting the answer

"Damn Pinzon," the Admiral shot back. My heart sank and surely the blood left my face. "He's gone inland without my Sovereign letter to the court of the Khan."

But how . . . I was baffled. Surely Martin would have waited to at least talk with me of a place to meet somehow. Perspiration beaded on my upper lips and a hint of tears stung my eyes. I turned from the group to hide them.

The Admiral walked away, reclaiming his letter, rolling it up and slipping it into this belt. He went back to *Santa Maria* without a word.

Diego looked totally dejected, but I had no strength to comfort him. Why hadn't the Admiral gone to the Court himself and left my lover to me?

The sun burned like a yellow coal, and I took no interest at all in anything now except sitting in a shaded place in silence. I crouched in the sand, and made circles with my bare toes. I did not even notice that the Admiral had returned, somewhat calmer, until he stood above me, his shadow rippling across the mounds of the beach.

"For someone who was so eager to stop sailing, you are hardly your usual exploring self," he noted, offering me his hand to pull me to my feet.

"It's too hot," was all I could reply.

"That's never stopped you before. I hope you are well," he remarked tenderly, taking my arm as we made our way back to the group of lieutenants.

"You have not seemed yourself lately," he said. It was true that, aside from my tension over Martin, I had been feeling weak from time to time and shiverish, but I had no ready reply. How could I tell my husband I was just exhausted with the disappointment of my lover being gone?

"The letter is not a disaster, Admiral," de la Cosa offered as soon as we reached the group. "Pinzon is merely on an exploratory mission. I myself helped him provision and he supplied for no more than two days anyway."

I bristled with impatience—two more empty days!

"You are right, Juan," the Admiral observed, then turned his attention to de Harana.

"I behaved badly, Diego," he apologized, the first time I'd ever heard him do so to someone in his command. "Perhaps I had not made it clear enough that Martin was to take the document."

For my part, I was totally confused. What plan was this and when had they hatched it? Listening gave the answers.

At some time during the voyage, outside my hearing, they had agreed to send an official exploratory party inland when and if we came to Asia. The Admiral had had a letter ready, about which I hadn't known.

"Here's a good opportunity to make sure the letter conveys the appropriate message," my husband said, unfolding the crinkling document again. He meant to make any revisions right here on the beach.

The letter had been written in Latin, the official diplomatic language of the courts of the Sovereigns, and he read it aloud, practicing his presentation of his credentials as if before the court and the Great Khan himself.

TO THE MOST SERENE PRINCE, OUR VERY DEAR FRIEND—FROM FERDINAND AND ISABELLA, KING AND QUEEN OF CASTILE, ARAGON AND LEON AND OTHER LANDS AND DOMINION, GREETING AND INCREASE OF GOOD FORTUNE. WE HAVE LEARNED WITH JOY OF YOUR ESTEEM AND HIGH REGARD FOR US AND OUR NATION AND OF YOUR GREAT EAGERNESS TO RECEIVE INFORMATION CONCERNING OUR SUCCESSES. WHEREFORE WE HAVE RESOLVED TO DISPATCH OUR NOBLE CAPTAIN, CHRISTOPHERUS COLON, TO YOU, WITH LETTERS FROM WHICH YOU MAY LEARN OF OUR GOOD HEALTH AND PROSPERITY.

I, the KING   and I, the QUEEN.

"Do you see any need for changes, Felipa?" my husband asked, uncharacteristically soliciting advice. He seemed genuinely excited at having the opportunity to present the decree.

"But how would you amend a royal document?" I said.

"Pen and ink, Felipa" he replied tartly, "as it was written in the first place."

In itself, the greeting sounded appropriate enough, though I didn't understand what the Sovereigns meant about having learned with joy and esteem of the Khan's high regard for them.

"Those tales were heard day and night at Cordoba," the Admiral explained, "everyone who travelled East regaled the Sovereigns with how eager the Khan would be to meet them."

"Since I wasn't there to hear them, I cannot question the statement one way or the other," I said.

"A pity, yes, Madame, that you could not hear the persuasive charm of the Admiral in Cordoba," de la Cosa added, somewhat gratuitously.

"That would have been quite inconvenient for my wife," the Admiral commented, putting an end to talk of the events of the Spanish Court.

He had perhaps hoped for more accolades for the letter, for he hesitated awhile before putting it back in his leather pouch. But none of us had anything further to say abouts its merits.

Caro and Yanez were missing, and I guessed that they had gone along with Martin Alonso. Still, it perplexed me that the Admiral hadn't himself headed the party inland as he was so eager for it.

Juan, the cabin boy, then came to shore with the tender loaded with broiled fish and fruits for lunch.

I resigned myself to the wait for Pinzon—two days would be the longest de la Cosa had said. While the men talked, I lay back to rest.

For awhile, I followed their conversation, but soon they drifted into counting barrels of water and discussions of whether this would be a good place to clean the hulls of the ships.

It seemed that when these men got together, even the simplest talk became a session for planning strategy. No one took pleasure in branch or blossom; no one stopped thinking of what came next.

De la Cosa's tympani drum voice bellowed above the others. He spoke again in favor of planting sugar here, and Luis Torres, who had so often previously resisted using his translation skill to serve de la Cosa's business planning, now seemed intrigued enough to wonder aloud whether he could convey such an idea to the Indians. Perhaps he too had begun to suffer from lack of purpose, for he had yet to master any of the languages here. Though he remained the official translator, the officers no longer left all the communication to him, frequently preferring to try to converse on their own.

How could this be the Orient, I kept thinking, for it felt exactly like every other island.

I listened again to de la Cosa, who again hoped to engage Luis in the task at hand.

"Luis, once it were accomplished linguistically, it would be no hard matter at all to move these people from one island to the another, wherever we need them most."

"You count a lot on discussion, Mr. de la Cosa. They must see some reason in it for I have the impression they don't travel just for its own sake."

De la Cosa was unconvinced, urging that "Pinzon believes those large canoes must serve them for journeys, not only fishing."

"They did say Colba took many canoe days to sail around," Luis offered, agreeing.

Colba? Was that the name of this place, I wondered to myself.

De la Cosa outlined how much he believed could be earned selling sugar grown here in Spain.

"And there are vast quantities of aloe and a rainbow of spices we've been collecting everywhere, Admiral," de la Cosa added, "we could make a fortune on nutmeg alone, I'd wager. These lands have their own rewards."

"Perhaps," the Admiral offered, "but the fabulous cities of Cipangu will make you forget all that, I assure you. And anyway, to be safe, I've claimed all of these interim ports for Spain, as you know."

"Yes, Admiral, you've approached these lands with unquestioning resolve, as one must pluck forbidden fruits," de la Cosa praised. The men laughed.

"Surely so would say Pinzon," the Admiral agreed, shocking me. Did my husband so blatantly know the truth? I cowered as I listened.

"Indeed Admiral. No surprise he volunteered to see if the Japanese court bore you any ill feelings," de la Cosa added. "He always manages to have a good time on land." The men laughed heartily.

My god. My heart pounded. What did all this mean?

I pretended to wake up slowly, as if from a deep sleep. And though the sun had lowered somewhat in the sky, I felt no cooler.

All the tension of the last few days returned to my body. Had the Admiral and the others found me out?

No one, though, seemed distressed that I had reappeared. Indeed, they kept on chuckling and laughing as if I was not there.

But that night aboard ship I could not hold back the question. While the Admiral made a second copy of his letter to the Khan, I asked him. "How is that Martin Alonso, and not you, made this overture?"

He seemed not the slightest perturbed by the inquiry.

"It occurred to me that though we were very eager to meet the Khan, the Khan might not bear us the same goodwill. Perhaps, for example, he has some dislike of Spain I could know nothing about. I thought it safer to risk Pinzon's life than my own, and as he had no fear of going, it seemed the ready solution."

But why didn't Pinzon warn me he would not be on land when we arrived? Did he think I would take his leaving as a signal that I should try to meet him? Surely that must be why he'd left without a word. Yes, I thought, that must be the explanation for why he'd gone off voluntarily. He expected I would find an excuse to follow!

The Admiral continued.

"The truth is, Felipa, I sent Caro also along to keep an eye on Pinzon's doings. I did not wish to rely solely on him, of course, for he still pushes his claim for the Queen's purse. He cannot be trusted entirely."

"Of course not," I replied, feeling I must seem to agree at least with something he said.

Juan knocked on the door to turn the hourglass. The Admiral made room at his table and stood up, looking out the window. He had ordered the fleet to anchor away from shore lest a wind come up at night and hurl our ships into the forest. Now from the tiny opening he could survey the positions of all three boats.

"Hm, perhaps, I've misjudged our Pinzon," the Admiral commented with not a little surprise, looking at the *Pinta*.

"A lantern is lit in his cabin. He must be back," he announced eagerly.

I need not say how my own heart rose.

Before we could ready *Santa Maria*'s tender, Pinzon and Caro had sailed up alongside us, rowed by de Triana who waited in the tender, gushing with news.

They climbed on deck and Pinzon stood in the yellow flicker of many candles, still my lover. His vehement eyes flashed at me, before he faced the Admiral and began his report.

A settlement existed, he said, larger than all the previous ones, a day's march through thick but penetrable woods. So it was just another island then, the Admiral said, disappointment saturating his voice. Not necessarily, Pinzon had offered.

"They speak of a human man dusted in gold, an El Dorado," Caro put in, "according to Pinzon's interrogation."

"How could you glean all that?" Luis interjected skeptically. He and de la Cosa had joined the group.

"By listening well, Luis," Pinzon replied, "though all I've got to show for our journey is this."

He reached into his vest pocket and produced a large nugget of raw pepper, handing it to my husband.

"But for God's sake, don't bite into it, Admiral," my lover warned, "I made that mistake and my tongue burst into flame!"

The Admiral examined the huge peppercorn closely, rolling it between his two palms. "So this may yet be some kind of portal land?" he asked, hoping for agreement.

"Yes, perhaps, Admiral, and it appears to be perfectly safe, though we saw no one who might be an Asian emperor," Pinzon described.

"All right," the Admiral announced. "Tomorrow at first light, I will go there myself."

Replenished with resolve, he then adjourned directly to his cabin. Caro and Torres and de la Cosa excused themselves, thank god, leaving just Pinzon and me.

Martin stepped closer immediately.

"Darling, I've been so so confused," I whispered, not daring to touch even his silken sleeve, for the others moved like chess pieces around the ship and any one might overhear.

"I had no time to tell you of the plan," he said, "we can meet tomorrow, while they go inland."

"But surely we will have to go with him," I declared.

"Not necessarily. I can make an excuse and he normally doesn't ask you along."

Chachu climbed to the foredeck now, to check the ties and anchor lines. We had to separate.

Pinzon bowed deeply, and turned away, leaving me in the shadows alone. My mind spun, and when I did return to the cabin, the Admiral was too enthusiastic about Pinzon's report to even think to ask me where I had been these last minutes. Instead, contrary to what Pinzon expected, he begged me to accompany his party.

"You must come, Felipa, for only you have a gift for penetrating these people. Luis is hopelessly confused about the language and I do not trust Pinzon, I've told you. Every word he says may be false. Say you will help me,'' he implored.

I agreed to him as well. Agree to my husband, agree to my lover. All lies become relative once you have lost your innocence.

Chapter Twenty Four

The Forest of the Khan

The morning came too early, with too much light, for even in the tightly shut-up cabin, the sun filtered in slivers through the boards.

Yet my sleep had been stormed by discontent and worry, not for where we were, but for where, I, Felipa de Moniz e Perestrello, found myelf.

Perhaps if I threw myself into the Enterprise again, right or wrong, I would drown the voices of infidelity in the sweet stream of exploration. Yesterday had been all too rushed, too confusing, and so certainly had last night with Pinzon. Take your own time, Felipa, I told myself. Nothing needs to be decided today. Start again.

I heard the clatter of preparations outside. By the sound of it, the Admiral was nearly ready to go ashore. Indeed, just as I finally stepped to the cabin door, Chachu tapped on the heavy glass window.

"The Admiral wants you to walk in his party," he declared "He is waiting for you before setting out."

The entire crews of the three ships except for a few needed to guard and clean them stood in soldiers' formation on the beach, the Admiral flanked by Pinzon and Yanez, Caro and de la Cosa. So that there would be no mistake, the Admiral read the Sovereign's letter aloud to everyone, announcing that he alone would present the letter to the Khan should we meet him.

Each man carried a stick or sword, and several men bent under the weight of crates belted to their backs, loaded with water urns, brass trays and other metal trinkets, planks of salted beef, even a cask of olive oil, strictly European goods for impressing the court.

I carried a few lighter items—a drinking cup, and a gourd of Coana's repellent paste—in a sack on my back of the sort Seixas used to wear on Porto Santo. I covered myself with the ointment and although I offered it to all, most declined, for it was still unfamiliar to them.

Only Pinzon approached me, holding out his arms as if to gesture that I should spread the salve on him. And though I would have given everything to touch him, even if only with my fingertips, I knew all eyes were watching and so simply handed him the gourd.

It had been folly to imagine the Admiral would have agreed to leave Pinzon behind—Martin had to lead the party since it was he who knew the way. Once Pinzon had turned his back to start the march, the Admiral came to me, asking for the insect paste. But unlike Pinzon, the Admiral tentatively sniffed it, and though my life with him had been drained of all passion, something made me wish to help him. Between the two men, the choice was only symbolic.

I rubbed the Admiral's neck and arms dutifully, thinking of other things. What if Pinzon had turned back too soon? Suppose the Khan's court did lie ahead. What then?

I stepped into the single file formation, the Admiral in front of me, de la Cosa behind. I could not see Pinzon.

At first we followed the course of a wide and slow but very deep river the Admiral had named Rio do Mares. Thick grasses grew waist high along its bank, so tightly packed that I still could read where Pinzon had earlier walked, pushing the green askew.

According to Falguero, who had split open one of the grasses in order to examine it inside, this was a field of wild tropical wheat, ripening in the hot sun, and the Admiral was greatly pleased for this was the first grain crop that we recognized from home.

"Perhaps it was brought to Europe from Asia," he speculated aloud, as he added his own form to the shadows left by my lover in the grass.

Ahead, the island rolled like the small of a back and tall palm trees stretched like harpstrings on the hillside. The Admiral declared this the loveliest land so far, and seemed genuinely to mean it.

I realized this was the first time he and I had explored a terrain together. Indeed this land was vaster than any we'd encountered. Yet it was hard to imagine that a great Asian city could be hidden here out of sight.

My mind's eye pictured Toscanelli's gold-dusted rooftops, held up by stubbled palm trees instead of marble pillars, and the constant encroachment of these gardens, for surely no settlement could long prevent these great green thrusting trunks from taking over any artificial clearing. Wouldn't the ropy roots, thick and tough as anchor chain, just rip up through the floors of any palace, wrestled by the servants of the Emperor himself, who used huge palm leaves to fan him in the heat?

We rustled through the river grass. But before leaving the river to turn into the woods, I loosened my bandanna, soaked it in the water and tied it around my neck.

The men, too heavily loaded for the weather, sat down at the riverbank, letting their feet soak, matting the grasses flat.

Where we had been looked like a field of bulls had grazed.

Once we were inside the forest, it was cooler immediately. So dense were the trees that it seemed the sun never reached the ground, for underfoot the soil was black and wet, as if it never dried.

I watched each placement of my foot carefully, for soft slimy moss wandered on every branch. I did not want to fall or give the impression I could not keep up. To let our phalanx pass, the men cut small trees and branches to the ground and I followed their slashings for several more hours.

Pinzon was nowhere to be seen, having kept his lead, presumably to take us over the same route he'd used before. But it was hard to believe he could have so easily retraced his steps. It seemed we had to cut an entirely new path.

The Admiral must have read my thoughts, and I was secretly relieved when he shouted "Pinzon, are you still ahead?"

"Indeed I am, Admiral," Pinzon's voice boomed through the forest, returning with a distant certainty. "I've sat down for awhile."

We stumbled into a small clearing exactly like Coana's—several houses around a larger one, but entirely abandoned. Pinzon and a few others were sitting on the ground, eating some stringy beef they had brought along. Pinzon dangled a piece before a small dog-like animal that fidgeted on his lap.

"It's a dog that does not seem to bark," Yanez reported, "no matter how my brother taunts it."

"I am not taunting it," Martin defended, quickly setting the animal on the ground.

It was an odd creature, black with close, tight fur, much like dogs at home except without yip or squeal. The site had been deserted recently, for there were heavily charred rocks in the fire-pits and uneaten fruit lying on the ground.

I noticed what looked like long blue-black stones in a pile behind Martin, and walked over to take a closer look, not daring to catch his eye. They were oysters, many still tightly clenched, unopened, ready to be eaten. The place still bore the palpable print of people.

"Obviously you've frightened them off," the Admiral said to Pinzon with some annoyance, scanning the empty settlement for any sign of lingering life.

"Your calling out to me through the forest would have accomplished that as well, Admiral," Pinzon shot back. Both were likely right, but how could everyone have disappeared from this village so fast?

"Is this the village you visited before?" the Admiral wanted to know, picking up an empty oyster from the pile, open but still bound together, like angel's wings.

"Hard to say, Admiral, for these settlements are not distinguishable one from the other, as you know. I believe so, but I would not write it to the Sovereigns."

Several of *Pinta*'s crew chuckled.

"These seem to be a richer people," the Admiral observed, changing the subject, noting a carved red clay pot with shining green stone eyes, hoping still to redeem the value of the march.

"This could be jade," he said, rubbing the green protrusions, his own eyes seeming weary.

There were also fishing nets and bamboo poles here and there, and a chalky white skull that could have been the headbone of a cow.

"Touch nothing and take nothing from this place," the Admiral ordered.

Ahead there was only a wall of trees. But my husband nevertheless declared that we would continue.

For nearly half an hour, as we advanced, I heard nothing but the hard thump of blades meeting jungle, and the swishing of feet and shoulders through the damp green labyrinth. I watched Caro hack and hack at the same piece over and over, all his effort brought to bear until the one branch finally gave in, falling to the ground, writhing in its last bend like a snake bleeding sweet yellow blood. Caro stepped over it and took on the next.

The prow of our convoy cut through, but then I became aware of a gradual thinning of the forest. Walking became easier.

Then ahead very bright yellow sunlight fell in a circular open area, as if filling a distant cistern. One by one, our men walked into it as I followed.

We had stopped dead in our tracks before a huge number of some fifty bohios, with one enormous central house. But there was no greeting, no welcome, no people. Instead we saw only the tawny backs of the last inhabitants as they escaped into the dense bush.

They vanished, untraceable, leaving meat skewering on fires, piles of precious tobacco leaves for the taking, grains half pounded in round gourds on the ground still spinning from the last hand to touch them, half-peeled papayas tossed around, even one large jutia, the boucan stick just barely thrust into its mouth, propped in a vacant useless snarl.

But none of this concerned me. I was captured by the sight of a small terrorized boy, no taller than the Admiral's knee, standing naked, tears streaming down his red-brown face. Did they fear us so that mothers and fathers left their children rather than face whatever and whomever we might be?

Some of our men gave chase into the woods to no avail, but no one approached the boy, whose crying did not lessen. My husband rummaged through the piles of cloth and statuary scattered throughout the large main house. Like a storm the Admiral could navigate around, the boy's horror stood alone.

Even Pinzon did not approach the boy, walking and looking from house to house instead.

But I could see only the tiny child. I walked to him and bent on my knees to comfort him, but only when I put my arms fully around him did he begin to quiet.

He tried to catch his breath in small gasps and for these few wordless moments, it was as if this child and I were the only people left in a trembling world.

But we weren't. As I held the boy close to me, his quaking now almost gone, I looked across the clearing to the perimeter of the woods, and saw the branches rustling. One by one, the people were returning, anxiously, slowly, as if with each step they were testing the land beneath them. In moments, it was as if they were blooming in the forest, so numerous did they become.

My husband now took notice of the boy. He dropped a huge stack of fiber-woven cloth on the ground, and walked toward me. But this frightened the people again, and they stopped short in their tracks.

242]

With one arm still holding the boy, I signalled my husband with the other to retreat.

"Leave us," I ordered, commanding him as I had never done before. I signalled him to keep away. "Let them come."

And they did, one by one, until a most beautiful tall man emerged from the group, thin red markings flowing straight down his nose, and a bright yellow cloth band around his head, braided with cobalt blue bird feathers. With him, an equally handsome woman with a bracelet on her arm that matched the band he wore.

They walked straight to me, and the boy turned, my arms still around him. I let him go, and he rushed to the woman. She lifted him to her bare chest, holding him as if trying to absorb him into her body.

She cooed and soothed him, and soon I was aware of relaxed talking among the people. Then the man, obviously the leader by his bearing and the way the rest stayed in place behind him, extended his hand to lift me from the ground.

With that, the people shrieked and shouted with pleasure, all threat defused. The woman, child, man and I were surrounded, and everyone proceeded toward the largest house. I was carried along by their sheer number and could barely see the Admiral, Pinzon and the others over the heads of my escorts, their glistening hair giving the impression of a field of black mushrooms.

Only when I had been gently goaded in to the huge central hall did the mass open to admit the Spaniards. Then the natives began to disperse to take up their daily occupations again. The small boy, free now of anguish, played delightedly at the feet of his mother, who waited patiently to see what the man whom I assumed to be her husband would do next.

My own husband stood speechless for a moment, not quite believing, I guessed, that so many people could be moved by attention to one so young. Would he have left his own son alone had he been set upon by this horde of naked strangers, or was he fortified as only Europeans could be, confident in the guns and axes these people did not know? What fears would drive him from his only heir, I wondered?

Still, it seemed amazing that so loving a people could have deliberately gone off leaving the boy behind, from all we'd seen so far. Why had they been so afraid, when the others with whom we'd mingled had not fled at all, except over the unfortunate accident with the Admiral's sword on the very first day.

[243

"That was ingenious of you," my husband complimented. Though I knew he had not understood my motives, I was startled by the depth of his misconception.

"I assure you it was my heart, not my mind, that drew me to the child," I replied.

"A woman's internal wisdom," he answered crisply, "but nevertheless you have won over an entire civilization for the Sovereigns with your tenderness."

"If you wish to see it that way," I acknowledged indifferently, for I knew, since Pinzon, that my husband had no real way to tap the well of feelings that bond two people, as this mother surely felt bonded to her son.

But Martin had not moved to the child either, and now I could not see him.

I took my first real look at where we had arrived.

This was no mere settlement, but a true city, dominated by the great hall in which we stood. Its roof was nearly as high as the Do Carmo Cathedral in Lisbon, built of tough fibrous wood and covered with tightly woven palm. Some thirty pure white net hammocks hung here, rolled up in balls, waiting for the night, when they would be stretched out between the corners of the building.

A backless throne of dark wood sat on very short legs in the center of the room. The stately head of an Indian man was carved into the front, with eyes and ears of glistening gold. The Admiral's eyes became as bright.

He pulled his declaration from his leather pouch, and read aloud the Latin greetings from the King and Queen to the court of Asia.

All the crew stood on in silence, but I could tell from the rapid, unceremonious tone of the Admiral's voice that, though he believed we were in the neighborhood of riches, even he knew we had certainly not reached Japan here.

Still there was no denying this was the most sophisticated civilization we had yet encountered.

Throughout the building large stone figures, many of women, stood in the corners. They were worked to smooth perfection, and had gold ornaments and what looked like opal or sapphire eyes. In the wooden pillars, there were carvings of snarling great-toothed cats or giant parrots with beaks protruding like hooks. Elaborate snakes slithered up the central poles as if seeking the roof.

One huge speckled turtle shell as large as a split water barrel, hung on the wall.

"This is the Colba we have been hearing about," someone whispered behind me, just as the Admiral spoke his last words. It was Martin.

My heart raced at the unexpected sight of him. We were the only two foreigners in a knot of Indians and so felt free to talk.

"Have you been in the forest?" I asked.

"No, I've been watching you from a distance. I wanted to join you with the child, but thought you'd be more convincing alone."

"Darling," I said with some exasperation, "why do both of you persist in believing I embraced him to win the Indians?"

"Both?"

"You and the Admiral. I was drawn to the boy by pure emotion."

"And I know how deep is that well," Martin replied warmly.

"We mustn't talk like this now," I demurred.

"No but I must have time alone with you to speak about. . . ."

"I'll try, my darling," I interrupted, terrified of being caught, "but that will not be easy to arrange here."

"We'll both try," my lover agreed, his firebrand eyes staring. Then he stepped discreetly away just as the veil of Indians around us began to drop.

The mother of the boy came and stood next to me, and her husband made a sign with his hands, suggesting he was about to speak. "*Cacique*," she uttered, a word I had heard before and that I had come to associate with "leader."

He was a leader indeed, and had no need of written speeches. He sat in the throne, which was then lifted into the air by about a dozen attendants. They carried him into the cleared area outside, where he gave orders and several young men whirled into action.

Caro meanwhile, smiling broadly, had returned from a tour of the area reporting to the Admiral that he'd observed gold ornaments in virtually all the buildings he had visited, even one thin gold plate, but that he'd learned that the most gold could be found at a place called Ceiba, still ahead.

Had he confused the name with Pinzon's "Colba," I wondered, deciding not to speak quite yet.

"They say it is ten days from here, and that a warlike people live on islands nearby," Caro added.

I wondered how he could have collected so much information so quickly, unless Luis had been along to translate, and I thought I had seen Luis go off in another direction. And anyway hadn't

Luis said it was ten days sail around Colba, not too different a sentence from "ten days to Ceiba."

But it didn't matter now, for it was certain we would not be sailing anywhere right away.

Night was already beginning to fall, and we could not march back through the woods in the dark. It had taken most of the day to get here.

But first there was a feast like none we had yet seen, since we were being accorded status as honored guests, it seemed. The *cacique*, still seated upon his throne which had now been placed back on the ground, continued to give commands as men and women brought in great round woven trays heaped with unknown foods. There were also piles of more familiar vibrant fruits, and some round orange tubrous vegetables new to me. Another tray was loaded with large shiny red crabs that had been split and grilled along with what looked like giant spiders, plus oysters and clams the size of human hands, and several large whole blackened fish, their heads cooked dry and eyes burned still. How could they serve such dishes when we were so far from the sea, I wondered.

There were also chunks of meat, also blackened. And all was decorated with flowers interspersed among the foodstuffs, and everything deliciously flavored with spices such as we never knew existed.

This banquet was set before our party, the *cacique* and the woman I had assumed to be his wife. All the attendants and other people—there were hundreds here—waited in a circle for us to begin.

The meat tasted like fresh pork, though did not have the same texture at all. The orange tubers had a sweet nutty taste. There was even a beverage that had perhaps been fermented from palm leaves, for drinking it recalled the scent of the woods.

The *cacique* spoke little. Two of his aides carefully removed the eyes from the centerpiece fish with a thin sharpened stick, and passed them respectfully to him. I assumed fish eyes were delicacies reserved for the king. He swallowed them whole, but otherwise ate with gusto along with us, with no particular ceremony. Once he had tasted from each plate, he signalled that it be replenished and sent it to the rest of his people.

In this way, the entire population supped well beyond the arrival of night. Women lit torches one by one in the great hall as we finished our dinner. The Admiral sat next to the Cacique, whose wife sat on his side next to Caro.

I sat next to the Admiral, and to my right was Luis, fortunately, for I could never have mananged to dine calmly, sitting between the Admiral and Pinzon. As it was, Martin sat well within my sight.

When at last we had finished, the king stood to give more orders. He appeared to have assigned each of his trusted aides to a group of our men, and they were led by torchlight to their respective sleeping quarters.

As for us—the Admiral, myself and the officers of the ships—we were to sleep in the largest house with the Cacique.

I watched the naked chieftain, his back muscles rippling, as one after the other he rolled out the finely woven hammocks for us, as if he were an innkeeper and we the guests he had been expecting.

The Admiral chose his hammock, gently pulling on the fiber rope ties to be sure they would hold, then awkwardly lifted himself into the unsteady bed—he had never tried the hammocks before. I took the one next to his, and had just lay down when I saw that Pinzon had scrambled into the next hammock, smiling craftily at me.

A light rain had begun to fall, gaining momentum that suggested it might well rain through the night, but there were no leaks through the towering palm frond roof.

For a long time, I listened to the pattering as drops fell and then exploded into mist, swaying between the history of my life with my husband, and the regular close breathing of my lover that eventually soothed me to sleep.

It was my father's face in my dreams that woke me the next day. That his eyes were the same sad almond shape of the boy who rocked away his tears in my arms was all I could remember of the night.

Chapter Twenty Five

The Mirror

When I woke up, the city was already busy with morning. There was the smoky scent of fires and foods cooking. I rolled my hammock back into its ready knot, and stepped into the sun.

Before I could think what to do next, the Cacique's wife, I should say queen I suppose, though she seemed without administrative role, approached me, offering a hollow gourd brimming with clear water for sipping and refreshing my face.

Children romped through the clearings, playing a game with flat paddles, hitting strange round objects that seemed to bounce. I picked up one when it rolled to my feet—it was oddly soft yet held its shape. Sensing my intrigue, the woman led me to the edge of the clearing and to some small trees whose bark had been cut into triangular patterns. A white substance dripped down the ridges.

She dipped her finger into it, making a tiny version of the ball the children were playing with, handing it to me. It was a soft pellet, a natural sealant like ships' caulk. The tree was a kind of mastic, and when I looked more closely at the leaves and branches, I could see we'd come across many of them on the trip. Stupidly our men had burned for firewood the branches of trees full of this useful sap, wondering why the wood burned weakly. How little our wisdom in the face of these forests. We had acquired no real understanding of the properties of the flora, except aloe.

I put the sap ball into my pouch, and rejoined the group.

The Admiral had announced that we would return right away to the ships in order to make for the place called "Ceiba," it having supplanted the tale of El Dorado in his mind, for which he had found no corroboration here.

I began to eat some translucent yellow berries, all that remained on the banquet plates of last night when Chachu came striding up to me with alarm on his face. Falguero was gravely ill, wretching and feverish, he reported.

He took me straight to where Falguero lay ashen-faced, surrounded in his misery by the Admiral and all of our crew. The *Cacique* stood outside the circle of our group, in worried stony silence.

I worked my way to my husband's side. A woman was wiping Falguero's body with fresh water. He was shivering and no sooner did he fall calm than he was compelled to vomit again, which in turn triggered new shivering. Each time, several Indians tossed gravel on his digestive mess and the cycle started again, though each time with less force.

"Where have you been?" the Admiral scolded me "Can't you see one of the crew's been poisoned? We must leave."

"My god," I replied, shocked at the theory, "no one here would poison him."

"Felipa, please swallow your innocent admiration. Do you deny the facts before your eyes?"

Why accuse me of simplicity, I thought, he who searched only for gold when alive in a palace of other treasures?

"What has he eaten, Chachu?" I asked, ignoring the Admiral's hypothesis.

"As we did, Madame," the boatswain replied, obviously frightened for his comrade.

"Nothing else at all?" I probed.

"No."

I wondered where Martin was, but the Admiral gave me the answer. "Pinzon is on notice that hostages may have to be taken," he said grimly.

I was startled. "Surely you exaggerate. That will accomplish nothing but a worsening of relations," I reminded him bitterly.

"You are not a good counselor on such matters, Felipa," he said, no hint of taking me seriously. "Just remain at my side. I do not wish to search for you if we must escape in haste."

I looked at Falguero's grayish face. Did the Admiral then plan to leave even the sick man behind in such an event?

Juan, the cabin boy, squeezed through the crowd to my side. He held a round object.

"He ate from this, Madame," Juan said quietly, holding out his hand to show me a gourd half full of yellowish *casaba* paste, half mashed.

Then I understood. Coana had always been fastidious with *casaba*, mashing it very finely and rinsing it constantly. I had gleaned that to do otherwise would have let some noxious substance remain. This was clearly unfinished *casaba* flour intended for bread, interrupted by our arrival. Falguero had doubtless eaten it unknowingly, for no Indian would have offered him a taste in its half-done condition, of that I was sure.

The *Cacique* had seen what Juan had carried to me, and also immediately understood. Before I could even explain to the Admiral, the Cacique had begun shouting angrily, throwing his arms into the air.

While the Indians dispersed, I quickly passed along to the Admiral my theory of what had stricken Falguero. But just then, a young woman was led into our presence by two Indian men, and the *Cacique* spoke to her in demeaning, reprimanding tones.

Juan, who apparently knew more than all of us about what had transpired, explained to me.

"That woman was with him last night, Madame, after dinner, but she did not serve him the food. He tried it while we were alone in the house before she came to him."

The *Cacique* continued to berate the woman in front of us all.

"But the she mustn't be blamed," I said, trying to find Luis to intervene.

"Say nothing, Felipa, I warn you," the Admiral instructed, who had also overheard Juan.

By then the *Cacique* had calmed somewhat, and the Indians were beginning to smile. Falguero had ceased his retching almost entirely and lay spent in his hammock, but surely not near death.

In fact he seemed now to be dozing rather quietly, the toxin fading from his system. He would recover.

Meanwhile, though, the Indians appeared to insist on some kind of amends. The *Cacique* had ordered a handful of women, each with gourd basins and soft white cloths, into the house.

The *Cacique* sat on the throne, the women kneeling before him. While the supplicants washed his feet, he gestured that the Spaniards too should remove their boots. Another group of Indians arrived with several small hassocks made of wood and turtle shell, and first the Admiral, and then de la Cosa sat down. The women moved in front of them.

To my amazement, the *Cacique's* own wife took my husband's feet in her hands, washing them softly, taking each toe and gently massaging it, as if to ask forgiveness through her fingertips. She moved on to de la Cosa, then to Yanez, who had arrived to take his place.

I was shocked at the Spaniards, now knowing the truth, still allowing the women to beg at their feet for the Indians to be excused.

Then the woman who had been accused of serving Falguero the tainted meal appeared, also carrying a basin and cloth.

She took Luis' feet into her hands, for he had sat down as well, and then as if to coax the final outrage from my heart, Martin too arrived, sat down, unlaced his boots and dangled his toes into the waiting hands of the woman who seemed desperate to be pardoned.

"You may not," I shrieked, my eyes flaring with anger.

"Felipa, do not speak," my husband ordered.

How could he, how could Pinzon submit himself, be party to this insult?

He would not look at me, and I could only watch in paralyzed disgust, for now, the washing finished, the Cacique's wife said a few words to the other women, and they bent their heads and put their dark lips first to my husband's feet, then one after the other to the feet of the rest of the men.

I watched a queen made to grovel before my husband. How dare he accept and demean her, knowing the facts?

I waited, heartsick, as the younger woman arched her neck to place her mouth on Pinzon's toes.

"I forbid you, Martin," I called out in shaking voice.

But he did not stop her. I was stunned. My lover let the woman kiss his feet.

"And I forbid you another word," my husband then declared.

I could not stand by anymore and raced outside. When I returned, the ritual had ended.

Our men were not to be seen, not the Admiral, no one, and I wondered if, after all, I was the one to be left behind.

But no, they were simply dispersed in various houses, collecting bolts of cotton and gourds of cinnamon, nutmeg, aloe, mastic, papaya and pepper and many many other gifts to take back to the ship. In return, they gave some porcelain baubles and a single leather thong. Most of the provisions we had carried here, we would bring back to the ships.

Twelve local people—men, women and several children—appeared to be readying to come along with us, and I did not understand why until Chachu told me the Admiral had given orders to collect people who would travel with us to prove the success of the voyage to the Sovereigns.

"He says though we haven't met the Khan, these are the Great Khan's soldiers," Chachu explained, somewhat unskeptically for him.

"I see," I replied, watching the dazed faces of the twelve, but when I saw that among the children was the young boy who had been the cause of the society's return from the forest, I could not contain my fury.

I went from house to house until I found the Admiral, who was waiting for Caro to return from his final tally of the number of gold ornaments in the village and their approximate value.

I strode up to him and glared, stating, "I forbid you to take that boy from this place."

The Admiral was unmoved. "He is insurance that we will not be attacked," he blandly replied.

"But he is the *Cacique's* son!"

"The *Cacique* has not objected, Felipa, though you have. Perhaps he relished the thought of the boy growing up in Spain!"

"You are being villainous to take such a boy," I declared caustically.

"Do you not remember the castle of Moura, and the children there who kept the peace between your country and Spain?" the Admiral slyly offered.

"This is hardly comparable," I replied in disgust.

"Felipa, will you for once act like an emissary of Empire?" he demanded in dagger tones. I turned my back on him.

All was ready for our leaving, and I was glad Pinzon was again in the lead for I knew I could not face him also in the wake of what was happening.

But my heart surely broke a little when, to coax the boy into leaving when he seemed reluctant, the *Cacique* placed him in the arms of a woman who would be walking in front of me. There, the boy would face me through the entire trip.

I had no words for farewell, and the *Cacique's* wife would not look at me as we left, her child betrayed. I walked numbly through the woods, one foot following the other without will.

Though it had taken us hours to travel inland, with our Indian guides we reached the coast in very little time. They picked out paths between the trees, cutting nothing. We had apparently hacked in circles to reach their settlement, which had been closer to the sea than we had understood.

The morning sun was still shimmering on the ocean when we again saw our ships.

Also while we had been inland, a group of Indians and several canoes had appeared on the beach. They dove for oysters and our men dove too for awhile, but lost interest when no pearls were found, and tossed the opened oysters back into the sea. In this resplendent garden where food was literally everywhere, the Spaniards had lost all memory of scarcity.

What to do with the time at hand? I wanted to be at sea again. Land had become too full of meaning.

But I ought to have known that fate would bring Pinzon to me as I stood by myself.

He approached, his face filling with apparent relief to catch me alone.

"At last," he murmured, "a chance to speak."

I said nothing, my love burdened by disappointment and the unforgettable events of the inland journey.

He wiped his perspiring brow with the back of his palm.

"You do not wish to speak to me, after we have waited all this time?" he questioned incredulously.

"How could you think so little of those women as to let them kiss your feet?" I challenged.

He looked at me with astonished eyes, and said, "Surely you did not think that I enjoyed it?"

"But you did not protest."

"How could I then? It was a cleansing ritual for them, to wash away the bad feeling between our races."

"But they were innocent. You know that the fault was Falguero's."

He agreed, but without language, how could we ever make such points understood?

"Forgive me if I did not listen to your entreaties," he said sweetly. "I saw no way to obey your protests and spurn the attention of the women without arousing suspicion about us."

If only we could have gone to the city alone, I thought, nothing untoward would have happened. I was thinking of what to reply, yearning to hold him again, to be cleansed, to wash the taste of sadness from my mouth by a swallow of the sea. How was I to know the truth now, when so many lies had been created? I wanted my lover back the way it had been before.

But he wanted no part of history. Pinzon seized the future.

[253

"Leave with me," he uttered with no hesitation.

My eyes widened with shock.

"You are mad," I said, "you could not mean it."

"I am perfectly serious," he replied. "I made up the story of El Dorado to tantalize them to the interior, thinking we could escape, thinking he would not ask you to go. But I had no chance to tell you. This is an island just like all the others. Surely you know we are nowhere near the East. If you care for this place, you will help me spare it from the money-hungry plans of the likes of de la Cosa."

My mind reeled. Such momentuous thoughts and propositions compressed in a single stolen conversation.

"I cannot say for certain now," I replied evasively.

"You must," he insisted, "do you not love me still?"

God spare me, I thought, or free me to answer.

"We'll have to accompany him when he next stops," I side-stepped.

"I don't plan to, and you can feign illness, anything. We'll be far away on the *Pinta* before they understand."

My God, it was treason that he wanted.

"You ask me now, here, to abandon my husband and my dreams?"

"Your dreams?" he asked skeptically "You do not believe in this Asian hoax, I hope."

I had never told him who had first had the Enterprise idea, and there was the Admiral's reputation to consider. At least I could leave him that.

"You ask too much in too short a time," I told him.

"Your husband uses you, Felipa," Pinzon declared, "he always uses you."

He squeezed my arm, and I flinched.

"Forgive me," he said, realizing how hard he had grabbed, letting me go.

At that, Chachu appeared out of nowhere to retrieve me, for the Admiral had asked him where I was.

But Pinzon would not be put off so easily. "Tell the Admiral Madame will join him shortly," he said boldly.

Chachu slipped away, and Martin looked at me again.

"I beg you to agree," he insisted, his eyes dancing. "At least admit it has some merit to you."

How to tell him all the merit that life with him could hold for me, and yet, foisted upon me here, the prospect seemed impossible.

Where would we go? Where would we live with our betrayal? But we were running out of time.

"Perhaps you are right to press me," I said at last, "perhaps only then will I find the courage to do it."

"Felipa, do not believe that such offers grow as easily as this island fruit."

"You would leave me?" I gasped, now terrified of that.

"Who can say when he'll call a stop again, but I will be waiting for your answer. We must return."

Now it was for me to grasp him, for I could not agree and yet dared not lose him. I reached for his wrist.

We stood on a small promontory of the beach. I looked behind him; no one approached. I led him by the arm over the slight rise, so we stood out of sight of the others.

I held him, kissing his neck and beard and whispering his name. I found his mouth and he kissed me back as fully, and then in an instant, we had to stop. We had stolen all the time we could.

"When we come to land again, I will find some way to see you," he plotted in a gritty whisper.

I watched him stride across the beach alone. I waited a moment or two, and then followed.

When I reached our anchoring site, the Admiral had returned to the beach and was trying to gather everyone to sail.

Sweetly he approached me.

"I regret my words to you at the city," he said softly, "but the moment there was tense."

I did not reply, still quavering from my last encounter with Pinzon and all it could mean.

My husband didn't notice my distraction, though, and said he thought the twelve Indians from the city should join *Santa Maria* now, before the other Indians tempted them away.

"Will you help me by boarding," he asked, "just one more favor so they follow?"

My heart was heavy and sick. Agree again to my husband, agree again to my lover. All lies were indeed relative once innocence had poured like wine into the beaches of worlds we had never intended to find.

I acquiesced and boarded the flagship, and the twelve Indians—five men, four women and three children, all boys—followed in the next tender.

Once they reached our large ship, they huddled together in the foredeck, like a knot of windblown leaves. Gradually they began to move about, interested in the details of what was for them a very unfamiliar complicated vessel. The men examined the heavy netting and rope with Chachu, keeping the children with them. The youngest boy was now quietly in the arms of one of the men, and the others, about seven or eight years old, kept their balance ably, one using a small canoe paddle he had brought along as a kind of walking stick.

I took the women to my cabin. I don't know why. Perhaps it was some instinct of modesty, for although the Spaniards mixed freely among the nude women on land, I wondered how such habits would fare in the ship's tight quarters. Immediately, the women began touching the cabin cabinets and gazing at the goblets and bottles. They sat upon the bed, giggling, and seemed perfectly at ease, all of them beautiful, each shapely and unblemished, darkened by the sun.

But then one of them spied the prize—my mirror. Baffled, she slowly approached it, and seemed to be dazzled at seeing her true image, not the subtle shimmer of herself as seen in a stream or river. She ran her long nimble fingers through her black hair, seeing that by some magic, the fingers too appeared in the mirror. She moved her hand across the glass, watching it enter the window of herself, smiling at her own face.

The others waited their turn patiently behind her. Though they made no request, I knew I should give the mirror to them, but they were four and perhaps it was best to wait until Spain where there would be mirrors for all.

I heard myself thinking and was again confused. Spain. Did the Admiral now plan suddenly to return or did he mean for these people to accompany us to yet another peninsula that would be in fact another island, another landfall? What were his intentions? As for mine, could I actually be giving thought to abandoning the husband who had been the sum of my life, in favor of treason and adultery. And what if the Admiral should sail directly home? What then of my prospects with Pinzon?

One of the women reached for the mirror to lift it from the hook on the wall, and I did not protest. She can take it if she wants, I thought, but instead she held the silvery smoky glass in front of me, moving it around in a circle, watching from behind me as my own face swirled before my eyes. Who was the woman there, moving at the whim of this alien hand?

She took my own fingers and raised them to my face. She ran a fingertip along the coast of my lips, the hill of my nose, up into the valleys of my eyes and the fields of my brows. Together we explored the new land of my own face.

We were equals in the magic of the mirror, their reflections as true as mine. Then the woman put the mirror back on the wall. She had no wish for it, and one by one, they left my cabin.

I felt the ship moving.

On to where?

The Admiral was elated, as if he had succeeded in reaching the Khan, instead of accepting the reality that, at best, we had found an island richer than all the rest.

The Indians disappeared once the sails were fully furled, finding niches in the ship, as if the vessel were the forest they slipped into at will.

We sailed all afternoon, and all afternoon, I lay on my bed, staring at the thick beams and weathered planks of the ship, curled in the bedcovers, thinking blankly, eaten by indecision and avoidance. How could I deny Martin, for I could not imagine existence without him. But could I leave the man to whom I'd sworn vows of marriage? How could I have come to even think of such a proposition? And yet I knew it was likely better to leave this land alone, return to Spain and admit the Enterprise had failed. Surely even the Admiral could see this was the noblest course.

Life with the Admiral against life with Pinzon.

Pinzon and I would have to begin again somewhere entirely new. Perhaps Italy or France, but certainly neither Spain nor Portugal. Take on yet another name, another nation? Somewhere where marriage could be imitated, where legality did not matter.

My musings were absurd. There was no place as free in all the world except right here.

I dozed, and then woke with a start, forgetting for a moment where I was, seized with panic that I had waited too long to decide. I ran to the small window and looked. *Nina* was there; *Pinta* too. Our formation was intact. I had not lost him.

I had managed to avoid most of the day, half dozing, half dreaming, for already Juan was knocking with the dinner tray.

"The Admiral said he will be joining you soon, Madame."

Smoke rose from the plates and the food smelled delicious—an array of fish, oysters, crayfish and the pork-like meat we had eaten on land.

"Be sure the local people with us eat as much of whatever they wish," I instructed Juan, but he told me that the Indians had already eaten an ample dinner and were now asleep below.

But the Admiral did not arrive as quickly as I expected.

I waited some time, but then decided to begin without him. I had eaten nothing since the berries of the village, and I began to peel the skin from a pink crayfish the length of my forefinger. The succulent flesh still tasted of ocean, and I stood to pour a goblet of water and one of wine.

Voices fell through the open window—the Admiral, Caro and de la Cosa. I listened.

Caro estimated there were forty separate pieces of gold at the city, of which he had managed to barter for twenty.

"I offered virtually nothing, Admiral, I assure you," Caro was explaining, as if deflecting an accusation.

"Be sure of that," the Admiral directed, "for we have more lands ahead, though I am certain we have never been as close to success."

"That was splended practice, Admiral, very well done at the great settlement," de la Cosa offered, ever free with praise. "You established our superiority with no difficulty at all. These twelve will now attest to it."

"Yes, Admiral, well done," Caro echoed. "You must take a land when you want it."

"Rather like taking a woman," de la Cosa put in, "if I may say."

All three laughed grotesquely.

"Indeed," my husband agreed, "though I'll leave that task to Falguero for now, poor man."

They laughed again.

"Or better to Pinzon," Caro quipped.

What was this?

"Yes, indeed Admiral," de la Cosa amplified, "one should perhaps adopt his habits of flouting customs to make life more satisfying, shall we say."

"Only some habits," the Admiral replied, "for he causes me much ill-ease with his highhandedness. I trust him less each day."

"Very wise, my Admiral," de la Cosa embellished. My heart sailed into a frenzy. Pinzon had a good time on land, they had said earlier today, and flouting customs? Martin did love the land, and he did spend nights there. Surely this was what they meant. It could not mean they had figured out my doings. No, the Admiral would never take that calmly, I was sure, never conceal his awareness of it.

Now they changed the subject.

I caught only Caro's statement that the twelve Indians aboard would be essential to the remaining voyage.

De la Cosa said Caro was right, and that there was no other way to ensure we would ever reach Ceiba.

"They must show us," de la Cosa observed, "and we must keep them as an example to the people ahead. We'll need them to convince their compatriots of the need to learn the Spanish way of labor."

My husband agreed that the system of taking local people had greatly aided the credibility of the Portuguese, so why not him?

"Yes Admiral, all the great captains took Negro captives. But who is to say these people here would not be more hearty slaves than even Africans, when necessary."

Caro did not like this thought.

"I never meant slavery, Admiral," he said, "that was not my . . ."

"Caro, don't be naive," de la Cosa interrupted. "You yourself say that gold mines here will be difficult to work without people who are used to the climate."

"But that was . . ."

The Admiral would hear no more.

"Gentlemen, it is too soon to quibble about the fate of these people. We will decide nothing until we sit once and for all in the kingdom of Cathay. Now enjoy your dinners; I must join my wife."

I sat down at my plate. Quibble, he had said, about the fate of these people.

He entered the cabin and gaily pronounced himself ravenous.

"Good thing, for here is a lovely meal," I said, acting as if I had not overheard. I poured him a full goblet of wine.

He kissed my forehead and sat down across from me.

"Have you slept all day long?" he asked.

I told him I had, claiming the heat as an excuse.

"Yes it is very humid today," he agreed. "Even the breeze makes no difference. The wine will soon send me to bed if I drink much of it in this weather."

He plunged his thumb into a crayfish, tearing away the glassy crunching shell, removing the dozen bent legs, lifting out the brown bulging eyes, one of which lodged under his thumbnail until he flicked it to the floor. Then another crayfish, then a mouthful of

[259

dorado, neatly slitting the browned back of the fish, pulling out the spine in one long piece. The white bones shook in his hand, a whole fish in mid-air, minus its flesh. Our plates were full of debris. He stood and tossed it all into the sea out the window.

We kept eating, and when he finished his glass of wine, I poured him another.

"You will have me drunk," he teased. I began my lie.

"Today is a day to celebrate, heat or not."

"Well, I'd never thought I would hear you say that," he blushed. I continued.

"I overreacted to all the day's events," I announced humbly. "Surely you are on the eve of Japan, and this we must salute."

He took a sip, but did not agree.

"I am not sure, Felipa, but I must return the Sovereigns something."

"Of course you must, and do not forget I am as well implicated," I said.

"Yes, of course, my wife. I know that you will help me bear the blame if we are wrong and the garlands if we are not."

He cleared his throat of a bone, bringing it to his mouth on the tip of his tongue, removing it with his fingers.

"It was extraordinary how the women treated us today," he began. "I can understand how it would surprise you."

"They had little choice," I said, now also struggling with a fish bone in my throat.

"But women are used to being on bended knee, Felipa. They were not as offended as you were."

I swallowed the bone.

"No, but you understand, I assume, how all of that would seem to a woman of my station."

"Of course, of course," he said, now full of animation. "But these are not our race, my dear, they value and enjoy supplication, though I must say that does seem to be a trait of your sex no matter the culture."

He poured more wine for himself. I eyed it like a messenger.

"A man of exciting experience," I flattered, the words as dead on my tongue as the fish bones piled on my plate.

"Hardly," he said, slightly embarrassed, "not like some." He looked absently into the yellow wine and the candle flicker. But no, he could not be referring to my illicitness, for surely if he had been aware he'd have spoken of it by now.

"You know," he said, drifting back, "I might rather enjoy that island of which these Indians spoke, Matinin was it? Inhabited entirely by women, only with your permission of course." He looked at me, with a wide and teasing smile, his eyes glowing from the wine.

"I didn't know they spoke of such a place," I commented.

"Caro was told of it, by Falguero, who heard it no doubt from one of them, perhaps the very one he so apparently enjoyed." He smiled to himself, avoiding my eyes. We had never spoken of women like this before.

"But the Indians also spoke of another, stranger island, one peopled with men who have no hair."

"You do listen well to Torres, I see. Who can tell myth from fact in these mysterious places," he remarked, admitting the one indelible truth about the journey so far.

"Can you not," I broached, "think of these lands as something in themselves, my husband, something of worth as they are, unchanged, something to count as success?"

"Only properly used, darling." He stopped, then started again abruptly.

"That is so female," he went on, with condescending self-assurance, now reaping the effect of several glasses of wine and quite proud to share what seemed to him some new dinner table insight. "That is such a womanly idea—acceptance of what is here. Those are the elements of womanhood—acceptance, compromise."

"Supplication, as you said" I goaded, feeding his bravado.

"Yes, supplication. It falls always to men to forge objectives, while women are satisfied with any little thing en route. These lands are in the way of the goal, Felipa, that is all, but they are not without value, once we've reordered things."

"More wine?" I offered.

"Yes, yes, damn the heat," he said easily, "Let's enjoy being on our way again."

I unwrapped a second smaller bottle and poured, giving myself less.

"So, our guests are also means to the objective," I asked, for I wanted to hear from his own mouth the plans he had.

"Yes, yes, gold mines need labor; sugar plantations need labor; spice gathering needs labor; shipbuilding needs labor."

"Shipbuilding?" I asked, for this was a new enterprise of the Enterprise to me.

"Indeed, have you not noticed how straight and tall these trees are. They will make superb masts and rigging, if this is not Asia." He stopped cold. It was the first time he had admitted it.

"If?" I asked, faking surprise.

He recovered, but the wine had loosened him.

"It surely is, but after all, I am not infallible. If I'm wildly off course, I must justify things to Santangel and the Sovereigns, in order to continue."

Someone knocked at the door.

"Not yet, Juan," I called, "we are still dining." Indeed we had not yet touched the oysters.

I poured more wine, and heard Juan say, "I'll return for the tray, but I've also come to turn the hour glass."

"I'll do it," I replied, not wanting interruptions. I stood and shifted the sands, watching them fall, white as a beach, whiter even than the skeleton of a fish.

"You were saying?"

"I do not remember now," my husband answered, probably not wishing to outline further his own doubts.

He gave a great yawn, but sipped to the bottom of his glass, dipping small, very sugary beach plums into the wine before swallowing them whole, and yawned again.

"I cannot eat another thing, my dear. Too bad, these oysters will be spoiled tomorrow. Do you want yours?"

I didn't.

"But let's finish the last of the wine," I insisted, pouring anew.

"Indeed, we'll drink to the future of these Indians in Europe," he announced, slurring his words. "May their glory surpass even the stallion riders of Senegal!"

He clinked his glass with mine and swallowed all his wine, his eyes now overflowing with drowsiness, satiation and drink. I took only a sip, and put my glass on the cupboard.

He stood to let me clear the table and threw some water on his face, but it was insufficient to undo the wine.

"I'll just lie down a moment before logging the day's route," he said.

He landed on our bed with a heavy thump and fell asleep.

I put the tray and dishes outside on the deck so Juan would not knock again, and sat on the footstool to see what the Admiral would do. He stayed asleep, his breathing heavy but very regular.

I waited longer, then stepped to the window in our door. I watched the men retiring one by one. But as I hoped would happen, the Indians had come up to the deck, probably fearing the bowels of the ship in the dark. They hung together near the stern, just beyond the entrance to the hold.

The Admiral did not stir.

Outside now, all was silent, except for the wash of the sea.

Juan, the cabin boy, had drawn watch this night, but he had not gone up to the crow's nest. He had once confessed to me his fear of the high rope, and he was now apparently delaying until the last possible moment. He milled around the deck, then finally climbed up out of the way.

The Admiral slept as soundly as a rock at the ocean bottom. The wine had worked with the heat as potently as a drug.

Then, they began.

A low moaning sound, one sad note, like the hum of a bassoon. One Indian man had started them chanting, a mournful incantation.

The Admiral did not hear it; so far Juan and no one else had taken note. I had very little time.

I molded my pillow lengthwise, as my own body would have been, then lay it against the Admiral, who had now turned his face to the wall. I prayed I would not wake him, but he made no motion.

Then, I unlatched the cabin door and slipped out. The Indians made no sound on seeing me, other than continuing their subdued wail.

Don't cry out, I beseeched them in my mind, and motioned that they be calm.

I walked toward the railing, gesturing them to follow. No one stirred on deck, and where we stood, those in the hold could not see us. Only Juan might, but not if he kept his eyes on the seas ahead, as he was charged to do.

The twelve softly made their way, lowering their song as if they now understood. One of the women held the youngest boy, who slept soundly on her shoulder.

"*Canoa*," I whispered to them, pointing to our tender tied up alongside, "*Canoa!*"

Their eyes brightened, and one by one they stepped over the side into our little boat, nowhere near as seaworthy as their own majestic craft, but sound enough to carry them back one day's sail in very calm seas, I was certain. I untied one of our own oars from the gunwale and handed it to the man who had begun the singing. It was the best I could do.

I saw as the last woman began to step into the tender, that there was a deep scratch on her thigh that had not been there when she had arrived, as well as red scratches on her back that seemed to come from fingernails. Seeing me notice, she glanced toward the hold.

My eyes burned with shame. Take land as you take women, de la Cosa had said. I signalled her to stop a brief second. I raised my hand to my mouth, kissing each of my fingers, and pressed them one after the other into her wounds.

Then they all settled into the tender that was just big enough.

A single heavy line still held them prisoner. I tore at the knot with both hands, looked at each revived face for the last time, and with all my strength, tossed the wound rope of my life on the black mirror of water.

Chapter Twenty Six

The Bell of The Cup

It had gone smoothly. The pillow was still unnoticed by the Admiral, and I climbed into bed, my heart pulsing with the success of what I had done.

At one point during the night, the Admiral turned over and threw a heavy arm like a gate closing across my chest. But he made no other movement, and once my heart calmed down, I slept the contented sleep of accomplishment.

In the morning, the Admiral was furious. He had left our cabin early, and I was still in bed, pretending to be waking up, when he came back bellowing that the Indians had again escaped, this time stealing his tender.

"They should have been tied up," he stammered, "that's what the others suggested. It's Juan's fault."

I hadn't anticipated he would be blamed.

"Well, he can't be faulted for keeping his eyes forward, darling," I argued lightly from the bed, "and wasn't the tender in the stern?"

"What? Yes, well, he should turn his head now and then, damn boy," the Admiral huffed. "From now on, with Indians on board, I will order double watch."

I dressed as quickly as possible, not wanting to linger for any more discussion or possible questions.

It was a glorious day outside, a blue dome of cloudless sky overhead, a stiff breeze and green, shining water.

Juan stood alone at the water barrel, a downtrodden look on his face. I tried to cheer him up.

"I've told the Admiral you are not to be blamed, Juan," I said, putting my hand on his shoulder. He stared silently straight into my eyes. Had he seen me do it after all?

"Thank you, Madame, but I confess I am only sad to be accused, not that they left, for I heard them singing as if they were about to die."

So, Juan was an unexpected ally.

"The accusation will come to nothing, dear boy," I soothed, "I can assure you."

"Yes, Madame," he replied, "but I've been forbidden to be on watch anymore. Chachu will give me the rudder at night instead."

This surprised me.

"But I thought the Admiral wished only the most experienced sailors to rudder the ship when he was not on deck?"

"True, Madame, but don't worry. Chachu will be with me always. This is just to allow me to be credited with deck duty, for otherwise I would no longer have any." Deck duty was quite important for the wage tally that would be made on the return to Spain, as well as prestige among the men. I was glad Chachu had, as usual, found a ready solution.

I took my place in the breakfast line, next to Diego.

"The Admiral woke up to a great disappointment, Madame," de Harana observed to me.

"Perhaps it was bound to happen," he continued, heaping a mash of turnip-like vegetable and papaya onto my plate. It was a breakfast meal Chachu had learned on Guanahani, our first landfall that now seemed so long ago.

The Admiral joined us, somewhat calmer than before.

He had tied his white hair, now terribly long, behind his head, and this gave him a rather foppish but more comfortable look. He had aged since Spain, acquiring deep lines around his mouth and eyes, no doubt abetted by the sun to which he had not yet, after so many weeks, become accustomed.

"I've named the last island Juana," he announced, "and by my calculations, another great land is within three days of here."

De la Cosa, Torres and Caro soon joined us, like bees to the honey of the Admiral.

"Too bad about last night," Caro said glumly, testing the depth of the Admiral's anger.

"There's more where they came from," de la Cosa added coldly. I suppressed my urge to bare my complicity to them all, filled with renewed pride in my secret.

"Yes, there are," my husband noted, "and we'll seize them when we next put into land."

266]

I bristled. "At least you do not expect me to do any more coaxing," I said.

"No, dear wife, I know you do not like to do it, and perhaps the time has come to employ more manly methods anyway," the Admiral said.

"Speaking of coaxing," de la Cosa then cut in, "where is our smooth-talking colleague, Pinzon?"

I had been so consumed by the aftermath of the Indians, I now looked hastily across the ocean and gulped in fear—Pinzon and *Pinta* were nowhere to be seen across the sheet of water.

Dear God, had I lost him with my indecision? Had he already turned back, already made the choice?

The Admiral shouted up to Falguero in the crow's nest to report if *Pinta* was visible.

"Nay, Admiral, both *Nina* and *Pinta* are gone from view."

"Damn him," the Admiral cursed, "no doubt he's tried to reach Ceiba and its gold before I do."

"Perhaps he too should be seized, Admiral," de la Cosa suggested, all too willingly.

That would be a devil's journey, to have my lover in prison on my own ship.

"Perhaps he's just found his usual distractions, Admiral," Caro offered with a slight laugh, and I turned quickly at his words.

"Perhaps, indeed," my husband said, smiling wryly, "though I detect no land nearby, nor ladies, my wife excepted, naturally."

They laughed as if in secret common understanding and the gathering broke up jovially. Only I was rattled to the core.

I followed the Admiral to our cabin. He installed himself behind his desk, as usual, and I needed to inquire without appearing too anxious.

"Do you think *Pinta* could actually reach Ceiba ahead of you?" I asked, accentuating the navigational aspects.

"*Pinta* has been speedier from the beginning, as you know," the Admiral replied, not looking at me.

"But would he actually attempt to outdo you?" I pursued.

With this, the Admiral paid more attention, and said in shrewd tones, "The truth is, Felipa, even if he tries, I do have insurance against Pinzon's insistence on recognizing his claim."

Was he about to lay my infidelity at my feet?

I took the bait, for I could not live with him another minute if he had found us out.

"You do?" I probed, my stomach knotted like a sailor's rope. "And what is that?"

"According to the men, Pinzon has had as many Indian women as there are islands in this sea—in total contravention of the Sovereign's rules. He could hang for his recklessness, using a Sovereign mission for lustful purposes. Apparently, his escapades make Falguero's indiscretion seem a monastic frolic by comparison."

I thought that I would die, that my backbone had been stripped from me as cleanly as the spine of a fish, and that I would now tumble in a heap of loose flesh to the floor.

"That is impossible," I heard myself utter, my voice hoarse with disbelief.

"Not at all, my wife. Just because I have not made it public knowledge does not mean I do not know."

"Has anyone actually seen him?" I asked, posing the one question I could think of that would save my bleeding heart.

"No," the Admiral reported dryly.

"Well then perhaps it isn't true." I stated.

"Felipa, not everything need be seen to be true," the Admiral reminded me.

"But there is no proof then," I insisted hopefully.

"Not in the strict sense," he had to reply, blotting a line on a letter he had begun.

If it were only that he stayed on land, why even I knew that. I was reprieved. No, if he had not been seen with women, then there was no proof he slept with them and it was not true.

But now, truth had become entirely relative, and I was becoming a specialist at lies.

In my dreams that night, a great palm branch wildly sprouted from the back of Luis Torres, straightening him as on a rack. Don't stretch, Luis, don't break. You are a good man, I heard my sleeping mind shout.

The forest was indifferent. His black hair swished like branches, wet, dripping as if oiled by the humid tropics. His face tightened in red-lipped agony. Torres could not speak.

The campfire smoldered. A sailor I could barely recognize peeled leaned his knee into a purple plum until it split apart like a broken porcelain pot, and he hurled the edible pieces like enemies into the woods. But there was no sound of rustling there, only in Luis Torres' hair.

I woke up hot and trembling from the dream I could no longer see but which felt like a fluid still coursing through my body.

I felt along the bed to the water bowl. I ran the tin cup along the bottom and heard the melodic ring of crystal, the bell of the cup, and though the water was too warm to quench my thirst, I had no choice but to drink.

Chapter Twenty Seven

The Incontestable Witness

For several days we were tossed by rough open seas, having left all coastal protections. We saw no land, no *Pinta*, no Pinzon, though *Nina* reappeared on the horizon.

Turmoil was my only steadiness. I swam in jealousy. I ached to know why my lover had left me alone to wrestle with the future, knowing I could share my anguish with no one. I yearned for him to return so that I could lay the rumors to rest. Then we would leave. I was too imprisoned by thoughts of him to pretend I had not made my choice.

But a verdant coast again drew into view, the land the Admiral had predicted, and he headed straight to it, again purporting that here, assuredly, was the Asian court. Skepticism was palpable.

As we prepared to anchor yet again, before terrain that seemed no different from any other, I found myself alone in the cabin. It was just as well, given the intimacy with which I was writing down these events. I had begun to be concerned about my journal being found, and had decided it best to hide it below a loosened board in the drawer beneath my bed, but I needed to protect the finished pages from the dampness.

I made several packets of pages filled with all I'd written since the beginning, then wrapped them in plain white paper and again in the thick palm leaves that so adeptly keep out rain, and tied it overall with bamboo grass strings.

I also poured some ink into several hollow reed tubes and sealed them with the sappy substance I had found at the last settlement, packing these capsules and a pen in one of the bundles, thinking that leaving hurriedly with Martin, I would have no time to prepare such items.

And so it happened that the morning I was taking advantage of solitude to secure my journal, I noticed the Admiral had left some documents loose on top of his flat letter portfolio.

Of course, by now I was no stranger to reading his papers, but still I hesitated, thinking he might burst in anytime.

Not wanting to be found behind his desk should he walk in, I tried to read his tight black writing upside down, slanting the parchment just enough.

To my shock, he had written reports to the Sovereigns, already! What could he be saying, if we were not yet headed home? But, it seemed he had begun with the end:

> Although all I have related may appear to be wonderful and unheard of, yet the results of my voyage would have been more astonishing if I had had at my disposal such ships as I required.

My indefatigable husband. So now he was blaming the ships we had been given and that had served us well. Writing this, was he already explaining why Pinzon might lay claim to being first?

I tried to read more, but nervous at being caught and craning my neck so uncomfortably, I abandoned the effort and walked out onto the deck just as *Santa Maria*'s anchor heaved out of its socket with a deep splash into the sea.

And here was a phenomenon to calm any quaking heart. Hundreds of tall rose-colored birds I had not seen before stood at the water's edge. They had spindle thin legs, long curling necks, shining black beaks, and they kept balance on one stiff leg, the other bent at the knee for minutes at a time.

I took them as a good omen, a sign that Pinzon's straying ahead was part of a larger plan he could not convey to me yet and that the rest was merely ugly rumor. The entire crew gazed at the spectacle of birds, circling and flying, then settling again as one crimson hue when we did not come closer.

But we could approach neither birds nor land. For *Santa Maria* was without a tender, thanks to me, and all, including the Admiral, were confined to the ship until *Nina*, at last, came into the cove.

Yanez rowed over right away, but was not warmly greeted.

"Give me your tender now," the Admiral ordered, "and tell me what has become of your brother."

Yanez was taken aback by the Admiral's brittle tone.

"He's gone scouting, sir, using his greater speed to spare us false course," Yanez explained as he roped his small boat to ours and climbed aboard, short of breath.

"I don't believe you," the Admiral replied, uncharacteristically blunt.

"I assure you, Admiral, he did not have the means to signal you—his powder was too damp with humidity to fire the cannon and he lost sight of you on one of these nights."

It was all so exquisitely plausible and believable to me, but the Admiral would have none of it.

"I'm taking the tender to shore, Yanez," he declared, "with Caro, Chachu, de la Cosa and Torres. Everyone else, including your brother, is confined to his ship until I return."

He stuffed a sack with trading items, and several machetes, and passed the parcel over the side to the wiry Chachu, who was already waiting in the commandeered tender. The four rowed off, dropping Yanez at *Nina* on their way.

Their little boat disappeared through the flock of birds.

Diego de Harana came up behind me on the railing. He had grown forlorn on our journey. Though he had the rank of marshall, Caro the goldsmith had displaced him as the Admiral's confidante, and Diego, much better bred and interested in the sovereign nature of our business, seemed a lost man.

The sun beat down, and he offered me a cup of water, dipping the ladle into the central barrel. I drank, then poured the rest down my neck.

"Do you think we will make soon for Spain?" Diego asked, his hopefulness barely disguised.

"I am hard pressed to say, for my husband still seems bent on Cathay."

"One cannot blame him, for that was his goal, but surely he has at least proven the western route has merit. He can leave it to others to . . ."

"To greet the Great Khan?" I provided "That is doubtful."

"Oh Madame, I long to return now," Diego confided. "I would be so grateful to return to my family, my cousin, and it is too tiring to keep all I see to myself. I have no role here anymore." We seemed to have a common situation.

"I haven't spoken very honestly, Madame, about my family," Diego continued.

Diego's family was, frankly, a long way from my mind at that moment, but he seemed to have the need to talk, and so I pretended to be interested when all I could think of was Martin, and how this was time to be alone with him and make our plans and clear the air and it was all being wasted.

"It's my cousin, Beatriz, who so pains me."

"She is much on your mind, I see, still after so many weeks," I said, my own thoughts wandering.

"She is more than my cousin. That is, once I longed to marry her."

"And you do no longer?"

"That's not . . . you know I suspected she took a lover, but worse—and this I haven't told you—-I believe she has a child with this man who has never married her. She could be at the heart of a scandal in Cordoba."

"Does the man know of the child?" I asked.

"Perhaps not," Diego replied.

"Diego, I confess my mind is on other matters now," I admitted, "but my advice would be, if you still love her as you seem to, insist either she marry the man, or that he give the child his name. Otherwise, she will drown in anonymity and despair."

"Cordoba is so small, Madame, such doings are as visible as royal monuments," he said.

"Be courageous, Diego, let it be seen. She has been victimized, that is clear, and you ought not let her remaining life be governed by the eyes of others." It seemed such easy advice to give, if I could only live it myself.

"Madame, you are so kind to take this time. If I can favor you with any service, please demand it."

I agreed, and he left me, greatly relieved to have unburdened himself. He loved his cousin who loved a man who would not marry her, but with whom she had a child. Poor Diego, I realized these facts must have been tormenting him the entire trip.

Nothing happened all afternoon, and the *Pinta* did not reappear. I retired to my cabin to wait.

It had been some time since I had brought order to our quarters, so much else had been on my mind. My nightdress lay tossed on the bench, a blue serge skirt I had yet to wear lay over a chair. The Sovereign letters were still there, of course, on my husband's desk, but I could predict too well their contents—accolades, excuses, pat conclusions about this unexpected place.

No, I would distract myself instead with cabinkeeping, hoping that Martin would return before the Admiral. My lover had been shrewd, for I pulsed for him all the more in this wicked unexplained absence. If he wished to torment me with the thought of never seeing him again, he had gone too far to make his point.

Surely he will come, I thought, and explain everything and clear the viscious lies.

I folded all my garments and flattened the sheets on the bed, wiping away the conjugal forms my husband and I had left that might as well have been those of perfect strangers.

The Admiral too had grown careless with his belongings.

I folded his face towel. Could I really be thinking of leaving him, this man who had been my home, my life, my fate, for as long as I had been a woman?

Spin the compass, I told myself, and I did. The Genoese rowers bobbed and shook, turning irrevocably to Martin.

My husband's leather doublet rested on the back of his chair, the one he had offered as the supplementary prize when mutiny seemed so certain. Brown as the earth of Spain, it was trimmed with the purest silk. Yet it seemed so bulky in my hands, a truly European garment—it had been months since wearing such clothes seemed remotely reasonable.

I tried to fold it compactly, pressing and patting, and as I did, a white sheet of paper fluttered to the floor, falling like a handkerchief from the breast pocket, creased in quarters.

I did not intend to read it, thinking it must be yet another letter bound for the Sovereigns, but it seemed brief, and I opened it in full.

The letter did not pertain directly to the King and Queen, but it was as important, as blindingly revealing, as the first words I had ever learned to read.

The neat black ink spread in ten unforgettable lines:

My dearest Beatriz,
I have missed your sweetness every day since our fortunate stop at Gomera. I will post this to you immediately I reach a point of European land, and in any case, I will communicate with you from Seville, as soon as the Sovereigns' heralding of me is over and I am free to travel. Perhaps you'll be invited, or could arrange to be there. (A crowd has never deterred us before.) The journey has been an unswerving success. I've little time to

explain Asia here, but suffice it to say no greater marvels could be imagined.

I embrace you, my darling Governor.

The note was signed by my husband.

I was stunned at its meaning, so unsteady I dared not move to sit down. Realization flooded me like a tropical storm. How had I been so so foolish, so duped?

Of course. Pinzon had almost given it away that night we walked at Gomera harbor, but I, deaf to him, had not listened. Though I hadn't wished to see it, the vivacious Governor had been my husband's lover at least since he had been trying to see the Queen in Spain and who knows for how much longer.

And our time waiting in the Canaries? My mind spun back to that miserable evening, the dinner I ate alone while the Admiral, I thought, made the rounds of his ships.

On land indeed. It was my husband who had begun the cycle of dalliances on land.

How lucky I saw the hateful message then, for I needed this push, this evidence.

During the days when I had loved him most, my husband had been involved with someone else. Poor foolish Felipa—I even believed his excuses that he had no proper home to receive me in Spain. Indeed, he had only the Governor's!

I had to remember that, and swallow it, for it was the food I needed to eat.

I put the letter back in the doublet pocket, and became more concerned than ever about the sanctity of my own records.

I quickly reached for the packets of wrapped journal pages that I had hidden earlier and put them in another wrapping of parchment, tied with ribbon.

I glanced in the mirror and saw my face was flushed with hurry. I needed to calm down. I had too many secrets to wash off.

Outside, Juan prepared to build the dinner fire, and Diego stood with Falguero and some others.

When I called Diego to my cabin, he came right away. I concocted that given the upheaval likely to ensue between Pinzon, when he returned, and the Admiral over Ceiba and where Pinzon had been, it was best that certain of the Admiral's documents not be in his cabin, lest Pinzon steal or damage his logs.

Diego, entirely disposed to believe my tale, took the documents he thought were the Admiral's for safekeeping with a true sense of mission. I made him swear he would never ever read them, nor open them before he reached home, and that he would deliver them only to the addressee whose name he would later find on the inside wrapper. Unquestioningly, he accepted and pledged not to even think of touching the package again until he was safely back in Spain.

I believed his word was worth the risk I was taking in giving him my journal. I had little choice but to wait for Martin now, to tell him my answer, that the Enterprise had emptied for me and I was free to go.

But the Admiral returned before Martin did, late in the afternoon. He and his party emerged from the forest and before signalling the tender to collect them, they planted a tall cross on the beach, the first time we had indulged in this ritual in quite awhile.

They reached the ship shiny with perspiration, hungry and craving a drink. Chachu especially seemed exhausted, and they gave him the first chance at water.

The Admiral announced they had seen no human being. Dare I confront him, I wondered, lay the truth at his feet before the entire crew? No, for now he held little awe for me and was thus little target for humiliation.

I was void of him, despite my own infidelity. Mine was nothing next to the unbroken tract of his.

I felt oddly released and free. That I had been betrayed when I had been at my most vulnerable, my most trusting, diluted my own act of betrayal. At last, in realizing that my husband and I were now equal in a sense, I felt relieved. For now I would say nothing.

I had not even been listening to what my husband had been reporting, picking up the conversation only in the middle.

"And the cross?" Falguero was asking.

"That was an amazing occurrence," the Admiral said. "We found nothing inland, and began to retrace our steps. But then, I spied these entwined tree branches in the form of a natural cross, and we cut it down to mark our passage here."

"And claim the land for Christianity, let us not forget," I added acidly, testing him.

"Of course," he said, indifferent to my sting.

"Yes, and Chachu here carried the cross on his back," de la Cosa explained, "a veritable Savior on Calvary."

Cheers to "Chachu the Christian" were ordered. But still no Pinzon.

I had only the words of Yanez to cling to now. Surely Martin would never have instructed him to lie so boldly to the Admiral. I had to believe Martin's brother, that Pinzon had only gone ahead to scout.

The Admiral, though, disbelieved Yanez outright, and did not summon him for further consultation. He wanted to plan the next few days, and commanded the usual officers to our cabin once again for dinner. After that, he proclaimed, we would sail immediately, with or without Pinzon.

I had no stomach for it, neither to eat nor to listen, for now I was already gone on my own voyage away from here, waiting for the vessel into which I had been poured. But I couldn't give my plans away yet. I had to endure awhile longer, as long as it took Pinzon to return.

The meal was served, and the Admiral filled our goblets amply with wine. Out of nervousness, I sipped my wine eagerly and took a second glass before the others. It was as yellow as straw in the glass, and I watched coolly through its golden prism as the Admiral drummed his fingers on the table.

At first, they talked of route and navigation. We had been away now several months, and the Admiral hinted that he would entertain the idea of returning, though he stopped short of saying when and if he planned to turn back.

Since no one pressed him on the point, he steered to another subject, the disappearance of Pinzon, intending, he said, to poll the officers for their views. My ears sharpened.

"I am not pleased with Mr. Pinzon's constant infractions," the Admiral declared, "for he undermines me."

The others listened intently, and I tried to read each face. The Admiral continued.

"Therefore I propose to charge Pinzon with several crimes," he announced, while he sprinkled salt and pepper on his fish, confident of his audience, enumerating "treason, sedition, and licentious behavior with subjects under Sovereign protection."

All the men, including de la Cosa, applauded lightly.

I moved the food around my plate, and swallowed the last of my third cup of wine. But now I had to speak up.

"There's no evidence of the latter. You've said as much yourself," I challenged, finding the courage in my glass. "For example you've found no incriminating document, no penned poetry, no confessions of love hidden in his doublet," I alluded icily, staring directly at the Admiral.

His face grew ashen, but my insinuation was drowned out by the group.

"Dear Madame," de la Cosa addressed me, "ironclad proof would be unreasonable to expect, under the circumstances. We could not lurk behind him in the bush."

"And anyway, Madame," Torres too insisted, "have you not asked yourself how he seems to glean so much of the day to day ways of these people, and how he knows so much of the language?"

I flushed with the truth of that. Pinzon knew these people better than any in the room.

"He did often sleep on land," I admitted, "but in itself that should be no crime. Most of you perhaps wished to indulge in that as well," I suggested, signalling my husband to fill my glass again by tapping it with my fork.

"You've not eaten anything yet, Felipa," he said, pouring nevertheless while the crystal still rang in the air.

I swallowed a tiny morsel of pure white fish.

"He bragged about it, Madame," Torres continued, "in the mornings afterward."

"To whom?" I insisted, Torres' face vaguely spinning before me.

"To any man who would listen," Torres replied, clearly trying to convince me.

Diego remained curiously silent.

Juan de la Cosa took up the conversation then.

"What irks above all, Madame," he said, "even if we were to put Pinzon's personal behavior aside, is that it was he who most pressed the commercial virtues of this place. Pinzon may well be en route to Spain with all our most secret ideas. Have you no fear for your husband's reputation?"

I laughed dizzily. "That's the most absurd charge of all," I exclaimed, my tongue thick. "Martin Alonso was the last to wish to exploit this place, so you are all entirely wrong."

I poured my own glass now.

"Felipa, I don't see why you rush to defend this man," my husband now interjected, "who has left us cold."

"Betrayal, my husband, as we know, must be planned over months, a palace of lies created, time taken. Pinzon is not the sort," I defended, launching more intimations. The Admiral seemed exasperated.

"Pinzon will be back," I insisted, gazing away from them to take a deep breath of air.

"I believe he intended exploitation of the most complete kind, Madame," de la Cosa insisted. "Why, his own men were ordered to inventory every spice, every plant, every new fruit they found, and daily he would ask me to calculate a value, which he then wrote down."

I bit my quivering lip. I was surrounded by lies and could not defend myself from more of them.

But then Torres flung the final arrow.

"Indeed, Madame, you who care so much for these people, do you not know it was Pinzon who first suggested we take some of them with us and that we avenge Falguero with hostages? In fact it was Pinzon who supplied him the woman in the first place."

My stomach rolled, but Diego now stood up, pushing the table away with a rough scrape, looking straight at de la Cosa.

"I see no reason to blame all this evil contemplation on one man alone, when it was you, Mr. de la Cosa, who conspired with Pinzon to split the gains if he would return to Spain and announce we had not found Asia at all. Sir, do you think this ship so vast that nothing is overheard?"

Diego trembled as he hurled his accusation, as if he had never imagined himself capable of such a confrontation.

De la Cosa's eyes glistened with shock. The Admiral's too.

"You insult me, de Harana," de la Cosa bellowed, staring at Diego with blades in his eyes. But everyone knew that Diego, of all people, had no reason to lie.

"I listened to you both, many times," Diego repeated, now more confident. "Pinzon is your acrid partner and you his! You are only turning coats now in case he's left without you," Diego said, his voice lowering as he sat down, spent from the charges that he could never retract.

But de la Cosa would not accept such exposure without response. He threw his glassful of wine straight into Diego's face.

"Admiral, this man may not travel on my ship another hour," de la Cosa declared. He lunged at Diego, reaching for his collar.

Diego, unruffled, slapped the hand away and wiped the wine from his beard. He uttered quietly, "I can move all my belongings to *Nina* this night, Admiral. That is no hardship."

But I had no mind for this duel of accusations and charges I could not accept. I filled my glass again. The Admiral was too engrossed in these loyalty issues and the disintegration of his crew to stop me.

"I deny these outbursts," de la Cosa stated flatly.

My husband said nothing.

"Think it through, Admiral," Diego began calmly, taking his turn to reason with my husband. "Alone, Pinzon could never dream of convincing anyone in Spain of facts contrary to what you yourself announced. Alone he would be ridiculed. Alone, he would be nothing but a traitor."

"Yes, he would be mad," the Admiral said at last, "for that would be political suicide for a man of his estate."

"Not unless he had an ally of standing willing to attest to what he reported," Diego noted, glancing at de la Cosa, but having no idea the potent implication of his words for me.

"Yes, perhaps," the Admiral agreed, eyeing de la Cosa with new suspicion. "He would need a partner of repute, someone entirely above all question. That he would come back for."

Now I stood, for my stomach was turning with the acid of this dose of bitter blood. It was not de la Cosa who was to have been the incontestable witness.

I ran from the cabin to the railing, my chair clattering to the floor, and hung my head overboard, letting the river of wine burn up from my stomach and out of my mouth, vomiting the realities I had been trying for days to drown in the sea.

Over and over I wretched, listening as everything I had swallowed hit in splashes in the ocean, all the liquid in my stomach and the lies in my heart, until my chest cramped in pain.

I cried and sobbed as I had never done in all my life, but when my husband came to see what had happened, I did not want him near me. "Please leave me alone," I whispered.

"But you are . . . "

I begged him to go.

"As you wish," he said, handing me a clean wet linen towel and a cup of water to drink.

I sipped it slowly, rinsing my mouth.

But crying had not unburdened me, only weighed me further with what was now inescapable, glowing like hot crystal.

Of course. I was to bear out Pinzon's claims before the world. He had even duped de la Cosa. Why bother with the Admiral's first officer when you could secure the Admiral's wife?

This was the source of his passion, his oath of love, his urge that I leave with him. Not for a new life together, not for this new world, but for his own aggrandizement. Could it all have been as fraudulent as that, as fake as Asia within our reach. I begged another time to believe it was not so, but there was no mercy tonight.

Soon, while I still tried to calm and clean myself outside the cabin, Pinzon's tender came up. It was Yanez and yes, Martin, Martin, Martin holding a torch against his winning face.

Yanez did not see me, and instead knocked directly on the cabin door.

But I could not lose this one moment with Pinzon, and before he too stepped inside, I called his name hoarsely in the night.

He moved the light over and picked me out of the corner.

"Felipa, what has happened to you," he demanded, rushing to me, touching my shoulder.

I kissed the back of his hand. I would complete my humiliation.

"Please, my darling, swear you have not deceived me," I said, searching his eyes for my answer.

My body shook and his eyes evaded.

"Swear you did not use me," I begged again, "swear you did not lie and sleep with other women, swear you loved me in truth, that you did not mean to conspire. Swear, Martin, please."

He was, of course, shocked, and failed to truly understand how far everything had gone. Had he kissed me fully, or whispered a single loving murmur to discount what I had accused him of, had he just denied it, I would have believed him.

But perhaps even for him lying could no longer come as naturally. Instead, as was his way, he tried to make a tease of it, thinking probably I would accept any trespass for the sake of my frantic love for him.

His face took on the beginnings of a rakish smile, and he ran his hands through his beard.

"My lady, all here was too easy," he began, his silver tongue taking charge once too often. "I am not to blame if the women here are beautiful. One woman could never have been enough in such a setting. You must admit it was a very good plan and if you could just allow me to explain the rest I . . . "

The sound cracked in the air. I slapped his face so hard that I will forever feel the burning in my own hand.

I don't know when Pinzon left the ship, or if he spoke at all to the Admiral. I remained sitting on the foredeck in its shadows until the last man had left. Diego was rowed to the Nina and the anchor of our flagship hoisted, its great chain links scraping one by one into place.

[281

I stepped into the cabin, where the Admiral was already in bed, having had his fill of confrontations. I was beyond all fury at him now, even beyond all pity. I felt curiously serene, now that all was said. Out of what darkness was I traveling, and into what light?

I sat for some time in my husband's chair, as our ship began to sail, and the quiet of the night spread like the vanquishing stain of truth.

I felt void of all emotion, all responsiblity, and this great emptiness enabled me to fill with new and selfish thoughts.

The Admiral lay there, as vulnerable now as I. I climbed into bed. Slowly I began caressing, kissing, not letting him speak or wonder or protest, exploring him the way I had learned to take pleasure from a man on the beaches of these seductive shores.

He was neither Martin nor my husband now, and so lost was I in the anonymous art of mastering this night, that I remember only those few moments of passionless power, as I lay upon him, taking without wanting, never feeling, never even hearing the slashing sea that broke our ship in half.

Chapter Twenty Eight

The Garden of the Queen

I clung to a yellow hill, my arms trying to embrace the trees and broken branches. It was not wheat growing, but straw hair. Hawks tore at the kernels from the scalp. My head was salty.

The sea hissed in my eyes. The earth waved under my belly, rising and falling underneath. My face was burning and my arms could open no further, for I had no wings to reach the garden of the queen.

I sucked the water from the back of my hand until I felt my tongue scraping sand, the grit of gravel in my mouth.

My mind began to clear.

My throat was cracked and dry, my forehead pouring beads of sweat, and the heat of the beach burning up through the tatters of my damp clothes.

I don't know how long I lay there, but when I opened my eyes, when finally the earth and hills and ocean ceased moving, there was no person, no ship, no convoy. There was no one else.

My face was pressed into the tawny beach. I turned my head from side to side, but there was no pillow here, no bed.

I arched my back like a cat's at first, to see if it would work again, for my body ached with soreness. I sat up, picking stones and glistening pounded seashells from my swollen lips.

I tried to remember what had happened, but I could recreate nothing of the wreck, and how I came to survive it.

Except for the evidence on the beach. In shards around me on this arc of sand, were pieces of my bed frame, and indeed parts of the drawer from underneath, now split and splintered, tossed with me, and some of the leaf-wrapped packages I had stored. I must have fallen unconscious, perhaps hit on the head as the ship fell to pieces. I suppose I had clung to the floating wood, until it washed to shore.

Santa Maria must have run aground on a reef or rocks or some unseeable bludgeoning blade, torn through the hull. Had, after all, Juan been left alone at the rudder? I don't know who had been in charge on deck that night, or who might have been hurt in the accident, but the Admiral was not.

I know that my husband and the others earnestly looked for me, for eventually I hauled myself to a high point on the coast and observed them. They shouted and shouted my name, searched the waters and the woods. They called to me each hour, until finally the Admiral ordered a mass said and the entire crew of all three ships prayed on the beach for my soul.

But I made no sign to them. I do not wish to be their tool any longer, and were I to reveal myself, I would have to unveil all that I have done, or silently bear witness to events as they wish to report them. They are as strangers to me now, and I do not wish to join their journey again.

And so I write to you, to finish what I started.

Perhaps the pages I entrusted to Diego have not yet reached you. But they will. He will eventually see they were not addressed to any royal official, but to you, and I am sure he will bring you the package. Some pages will be missing. For example, you will not know, until now, of other things I read in the Admiral's documents on my last afternoon in my cabin that I should explain.

His letters to the King were full of glowing reports and precise details, and yet he continued to invoke Asia, knowing as he did that he had not found it, but insisting we were close.

Perhaps we are, but it is unlikely. For this land is like no other ever known, like nothing for which we could have been searching.

And so I write to you finally, Beatriz de Harana, companion of the western route though we have never met, for it is also of you that I read among the Admiral's possessions.

As I gathered the green tufted cloak that he had spread across his sidetable to cushion his compass pins, I felt some more papers, and opened them—a long letter to you.

I saw that the Governor of Gomera was not his only Beatriz, nor was she his only lover. I read his loving report to you, the woman of whom Diego had so much spoken.

How was it possible, I wondered, to have been so bonded to my husband that I could be so foolish, so totally blind and believing.

But I am beyond all pain of that. I believe you will understand, as another woman, having no tendency nor wish to judge me.

I don't know whether Diego realized you were my husband's lover in Seville while I waited in Lisbon. Perhaps in his way he was hinting it to me since he found a way to bring you up many times. Probably, he loves you still. But what matters here is that you and I have both loved the Admiral who, now, has brought us irrevocably together, and in this, I feel free to speak.

You will make your own choice, your own life. I give you the story only so it does not remain solely with me.

You could not know of me, or that, had he wished to, the Admiral could not have married you, because he already had a wife. I wonder if he told you anything at all about me, or the Governor, but I feel that you would want now to know what I have learned. His will be the tale of glory, but our story will be more true. You and I have never looked into a mirror together, but rather into the eyes and face of the same man.

Sooner or later, there is bound to be movement between one continent and the other. And so when there will be traffic with this new world, these remaining pages will reach your hands as I will leave them where they can be found. Such lost letters have a way of turning up, and you can make the parcel whole.

My husband, my lover and most of the rest of the crew returned on the two remaining ships, but not before the Admiral commanded a few men stay behind to build a fort with the timbers of the wrecked *Santa Maria*. This camp will surely serve to begin the empire that the Enterprise has become. But I will not go down to it.

Pinzon too searched for me before leaving. Perhaps he thought, should he find me, he could reconvince me, reseduce me. I took a bold, unashamed but bitter pleasure in watching him call and scour, and find nothing. It was my turn to laugh.

His lies were both the foulest and greatest. Commandeer the Admiral's wife—how audacious. In striking him, I struck my own history. I would do it again.

But blame transcends such a man, really. After all, how could he and the Admiral shed their breeding in bankrupt notions, royal competitions, petty greed, lies. I cannot go back to that Europe, for the dream has been broken into too many pieces of truth. How to repair the scattered rose?

My husband is no longer mine, of course. We could not divide him anyway, as the wealth of these lands will surely be divided between my country and yours for the prizes fall too easily.

My husband wrote to the Sovereigns that he too was made a king here, that the Spaniards were received as celestial beings by the people of this new world. But what will the Spaniards make of this godliness; what will they plant here but the same deception they brought with them?

My husband made several copies of his Sovereign letters, and wrote that he had sealed one copy in waxed cloth and put it to sea in a barrel, in the event he or his records should fall into the hands of foreigners. He meant the Portuguese, most likely, though surely I must have been expected to help there, should there have been a need. He offered a reward to whomever would find the floating letter and deliver it to the King and Queen. I merely trusted Diego, the wrapping of leaves, and you.

My husband made grand promises, not of passion but of territory, writing that with a little more assistance afforded him by his most invincible Sovereigns, he would procure for them as much gold as they need, great quantities of spices, cotton, and mastic, and as many men for the service of the navy as their Majesties may require. He predicted a thousand other things of value, promising material benefits, refreshment and profit for not only Spain but all Christians.

What is Pinzon's single empty promise to love me against this litany of expedient promises?

I am tainted now with the knowledge that no good will come of our travels here, not soon anyway. In that, I cannot go back.

I know you have a child, my husband's child. My own body had begun seeming strange to me of late. It is supposed to be impossible, but perhaps I too will have a child in some months, though the doctor said long ago I could not survive a birth. As to lineage, I could not be sure—the Admiral or Pinzon. But the father would certainly be these lands, and so my child and yours would share at least the blood of the same voyage.

I cannot stop what will happen here, but I cannot resume my life as before. I did not show myself to the searchers, for I do not wish to return, to become their convenience again, merely their colony at home. Pinzon was only the costume of my escape.

There are surely people here, silent in the branches that shield them, yet neither am I one of them. There is enough to eat here and water to drink. I will live until my life runs out.

Silver raindrops shine in sunlight on the leaves, like drops of mercury. The moist forest breathes my breath.

But this new universe too will soon elude me. In exploring the world, I have lost my place in it. Such is the risk of discovery.

I found a fire that once had been, now a pile of cinders of gray wood polished by the sea and cast on the shore. I rubbed my finger along a sliver of driftwood branch that fell to ash at my touch.

It is odd that I would consign all this to you, but in all that we have lived, we are opposite poles of the same earth.

Everything I describe here happened, or was told to me. The rest it was never known I knew.